BESTSELLING AUTHOR COLLECTION

New York Times and *USA TODAY* Bestselling Author

HEATHER GRAHAM

FOREVER MY LOVE

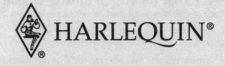

HARLEQUIN®

TORONTO • NEW YORK • LONDON
AMSTERDAM • PARIS • SYDNEY • HAMBURG
STOCKHOLM • ATHENS • TOKYO • MILAN • MADRID
PRAGUE • WARSAW • BUDAPEST • AUCKLAND

Recycling programs
for this product may
not exist in your area.

ISBN-13: 978-0-373-38991-9

FOREVER MY LOVE

Copyright © 2010 by Harlequin Books S.A.

The publisher acknowledges the copyright holders
of the individual works as follows:

FOREVER MY LOVE
Copyright © 1990 by Heather Graham Pozzessere

SOLITARY SOLDIER
Copyright © 2002 by Debra Webb

For questions and comments about the quality of this book
please contact us at Customer_eCare@Harlequin.ca.

® and TM are trademarks of the publisher. Trademarks indicated with ® are registered in the United States Patent and Trademark Office, the Canadian Trade Marks Office and in other countries.

www.eHarlequin.com

Printed in U.S.A.

CONTENTS

For Chynna Skye Pozzessere—
who came into the world right around
the original publication of this story!

FOREVER MY LOVE

New York Times and *USA TODAY* Bestselling Author

Heather Graham

HEATHER GRAHAM

New York Times and *USA TODAY* bestselling author Heather Graham has written more than a hundred novels, many of which have been featured by the Doubleday Book Club and the Literary Guild. An avid scuba diver, ballroom dancer and mother of five, she still enjoys her south Florida home, but loves to travel as well, from locations such as Cairo, Egypt, to her own backyard, the Florida Keys. Reading, however, is the pastime she still loves best, and she is a member of many writing groups. She's currently vice president of the Horror Writers' Association, and she's also an active member of International Thriller Writers.

She is very proud to be a Killerette in the Killer Thriller Band, along with many fellow novelists she greatly admires. For more information, check out her Web site, theoriginalheathergraham.com.

Chapter 1

Kathy heard the music long before Shanna called her to the living room to watch the television. And despite the years, the pain and the endless things that had gone wrong, she felt the poignant tug on her heart that she always felt whenever she saw Brent, heard a piece of his music, saw his picture in a newspaper or heard the husky whisper of his voice.

"Mom! Come out and see Dad!"

Kathy gritted her teeth and smoothed out the comforter she had just tossed over her bed. Don't growl, smile, she warned herself. If there had been one decent thing she and Brent had managed to do, it was their raising of Shanna. Neither of them had ever said a negative thing about the other to their daughter.

And now she was almost grown up, a beautiful young woman with white-gold hair, fabulous blue eyes and a figure that was both slim and curved, and entirely enchanting.

It was getting harder and harder to believe that she was no longer a child, Kathy thought. Sometimes she found it amazing that she and Brent had created a child with such startling beauty, and then again, sometimes she smiled wistfully and thought, why not? Had she been so very different herself way back when?

And hadn't Brent been the most gorgeous man she had ever seen when she had first met him?

"Mother!" Shanna called.

For a moment Kathy's fingers curled tightly around the quilted comforter, then she straightened, inhaling, exhaling. She knew Shanna was watching Brent's new video.

He and the other four musicians that formed the Highlanders had just cut a new album. She had read about it in *People*. She knew Johnny Blondell fairly well, and had never been especially fond of him. He had a penchant for high living and verbally abusing his wives—she had lost count of how many. Keith Montgomery was originally an Iowa farm boy, and he had never lost the sense of home and old-fashioned values. Kathy was sorry for Keith. He was the one who deserved the breaks, and she had read that his wife had recently been killed in a car accident, leaving him with an infant son. Then there were Larry and Thomas Hicks, brothers famous for their haunting harmonies. Kathy knew them from the old days but knew practically nothing personal about them except that they were both very talented, and as rumor held true, equally temperamental.

The band was quite an array of talent all the way around, Kathy thought. Brent was supposed to be one of the top five guitarists alive, ranking number one at times, depending on the opinion of the reviewer. Johnny was an ace drummer, Keith was extraordinary on keyboards, and the Hicks brothers had their fantastic harmony. The group was destined for success once again.

If only she could distance herself, their new video would probably be wonderfully entertaining to watch.

If only Brent wasn't among the company....

It wouldn't be as bad as watching the old videos, Kathy assured herself. She wouldn't see the Brent she had fallen in love with—the tall, rangy man with the sensual amber eyes, the rugged face, the dark sandy hair that fell so seductively over one eye.

This was a new video. With any luck, Brent would be half-bald, liver-spotted, bent over and full of warts.

In the doorway she paused with a certain amusement. She'd better hope that he wasn't in that bad a condition. He was only four years her senior, and she didn't want to think that she was rotting away herself. Not quite yet, anyway.

She hurried down the hallway to the large living room. The television was against the wall néar the brick fireplace. The floor was laid with Mexican tiles and little studs of old English coats of arms at the angles where four tiles met. Shanna was stretched out on a rug that she had dragged to within a few inches of the television set.

"Dad let me watch them filming one day," Shanna

said excitedly, aware that her mother had come at last, but not turning her glance from the television. "Of course, it isn't the same at all, because all the images have to be combined. Well, you know!"

Kathy knew. She still knew something about the business, even though they had been divorced for three years.

Three years didn't erase fifteen. She had never realized that more thoroughly than now, standing barefoot, her hands shoved into the pockets of her cutoffs, staring at the television.

He hadn't gone bald. He hadn't changed a bit.

And the video might be a group effort, but this particular song was Brent's. All Brent's. He was the one singing. His distinctive voice carried the melody with a husky hypnotism that was his trademark.

He was seated on a tall stool, his old guitar on his lap, his smile easy and friendly as he strummed the strings or glanced at one of the other musicians. If anything, his shoulders had broadened in acceptance of the fact that he was forty-one now, and she had a sneaky suspicion that his chest was more richly haired. He wore age well, she thought, very well.

He was even more striking than when she had first met him. Some of the years that had gone past were evident in his eyes. They were still full of enigma, but she thought their whiskey-colored depths betrayed a few other emotions—pain, loss, wisdom and acceptance. Did her eyes look like that? she wondered.

"Doesn't he look great, Mother?"

"Yes," Kathy answered evenly. "Yes, he does."

As videos were prone to do, this one changed suddenly. The musicians were no longer in the studio. They were out on a yacht. Brent was in a chair, lounging. A young bikini-clad beauty was behind him, laughing delightedly, draping her near-naked body over his naked back.

She had been right, Kathy thought. That chest of his was more richly furred than ever with fine gold-tipped hairs. He was tanned and bronze, and his stomach was still as lean as a whipcord. She felt a tremor somewhere in the pit of her belly and for a moment she intensely hated the blonde girl.

It's over between us, Kathy told herself. It had been over for a very long time. Their marriage had fallen apart just like Humpty Dumpty. It had shattered in so many pieces that no one could ever put it together again. And it hadn't been the music business or a blonde or a brunette that had caused the breakup. It had been the big blows of life, followed by the darkness that had suddenly covered them. They hadn't been able to pull together, and so they had fallen apart. Only then had the blondes come into it, and they had both known it. They might have remained friends if they hadn't quarreled quite so passionately at the end.

There had been the last awful fight with its tragic consequences. Afterward he had treated her like a fragile rose, and he had kept his distance. If he had cried, he had never let her see. She knew he had sworn he would never hurt her again, but all that really hurt was that he wouldn't come near her.

Yes, it was over.

Kathy gritted her teeth and managed to put a tight clamp on the emotions that should have passed away with the years. She swallowed the hurt and tried to remind herself that she really wished him well. She wished Brent happiness.

But she still hated the blonde, she decided.

"Marla Harrington. She's a twit!" Shanna said disgustedly.

"You know her?" Kathy curled up on the leather sofa.

Shanna's golden head was nodding. "She's a twit," she repeated.

"A good-looking one," Kathy commented.

"She hangs all over Dad, and he isn't interested."

Kathy doubted that. Brent was looking at the woman, smiling, laughing. Marla Harrington was tall, with short silky hair that moved with her, like the hair in a shampoo commercial. She was lean and lithe, except around the cleavage area. She had a beautiful smile and mahogany eyes. Laughter was touching those eyes, just as it touched Brent's. It was a fun song they were singing, with an easy pop rhythm. Kathy knew already it would be a big hit. The single would probably reach number one immediately. Shanna had told her that the album had several great songs and that she would love it. Kathy believed her daughter, but she didn't want to hear the album.

"What makes you think your dad isn't interested?" Kathy asked idly. She stared at her toes.

Then she had Shanna's attention. Shanna turned from the television to stare at her. "He just isn't. I know it. He hasn't been interested in anyone since you two broke up."

"Oh." Kathy tried to speak lightly. "That isn't true. Give him a chance. He'll find the right woman."

"He's still in love with you. And you're still in love with him."

She breathed deeply. "Shanna," she said very softly. "Children of divorced parents always want to believe that. But it just isn't true. I haven't even seen your father in three years."

"It doesn't matter," Shanna said. She turned to the television. The video had come to an end, and the DJ was announcing it as a surefire hit. She went on to introduce the musicians, ending with Brent McQueen. "The master is surely back to it here! Some thought that he'd never really be back after the death of his infant son four years ago, but as you've heard today—"

The television was off. Shanna had leaped to her feet to flick it off. Now she stared at Kathy. "Mother, I'm sorry, I didn't mean—"

"It's all right," Kathy told her. She managed to smile and get to her feet. "It's all right, really, sweetheart. It happened so long ago, and I've still got you." She gave Shanna a fierce, tight hug, and her daughter, warm, protective, giving, hugged her back. Suddenly, there were tears stinging Kathy's eyes. She held tight to her daughter. "Honestly, Shanna, I have you, and you're precious to me, you know that, don't you?"

She pulled away and managed a huge smile. "And you're taller than I am, too, now. That's not quite fair."

Shanna laughed. "Mom, neither of us is exactly an Amazon."

Kathy grinned. It was all right. She had control again. She could push it all into a far corner of her heart, where it belonged. She released Shanna, certain that no matter how good and loving her daughter was it wasn't good to hold too tight. "Aren't you going to be late for that trip of yours?" she asked Shanna.

Shanna glanced at her watch. "Oh! Gosh, I just might be running late. David should be here any minute. Now, Mom, you're really not going to worry, are you? His parents are both wonderful sailors, and you know that I'm a darned good diver and—"

The doorbell rang. Patty McGiver, Kathy's secretary and housekeeper, chirped merrily, "I'll get it!"

Patty had a pretty, wholesome face, but she insisted on wearing her steel-gray hair in an old-fashioned bun on top of her head. She had the look of a resolute old maid, and though Kathy wondered why Patty had never wanted a family of her own, she was too grateful to have the woman to ponder the question often.

Kathy went by her maiden name, O'Hara, and she lived in an old, quiet section of Coconut Grove, Florida, where her neighbors were discreet and respected their privacy. She had her own business, an advertising firm, and needed the help at home. She liked the house, and she even liked cleaning—it helped her think—but there just weren't enough hours in the day for everything. Patty was a godsend.

"Hello, there, young man!" Patty greeted David Brennan.

"Mom, now—" Shanna began.

"I'm not worried. I know the Brennans are exceptional sailors, and I trust you and David." She had been an overprotective parent for a long time. She hadn't been able to help it. Now she was trying very hard to let loose a little. If she didn't, she knew she would smother her child. And Shanna was an angel. She'd seen enough of some of the music crowd to stay away from drugs. A senior in high school, she got excellent grades, and she seemed to love her mother and father equally. She lived with Kathy, but she spent every other weekend with her father, and shared her holidays carefully.

Brent had always been there for Shanna, Kathy thought. No matter what he had been doing, he had never failed his daughter. She would have to say that for him.

There was much more to be said for Brent, she knew. She also knew she was still in love with him, that she always would be.

But life went on. She had learned that the hard way.

"Honest, I'm not worried," Kathy reassured Shanna. She walked with her daughter to the doorway where David—six foot two, blond, all-American with a wide grin—was waiting.

"Hi, Mrs. McQueen." David never had comprehended why she chose to use her maiden name. "Please don't worry—"

"I'm not worried," Kathy vowed again.

Shanna laughed, stood on tiptoe and gave David a kiss on the cheek. "She's already been through it, Dave. I'll just get my things."

"You're going out from Key Largo, right?" Kathy asked as Shanna ran to her room.

"Right. We can be reached by radio, you know," David assured her. "And you are still invited."

Kathy shook her head. "Thanks, David. I'm having dinner with Axel Fisher."

Shanna had appeared with a duffel bag. "Of Axel Fisher Skin Care Products," she said sweetly. Shanna didn't like Axel. He was tall, urbane and attractive, but he knew very little about dealing with young people. He was attractive in a very studied way, like the male models who showed off his products. He was tanned, his hair was styled, not just cut, and he carefully allotted so many hours of the week to his health club.

He was nice, though. Attentive and caring. Kathy wondered if she would find fault with any man, and if Shanna would do the same. Shanna had found fault with Marla Harrington on her mother's behalf, and she found fault with Axel on her father's behalf.

"You could have brought along Mr. Fisher—" David began.

"No, she could not!" Shanna said emphatically. Then she flushed and apologized. "Sorry, Mom, it's just—"

"That's okay!" Kathy laughed. "Go out with your father and the twit, but draw the line on me."

"Oh, Mom."

"I'm teasing, I swear it. Now go on, and have a great time. And David, give your parents my regards, and my thanks for the invitation. See you Monday sometime."

"Bye, Mom, bye, Patty." Shanna gave Patty a quick kiss on the cheek, then hugged her mother fiercely. David solemnly shook her hand then told Patty goodbye. Patty and Kathy stood together waving as the two went down the walk and out the high gate that surrounded the property.

"You should turn on the security system now," Patty told her.

Kathy shrugged. She didn't worry much about security. There was a gatehouse at the front of the exclusive housing estate, and the entire area was off the beaten track. They were old houses for Miami, built in the early twenties, and most of the houses were still owned by members of the original families. Besides that, Sam, her fiercely loyal Doberman, guarded her house, and only friends could walk by Sam. He knew who belonged at the house and who didn't.

"I'll set the alarm once you head for your sister's, Patty," Kathy told her. "I'm going to have a bath, but I'll be out in time to say goodbye."

"Make sure you set that thing!" Patty warned her, hurrying to her room behind the kitchen. "Alarm can't be any good if you don't bother to set the darn thing. And a high-crime district like this one—"

"The area has a high crime ratio," Kathy said, smiling. "Not our little neighborhood."

Patty sniffed and disappeared. Kathy walked to her bathroom, determined on a long soak in a bubble bath. Then she realized that the scented salts she had just bought were still in the kitchen cabinet where she had stuck the department store bag to get it out of the way.

She went into the kitchen, found the bath salts and took the glass of wine that Patty insisted she bring with her. When she was ensconced in the big oval tub, she took a long swallow of the wine. It was therapeutic. It warmed her to her toes. It warmed away some of the tension deep within her.

She leaned her head back and closed her eyes. Her heart was thundering. Close your eyes, she told herself. Relax. She had to relax.

But trying to relax made her think more. About the tub, about the house, about Brent.

She'd always loved the tub. She loved the bathroom—it was huge and had been redone before they bought the house from her mother's cousin. There were his and her toilet stalls, a giant marble island with a skylight above and double sinks, a shower stall and the tub. It, too, had a skylight, plus a glass wall beside it. Outside the glass wall were shrubs and flowers and a high redwood privacy fence. The back of the property faced the bay, so a breeze was always touching the shrubs and flowers, moving them gently.

She opened her eyes. The hot steam of the bath rose around her, and she felt her tension begin to ease. She took a long sip of her wine, then closed her eyes and leaned her head against the rim of the tub.

If Brent were still her husband, she could have opened one eye and found him standing there. He seemed to sense when she was going to settle in for a long bath. And he would appear in a terry robe, its V-neck displaying his chest, with the mat of sandy and gold hair and taut muscles and the pulse at the base of his throat. He'd show up with a lazy, wicked gleam in his eyes and say her name so softly that it would seem to come off the breeze. She'd smile, and before she'd know it he was stepping in with her, heedless of his robe, which would be soaked and floating around them. He'd hand her a glass of wine and pull her into his arms. Then he would ask her huskily, "Isn't it fun to have a little money at last? It can't buy happiness, but hey, it did buy one hell of a bathtub, huh?"

She would laugh, and he would kiss her, and their

legs would tangle together. She always thought it had to be hard for him to get comfortable. She was a mere five foot three, whereas Brent was six foot two or more, but he would tell her it was impossible to be uncomfortable with her in his arms.

They would laugh and remember what their first place had been like. She had been eighteen and he had been twenty-two and they were trying to live off his club-date fees while she went to school and worked part-time at the Burger Barn. She had been desperately in love with him right from the very first time she had seen him playing his guitar at a friend's wedding. He had been so tall, lean, fascinating with his deep, penetrating eyes that seemed to gaze upon her with ancient wisdom, to sparkle with laughter, to deepen with something more intense. He had appeared older than his years, or maybe it was just that he had already been through so much—a wretched childhood as an orphan, three years in the service, a third of that time in the volatile Middle East, then attendance at a college and survival with his music at the same time.

Kathy had been a senior in high school, and from the first time his eyes had met hers across the room, she had been in love. Later, when the band had stopped playing and pre-recorded music filled the break time, he had walked straight to her, and he had danced with her. She had stared into his eyes and slowly smiled. When he had gone to play again, he sang a song he had written, a soft, romantic ballad he called "Forever My Love." She had felt his voice touch her. It was husky, sure, a tenor with just the slightest hint of a masculine rasp. His eyes had been on her, and she knew that the song had been sung just for her. He admitted later that he'd never sung it in public before, that it had never come together before, but when he had met her, the words, the music, everything had just fallen in place.

Forever, my love…

Well, they had tried it, they had vowed it, and maybe a certain amount of the love would always be there. But on that night so long ago when they had first danced they hadn't known all that was to come between them, the good times and the bad, the heaven and the hell. Nor had they had any way to see the pain that was to befall them.

Kathy sighed softly, opening her eyes. Darkness was falling rapidly. She looked up and saw a murky sky with the stars just beginning to dot the gray.

She started suddenly, thinking that something had tapped against the redwood privacy screen. Sam, she decided. It had to have been Sam. Still, she straightened and stared out. All she saw was the darkness. She rose out of the tub, passing the gilt-edged Victorian mirror by the closet. She paused and smoothed a stray strand of hair. She was still staring at herself seconds later, she realized. Looking for age lines? she taunted silently. Standing away from the mirror, she saw that she did resemble her daughter a great deal. They had the same huge blue eyes and the same soft blond hair, which they wore layered just past their shoulders. And they were both lean and petite with moderate but ample curves, as she liked to call them.

It was when she stepped closer to the mirror that the differences became obvious. Shanna lacked the tiny lines and grooves around the eyes that defined Kathy's age. Maybe it was more than the lines. Maybe it was something in her eyes that betrayed her so quickly. Maybe she needed something to clear them away....

"No," she told the mirror. "Those are character lines, and I earned every single one of them." Managing a rueful smile, she told herself she was not going to wax nostalgic any longer.

She started down the hallway and across the living room. It was only when she was halfway to the kitchen that she realized the television was on and that Patty was standing stock-still in the middle of the room, staring at the screen.

"—and it is believed at this time that Brent McQueen was also aboard the yacht *Theodosia* when it exploded. McQueen and Johnny Blondell were reportedly having serious problems, and McQueen was expected to lay his grievances before Blondell. The body of Johnny Blondell has been found, but not McQueen's. The search team will have to wait for the fire on board to die down before they can look for the remains of any further victims. No one knows the cause of the explosion at this time, but arson is expected."

Kathy inhaled sharply, unable to comprehend

what she was hearing. She walked closer to the television. The anchorman was still talking. A picture of Brent was flashed across the screen, a picture almost twenty years old, one with her in it. His arm was protectively around her, there were conspiratorial smiles on both of their faces, and they were both very beautiful in the simple happiness that radiated from their faces. The picture had been taken at the airport, right after their marriage.

Her hands clenched into fists at her side and she fell to her knees, a ragged, anguished cry wrenched from her lips. Patty walked to her and patted her shoulders. "Kathy, they don't know anything yet. He probably wasn't aboard the yacht. You can't jump to conclusions like those stupid newsmen."

Kathy looked from the screen to Patty, dazed.

"He was having problems with Johnny and he might have died because of them. That little rat! Johnny Blondell was a junky, a womanizer, a slime and an abuser—"

"Kathy, the man is dead."

"And he might have taken Brent with him! Oh, my God!" Kathy breathed. "Shanna! Thank God she can't have heard anything yet!" She hopped to her feet, raced to the phone and tried to call the television station to find out more information. When she finally got through, they were vague, saying that the police didn't know any more yet. "Watch at eleven, and we'll bring you up-to-date information," a deep male voice told her.

"Wait a minute! You're reporting very irresponsibly!" Kathy swore. "You're saying a man might be dead—"

"Honey, wait till eleven. What does all this matter anyway?"

"It's going to matter tremendously to his daughter, in whose name I intend to sue you!" Kathy said, and slammed down the receiver.

"Kathy—" Patty began sympathetically.

"I'm all right!"

She wasn't all right. She was ready to burst into tears. She was torn apart for Shanna. And she was bleeding herself.

A bell clanged, warning them that someone was at the gate. Kathy frowned and hurried to the door, looking through the peephole that showed whoever was on the porch and also magnified the scene at the gate.

A man was standing there.

"My God!" she whispered. "It's about Brent, I know it!"

"Kathy," Patty began again. "Wait—"

Kathy threw open the door and hurried down the porch steps and along the flower-bordered tile path. The dog barked, and Kathy told him to get back. She swung open the gate and cried out when she saw that it wasn't just a man, but Robert McGregor, a plainclothes cop who had gone to school with her and been a friend to both her and Brent.

Fear rushed through her. He had come to tell her

that Brent was dead. The world spun, and she thought she was going to crash to the ground.

"Kathy! It's all right. Listen to me, please. I haven't got much time, I've got to get back to the marina. Listen, he's not dead, I'm sure he's not. I talked to Brent tonight."

"What?" she gasped and sagged against him. He caught her.

"Let me get you back to the house."

"No, no. Tell me now. Talk to me, Robert, please."

"Brent called me. He wanted to talk with me about something. He said he wanted to see me before he saw Johnny. So I know he's all right."

"But you haven't…you haven't seen him?" she whispered.

He shook his head. "But I saw the newscast, and I knew you must be going insane. Now listen to me. I'll find Brent."

She nodded stiffly. "I'll go with you."

"No. You'll go into the house and you'll calm down and relax. *I'll* find Brent."

"But—"

"Please, Kathy. Come on now, I'll take you in."

She straightened and offered him a tight smile. "No, I'm fine, I promise. Go on. And thank you! Bless you!" she added in a whisper as she watched him go down the walk. Then she hurried into the kitchen. "It was Robert McGregor," she told Patty. "He says that Brent wasn't on the yacht. He talked to Brent."

Patty nodded. "Why don't you lie down for a few minutes?"

"If you promise to listen for the door or the phone."

Patty smiled her agreement, and Kathy headed for her bedroom. She was numb. She had to believe Brent was all right. She had to.

She entered her room and closed the door behind her. She had never changed the room. There was the huge closet, the entertainment center, the stereo, the bookcases, the television and DVD machine. The woodwork had been carved to complement the turn-of-the-century dresser set. Old and new, masculine and feminine touches, were combined. It was a room designed for a couple to share. A place to laugh and dream together, to hide away from an intrusive world.

She covered her face with her hands.

The room almost looked as if she had been waiting for Brent to return for the past three years. But now it seemed he never ever would.

Nonsense. Robert had said that Brent was all right.

She was too jittery to sleep. Knowing only another bath would calm her down, she hurried into the bathroom, trying to function normally. After turning on the tap, adding more bubble bath, she pulled the drape on the window of the door that led out to the pool and cabana, and mechanically stripped off her clothing. She stepped into the water.

There was a whirl of darkness in the shadows of the night, and before her scream could find voice, a hand clamped hard over her lips. She threw up a spray of water, flailing with her fists to free herself.

"Kathy!"

She heard her name in a hoarse whisper and still she struggled desperately. When she was dragged against a rock-hard chest, she thrust her knee forward in terror and heard a soft grunt.

She managed to escape the arms, but before she could step from the tub the arms were around her again, dragging her back. She opened her mouth to scream but her assailant's arms and hands were on her mouth once again. He was holding her in a vise-like grip. She writhed and twisted to no avail, panicking when she felt fingers just beneath her breast.

"Kathy! Kathy! For the love of God, it's me!"

She froze. Hysteria rose within her. She had conjured him from the illusions of her mind. She had thought about him stepping into the tub with her….

And now he was there.

He wasn't dead at all. He was there, in her bathtub.

He eased his hold. She drew quickly away from him, gathering bubbles around her, staring at him incredulously.

He was real. A lock of dark, damp hair had fallen seductively over his forehead. His eyes were the same deep rich amber, the lines around them a bit deeper, but attractive. He had a handsome face with a fine bone structure that indicated integrity. The face had aged remarkably well, and it was even more fascinating now for all that character etched into it. She stared at him and knew his death would have killed her deep inside, and that life would have lost all meaning for her. She was still in love with him, and she always had been.

"Brent!"

"Kathy." His voice was husky and low. It was sexy and sensual and deeply masculine, and it touched her as it had always touched her. "Kathy, shut up, please. I need your help."

"Why did you attack me?"

"Why did you scream?"

"I always scream when strange men enter my bathroom."

He grinned. "I'm not a strange man."

"Oh, I do beg to differ!" she retorted. "You're an extremely strange man!"

"Kathy—"

"Brent, for the love of God, would you please get out of the bathtub?"

His smile remained in place. "Brings back memories, doesn't it?"

"Out!"

"Kathy, I need your help."

"Get out of my tub!"

He rose and stood dripping on the bath rug. He pulled off his sneakers and socks. "I hope there's still something of mine around here somewhere," he muttered, unbuttoning his shirt.

"What are you doing?" she nearly shrieked. His sodden shirt fell to the floor. He was half-naked, his jeans clinging tightly to the line of his hard, lean thighs and the muscled curve of his buttocks. The bronze chest that she had ached to touch was suddenly before her, and she was so unnerved she could scarcely bear it.

She leaped up, heedless of her nudity, grabbed a bath towel and wrapped it around herself. But her fingers were trembling and she dropped the towel. He reached for it and handed it to her. Her eyes met his. Then all the emotions that had surged through her in the past few minutes exploded to the surface.

"Damn you! Damn you! You need my help? You broke into my house, you attacked me in the tub—"

"Kathy, *our* house, I still own part of it, remember?"

He was smiling. He was actually smiling. Of course. She was standing there with the towel between them, swearing away, stark naked. Slowly, his lips curled in the way that was so Brent McQueen, and he gave her an easy sensual smile like the one he had given the young woman in the video.

She snatched the towel, then slammed the palms of her hands hard against his chest.

"Kathy—"

"Brent McQueen, how could—"

She broke off as a voice from outside the bedroom door interrupted them. "Kathy!" It was Patty. "Kathy, if you need me…"

For the third time Brent slapped his hand over

her mouth. "Tell her you're fine!" he warned her. She stared at him, her eyes narrowing. He was tense and deadly serious. There was something very hard and lethal about him, and despite herself, she shivered.

What in hell was going on?

He had always been hard; the service had done that to him. And he had always been smart, so he had sometimes been cynical. And he had always been more than a bit of a chauvinist, demanding, autocratic.

But this was something new.

"Kathy?" Patty's anxious voice sounded again.

His eyes glittered, dancing in the false light of the room. "Kathy, so help me God!" he said. His hand rose carefully from her mouth, but he still held both her arms in the vise of his fingers.

"Patty wouldn't hurt you!" she whispered.

"Tell her to go away!" Brent insisted in a soft growl.

"You know you don't live here anymore and we're not married anymore and I'm not at your beck and call—"

"Kathy!" He towered over her, his features taut and strained. "Tell her you're fine. Tell her to go away!"

"I can't—"

"You will!"

She stared at him a moment longer, thinking that she ought to tear every hair out of his head. Then he would be bald. And maybe he wouldn't be so attractive.

No, every hair could be out of his head, he could be painted purple and he would still have the raw, masculine charisma that so easily attracted the adoration of women and the admiration of men.

She breathed deeply, then called out softly. "Patty? I'm fine, just getting dressed. I'll be out in a minute."

"Oh! Thank goodness. I heard some noise. I was getting so worried."

Staring at Brent, she listened to Patty's soft footsteps on the carpet as the woman moved away. "So you are alive," she whispered to Brent.

"Disappointed?" he asked her.

"Of course not. Shanna would have been terribly hurt if you had died."

"Just Shanna?" His hands were on her, still holding her close.

"Well, of course, your death would upset me, too. For old time's sake." Once again, she shoved her fists hard against his chest. "Let me go, Brent, and for God's sake, tell me what the hell is going on!"

He didn't let her go, not right away. He caught her hands, and his fingers wound around her wrists. Then he stared at her for what seemed like aeons. His eyes flashed gold and fire as they moved over her face, then her form. For a moment, she thought he was going to kiss her. That his lips would touch hers with their special, intimate seal, and all the hurt and pain would be gone, erased, like magic.

There was no such thing as magic, and nothing could erase the things that had gone between them.

He released her and walked out of the bathroom.

She followed him, grasped her robe from the bed and quickly slipped into it. Her towel fell to the floor and she realized she could not stand. She sat at the foot of the bed.

He paced, rubbing his temple with his thumb and forefinger.

"Brent?"

He didn't seem to hear her, and only continued to walk across the room.

"Brent?" she repeated. "I've played it your way. Now I asked you to tell me—"

"Dammit, Kathryn, I don't know what is going on."

"But you're alive and—"

"Yes, yes! And I'm alive because I wasn't on that boat. But Johnny's murderer is after me, and I can't quite figure out what the hell is going on." He had stopped pacing and stood before her tensely. Then he dropped to one knee and caught her hands. "You're going to listen to me, Kathryn, and do what I say."

"Brent—"

"You don't owe me anything. But you're going to do what I tell you now!"

It was an order, not an appeal. He really hadn't changed at all.

She pulled her hands away and curled her feet beneath her. "Am I really? Tell me, McQueen, just what it is you're assuming I'm going to do."

Chapter 2

This really wasn't going at all well, Brent thought, staring at Kathy as she stared at him. He hadn't expected to find her in the bathroom, and he hadn't expected her to scream at the sight of him. Well, all right, so maybe he hadn't expected her to jump up and down with joy, but he hadn't thought it would get so damned physical.

Or that it would hurt so much. As if his heart was being torn out all over again.

He stiffened his spine and squared his shoulders. This had to do with life and death, and she was going to have to listen to him. She had to quit with that imperious stare. But then that was part of Kathy's charisma. She looked like a snow princess with her startling blue, almost cobalt, eyes and silky blond hair. Her features were near perfect. Her face was oval, her cheekbones defined, her lips generous but beautifully shaped, and her eyebrows with a little arch that could give her a look of annoying superiority. Despite that, there had been times when his need to protect her had been enormous. And it could be just like trying to protect a barracuda at times, he reminded himself.

She was still staring at him, waiting.

"Kathy, where is Shanna?" he asked.

She seemed startled. "Out with her boyfriend," she replied. "I get the first questions, Brent. Why the bathroom? After three years apart, most men would have rung a doorbell."

And after three years, most men might have found a new life, he thought bitterly. He never had. No matter where he went, or what he did, images of Kathy were always there. She intruded on a dance floor, she intruded in bed. Sometimes, alone at night, he'd stare at the ceiling and try to remind himself that they'd had an uncanny ability to fight like warring politicians. But the memories would keep going, and he'd remember the way the fights would end, how they would both be so alive and on fire with passion. And that made the love and tenderness that followed so much sweeter....

But in the end, the pain had just been too much. When he couldn't bear it any longer, he had walked away.

She could have had the decency to change, though, he thought. She hadn't, not a whit. She should have gone gray, or gained fifty pounds, sagged somewhat with the gravity of time. But she hadn't. That was one fact he was sure of from their encounter in the bathtub. She was browned from the sun, slim and still beautifully curved. Her eyes were enormous and exquisitely blue. Her blond hair was soft and curled over her shoulders, looking sleek and achingly inviting.

"Kathy," he said wearily, "you're not getting the drift of this—"

"Because you're not telling me anything!" she flared.

He swore softly and turned from her, padding to the closet. With any luck, she wouldn't have burned every single thing he used to own.

"Brent, you're dripping all over the place!" she called irritably after him. "All over my rug—"

He poked his head out of the closet door. "My rug, too," he reminded her pleasantly.

She was on her feet, hands on hips, staring at him. "We agreed to keep the house together until Shanna was twenty-one. I'm to live in it, and we both have the option to buy the other out, or share in the profits if we sell it to someone else. The agreement does not mean that you can enter via the bathroom at any time and soak the place! You're walking all over with those drenched pants."

She knew the second the words were out that she shouldn't have spoken. He stared at her hard, smiled slowly, then unzipped his pants. She turned with a soft oath on her lips because she knew damned well that he was going to strip his pants right off and throw them on the floor.

He did. She heard them fall. "Happy?" he asked her softly.

She strode quickly to the dresser that had always been his, and hunched down to reach the bottom drawer. She found a pair of his briefs, socks and jeans and threw them in the general area of where he was standing.

"Fifteen years and you suddenly want modesty?" he queried in the same soft tone.

"Fifteen, and then three!" she reminded him, her back to him as she fished through her own dresser for jeans and a soft blue knit pullover. She could sense that he hadn't picked up his clothing.

"Am I disturbing you?" he asked, and despite the circumstances, she could hear the humor in his voice.

She turned and looked him straight in the eye. "No." Her gaze started to slip down his body. She couldn't stand there much longer. "Excuse me, I'll take the bathroom. If you think you can refrain from entering it for a few moments, that is?"

His smile slowly deepened. "Well, I'll try, Ms. O'Hara. I'll certainly try."

She headed into the bathroom. She brushed her hair before the mirror over the sink and realized that her hands were shaking badly. She gripped the sink hard to make them stop. *He was alive.* The thought filled her completely. But he was talking in riddles, and she wasn't getting anywhere with him. The past kept leaping before them.

And desire, she reminded herself ruefully. She felt as if she hurt all over and she closed her eyes, wishing desperately that she had fallen out of love, not just out of marriage.

She took a deep breath, swung around and went into the bedroom. Being clothed was much better. Brent was in the closet, but his wet jeans were hanging on the bathroom doorknob. His dry jeans and briefs had disappeared.

He appeared in the doorway a second later, buttoning a tailored striped shirt. "You kept things," he said bluntly.

She shrugged and sat on the bed. "I meant to have you pick them up, or else send them to you. Then I decided you probably didn't need them anymore. So I was going to have them all sent to the refugee camps, but I never did. Brent, tell me what—"

"Exactly where is Shanna?" he demanded, interrupting her.

"She's out with David. I think you know him."

"Where?" he snapped.

"You should have stayed in the army! You would have made a wonderful drill sergeant."

He strode across the room and leaned over her, bracing his hands on the bed. "I need to know where she is," he said tensely.

Before she could reply, there was a tap on the door. "Kathy? Are you all right? I'm not going to leave you alone tonight, you know that," Patty called to her worriedly through the door.

Brent backed away. "She's not going to leave you alone tonight?" he whispered in dismay.

"We thought you were dead, remember?" she whispered.

A smile crooked his lips. "And you were that upset?"

"I couldn't begin to imagine having to tell Shanna," she retorted.

"Kathy, please! Are you all right in there?"

"Why can't I tell Patty?"

He shook his head vehemently. "Tell her to go home. Or to her sister's, or the movies, I don't care where."

With an exaggerated sigh she hurried to the door while Brent flattened himself against the wall. She opened the door. "Patty, please, go on. I know that Brent is all right, and I'm fine. I might even take the boat out to join Shanna just in case she hears something. You go on now."

"But Kathy," Patty protested. "I couldn't leave you alone, not when you were so hysterical."

"But I'm not hysterical now," Kathy insisted, gritting her teeth. "Please, Patty, I'll be fine."

"Well, all right then, but you know where to reach me if you need me," Patty said at last.

"Of course." Kathy gave her a warm hug and a kiss on the cheek.

"And you come out and put on that security system, do you hear me?" Patty charged her.

"Yes," Kathy said dryly. "Yes, I think I should." She followed Patty into the living room. Let Brent pace and fume for a few minutes. He was darned lucky she hadn't set it before. Sam was still the best security in the world, she thought, except that Sam had always loved Brent and apparently hadn't forgotten that for a single moment. The dog had probably licked Brent's face and hands the entire time Brent was sneaking into the bathroom.

Even dogs were traitors!

Kathy spent ten minutes assuring Patty she was fine, then another ten getting her out the door. She started to set the alarm when Brent's voice suddenly made her jump nearly a foot.

"Who the hell is that coming now?" Brent demanded at her shoulder.

She stood on her toes and looked through the peephole.

Axel was at the gate. Sam didn't like Axel very much, so he had started to bark. Axel, very tan, very tall and looking perfectly urbane in very fashionable clothing, was at the gate, swearing.

The bell rang.

"Who is it?" Brent demanded.

"A friend," Kathy murmured.

"A friend?"

"Okay, a friend with whom I have a date," she said.

Axel was still swearing at the dog, and Brent was swearing at her under his breath.

"Couldn't wait for my body to grow cold, huh?"

"I made the date last week," she answered. "And we've been divorced for three years, Brent."

He wasn't going to argue with her over that. Leaning against the door, he stared at her and charged her, "Get rid of him."

She glared at him. "You know, Brent, I did have plans—"

"Get rid of him, Kathy."

"Don't you talk to me like that and—"

"All right, please get rid of him, Kathy." He didn't wait for an answer, but turned and looked through the peephole. He smiled at her. "Natty dresser, huh?"

"He dresses quite nicely, actually."

"Yep. Just like dating a Ken doll, eh, Barbie?"

"Speaking of Barbies, where is Miss Harrington? Marla, isn't it? Couldn't you have gone to her for help?"

He didn't blink or betray a single emotion. "She isn't the mother of my daughter," he told her simply. "Kathy, please go do something with Mr. Sunshine. I want to get to Shanna as soon as possible."

Her eyes widened with alarm. "Why? What's wrong? What's going to happen to—"

"Kathy, I'll explain, I promise. But Sam is barking loudly enough to wake the dead, and if you don't answer that door, your, er, friend is going to call the police."

"You're blocking my way," she said.

He stepped quickly aside. Kathy hurried down the walk to the gate. "Down, Sam, down!" she told the dog. But Sam was still jumping at the gate, no longer barking, but whining unhappily. He knew

Brent was in the house. He was worse than a mother, Kathy thought.

"Sam, down!"

"Kathy, that dog is getting dangerous," Axel warned her.

"He's supposed to be dangerous. He's a guard dog," she said sweetly as she opened the gate. Axel would have come in, but she slipped out quickly, closing the gate on the dog. Axel was frowning, looking at her casual attire. "I know I said that we didn't need to dress for dinner, but—"

"I can't go, Axel," she said.

"What's the matter?"

"Nothing, really. There's, uh, there's been an accident, and Brent's name has been linked with it and I want to stay here in case Shanna calls."

"Oh!" Startled, Axel looked at her worriedly. "Oh, Kathy, I'm really sorry. Of course, we'll cancel dinner. I'm sure you must be very concerned. I'll stay with you—"

"No!" she said quickly, then instantly regretted her outburst. There were nice things, really nice things, about Axel. His concern for her was one. "Axel, please forgive me. I have a horrible headache. I just want to get some rest and be alone. Please. I appreciate your concern and I am so sorry, it's just—"

"Hey!" He caught her face between his hands and held it tenderly, staring into her eyes. "Kathy, it's all right. I understand. Call me if you need me, if I can do anything, anything at all."

She nodded, feeling horribly guilty. He bent and softly kissed her lips, then urged her toward the gate. "Get on in there now."

"I will."

"Set the alarm."

"I will. Right away."

"Call me!"

"I will."

He nodded and started toward his bloodred Ferrari. "You do have Sam!"

Yes, she did have Sam. And Sam could protect her against anyone. Except the one man she most needed protection from.

She locked the gate and waved at Axel, then hurried to the house. The door opened when she reached it. As soon as she stepped inside, it closed behind her. Brent was leaning against it, watching her with a wicked gleam in his eyes.

"A friend, huh?" he asked.

"Yes."

"What a tender farewell."

"He's a tender sort of guy," she said, waving a hand in the air.

He stepped away from the door, and in a second he was standing before her, looking into her eyes. They might have been kids again, volatile, very passionate and insanely jealous.

"So just how serious is it with you and Ken?"

"Axel. His name is Axel," she said sweetly.

"Well?"

She smiled slowly, enjoying the moment. At least she didn't appear on videos with Axel with her chest bared. Maybe it wasn't quite the same thing, but…

"He's a friend. And what is it to you, Mr. McQueen?"

"I'm concerned for your welfare, nothing more, Ms. O'Hara," he told her. But his eyes were on her mouth. He wasn't touching her at all, but she felt the warmth that radiated from him as if it was the glow of a fire enveloping her….

"I just wondered if it was the same," he said.

"The same?"

His head lowered and his mouth caught hold of hers, and waves of sensation, memories and more, flooded throughout her limbs and her torso and rushed wickedly along the length of her spine. His tongue flicked softly over her lips and gained entrance. She should have denied his gentle assault, but she could not. She trembled, wishing it wasn't the same, wishing she wasn't so easy. Wishing that Axel's kiss was something pleasant, not unstirring. Wishing that the mere contact with Brent's mouth didn't cause such an explosion of passion and desire….

He stepped back. If she hadn't caught herself instantly, she would have fallen. Her eyes flew open, and she could still feel his mouth touching hers. He was studying her so intently, and she was afraid she would betray her feelings.

"Well?" he said very softly.

"Well, what?" she demanded.

"Is there a difference?"

"Well, no, you haven't changed."

"But you don't love me anymore."

"I did for fifteen years. Perhaps now I don't know, but the thought of your kiss—"

"Or the reality of it," he interjected.

"Hmm. Anyway, it doesn't make me want to throw up or anything," she said sweetly.

He groaned softly, then he laughed, and he pulled her to him. She felt the bulge of muscles in his arms and the hardness of his chest, and she suddenly knew that if he came a single hair closer to her, she would burst into tears and beg him to try to explain to her what had gone wrong.

She wound her fingers around his wrist and stepped back. "Brent, what about Shanna? You broke into my bathroom, you made me send Patty away and break a date and now you have me worried senseless and I still haven't the faintest idea what is going on. Tell me!"

He released her. Still comfortable in the house, he strode across the living room toward the kitchen. He opened the refrigerator and pulled out a beer, casting her a curious gaze at the change in her brand.

"Brent—"

"All right," he said. "I'll start with tonight. I was supposed to have dinner with Johnny on that yacht of his. Johnny wanted to keep the Highlanders going for another album and I didn't want to have anything more to do with him."

Kathy pulled a soda from the refrigerator, sat on one of the kitchen-counter bar stools and nodded. Brent and Johnny were entirely different people. "He's still late to rehearsals, pulls no-shows and the like?" she said.

He nodded. "Well, he was still that way," he said softly. "But there was more than that going on."

"Oh?"

He leaned over the counter toward her, and she saw tension tighten his features. She wanted to ease it away. There was so much she loved about his face. It wasn't just that he was handsome. It was the character in his features, and the wisdom and determination in his gaze, even the penetrating golden light that sometimes seemed to impale her. In an argument it was awful. But when they did manage to speak, it was wonderful and understanding, and could enter her soul and see the things she couldn't quite say.

She closed her eyes tightly. Something horrible was going on. Shanna could be in danger.

"Johnny was afraid of something or someone. I don't know what. He didn't want to be alone."

"So he knew someone was after him. Is that why you called Robert?"

He glanced at her sharply. "He's a cop and a good friend. I knew he would be discreet."

"So why didn't you go see him after all?" she demanded.

He sighed and took a deep swallow of the beer. "I am going to see him. Just as soon as I get you and Shanna out of the country."

"Out of the country!" Kathy exclaimed. "But Brent, Johnny could easily have had lots of enemies. Why would anyone—"

"Kathy, there were all kinds of news reports about the fact that I was going to be with Johnny tonight. I have reason to believe that I was supposed to go up in smoke with Johnny. Someone didn't just want him dead—whoever it was wanted something from him, too."

"Wanted what?" Kathy demanded.

"I don't know, I don't know." Brent set his drink down and rubbed his fingers wearily through his hair as he paced the kitchen.

"Just because—" Kathy began.

"That's not all!" Brent interrupted harshly. "Do you remember a man named Harry Robertson?"

She thought for a moment then nodded. "He was the backup musician who went to prison for smuggling, right? He worked with you when you and Johnny and the others got together for that benefit concert right before…" Her voice trailed away for a moment. It had been right before Ryan had died, right before she lost the new baby, right before…

"Right," Brent said harshly, then continued quickly. "I always felt kind of bad for Harry. I had this feeling he had been coerced into his smuggling activities. Except that I was in the group when he was trying to steal Mexican treasures from the time of the conquistadores. Still…I think he was pressured from the outside, but he wouldn't say. He seemed scared to death all the time. He played and played and played that tune of mine, 'Forever My Love.' He wouldn't talk. He wouldn't let any of us help him at his trial."

"So he went to prison," Kathy whispered.

"And he was murdered there a year later," Brent said.

Startled, Kathy sat back. "Murdered?"

"Well, the papers said he died in a prison fight. That he was stabbed to death. No one was ever prosecuted for his death, but—"

"Maybe he wasn't murdered. Maybe it was just a fight."

Brent shook his head. "No, I don't think so. I've been remembering who was in the group back then, Kathy. It was Johnny and me, the Hicks brothers, Keith Montgomery—and Harry Robertson and Larry Jenkins. And guess where Larry Jenkins is right now."

Kathy shook her head, a chill sliding up her spine. "Dead?" she whispered uneasily.

Brent nodded. "Larry was killed in a car accident, all alone, out on the highway, not a month ago. Then Keith's wife was killed, too, the same way."

Kathy gasped. "You think she was murdered, too? Oh, my God, why?"

"I don't know, Kathy. I don't know. But can you understand now why I want you and Shanna out of here before I do anything?"

"Do anything!" Kathy protested. "You've got to go to the police—"

"Kathy, I am going to go to the police. But I'm not going to be a sitting victim for whatever it is that's going on."

"Don't you dare think you can take care of this by yourself."

"Kathy! I just said I'm going to the police, all right? But I don't want anyone to know where I am until I reach Shanna and get the two of you away, do you understand?"

Kathy exhaled slowly.

"You got an ice chest here?" he asked her.

"What?"

"She's gone with David to the Keys, right?"

Kathy nodded.

"Well then," Brent said softly, "we've got to catch up with them and bring her home so I can make arrangements to get you both far away."

"I can just radio to them from the boat," Kathy said.

"Radio! You want to announce all this over open airwaves?"

"I—"

"No, we've got to sail down there and get her ourselves. And we should go now, right now. What have you got in here that we can take to eat?"

She stared at him. She couldn't go off with him alone in the boat—she just couldn't. She had a forty-foot sailboat with a great motor that would get them wherever they wanted to go no matter what the weather, but that wasn't the point.

Once, it had been *their* sailboat. He had been the

captain and she the first mate and they had spent hours and hours of their free time sailing her—to the Keys, to the Bahamas, wherever they had time to go. They had spent long, lazy afternoons on the boat, sunning, fishing, snorkeling, diving…

Fighting, and making love.

"Kathy, what's the matter with you? We've got to go! What can we pack—"

"We don't need to pack anything."

"What?"

"The—the galley is stocked."

He seemed to freeze for a minute. Then his eyes became darker than amber, and she knew he was holding a tight rein on his temper. "I see," he said coolly. "You and What's-his-name spend a lot of time aboard her now."

"Axel. And we were just going to go out on Sunday," Kathy said. Then she leaped off her bar stool and exploded. "What business is it of yours, McQueen? You walked away. And you seem to be spending all your time with that little twit—"

"Little twit?"

"Marla Harrington. And twit's your daughter's term, not mine!"

He stared at her as if he was going to explode. Then the darkness left his eyes and a golden flame of humor sizzled in them. "You should hear what she calls your good friend Axel," he warned her.

"What?"

He twisted his jaw and shook his head, silently

laughing. "Never mind. Let's go. Call Patty and make sure she'll feed Sam for the next couple of days in case we have trouble finding them."

"You want me to call Patty after—"

"Yes. Tell her you just want to be with Shanna. I'm sure she'll understand."

"But not good enough for me to tell her the truth."

"Dammit, Kathy, I don't want to drag anyone into this if I don't have to. You and Shanna are known quantities in my life. Patty isn't. Don't tell her anything. Then let's go. It's dark. We should be able to get to the docks without being seen. And we'll slip out really quietly. And find Shanna."

She nodded, but she still wasn't moving.

"What's the matter?"

She shook her head. "I just—I just wasn't planning on a cruise with you this evening," she murmured. And certainly not on the *Sweet Eden*, the vessel that had played such a very important part in their lives….

He came close to her, a wicked grin on his lips, and he leaned low to meet her eyes.

"What's the matter, Kath? Frightened of the things going on? Or of me?"

She shook her head, smiling. "Uh-uh."

"Hmm," he murmured. "Maybe you should be. 'Cause you know what, my love? I can still kiss you without thinking that I should throw up, either."

"How sweet. You always did have a way with words."

His smile deepened. "They were your words, remember? Actually, when I kissed you, there were other things I was thinking about. Lots and lots of other things. Maybe we should both be afraid," he said huskily. Then he turned away from her. "Come on. We've really got to go. I need my wallet. Get whatever you need and let's get out of here. I'll lock up the back where I came in through the bathroom. You still have that little secret door for Sam?"

"Uh, yes. He can come in or out if he wants. He usually likes to be out, though."

"Patty has keys?"

She nodded jerkily. "Brent—"

"Kathy, move!"

He was already past her, on his way to the bedroom.

She gritted her teeth. She wanted to fight and argue and deny any time with him at all. She wanted to deny any feeling for him!

But she had to reach her daughter. It was a desperate situation, and he did seem to have it all figured out.

It was just that she was going to go with him. Alone. Aboard the *Sweet Eden*.

A curious warmth snaked along the length of her spine, and for a moment she could barely breathe. She couldn't be alone with him. They'd been apart for three years and she'd barely seen him again and already…

It was almost as if they had never parted. His kiss, his touch, were every bit as evocative, as seductive, as they had ever been.

They'd been apart. They were divorced. Their daughter was at stake. Surely, she could go with him and hold her own.

Surely, she could…

"Kathy!"

It seemed that she jumped a mile at the sound of his voice. She spun. He was at the door, ready, his gaze sharp, his voice commanding.

She could hold her own.

She smiled sweetly at him. She just had to remember that he could be a temperamental, domineering son of a gun, that was all. Then she'd be just fine.

She collected a purse, slipped into a pair of sneakers then hurried to the door. He was there waiting.

"Let's go!" he said impatiently.

She sailed past him, her jaw clenched tight, her smile still in place.

"Fine! Let's go!"

She was holding her own, all right.

She was trembling like a leaf as the warm night air embraced her and they slipped away into the darkness.

Chapter 3

The moon was full, casting a surreal glow on the stately old houses along the way to the water. There wasn't another soul around as Brent led the way down the dock and leaped aboard the *Sweet Eden*. "Get the ropes, Kath, will you?"

She paused, arching a brow, then decided that she would help cast away without arguing.

The *Sweet Eden* was hers, though. They might have owned it together once, but it was all hers now. Yet he seemed to think he still owned it!

By the time she had tossed the ropes to the deck and jumped aboard, he'd switched on the lights and started the motor. As she moved to take a seat at the helm, she found he had beat her to it.

Not that he wasn't an excellent sailor. He always had been. He loved the water and everything to do with it.

He smiled at her as she approached him. "Have a seat, Kathryn. My God, it's peaceful out here, isn't it?"

Kathy sat on the curve of the seat beside him. The

Sweet Eden was a nicely shaped and compact sailboat with all the pleasures of home—well, almost all the pleasures. There was no gigantic bath aboard. The heads were small and compact. The helm was situated at the rear with topside space for about ten people. Down a flight of six steps were the galley, dining area and two cabins, one portside and one starboard. Each had a tiny head with a toilet, shower and sink.

Despite the fact that there was plenty of space between them, Kathy sat gingerly on the edge of the padded fiberglass seat. "It's quiet because very few people go on pleasure cruises at this time of night."

"Really?" he drawled.

"Mmm. And would you like me to take over? It is a little tricky here out to the bay—"

"I'm fine."

"It's been three years—"

"Kathy, I've done this hundreds of times. I know what I'm doing."

"It's my boat!"

His teeth flashed white in the shadows of the night. "So it is, Ms. O'Hara. Indulge me."

She threw up her hands. "Indulge you? Brent, I'm indulging the hell out of you as it is! Think about it. We haven't exchanged a single word in three years and the next thing I know you're in my bathtub."

"My bathtub, too."

"Your use of the facilities for bubble baths was not in the agreement!" Kathy reminded him indignantly. "Nor do I owe you this, any of this. I'm not even sure if I agree with what we're doing! And at the very least, you might want to recall, Brent, you walked out on me!"

"You filed for the divorce."

"You left—"

He exploded suddenly with a long, passionate oath, his fingers winding white-knuckled and tense over the wheel. "We'd lost one child and I'd caused you to lose another. How the hell long was I supposed to stay?"

Kathy gasped and leaped to her feet, stunned by the fury and passion—and the anguish—of his words. This was a mistake. There was nothing left between them except for old wounds. Agonizing wounds, barely sutured, that bled at the slightest brush.

"You're right!" she snapped. "There was nothing to stay for, nothing at all."

Tears were nearly blinding her. She left him and hurried below. He did know what he was doing. He could fend for himself.

She entered the first cabin and fell upon the bunk, clenching her teeth hard to hold the emotions surging inside her at bay. She didn't want to remember, she hated to remember. Maybe it had all started with the television today, maybe Brent's last words really had very little to do with it. But it was all there, rushing over her.

Ryan had been so little. Just two months old. And they had tried for him for so long, Kathy becoming concerned, Brent telling her that trying was the most fun in the whole world. And then they'd had him and he'd been the most beautiful little boy in the world, with huge blue eyes and dark blond curls, and they'd all adored him, Shanna included. But then the night had come when he should have started crying at his feeding time and Kathy had lain there awake smiling, just waiting. She waited and waited, then she got up and walked down the hall to his room and to his crib. She found him lying on his stomach, his little rump up in the air, as he slept so very often.

But when she reached for him, he was cold. So cold. She turned him over and his tiny lips were blue, and it was then that she started to scream.

In seconds Brent was down the hall and in the room. He shocked her into action and between them, they tried to revive him while Shanna called 911.

There was nothing anyone could do. It was sudden infant death syndrome, the doctor explained, so tragic, a horrible loss, and only God could understand. And she had cried and cried and hated God with all her might, and Brent, immersed in the loss, had held her. He'd been the rock she so desperately needed.

It was only later that she began to lose him, and she never saw it. Maybe she had begun to lash out first, maybe she'd been trying to crawl out of the lonely well of pain. Maybe she had wanted to fight because fighting made her feel as if they were still alive....

"Kathy."

She started, amazed to see him silhouetted in the doorway. She hadn't turned on the cabin lights, and they were in darkness and shadow. She realized the engine had stopped.

"Brent—"

"It's all right. We're hugging the coast and I'm anchored."

"You're sure—"

"Kathy, I'm sure. Honestly, I do know what I'm doing." She could see the flash of his rueful smile in the darkness. "Maybe I haven't been aboard this boat in a while, but I have been on others."

Yes, he had. He'd been on one in the video, with Marla Harrington draped all over him.

He took a step into the room and sat on the bunk beside her. Before she could stop him, before she realized what he was doing, he reached out and touched her cheek, then rubbed his fingers together after finding the dampness there. Quickly she wiped away the tears.

"Kathy, I'm sorry, really sorry."

She wanted to speak quickly. She wanted to escape the close confines of the cabin. She didn't want him so near, and she didn't want him touching her because it all felt so natural and so right. She wanted him so badly, wanted to be held in his arms, wanted his kiss, wanted his naked body next to hers, wanted to make love…

And it wouldn't be right. It would be very, very wrong. It hadn't been a casual affair that had ended, maybe to be resumed again. It had been their whole lives, and their lives had been shattered, and she wasn't playing with that kind of fire ever again.

"It's all right, Brent."

"You're crying."

"It's not your fault."

"It is, and it was."

"No, it was nobody's fault, remember? That's what they said."

"Kathy, I didn't mean to do this to you, I just wanted to get you and Shanna to safety. Want to try to start over for the evening?"

What else was there to do? She couldn't go home because they still had to find their daughter. And she couldn't stay in the cabin because she would throw her arms around him and burst into tears and beg him to make love to her just one more time, and give her one more memory to live on during the empty years to follow.

If they survived this, she thought fleetingly, then pushed the thought furiously away.

They would survive. She'd make Brent be careful, if nothing else. If he was going to make them go away, she was going to make him go away, too, she decided firmly.

"Dinner," she breathed.

"Pardon?"

"You said that you wanted to start the night over. All right, you muscled your way to the helm. Want to muscle your way to the galley?"

"Sure." He stood, reached down a hand to her and pulled her to her feet. Then he paused for a moment and she thought her heart stopped beating, that the whole world and time had ceased to exist. She thought he was going to touch her again, to say something, but he did not. He left the cabin and strode down the aisle to the galley.

"All right, Ms. O'Hara, what am I cooking?"

"I'm not sure," she admitted. She opened the tiny refrigerator behind the carved oak counter and started looking through the provisions. "Omelets!" she said at last. She set a dozen eggs on the stainless steel counter by the sink then began adding other ingredients. "Mushrooms, peppers, onions, cheese, sausage—"

"Hold up on the sausage, Ms. O'Hara," he instructed her. "That must be for the new love of your life. I detest sausage, remember?"

He spoke lightly but there was an edge to his voice. And when she glanced at him, he was leaning over the counter, watching her, a golden light glistening in his eyes. She hadn't forgotten the danger signals. She smiled sweetly, wondering why she felt such a rush of excitement at his anger. Was he jealous? If so, it was damned nice. He hadn't a thing to be jealous about, but he didn't know that. "Sorry," she told him casually. "I guess I did forget."

"Do you have any normal beer in there?" he asked her.

"Normal beer?"

"Good old American brew. Instead of your, er, friend's trendy water?"

Shanna had done some of the stocking of the

galley, and all her life, she had stocked it with her father's favorites. Kathy tossed Brent a beer.

"Thanks. I guess memory does survive at times."

"In your daughter's heart."

"So is he much of a sailor?" Brent asked politely.

"He's fine."

"Just fine? I would have thought that you would have demanded so much more out of life."

"We were talking about sailing."

"Were we? I had the impression we were talking about something else. Everything about him seems to be fine. Not good, not great, not wonderful. Just fine. You ought to be shooting for wonderful, Kathy."

"Ah. Because you were wonderful?" she challenged him.

He smiled, his lip curving slowly. He bent close to her and lifted a lock of her hair, then slowly let it go. "Yeah. At some things. We were pretty wonderful."

She pulled away from him, bumping her head against the cabinets. He started to reach for her, worried, and she pulled away again. "I'm fine! It's okay. Hey, you're supposed to be doing the cooking remember."

"Yeah, sure."

He sipped his beer, set the can on the counter and started to rummage through the cabinets. "Where the heck is the frying pan?"

"Amazing, isn't it? You remember the docks and the ships and everything else—but not where the pans are kept!" Deciding they were never going to eat if she didn't get him started, Kathy found the large frying pan and a cutting board. Brent managed to find some butter in the refrigerator, then the bread basket, and while she chopped peppers and mushrooms and onions, he cut slices of bread. As long as she was busy with the work before her, her eyes on her chopping, she thought she could manage a few queries.

"So tell me, Brent. How about you? Is Marla... just wonderful?"

He made a grunting sound. "Marla isn't anything at all," he told her briefly.

"Whoops. Trouble in paradise?" she asked sweetly.

He cast her a glance. "Where are you getting your information?" he asked her. "If you've been reading those rag magazines, you should recall that they once had a story about the two of us breaking up because you were having an affair with an Arab prince."

She had to smile, the story had been so ridiculous. They had both laughed over it, wondered whether to sue or not. Then Brent's lawyer had demanded a retraction and it had been given.

Kathy tossed the peppers into a little glass bowl and started on the mushrooms. "No, I haven't been reading rag magazines. I only read the front pages in the supermarket, and I try to refrain from reading about you at all."

"Do you?" he asked wickedly. "You mean you're never just the slightest bit interested in what I'm up to?"

"Nope," Kathy said, meeting his eyes, tossing a handful of mushrooms into the bowl.

"Ah, yes, that's because you're so involved with Mr. Fine."

"He's a very considerate man."

"That must be exciting."

"Not as exciting as Marla Harrington, I'm sure."

He sipped his beer again and leaned over the counter, watching her. "So what do you know about Marla? And if you're not interested, why do you know anything?"

"We share a child, remember?"

"I see. So what did our shared child tell you?"

"Just that she's a twit," Kathy said sweetly.

"What makes you think I'm involved with the twit?" he asked.

"Well, if you're not involved with the twit, she's involved with you. She was draped all over you like curtains in that video."

He started to laugh, straightening. She cast him a glance and nearly chopped off her fingertip. "It's nice to see you still have claws!" he told her.

"I haven't," she denied.

"But that sounds like such a jealous comment!"

"It's not jealous at all. It's just a comment."

"And you don't read anything about me, but you did see the video."

"What did you want me to say to your daughter when she insisted that I come out to see it? She's very proud of you, you know. And I've never discouraged that."

He was silent for a second, then she felt his eyes again, very warm upon her. "I know," he said huskily.

Again, it seemed that the space around them was too tight, that he was too close. She could smell a hint of his aftershave, feel the warmth of his body. It was so easy to let the years apart disappear, to pretend that this was like many a voyage they had taken, to imagine that she could drop what she was doing, forget the omelet, cry out and throw her arms around him, and damn everything else.

"So," she said quickly, desperate to break the spell, "is it on or off with you and Marla?"

"Marla? Not the twit?"

"Even twits have names," she said pleasantly.

"It was never on," he said.

"You should tell that to Marla."

"I have."

"I think she's in love with you."

"All that from a video?" he demanded. "Are you sure you haven't been reading rag magazines?"

She smiled. "Women don't drape that way unless they're in love."

"It was a video. She was acting."

"She is a…friend, though, I take it?"

"I met her through the Hicks brothers. They always have lots and lots of friends around them.

Why don't you just come right out and ask me what you want to know."

She gazed at him, startled. "And what is it that I want to know?"

"If I'm sleeping with her or not."

She kept staring at him. She wanted to tell him she could care less who he was sleeping with. "All right," she said blandly. "Are you sleeping with her?"

He picked up a piece of pepper and popped it into his mouth. "No, and I never was. My turn. Are you sleeping with Mr. So-so?"

"Brent, that's none of your—"

"Are you?"

She exhaled. "I—no."

He smiled and turned away, coming around the counter to pick up the eggs. He broke them into a large bowl. "I'm glad," he said quietly.

"Oh? Was I supposed to remain celibate forever?"

"Hardly," he said, whipping up the eggs. "But if you're going to have an affair, it should be a lot better than just fine."

"Thanks. I think." She hesitated. He'd turned on a burner and begun to cook. Once he'd flipped the omelet he glanced up to find her staring at him.

"What?" he demanded.

"I was just wondering about the rest of your life."

"What about it?"

"Oh. Just what you've been doing with it."

"And who I've been doing it with?"

"It's really none of my business, is it?"

He offered her a crooked smile, lowered his lashes and slid the omelet onto a plate without answering. He poured in the remaining mixture. "My life is rather at a stalemate," he told her.

She didn't say anything, but picked up the plate along with napkins and silverware and asked, "Want to eat topside?"

"Sure. There's a great moon out there tonight." He was still staring at the frying pan, and still grinning, she thought. Then his eyes rose to hers. "You're not afraid to be with me, up there, in all that moonlight, are you?"

"Have you taken up turning into a wolf during the full moon?" Kathy asked. Then, before he could reply, she answered herself. "Never mind. You always were a wolf by the full moon. And any other moon, at that."

"Not always."

"Oh?"

"It depends on the available prey," he told her.

"Ah, I see. Where do ex-wives fit in?"

"I've only got one," he reminded her.

"So?"

"It kind of depends on the ex-wife," he said. He flipped the omelet, slipped it onto a plate and smiled innocently at her. "What are you drinking, Ms. O'Hara? Wine cooler or a foreign beer?"

"A domestic beer will be fine, thank you, Mr. McQueen," she said sweetly, then quickly preceded him up the steps. She felt the warm breeze touch her, and she was instantly aware of the moon. It was very full, glowing with a soft shimmer over the water. The *Sweet Eden* rocked gently at anchor. Across the lightly rippling waves, Kathy could see the lights of the shoreline. It was a beautiful view, stunning. And they were all alone within it. She couldn't see another boat anywhere. There was nothing to see except for the lights on the shore, the velvet darkness of the sky and the beauty of the moon and the stars. And there was the water, too, seemingly eternal. The shoreline was the only touch of civilization, and it seemed a long way away.

She perched on the padded fiberglass bench, and in another moment, Brent was with her. He sat down on the curve of the seat, so that they weren't touching, and yet they weren't very far apart. He offered her a beer and she silently passed him a fork and napkin in return.

"What a stunning night," he murmured.

She nodded, watching the stars. "Where would you be, Brent, if you weren't here?" she asked him impulsively.

"What?" he asked softly.

"If you weren't so worried about Shanna. Where would you be, what would you be doing tonight?"

"I thought you weren't really so interested in my life."

"What would you be doing?" she repeated.

He shrugged. "Well, I was supposed to be meeting with Johnny, remember? And I was supposed to be meeting Robert, so I would have been doing one of those two things."

"And if not meeting with people?" Kathy persisted.

He smiled. "This particular Saturday night I was invited to be out with Shanna and David and his parents."

"You were!" Kathy exclaimed. "I was invited, too."

"And Shanna probably knew that neither of us could come."

"Well, actually, David invited me. Shanna didn't want me to come because—" She broke off.

"Because of What's-his-name, right?"

"Axel," she said dryly, "and I could swear that you do remember that name."

"Maybe." He finished his eggs and set the plate aside, stretching his arms across the seat and sitting back comfortably. "Speaking of Mr. Fine, where were you and he supposedly headed tonight?"

"Dinner."

"Ah, dinner."

"Yes, it's a meal you eat at night."

"And I'm sure he does it very well. Only in the best restaurants. He probably speaks French with a very American accent but likes to impress his dates by using the language to order wine, right?"

Kathy put down her plate, feeling her temper sizzle. It didn't help one bit that what he was saying was the truth, right to the bone. She stood and stared at him, her hands on her hips. "At least he never walked out on me."

"What?"

It was a mistake to be sarcastic, she quickly realized, a mistake to give away the least emotion— because he was up and on his feet, too, and staring her down.

"Dammit, I never just walked out on you!"

She spun around and grabbed the plates and started down to the galley. He was right on her heels. "Kathy, don't walk away. I'm trying to talk to you."

"I tried to talk once, too," she snapped. He wasn't going to leave her, he was right behind her, watching her every move. She'd meant to wash the plates, but he was too close, so she hurried up the steps.

And he was still right behind her. He was going to touch her. She turned, her fingers clenched at her sides, staring at him. "I don't want to talk anymore, Brent. We had that argument and when I wanted to try to understand it, you were gone! So don't start with me—"

"Kathy." He took a step toward her and she knew he was going to touch her. That was when she made her ridiculous mistake. She took a step backward.

She hit the starboard rail, and before she could cry out or scramble for balance or do anything at all, she was pitching into the darkness of the night sea.

She plunged into water and immediately began to go down with the weight of her clothing and shoes. Kicking hard against the water, she started to surface. She was an excellent swimmer, and she wasn't frightened, although she couldn't see a thing. There could be sharks in the area, not that she'd ever heard of an attack here. Still she didn't like the darkness all around her. And more than anything else, she felt like a complete idiot, which was the last way she wanted to feel around Brent.

"Kathy!"

As she broke the surface, she heard his voice and realized he had plunged into the water after her. His face was bobbing in the waves right before hers, then she felt his fingers gripping her shirt at the back of her neck.

"I'm all right!" she assured him.

But he didn't let her go. He was swimming strongly to the boat, dragging her along like an errant puppy.

"I'm all right!" she insisted again, but a rise of water splashed into her mouth and she started choking and coughing as he thrust her toward the dive ladder at the aft of the boat. She grabbed hold of the rail and lifted herself from the water, feeling his hand on her derriere propelling her upward. She leaped aboard and turned, watching as he came aboard, dripping sea water in gallons just as she seemed to be doing herself.

She put up a hand in case he thought of coming near again. "I'm going to take a shower and put on dry clothes. And I suggest you do the same. Then I think that we really have to get out of here and find Shanna!"

Without another word she turned and fled down the steps to the starboard cabin. After slamming and locking the door, she peeled off her sodden clothing and stepped beneath a tepid shower.

Industriously she scrubbed her hair and lathered her body. Then she leaned against the walls of the tiny stall and just let the water run over her. She'd fly to China to escape from all the things that were already simmering between her and Brent this night. They couldn't talk any more, the talking was over, the past was gone. The divorce was the most painful, bitter thing she'd been through in her life, and she could never, never set herself up for such misery again. She had to remember that.

Yes, she had to remember that....

But all that she seemed to be able to remember was the way he could touch her. How she loved the sound of his voice, how she longed to sleep in his arms.

Abruptly she turned off the water and groped for a towel on the nearby rack. Then she dried herself briskly and opened the dresser door in one of the built-in cabinets.

She stared blankly at the emptiness there before remembering that she had moved all of her clothing into the other cabin when she had planned the outing with Axel. This was the nicest cabin, and she had wanted to offer it to her guest.

She stood, perplexed, certain that she didn't want to go walk out clad only in the wisp of a towel. Then she looked at the door and exhaled with a certain relief because she had a terry robe hanging there. It wasn't great, but it was better than a towel. In fact, lots of women probably felt fairly well covered in a floor-length terry robe.

But they were women who didn't know Brent, who didn't already feel as if their flesh and blood and limbs were already half afire, women who didn't feel as if they were already touched, already naked, waiting....

She wrenched open the cabin door and stood in the narrow hallway. She couldn't hear a shower running so she hesitated, then knocked on the door.

It was thrown open, and there was Brent, in a wisp of a towel himself, his dark blond hair slicked back from the shower, an expression of irritability naked on his face. "I see that you did clean out in here," he said curtly.

"What?"

"I can't find a thing in here to wear."

"It's my boat! And you've been out of my life for three years!"

"Any suggestions?" he asked her.

"Yes! Yes, I've lots and lots of suggestions for you but I'm really not certain that you want to hear them!" She flared. "Yes, I've dozens of suggestions! You could start out by locking yourself in a closet!"

"Kathy, you little brat—"

He didn't get any further. She shoved her hands against his chest, thrusting him into the room, then she swung around almost blindly, wanting to escape him once again.

She didn't hear him behind her as she passed the galley and mounted the steps. She didn't sense him until his hands were on her and he was spinning her around. She cried out and fell down to the floor beneath him.

He was sprawled over her, taut, tense, his chest naked and the muscles rippling. The moon glowed on the bronze of his flesh, the harsh constriction in his features. His eyes seemed to blaze gold, searing her. "Kathy!" he began, then fell silent. Then he groaned as his fingers moved into her hair…and he was kissing her.

Not as he had kissed her earlier. Not lightly, not tauntingly. But with hunger, raw and ravenous. Openmouthed, his lips moved upon hers, wet, hot, eliciting. His tongue swept her mouth, thrust, demanded, tasted and thrust even deeper. Then he drew away and his lips touched her face. His tongue rimmed her lips before slipping inside her mouth again, so deeply that the heat and fever spread throughout her body. His fingers were in her hair, but there was no pain, even though he held her so tautly because of his need. She didn't want to touch him…but her fingers were upon his shoulders.

She didn't want to feel the warmth of his body, didn't want to recognize the length of it, the hardness of his thighs, the tautness of his belly…the bulge of his desire. She didn't want to feel the overwhelming urge, the fire, the desperation to have him at the cost of peace and sanity and life itself.

She didn't want to...

His lips rose above hers just a fraction of an inch. She touched them delicately with her tongue, encircling them, nipping lightly. He held still to her gentle assault, then swept his arms around her. Once again their mouths melded and the tasting and sweeping and hunger were shared. When they broke apart again, his hold on her hair eased, but the tension in him seemed even greater, explosive, anguished. His breath fanning her cheeks, he whispered, "Kathy, I didn't mean it to come to this. The last thing I ever wanted to do was hurt you again. And by God, I sure as hell didn't want to do this to myself!"

She lay still, thinking that he couldn't mean it, that he couldn't manage to walk away now. The kiss was a mistake, but she'd live with the mistake, she swore silently. She'd live with the agony of all the tomorrows...

If she could just have this moment beneath the black velvet darkness of the sky and the ethereal glow of the silver full moon.

He was standing, reaching down to her, helping her to her feet. She stared at him, her fingers still entwined with his, her lips swollen and soft and wet from the kiss.

"Brent!" She whispered his name. He didn't speak, and his eyes remained hard upon hers. "It's a mistake, I know it's a mistake...." Her voice trailed away miserably. She knew him still, knew him so well. But he wasn't hers anymore, and she wondered if his desire was great enough, if she could seduce him, if she wasn't making a fool of herself again.

"What, Kathy, what?" His voice was nearly a growl, his words fraught with tension.

She shook her head and tried to whisper more softly. "It's a mistake, but…maybe it's not a mistake. Maybe we can just touch and then let go. I mean by the light of day we can turn aside, we can see all the truths, we can know that it's over, that we can't take the pain again. But I was just thinking that tonight…"

She freed her fingers from his. She couldn't go on any longer, not without some help. She stepped back and turned around, her cheeks flushed with embarrassment, her back to him.

He was silent. She felt the cool night breeze sweep around her and heard its soft whisper. She listened to the gentle lapping of the water against the hull of the boat.

Then he stepped toward her, and she felt his hands upon her shoulders.

The terry robe that had never seemed much of a barrier went sliding to the deck at her feet, and she felt the searing fire of his lips against her naked shoulder.

Chapter 4

Kathy caught her breath as she felt the touch of the night breeze combine with the caress of his kiss against her flesh. He lifted her hair and pressed his lips to her nape, and his kiss moved once more over her shoulder blades. She stood naked in the moonlight, thinking that they had never made love quite like this. She felt as if she should drape something around her, but then she felt the eternity of the night and the stars and the sea, and it suddenly seemed the most private place in the world, just as his touch with that of the night wind seemed to be the most sensual she had ever felt.

His arms swept around her from behind and she felt the erotic brush of the golden mat of his chest hair against her back. His hands swept upward, encircling her breasts, cupping them tenderly, his thumbs moving in seductive rhythm over her nipples.

Then his kisses began to move down the length of her spine. Slowly his lips moved, touching each and every vertebra. Warm moisture burned her flesh, then the liquid fire was enhanced by the coolness of the breeze. Finally he was on his knees behind her, his fingers brushing her belly, his lips teasing her buttocks. Then she gasped as he turned her around. His face and hair lay buried against her abdomen, and the soft flick of his tongue began to touch her there. His hands stroked downward, over her hips and calves, then swept up her kneecaps and upper thighs, until she parted her stance for balance. He held her taut against him, and his searing, moist caress moved over the apex of her limbs, to the intimate center of her desire.

Three years were nothing….

The sensations that ripped through her were wild and sweetly primeval, as natural as the swell of the waves in the sea. She felt a raging ecstasy so swift and overwhelming that nothing else existed. Her fingers tore into his hair but she did not seek to pull him away, only to hold tight lest the storm of desire send her spiraling into darkness. He brought her ever closer, ever more intimately against him. And he parted her further with his touch, stroking her endlessly. Torrents of pleasure, wilder than any tempest on the ocean, came sweeping through her and she twisted and moaned. The sweet liquid fire simmering deep within her rose and rose, until it burst explosively, until she did see darkness, and came sinking down slowly before him, spent, exhausted, emptied. Then brilliant lights and sparks of fire seemed to cascade around her. She closed her eyes, still shaking, and embraced him, her lashes lowered. A rosy color crept into her cheeks because she had responded so uninhibitedly to his intimate touch after so many years had passed.

But he didn't allow her any regrets. He caught her lips and kissed her deeply and passionately, slowly lowering them to the deck. He whispered to her decadently, demanding to know if she could taste the love between them on their kiss. Before she could regain her senses from the first explosion, he had slipped inside her. He was magnificent, and just feeling him inside her as he whispered so erotically brought her near to a second climax before he even started to move his body.

Then he did so, languidly, nearly leaving, then entering her again deeply. The quickening deepened inside her again; the sparks of fire left behind were incredibly fanned. As he held his weight above her carefully on the palms of his hands, their only contact being where his body was immersed so deeply within her own, she began to meet his slow, demanding thrusts.

The world took flight all over again. As he moved within her he leaned down and took the hardened peak of her nipple into his mouth, and he sucked it hard as the speed of his rhythm increased to a frantic beat. She clung to him. She bit and kissed his shoulders, she pushed her fingers into his hair.

Then it seemed that the sky exploded above her, and the darkness was filled with myriad multicolored stars and lights. The exquisite pleasure of her body was seeping into his while he held still, emptying the tempest of his own desire deep within her.

Then he fell by her side, gasping, and she fought to regain her breath, her sanity and her reason.

She didn't know what to do or what to say as she lay sheened with sweat, glistening in the moonlight. Hundreds of little things she had seen in the movies swept through her mind, but she knew none of them was right. Was it good for you? It was magnificent for me. No, no, those were things that strangers said, or near strangers, and they were not strangers. But neither was he her husband anymore, nor could this magic last. It had been stolen, a few snatched moments.

Still it seemed that something should be said, but not the truth. She would babble. My God, I didn't remember just how sweet, how wonderful, how shattering, how volatile making love with you is. How it could make the entire world seem to disappear, and I wonder, is it because I'm still in love with you, or are you really such an incredible lover?

And maybe it's both...

It wasn't going to be awkward, and it wasn't going to be hard, she realized. He wasn't going to let it be so.

His arm came around her, pulling her close beside him. He brushed a kiss against her forehead and held her beneath the stars. She stared at the stars as the silence stretched between them, then he spoke. There was a husky trembling to his voice that seemed to reach inside her and squeeze her heart. "Kathy, I remember so much, and yet...God, I've missed you."

She smiled slightly and buried her face against his ribs, slightly stroking his naked belly. "I've missed you," she admitted softly. Then she sighed, because she was so replete. She didn't want to move, and she really didn't want to talk anymore, not that night. She didn't want the past to intrude, she didn't want to remember any of the pain. She just wanted to lie there, beneath the stars, secure in his embrace, and remember what it had been like when he had loved her, too, when he had really been hers to love.

But she inhaled on a shaky breath and said, "We should go."

To her surprise and pleasure, she felt him shake his head. "It must be one o'clock by now. Even if we managed to catch up with them in the next few hours, we'd probably wake everyone up and scare them all half to death. We'll start out at first light."

"Oh," she murmured. Her heart was thundering. She didn't want to move. And he didn't move. She felt his lightest touch, and the touch of the breeze, moving over her naked flesh. She closed her eyes. She had slept so many nights of her life in his arms, just like this. It was all new, and yet it was all so familiar....

She must have closed her eyes and dozed. She was vaguely aware that he dragged the cushions down from the fiberglass seats and that he laid her upon them. Sometime during the night he must have gone down to one of the cabins, because a sheet was wrapped around them both, a gentle barrier against the slight coolness of the breeze.

When she awoke, the stars were still in the sky, but the darkness was fading fast. The dawn was coming in curious, soft pastel shades. A filter of pink was stretching across the heavens before any touch of the sun's gold.

Brent was still sleeping. His bare back was to her; the sheet had fallen from his shoulders. She stared at the breadth of his muscles, and she felt like smiling just because she liked the way he was built. His back was bronzed from the sun, and it tapered to a narrow waistline. Below that his flesh was a lighter shade, and his buttocks were rounded and hard-muscled and very sexy, she thought. She wanted to reach out and touch him. Despite the fact that so much had been drained from her the night before, that so much desire had exploded with such tremendous force, she wanted to taste his flesh. See if it was salty, if…

He turned his head suddenly, and she realized that he was awake. His heavy-lidded golden gaze was upon her with a certain amount of amusement. She met his gaze, then moved toward him. Her lashes fell at the very last instant, as she touched his flesh with her lips, then grazed it slightly with her teeth. He didn't move; he waited. But she was certain she felt the beat of his heart, felt his pulse at his nape, felt the intake of his breath, the hardening of his body.

As he had done the night before, she began to move against him. She kissed the breadth of his back, caressing it with her fingers. She teased his spine, up and down, with the moist pink flicker of her tongue.

She caressed the small of his back and nipped at his buttocks and bathed them with her kiss.

He rolled to his side, and she was face-to-face with his hardness, the result of her assault. She felt a delicious power surge through her with an unbearable sweetness as she realized that she could still affect him as deeply as he could her. But it wasn't just with that sense of power that she continued to touch him, it was also with love, with memory. Once he had been hers. And on this shimmering pink morning, he was going to be hers again.

She closed her fingers around him, teased and caressed him and stroked him with her tongue. She heard his ragged cries, and the molten fire took hold within her own body. A fever began to rule her movements. She tasted his ecstasy, and still she held him with her caress, until his hands were on her and he was lifting her and she discovered herself seated on one of the fiberglass benches. His hands were upon her, parting her thighs. His eyes were glittering with passion. Then he began his own assault, searing her to her very center with the hot thrust of his tongue, then rising to impale her and take her with reckless fury. Cries tore from their throats, and spasms shook them as they peaked in an exultant climax together.

He held her very close, burying his face against her hair and throat. "I had forgotten how nice it could be to wake up beside you," he said softly.

To wake up…

It was morning, and there was no more darkness

to use as a shield against the past. She had wanted him, and she had had him, but it had been a horrible mistake. No matter how deeply she had been filled, she was still hungry. Their union wasn't as complete as she had thought it would be.

She had wanted a memory. And in the light of day, the pain from the past would come back. Sex had never been their problem. It was life that had come between them. It had been his temper, and her temper, and the awful things they had said. Nothing could erase the things that had happened.

"We have to go," she whispered painfully.

He nodded.

She started to rise, but he pulled her back, his eyes questioning as they touched her. "Kathy, tell me, are you sorry?"

She wanted to pull away. She didn't want to answer a question like that.

But he wasn't going to let her go.

"I don't know, Brent. I really don't know. It was probably the biggest mistake either of us has ever made. And—" She broke off, then she inhaled quickly and lowered her lashes. "That's all a lie. Maybe not all a lie. No, I'm not sorry. I wanted you last night more than I can remember ever wanting anything or anyone."

"What about this morning?" he demanded.

"I...wanted you this morning."

He inhaled quickly and seemed to catch his breath. He looked at ease and very handsome, sitting naked on the fiberglass by the hull. Was she so natural and easy, standing there in the buff, now in the sun and the early morning light? She tugged his hand. "Brent, it's daylight. Fishermen will be coming out."

He smiled. "You look great."

"Thank you."

"You always did."

"Thank you. So, uh, so do you. Brent, let go, please, we've got to get clothes on."

He shook his head, holding her tight. "Uh-uh. Not yet."

"What do you want?" she demanded desperately.

"I don't want to pretend that it didn't happen, that's all."

"I never meant to pretend."

"Or that it wasn't good, Kathy. And I don't mean that in any casual way. It was good for the past, and good for the future, and when I'm with you, you have to know that I want you."

She tugged more desperately on his hand. "Brent, we're not going to be together, remember? It's too damned dangerous. And not because of Johnny Blondell."

He dropped her hand slowly, and his eyes were heavily shaded as they brushed hers once again. "That's right. Damned right," he said coolly. He rose, relaxed again, able to swing in the breeze with the best composure. "Let's shower and get going. I'm really sorry. I guess I did forget some of the past."

He walked past her and disappeared into the cabin. She held still a second longer, wanting to scream. He didn't understand. He didn't understand what she had been trying to say at all. "Oh, Brent!" she said to the breeze. There were tears on her cheeks. She wiped them away furiously. She had taken what she wanted, and now it was time to pay. She'd made her bargain with herself openly, knowing the consequences.

She hurried down the steps to her cabin and into the shower. She turned on the water and leaned against the wall.

He thought he had hurt her, and he thought he was going to hurt her again.

The water poured softly on her and she leaned there, trying to reason, trying to understand herself.

He thought he had caused her to lose the new baby that had meant so very much to them both after Ryan had died. He had thought that the argument had caused her miscarriage, that he had been too rough, that he couldn't give what she needed anymore. And she had been too hurt herself at the time to realize he was slipping away with every remote, polite word. He had moved out of the house, and he hadn't been able to talk to her. Her pain had turned to fury and she had filed papers, and suddenly all that had been left was the pain.

He hadn't left when she had been sick. He had been there, white-faced, every day. He hadn't left her alone for a minute in the hospital, not when she had hemorrhaged, not when she had hovered so dangerously on the line between life and death. She could remember trying to promise him that there would be another son, and she had thought then that he was bitterly disappointed because he had seemed to decide, all on his own, that there never would be another one.

When Ryan had died, he had been tender at first. Then he had dragged her back into life, and that had included arguing—and making love fiercely, desperately. It had been good for her. She had wanted to live again, but then she had found out that she was pregnant again.

Kathy sank down slowly in the shower stall. He had never realized she hadn't wanted his temper to change. They had been wild as kids, neither one of them willing to give up a battle, and yet neither one of them walking away.

They had argued right down the aisle, so it seemed.

And he thought it was his temper. The doctor couldn't convince him that things just happened. She could remember now the way he had listened, his face so taut, his words betraying nothing, the denial within his heart.

"It is the past!" she whispered vehemently. Then she stood, wondering what in hell they were doing. They were forgetting their surviving child, the daughter that meant everything in the world to both of them.

She wrapped up in her towel and hurriedly opened the door to tap on the one across the narrow hallway. There was no answer. She didn't hear the water running so she carefully cracked open the door, then entered the cabin. Brent was gone. Within a few minutes she had pulled out a pair of shorts and a sleeveless cotton shirt with a mandarin collar. She paused as she dressed, listening.

Brent had already brought in the anchor and started the motor.

She walked across the hallway and crawled into the bunk, balancing with just her toes on the bed, to dig into the wall cabinets above it. She had a few things left that belonged to Brent. Cutoffs and old T-shirts. She'd kept them because, with a boat, you never knew when you would need something dry for a guest, male or female.

Maybe that was a lie. Maybe she'd kept them for the same reason she'd kept so many of his things at the house. She hadn't been able to part with them.

Leaving the clothing on the bunk, she hurried out to the galley, then paused. Before going topside she put on a pot of coffee and quickly cleaned up the mess from the night before. She wondered if she was stalling, if she was afraid to see Brent after everything that had passed between them. No, she determined, and hurried topside.

The magical pink lights of the dawn had faded. It was still early, but full daylight was already upon them.

Brent was at the helm. Barefoot, naked-chested, he had donned the damp, salty jeans of the night before. His eyes were focused on the sea, straight ahead. He was determined on making up for lost time, it seemed.

"Brent!" she called to him over the hum of the engine. He turned her way, curiously, politely.

A stranger watching would have never believed that they had been incredibly close and intimate on this very deck less than hour ago.

It was the way he had behaved all through the divorce. She could see it in the coldness of his eyes and she couldn't stand it. But she didn't know how to change it; she hadn't know then, and she didn't know now.

"What?"

"I found some of your things. Let me take the helm, and you go change. You can't be very comfortable."

For a moment she thought he was going to argue with her just for the sake of arguing, but then he shrugged and moved aside. Kathy slid in next to him, taking over at the tiller.

He disappeared down the steps. Kathy held steady to his southward course and estimated it shouldn't take them more than a few hours to reach Shanna, assuming she could find the Brennans' boat among the many pleasure craft that would be out on a day like today.

Brent returned, still bare-chested and barefoot, a dry pair of cutoffs hugging his hips. He hadn't bothered with a shirt. He had brought up coffee and he silently handed her a cup, moving to take his place at the tiller. Kathy had little choice but to give way.

She moved several inches down on the bench, noting that he had returned the cushions to their proper places. It was all over, really. It was almost as if everything that had gone on had been a fantasy. She might as well have slept in her own cabin and dreamed the entire episode.

Brent didn't say a word, he just watched the sea. After a few minutes Kathy couldn't bear the silence any longer.

"Do you think we'll have any trouble finding them?"

"No."

It was a flat answer. "The Brennans' boat is a beautiful sixty-five footer. The *Cary-Anne*."

"I know, I've been on it."

"Oh," Kathy murmured, startled. Shanna had never mentioned that her father had gone with her and the Brennans anywhere.

Maybe she didn't want to talk, after all.

But she didn't seem able to let anything rest, either. "Brent, are you sure this is all necessary? It's beginning to sound a little…silly. I really should have radioed to her. If she has heard something, she must be terribly worried. And if—"

She broke off because his eyes were on her, hard, cold, disdaining. "You think that what happened to Johnny Blondell is silly?"

"No, of course not! But even if we say that something is going on, I still don't understand—"

"Okay, Kathy, listen carefully. Several years ago

we were all together as a group, touring South and Central America and the States. We came through customs and Harry Robertson was arrested. The rest of us were furious because musicians seem to get a bad rap to begin with and because—to the best of my knowledge—no one else had had anything to do with it and we all had our private lives, our families and our careers. I felt kind of sorry for Harry because he wouldn't talk, and because he seemed so afraid, and I remember thinking Harry had been coerced into what he was doing. We couldn't really help Harry, no one could. He went to prison—he died in prison. Then Larry Jenkins was killed. Then Keith's wife was killed. Then Johnny Blondell was killed. It seems to me that someone out there thinks we all know something about something, and either they want information no one has been able to give them yet, or they just want anyone who might have any information to be out of the picture. I don't want to use a radio. I don't want anyone to know where Shanna is, I don't want to lead anyone to her."

"Brent, maybe you should be worrying about Marla Harrington."

He cast her a glance that sent daggers. "Why?"

"Well, most people would assume that you were involved with her now, I would think."

He kept watching her. The wind ruffled his drying hair, and he shrugged. "These people aren't fools. Whoever is doing this is not small time, and not a fool."

"But we're divorced—"

"Yes, we're divorced. The only people who have ever been my family, who could be used as a threat against me, who have really mattered in my life, are you and Shanna. A divorce doesn't change the past, Kathy. Whoever is up to this surely knows that."

Despite their tone, his words thrilled her deep inside. Maybe they couldn't put together the pieces of their lives, but it was exciting, it was wonderful, to hear him say that she was the only woman who had ever really mattered.

"Besides," he added curtly, somewhat dispelling the moment, "we were married at the time. And you were with me during a part of that tour. You could be a target yourself. I want you and Shanna out of it as fast as possible."

"So what are you going to do with us?" Kathy inquired sweetly. "I own a business, remember."

"Patty will run your business for the next few days."

"Where will I be?"

"I'm going to take you both out to a private airstrip and get you flown far away."

"We haven't got our passports."

"I've got a pilot friend who's going to take you to a retreat in rural Virginia."

"With some kind of security, I imagine."

He nodded. Then he grinned at her. "I've given a lot of support to one of the senators there and he's going to see to it that you've got lots of protection."

She threw up her hands. "This is crazy, Brent! You

don't know what is going on. You have no idea of how long it's going to go on—"

"It doesn't matter how long it goes on!" he snapped savagely.

"And what are you going to do?"

"Go back. I have to."

"So this maniac can blow you up, too?"

"So we don't all have to spend the rest of our lives looking over our shoulders."

She rose irritably. Maybe he was making sense, she couldn't tell anymore. But she didn't want to go to rural Virginia and be a prisoner.

Maybe that wasn't it. She was very frightened for her daughter, and she did want Shanna in safe hiding as soon as possible. She just didn't want to go herself. She didn't want Brent playing cat and mouse, alone, with murderers. Maybe he wouldn't be alone. Keith Montgomery and the Hicks brothers were still alive and well—and maybe targets, too.

If Brent went to the police, they'd have protection in Miami. And in Miami they had Sam, and her walled estate, and the alarm system.

They…

She didn't know if he meant to go to the house. He had his own big place on the water, with studio equipment and everything he needed. He didn't have Sam, though. He would need Sam.

"I'm not sure about this at all, Brent," she told him.

"What do you mean, you're not sure about this?"

he exploded. "You've got to do exactly what I'm telling you."

"Oh, no, I don't. We're divorced, remember. I can do whatever I please."

"Kathy—"

"Brent!"

He looked as if he was about to leap for her throat. The tiller lay between them.

He clenched his teeth. She saw him fight for control. "Kathy," he said her name very softly. "You are the most stubborn and obstinate and argumentative woman I have ever met. But you are going to do what I ask you this time, even if I have to tie you hand and foot and mail you north in a box."

He wasn't going to lose his temper. He was going to try damned hard not to lose his temper.

She lowered her head, suddenly aware that she wanted him really angry. She wanted him to leap for her, and she wanted the fight and the passion, and she wanted him to know…

She felt warm, flushed, and she realized that she wanted something very much like that last argument between them. She wanted the furious, cutting words, she wanted the tempest….

And she wanted him to grab her and carry her away and make love to her with that same fury and passion. It was the only way he would ever understand that he hadn't hurt her. But maybe the pieces couldn't be put back together again.

Last night had put the longing and the passion and

the sweetness and magic back into her heart when she had tried so hard to forget it had all existed. And now, this morning, there was all the anguish again.

She didn't want to hurt him....

Yes, she did. She wanted to shake him, and she wanted to make him see that he had been wrong. She wanted him to understand that she had been bleeding deep inside, and that had been why she had filed the papers against him, not because she had ever believed for a minute that what had happened had been his fault.

"We'll see," she said sweetly.

"I mean what I'm saying."

"Are you threatening me?"

"I'm just telling you the situation. Take that however you want to take it."

"Maybe I've got my own ideas on what should be done, and how it should be done, Brent."

"Damn you, Kathy, you would try the patience of a saint."

"And you sure as hell aren't any saint, right?"

"Kathy—"

She leaned close to him and smiled sweetly. "Get this, Brent. I'll decide what to do with my own life and you haven't got a single say in it, understand?"

A golden, furious fire leaped into his eyes. She heard the grinding of his teeth and she knew he was going to reach out and wrap his fingers around her arm.

She moved just in time. "I am going to have more coffee. Let me know when you've sighted the *Cary-Anne*."

She spoke hastily and decided on retreat for the moment, tearing down the steps to the cabin below. She paused, gasping for breath, her heart thundering.

What in God's name was she doing? she asked herself.

She was goading him. Because she wanted him to know...

No, that wasn't it. She didn't want to leave him. She loved Virginia, and Patty could take care of business for a few days, and...

She just didn't want to leave him again. Not now. Not after last night. If she let herself be shipped away, awful things could happen. He could be killed; she might never see him again. And even if he could figure out what was happening and survive it, she still might never see him again. Except at Shanna's graduation ceremonies, or at her wedding. And they'd both have escorts, and they'd speak casually and politely....

And it would be as if this thing had never happened between them, as if the full moon hadn't cast its glow upon them and reminded her that she loved him and that there could never be a love such as they shared for her again.

She inhaled sharply.

Was she trying to get him back? She couldn't be doing that; she'd be a fool. There had been so much agony between them in the past.

Her heart slammed hard against her chest.

Maybe it was exactly what she was trying to do. She didn't understand it herself.

Chapter 5

It was still morning when they reached the waters off the Keys. By ten o'clock, Brent could see the Brennans' beautiful *Cary-Anne* anchored south of Key Largo. His heart quickened with anxiety, but it seemed that everything was all right. No one had gotten to Shanna. Yet.

He pulled as close as he dared and tossed his anchor. He was going to take the dinghy over. Then he saw that the *Cary-Anne* was set with her ladders down and her dive flag up. Maybe he'd jump in and swim over, he was so anxious to see Shanna.

But he paused, remembering Kathy, wondering how he had managed to forget her for a moment. He twisted his jaw, thinking he'd like to hog-tie her at that very moment. What the hell had happened? She'd been so reasonable at first. She couldn't stay—she'd be risking her life. And if anything ever happened to her…

He inhaled and exhaled slowly. If anything ever happened to Kathy, he wouldn't be able to bear it.

Time and distance should have made him stronger where she was concerned. But time and distance hadn't done a damned thing.

He'd wanted her more last night than he ever had, more than he'd ever wanted any woman, more than he had wanted life itself. Just as he had known from the first time he'd seen her, when they'd both been little more than kids, that he wanted her, and no one else would ever do.

He'd known he loved her, that he'd always love her. Two people couldn't live as closely and love as intensely for as long as they had and walk away without any emotions remaining. He had believed that the emotions would change, that he could come to care for her in a gentler way.

It hadn't happened.

He closed his eyes and clenched his teeth. It had to happen, because they couldn't go back. Ever. Because he would never forget her miscarriage, the shock that filled them both, then the terror when it had seemed she would never stop bleeding. He remembered the sounds of the sirens clear as day, he remembered pacing the hospital floor and praying as he had never prayed before that she would live. If God didn't want them to have any more children, he didn't give a damn. There were lots of needy children in the world, they could help a few of them. He'd never touch her again, he swore, not in anger, not even in that kind of passion....

Well, he had. Last night. The desire beneath the

starlit heaven had been stronger than memory, stronger even, than a vow.

And now they were fighting again, too. Just as they always did. Only it hadn't seemed wrong when they had started out. They were both opinionated, stubborn and determined. They'd had an argument walking down the aisle right after their wedding. With his best man and her maid of honor laughing away, he'd had to lift her and practically throw her into the limousine that took them to their reception. Their anger had dissolved into laughter, then kisses, and he carried her away to their honeymoon suite in his arms. It had always seemed it was all right because they had both known the love was there. And that love had carried them through so very much.

He'd had nothing when they married. He'd made it through his tour of duty, then the G.I. Bill had paid for his college, but little else. He'd had only Kathy and his music. Then they'd had Shanna right away. Those years had been a struggle but they'd weathered them together, both getting through school, while he'd started getting a foothold on his career. When success burst upon them, life became good, and a whirl. They still fought wickedly, made up passionately, yet no matter what, they remained the main core of each other's lives. They'd been so busy, but wherever he went, Kathy usually came along, and Shanna, too. They'd always been a family.

Then they'd had Ryan, and it had seemed that

they had everything in life. When they lost Ryan, he'd wondered if they had just had too much. But even then they might have survived. It was just that after this loss, the next baby had meant so very much to Kathy. She'd fallen too quickly into a depression, worrying that the same thing would happen again. She spent hours in the darkness alone.

The doctors had told him he had to shake her out of it. And so he'd snapped at her like a drill sergeant, and he had touched her at last, touched her fury. It had exploded between them and they had argued until he'd dragged her into his arms and into their bed. All the hurt and fury and every other emotion they'd experienced had flared between them, and he had lost control and made love to her fiercely, almost violently. It seemed wonderful right after because she had remained in his arms and they talked again, talked about the new baby, about the future.

But three days later, she had started to scream. And he had burst in upon her to find her in a pool of blood. It hadn't taken long to realize that they hadn't just lost another child. He was about to lose her, and it had been his fault, because of his temper.

He opened his eyes and stared at the sun, shimmering hotly, hovering over him. Dear God, what was he doing to himself? He'd broken out in a cold sweat despite the heat of the day; he was shaking.

"Kathy!" he yelled down to the cabin. "We're here. I'm going over."

He dived into the water and swam with strong

strokes for the *Cary-Anne*. He reached the ladder and climbed up, his heart hammering as silence seemed to weigh down upon him.

"Shanna!"

He bellowed his daughter's name, much like an animal in pain. Then he exhaled with relief as he saw her come flying out of the cabin, her blond hair, tied in a ponytail, bouncing behind her. She pitched herself into his arms. "Dad! What are you doing here?"

He hugged her so hard that he felt her squirm beneath his hold, then he released her and framed her face with his hands, trembling inside. "You hadn't heard anything?" he asked her quickly.

She shook her head, her eyes narrowing with concern. David Brennan was on the deck by then, concern written across his features, too. "Mr. Mc-Queen? You're all wet. Where the heck did you come from?" He stopped, confused, then added a hasty, "Sir!"

Brent smiled, wondering if this kid was going to be calling him "Dad" one day. There could be lots of worse things, he thought. David Brennan was a sharp kid with a keen mind who happened to love the water and sports a lot, too.

"I came from the *Sweet Eden*—"

"Mom's boat?" Shanna shrieked. "Oh, I knew it would happen eventually. I just knew it."

"No, no, sweetheart, sorry," he told her softly. "Shanna, David, I've got to talk to you both, and to your parents, David. I've—"

"Where's Mom?" Shanna interrupted anxiously.

He smiled. "I didn't feed her to the sharks, don't worry," he assured her. "I'm sure she'll be over any second now."

"McQueen!" By then David's father, Justin Brennan, had appeared on the deck, a coffee cup in his hand, a broad grin on his face. Brent had hit it off with Justin from the first time they had met, right after their kids had started dating. Justin was a tall, husky guy with white-blond hair and the look of a Viking. He had also served in the army, joined the Dade County Police Force, been shot up badly, then retired. He'd taken to writing police novels, which had gained a steady following. He had reached a point where he always made the best-seller lists. He'd made a small fortune, remained entirely unpretentious and liked nothing more than a day with his family out on his one new toy—the *Cary-Anne*.

Justin walked across the deck, his hand extended in pleasure. "McQueen, what the hell are you doing here? I'd heard you had some meetings this weekend about a new album."

"Well, those didn't quite come off," Brent explained briefly. Justin's wife, Reba, was coming up the steps. She was a short, cute woman with dark curls, a beautiful smile and lots of ample curves. "More to love," her husband always told her affectionately when she worried about her weight.

"Brent!" she said with pleasure, taking his hand. "We hadn't thought you could make it! How nice to see you. But you're all wet! Where on earth did you come from?"

Brent grinned. Explaining this situation wasn't going to be easy. "There's been some trouble, and I have to take Shanna with me. And yes, Reba, I'm wet, I swam over."

"From where?"

"From Kathy's boat." He started to point to the *Sweet Eden*, but when he turned his voice died and he forgot what he was saying.

Kathy was just coming out of the water. She had decided to swim over, too. And she had dressed for the occasion.

She was wearing a black-and-teal bikini, a two-piece concoction that seemed to enhance the perfect roundness of her breasts and maybe display just a little too much of them. The bottoms of the suit had those high-cut thighs, and despite her diminutive height, her legs seemed to go on forever beneath them. Her belly was flat and her waist slim, and the little string tie that held the suit together seemed to enhance everything on her body.

He'd liked her naked last night. He'd known then that she was still uncannily perfect and sensual, and he loved the silky feel of her flesh. The suit shouldn't have had any surprises for him, except that...

She shouldn't be wearing it. That was it. She shouldn't be that close to naked in front of strangers.

She climbed out of the water, pulling herself up

the ladder, a near replica of her teenage daughter. Or Shanna was the replica of her. Something like that.

"Kathy!" Reba seemed even more delighted.

"Mom!"

"Isn't this just wonderful!" Reba said.

Justin was walking over to help Kathy up the ladder. Brent almost brushed past him to do so himself, then managed to control the urge at the last minute. He didn't want anyone else touching her.

It was that damned suit.

She was on the deck, dripping wet, smoothing back her hair, flashing her warm smile at Justin and Reba.

"I can't believe the two of you are here together!" Shanna said.

"We're not," Brent and Kathy said simultaneously. They cast each other a quick glance.

"Did your father get a chance to explain yet?" Kathy asked Shanna anxiously.

There was a pile of towels on a deck chair next to the Brennans' scuba equipment. Brent grabbed a towel and practically threw it over Kathy's shoulders, his fingers taut as he stood behind her, trying very hard to smile and not snarl.

"I haven't had a chance, Kathy. Justin, Reba, I think we'd better sit and I'll try to explain."

A few minutes later they were all in the cabin at the round booth to the starboard side of the very impressive galley. Justin listened in silence, nodding when Brent started with the Harry Robertson case, frowning intently when he heard about Larry's death, then knitting his brows still more tightly when he heard about the explosion. Shanna gasped in horror, realizing that her father should have been there.

"It's all right," Brent assured her gently. It was good to focus on his daughter. Kathy was sitting beside him, and she wouldn't hold on to the towel. It had slipped down her back. And her thigh was touching his. They were all sipping coffee, and her fingers kept brushing his.

He should have hog-tied her and left her on the *Sweet Eden*. He'd be making more sense now.

"I'm all right, and everything is going to be all right," he added, smiling at the anxiety in his daughter's eyes. God, she was precious to him. "But I want you and your mother gone."

"Why?"

He inhaled and exhaled. Damn, but she sounded like her mother!

"Because I don't want you hurt or killed by someone trying very hard to get to me. Shanna, weren't you listening, don't you understand? I tried to disappear the second I saw what had happened to Johnny because I knew I had to get the two of you away before they came looking for me. I called a friend in Washington and I managed to get everything arranged for the two of you."

"Washington! I don't want to go away. I want to stay near you!"

"Shanna, you can't—"

"You're going to go back! You're going to try to be some kind of bait—"

"Shanna—"

"Wait a minute, wait a minute," Justin interrupted. Brent looked at him. Justin knew he had to go back, that he didn't have a choice in the world.

He also seemed to understand how concerned Brent was for his wife and daughter. *Ex*-wife and daughter.

"What you want is absolute safety for Shanna and Kathy," he said.

"Right," Brent agreed.

"Okay, then listen to this. And you listen real good, young lady," he advised Shanna. "We've got a little place on a private island. Walled in, electric gates, a fine pack of trained shepherds, security guards, the works."

Kathy and Brent were staring at him. Justin flushed, his cheeks going very red. "I have a publisher friend who was in real trouble. Lost his job and everything, and we're always in the islands, so I bought the place from him. The people I've kept on I trust implicitly. I can take care of Shanna and Kathy. We'll still be real near just in case you need us, and Shanna will be a lot happier with David around, and I think Kathy will be happier with us than she would be with strangers, right?"

Brent hesitated. He didn't know what to say. "Justin, I can't put you in this position."

"Hell, Brent, I was a cop for years!"

"But your own family—"

"I'm telling you, this place is like Fort Knox!"

"We'd be delighted to have Kathy and Shanna. Honestly!" Reba said.

David looked at Brent. "Sir, please, we wouldn't have it any other way." He hesitated. "I can't let you take her otherwise, Mr. McQueen."

"Oh, you can't?" Brent said, his temper rising.

"Daddy!" Shanna pleaded. "I won't go unless I go with David."

Brent smiled. She'd been going to fight him the whole way. Then she'd jumped to David's defense, and now she was stuck.

"So you will go with the Brennans."

"You tricked me!" she wailed. "I still don't like this, I don't like it one bit. I want to be with you."

"Shanna," he said, sighing impatiently, "you can't be with me!"

"You could take the boat back and they could be waiting for you."

"I won't take the boat to your mother's place. I'll dock her somewhere else. Shanna, I'll be all right. As long as I'm not worried about you and your mother, I'll be fine."

"Then it's settled!" Justin announced, pleased.

Brent felt Kathy shift beside him. He looked into her eyes, ready for the biggest argument of them all.

"Is it settled?" he asked her tensely.

She smiled. "If this is what you want," she said sweetly.

Her smile was absolutely beautiful, totally innocent.

Her eyes were wide and very blue, and her hair was just beginning to dry. It was framing her face with soft, near platinum tendrils.

She was being too agreeable. Maybe she just wanted to get rid of him as soon as possible.

"It's not so much a matter of what I want," he told her. "It's what's necessary."

"All right."

She'd never said "all right" to him in all the years he had known her. Still, he couldn't argue with her because she wasn't arguing with him.

"Maybe we should all start moving," Justin said. He rose. "I want to get these two there as soon as possible."

Brent nodded, rising. He offered Justin his hand. "Thanks."

Justin nodded. "You be careful. Real careful."

"I will be."

He started up the stairs to the deck with the others behind him. "Do you need to get your things?" Reba asked Kathy.

"No, I don't think I need anything at all," Kathy said. Brent narrowed his eyes at her. She smiled at him again. "Really. Shanna and I wear the same size, and I'm sure she has plenty of clothing with her. Do you, Shanna?"

"Of course, Mom," Shanna answered, barely glancing her way. Her eyes were all for her father. "Oh, Dad!" she cried softly, and she threw herself into his arms.

Brent held her long and close, then set her down. "I'll be all right."

She nodded. There were tears in her eyes.

He looked beyond his daughter to his wife. *Ex*-wife. She was standing silently several feet behind Shanna. At long last she'd wrapped the towel around herself. Her eyes met his.

He wanted to sweep her into his arms, to hold her just as he had held his daughter. He couldn't. Not anymore. He lifted a hand to her.

"Take care."

She nodded, her blue gaze haunting him. She didn't say a word.

Justin moved to Brent and handed him a card. "This is the name of the guy who used to own the place. The phone and address are still right, in case you want to reach us."

Brent thanked him and stuck the card in his pocket. As soon as he returned to the *Sweet Eden,* he would memorize the numbers and destroy the card. "I'll call from a phone booth and make sure you all got there okay," he said. Shanna was going to start to cry, he thought, if he didn't leave quickly. He kissed her one last time, waved to the others, then felt Kathy's eyes.

She was still staring at him steadily, betraying no emotion whatsoever.

He turned, smiled and dived from the boat into the water.

The second he was gone Kathy dropped her towel

and spun her daughter around to face her. "I'm not letting him go back alone, Shanna. I'm going to get on the *Sweet Eden*."

"Kathy, you can't!" Justin protested.

"You can't stop me. And if you waste any more time, you might be risking Shanna." She smiled at him and Reba. "Thank you both so much. For Shanna and for me. Now, I'm awfully sorry, but I have to move fast. He's a stronger swimmer than I am."

She pulled her daughter into her arms and hugged her, then hugged David impulsively while she listened to her daughter's protests.

"Hang around for just a minute, will you?" Kathy asked wryly. "Just in case he has a chance to pull out before I can sneak aboard!"

"I'll stay around," Justin assured her. "I should warn him—"

"Please, don't!" Kathy whispered.

"But, Mother!" Shanna wailed. "Now I'm going to have to worry about both of you."

"Serves you right," Kathy retorted. "Now you'll know how I feel when you ignore the time I tell you to be in at night!"

She couldn't waste any more time. She crawled over the side, not wanting to alert Brent with a splash. She smiled at her daughter. "I love you. We both love you."

"I love you, too!" Shanna cried.

The last sight Kathy had of her daughter then was

bittersweet. David stepped up behind her and put a supporting hand around her. They were both very young and very beautiful, and maybe it was just as it should be. There was so much caring between them already.

I'm losing her! Kathy thought, but she wasn't really. Shanna was loving and would always care for her, just as she would always worry about her daughter. But she was going to have to hand her over to David Brennan, it seemed. Maybe much sooner than she had expected.

The water closed around her. Kathy didn't look back. She swam as hard as she could for the *Sweet Eden*.

Brent climbed aboard the *Sweet Eden*, anxious to move as quickly as possible should anyone have tried to follow him and recognized the boat as one belonging to his ex-wife. He wanted to make sure the boat was far, far away from his ex-wife and his daughter.

He was worried. He trusted Justin Brennan, he had a lot of faith in the man, but he would be happier once he placed the call and found they had all reached the island and were behind the gates and walls and protected by the pack of shepherds.

Still, he didn't pull the anchor right away. He took the wet card from his pocket and read the address and phone number, closed his eyes and committed both to memory. Then he ripped the card into tiny shreds and let them fall into the ocean. He walked into the cabin for a towel, then came up and pulled in the anchor.

The *Cary-Anne* had not started out yet. He saw Shanna on deck, watching him, and he waved. She waved in return. David was with her.

He didn't see Kathy anywhere.

He sat, turned the key and listened to the motor rev. Then he slightly angled the tiller and waved again as he headed the *Sweet Eden* toward Miami.

Well, it was over now. Their time together. He didn't have to burn inside and hope he could refrain from grabbing her and demanding to know what the hell she was doing in that bathing suit. He didn't have to worry about the overwhelming desire to touch her, to hold her, to make love to her.

She had very silently, very agreeably stayed behind. She wanted him, she'd had him, and she'd walked away damned easily, ready to resume her life. With Mr. Fashion Plate, Mr. Hair Mousse, Mr. Wall Street Type. Maybe it was just what she wanted, just what she needed. A guy with no passion whatsoever inside, a guy as straight as an arrow....

No passion, no life! He wasn't right for Kathy at all. There was no music in his soul, and Kathy was music, a sweet beat of laughter and impulse and challenge and never-ending curiosity, always willing to take a chance, to travel to new places, to meet new people. She was the pulse, the beat of his life. He hadn't lost his touch when he had lost his son, although the anguish had been terrible. He had lost it all when he had lost her, and he had barely managed to regain it.

Maybe it was better that she dated this guy, this Axel. Maybe they would never walk down island shores together while listening to the drumroll of a different lifestyle. Maybe they'd never find a private cove and throw caution to the wind. Maybe he'd never make love with sand between his toes.

But then again, maybe he'd never hurt her, either.

She'd walk all over him eventually, Brent thought sourly. Kathy had her own temper. And her own will. And both were powerful. She'd tire of this guy soon enough.

Hell, they were divorced. He should be wishing her happiness. He loved her still, didn't he? He wanted her to be happy. That was what loving was.

Hell, no. He hated Axel, hated the way the guy looked. Hated him touching Kathy.

But then, there wasn't anything he could do about it, was there?

The sun beat down on him as the morning waned to afternoon. He held a course for Bear Cut, determined to drop anchor for a while, then move in at night. He wasn't going to bring the boat in to any dock. He'd drop anchor right off some private property in the grove, then swim in. He'd have the boat picked up by a towing company.

Nightfall was coming. He stood, stretched and stared at the shallow waters before the island. There were still bathers on the darkening beach—lovers, picnickers, kids playing with snorkel gear.

He swung around suddenly, startled, as he heard

something. He wasn't sure what it was. Something. Maybe he hadn't heard it. Maybe he'd just sensed it.

Then he did hear something. Below.

Someone had gotten onto the *Sweet Eden*. When he had been with the Brennans?

Or worse, he thought, feeling an unease sweep up his spine. Maybe he'd been so involved with his thoughts that someone had crawled aboard as he'd set out, with him already at the helm.

He was slipping! He'd never stay alive at this rate.

There was a gun in the overhead compartment in the starboard cabin. He'd checked it before, the first chance he'd had last night. Kathy had never moved it. She didn't like guns, but she was a decent shot, and when it had seemed the crime wave across the country was here to stay, he had insisted she do some target practicing with him.

And now someone was in the cabin with his gun.

Well, he still had his hands and his wits and there had been a few too many times in the army when he'd had to use them. It was just that that had been a long time ago.

He moved toward the stairs, then silently moved down them in his bare feet.

There was no one in the galley or in the salon. The intruder had to be in one of the cabins.

He moved to the starboard side. The cabin door was slightly ajar. The shadows had become so deep he could barely see. But then he caught the movement. Someone was in there, moving furtively in the darkness.

He didn't dare make a sound. He catapulted forward, his arms outstretched. The shadow moved then, turning, seeing him.

A scream ripped through the air and the shadow tried to move. An elbow caught him in the chin. His arms wrapped around a warm body and held. Limbs thrashed and flailed as he dragged the body into the hallway, grunting. Then he tackled the body to the ground, straddling it and locking its wrists high above its head.

He blinked against the shadows and darkness. "Kathy!" he exploded.

"Brent!" She was furious, shaking. "You scared me half to death."

"I scared you! I'm supposed to be aboard this boat. You are not!"

"You could have just said that it was you!"

"I thought you were someone trying to kill me," he told her.

"Well, that just might be true at this moment! Why didn't you say—"

"I try not to announce my presence when I think someone might have a gun," he drawled wryly.

"You didn't have to manhandle me! Now get off me!" she snapped, her blue eyes flashing with fury.

He was about to do so, but then he shook his head with a grim smile and sat, still holding her wrists, still straddling her hips, his weight settled comfortably on his haunches.

"I don't think so."

"What?"

He leaned toward her. "Not until you tell me what the hell you think you're doing on this boat!"

Chapter 6

"I'm going with you," Kathy said.

"What?"

She inhaled and exhaled, feeling the pressure of his hands and thighs upon her. She could see an angry tic at the base of his throat. "I'm going with you," she repeated.

He exploded with a swift, precise oath.

"Will you please quit that and listen to me for a moment? And while you're at it, would you please let go of me? This is not the most comfortable position in the world."

"It seems to be the only position to have you in, Ms. O'Hara, to know where you are and what you're doing!"

"Brent!"

He got up and none-too-gently and very ungraciously dragged her to her feet. He stared at her in the growing darkness, turned and climbed the stairs. Kathy quickly followed.

"Brent, will you listen to me?"

He was standing there, his hands on his hips, staring out at the beach. In the coming darkness, the place was almost deserted. All the children had returned to their various boats with their parents and were heading to the marinas. The picnickers were all gone. A lone couple walked the sands hand in hand.

"Kathy, I'm putting you on a plane out of here," he told her flatly.

"No, you're not!" she retorted furiously. "Do you want to know what the problem is, Brent? I know what you're trying to do. You don't want to go home and play it safe. You want to go back and make sure you're incredibly visible. You want to draw this person or these persons out."

He turned to stare at her. Even in the darkness she was certain she could see a glitter in his eyes. She had hit upon the truth. "Kathy—"

"I'm right and I know it!" she said stubbornly.

"Kathy! I don't know what I'm doing, and I don't know just how good these people are. I—"

"My house is probably the safest place in Miami for you, Brent. Had you thought of that?"

The moonlight was growing stronger, cutting through the shadows of the night. He inclined his head, watching her with a certain amusement. "Is it?"

"Yes, it is. And don't laugh at me. I know what I'm talking about."

"*Our* house, remember? And if it's so safe, why was I able to walk right into the bathroom?"

"Because you know about that entrance. Because I hadn't bothered with the alarm because I knew Sam was out there. No one gets past Sam."

"I did."

"Because I never managed to explain the terms of the divorce to him!" Kathy snapped. "Brent, that foolish dog loves you. But he's wonderful otherwise. And the alarm system is connected directly to the police station. And we can even bring in a cop or a security guard or—"

"Kathy, don't you understand? You would be safest if you were far away," he said with exasperation.

She was silent for a moment. "No. I can't go away. Don't you understand?"

They both felt the rocking of the boat, the gentle movement of the waves, the coolness of the night breeze. He stared at her then sank onto the bench, sighing. "Kathy, I wasn't going to even bring the boat into her berth. I was going to ditch her somewhere close and—"

"I know the perfect place!" Kathy said enthusiastically. "Mrs. Fenniman's property."

"Whose?"

"Mrs. Fenniman's! She lives at the little curve in the arm of the peninsula. She's ninetysomething years old, lives with a sweet young nurse and has the most overgrown acre of land I've ever seen. And you can run along the back of it and right up the side of our wall to the gate and be inside the house before anyone could possibly know you'd been outside it!"

He watched her for a long moment, knowing she was absolutely right.

Then suddenly the moon touched his eyes and Kathy saw that they were flashing with fury again. He stood and walked over to her and caught her shoulders and seemed to be fighting the temptation to shake her hard.

"Why are you doing this?" he demanded harshly.

She let her head fall back and met his gaze with an equal fury and challenge. "For old time's sake," she snapped.

"Kathy—"

"Because I don't want to be forced out of my own house, all right? What difference does it make? You cannot force me to go anywhere, Brent!"

"Don't bet on it. I thought earlier that I *should* have tied you up and sent you north in a cargo box."

She wrenched back from his touch, taking a step away from him. "I'd never speak to you again."

"Well, you haven't spoken to me in three years."

"I'll have you nice and safe in jail on charges of physical harassment or whatever it is you call it!" she warned him.

He laughed and before she knew it had caught her by the shoulders again, swung her around and set her on the bench by the tiller, then stood towering over her, locking her in place with a hand laid flat upon the fiberglass next to each shoulder.

"This is my party you've crashed, Kathy. And things are going to be done my way."

"I beg your pardon! You crashed into my bathroom, remember?"

"*Our* bathroom!"

"Brent—"

"It's almost like you're inviting me to play man and wife again. Is that what you're doing, Kathy?"

"Get off me, Brent. I'm trying to help you. For Shanna's sake. For—"

"For old time's sake. Yes, I know." He straightened suddenly and walked away from her. He stared at the water, then said, "All right. All right, you can stay, but we still play it my way. I make all the rules. Agreed?"

"No, you do not—"

"Kathy, trust me, I wouldn't feel a bit guilty exercising a little physical harassment to get you to safety."

"What are these rules?" she demanded. Muttering beneath her breath, she added, "I don't believe this! I've done my very best to be an extremely decent ex-wife, and here you are—"

"Making rules. Right. That's the way it goes. Agreed?"

"I told you—let me hear the rules."

"Once we get to the house, you stay in it. You don't even walk to the pool unless I'm with you, understand? You don't bring in the mail. You don't do anything."

"Brent—"

"Anything at all. All right?"

She clenched her teeth and nodded. "All right!"

"And," he added softly, "if you want to play house, Ms. O'Hara, we play house."

"What?" she said.

"I'm not sleeping on any couches. Or in Shanna's room or on the floor."

Warmth sizzled through her. She knew what he was saying. It was just that her tongue had gone very dry and she wasn't at all sure of how she should respond.

"I—I don't mind couches or Shanna's room," she said softly.

"That's not what I meant and you know it. I can't live with you and not sleep with you. You're not my wife, but you were for a very long time, and I discovered years ago that I didn't seem to be able to manage any halfway situations with you. If you want me in the house, you get me in your bed. Understood?"

She stared at him blankly and wondered if he had just given her exactly what she wanted. Or if he had frightened her beyond anything she had expected.

What had she wanted? Flowers? Soft music? A careful seduction? Maybe she was pretending. And maybe she had wanted him to play the game, too. Perhaps there was no getting back together, ever, because the desire they shared blanketed the pain, but in the harsh light of day, it could never erase it.

"Kathy!" His voice was curt, nearly brutal, and cold as ice.

"I'm thinking!" she snapped.

"You didn't have to think so long last night," he reminded her bluntly. "Last night you were just about as hot as—"

"You bastard!" she gasped, leaping to her feet and staring at him furiously, her fingers curling into fists at her sides. They wouldn't stay there. She took a step forward and slammed them against his naked chest. He caught her wrists and dragged her hard against him, his eyes sizzling as they bored into hers.

"I'm just trying to keep this blunt and true and in perspective, Ms. O'Hara. I told you before I won't play games. I wouldn't pretend that what happened between us didn't. And I won't turn anything into a game, either. I won't bed down on a couch then come wandering around in the middle of night pretending I'm looking for something I can't find. You wanted me last night, I wanted you. I still want you. And if I'm going to sleep in that house, I'm damned well going to sleep with you."

She couldn't stare at him much longer. Maybe he was right, maybe it should all be kept strictly on the surface. It would be foolish to pretend, even to herself, that she didn't want him desperately. Even if it was just for this brief time.

It had been his house, too. Technically, it still was. Maybe he couldn't live in it and keep his distance. She knew Brent well; he wasn't going to date her at this time in their lives.

She wished he hadn't been quite so blunt, but he

meant to be. Blunt, crude, basic. He didn't want her to expect more out of him.

She wrenched from his hold. "All right."

He arched a brow. "You agree?"

"I just said so."

He smiled slowly. She tossed her blond hair, turned and started for the steps.

"Where are you going now?" he demanded harshly.

She had reached the stairs. She swung around, angry. "You've got a bit of a ride to the shore. I'm going to bed. Alone. We haven't reached the house yet!"

She started down the steps, infuriated. She heard his soft laughter follow her, and it didn't help one bit. She slammed her cabin door and flung herself on the bed, her heart racing. She waited tensely, wondering if he would come after her with some new ultimatum.

But he didn't. She heard the motor rev, felt the motion of the boat, and she knew they were under way. He hadn't come near her.

He didn't need to, she reminded herself. He already had her exactly where he wanted her. All he had to do was bide his time.

She hadn't thought she would doze off, but she'd probably had less than four hours of sleep the night before and, to her amazement, once she closed her eyes, the rocking of the boat allowed the world to slip away.

She was startled when she heard Brent's voice awakening her. "Kathy! Kathy, we're here."

She sat up and saw his silhouette in the doorway. She blinked, trying to leave the fog of sleep behind her. It was so dark. They hadn't come into a marina.

No, no, they weren't supposed to be at a marina. They were on the shore of Mrs. Fenniman's property. It had been her idea. Whatever had possessed her?

Despite the moon, it was still very black out. And there was no nice clean beach here, just weeds and high grass and all kinds of trees and yucky underwater plants.

"Come on!" Brent urged her. Even in the shadows, she felt his eyes wander over her. She was still dressed in the bikini—Shanna's bikini—and nothing else. Well, it was appropriate for a swim.

"Have you got your sneakers and the keys?"

"Sneakers?"

"Yeah, you never know what you might step on trying to get out of here."

"Oh, yeah, right!" she agreed miserably. She found her sneakers beneath the bunk and tied them on. Then she dug into her bag to find her keys and wallet. Brent reached for them and she stared at him blankly. "I've got pockets," he told her curtly. "You've barely got room to breathe."

After handing him her things, she waltzed past him and hurried up on deck.

There wasn't a soul around, not for miles and

miles. Brent had turned off all the lights and brought them in to hug the shore. The tide might ground them by morning, but that didn't seem to matter much right now.

"Ready?" he asked her.

If only it had been a nice clean beach.

"Sure," she murmured. She didn't want to dive into the water. They were close enough to the marina for the water to be filled with oil and garbage. They were far enough away for it to be filled with all kinds of creatures she didn't mind at all by daylight—but hated in the darkness.

"Let's go."

She must have hesitated too long. He swept her up and tossed her over, then followed quickly.

She was a good swimmer. She clenched her teeth and headed in, trying to ignore the muddy sand and slimy feel of the sea grasses. She stumbled for a foothold when she neared land. She almost slipped in the stuff but Brent was right behind her, taking her elbow. They walked to the hard earth together. Then he had her hand and was leading her silently through the sea brush, through the stands of mangroves and deep into the foliage of the yard.

She could see Mrs. Fenniman's old Spanish mansion up on a rise. They came to the row of pines at the base of the ledge and ran along them until they reached the back wall of their fence.

"Don't bark, Sam! Don't bark!" Brent muttered. He paused just a second, then led her to the front of the property. He glanced quickly at Kathy as he looked at the alarm box.

"I haven't changed the code," she muttered.

He punched in the numbers, then opened the wrought-iron gate with her key. He shoved her inside and followed quickly, locking it behind him.

Kathy nearly screamed as something cold touched her hand. She jumped a mile before she realized it was Sam.

"Good dog!" Brent said, patting him affectionately. "Come on," he told Kathy.

They hurried up the path to the door, which Brent opened. Sam started to follow them in. "All right, just for a few minutes," Brent told the dog. "We need you out there tonight, my friend."

Kathy sighed and leaned against the door for a moment, then moved away as Brent continued to pat Sam. "Where are you going?" he demanded sharply.

"For a glass of wine. And then I'm going to take a bath. Every creepy thing in the sea seemed to have touched me."

"Wait a minute," he told her curtly.

She stood and watched him while he disappeared into her bedroom.

Their bedroom.

He came back a moment later. She stared at him curiously. "I was just checking the back door."

She smiled sweetly. "The riffraff has already come in that way."

He ignored her and picked up the phone. She walked into the kitchen and poured herself a glass of wine, then decided to be generous and pour him a glass, too.

When she emerged from the kitchen, he seemed to be on hold. The receiver was between his head and his shoulder and he was busy loading a gun.

"Where did that come from?"

He glanced at her, arching a brow. "It's a police gun, fires fifteen shots."

She shivered despite herself. There was a gun on the boat; he'd always kept a gun in the house. This was a new one, though.

"Robert gave it to me a while back. I have a permit, and it's nice and legal." She was still staring at him. "Kathy, if someone comes in and tries to shoot us, I'm going to shoot back. Okay?"

"You brought that off the boat?"

"I brought it with me the other day, when I came in through the bathroom."

Just how long had he been in the house before she had seen him? she wondered. Not that it mattered anymore. She set down his glass of wine.

He cast her a quick glance. "Thanks."

"Sure."

"Robert? Yeah, it's Brent," he said suddenly into the phone. He had called Robert; he was bringing the police in on the situation.

She could hear Robert's voice, demanding to know where he was, where he'd been. "Robert, hang on just a second," he said as Kathy started to turn away. "You're taking a bath?"

She nodded, wondering if he thought she was giving him some kind of an invitation. She wasn't— she felt dirty from swimming in dirty water.

"Good," he said bluntly. "Burn that suit when you're done, will you?"

She arched a brow in surprise, but he had already turned his attention to the phone conversation. She walked into the bathroom with her wine, turned on the water in the tub, poured in an ample amount of bubbles, then lowered herself into it.

The heat was delicious. The clean water was delicious. She sank beneath the water, soaked her hair and scrubbed it assiduously. She leaned back, content, and took a long swallow of wine.

Was this an invitation?

It hadn't been that long ago when she had lain here dreaming of the past. Then the past had intruded upon the present. She had thought about Brent crawling into the tub with her. And he had stumbled into it, jeans and all. Not exactly what she'd had in mind.

None of this was what she'd had in mind....

Would he come in now? she wondered. Come in now as she had dreamed, stride in, peel away the cutoffs, sink down with her. Touch her in the midst of the bubbles, do the things to her he'd done the night before...

Her eyes closed. He would come, he was the one

who insisted he would. He would sweep her up as
he had so often before, and lay her on the bed they
had shared. Against the whiteness of the cool, clean
cotton sheets. His body would look so bronze.

It would be like playing house all over again.
Playing man and wife as Brent had said.

They could never go back. But that was all right.
She only wanted these few nights....

Brent came in, talking. "I'll see Robert tomorrow," he said. "They'll have a man watching the
house tonight. They had a patrol car going around
when we came in, but apparently the man didn't see
us. I don't know if that means we're very good, or
he isn't quite so good. But between the alarm and the
dog and the cop, I guess we should be in pretty good
shape."

She didn't respond. Her head was on the rim of
the tub, her eyes were closed, her dark honey lashes
sweeping her cheeks. He smiled suddenly, realizing
she was sound asleep.

"You can drown yourself that way," he whispered
softly. He pulled a towel from the rack and bent to
lift her. Her eyes flew open with alarm.

"It's all right, don't be frightened. It's just me. You
were sleeping."

Her eyes fluttered, and her arms wound around his
neck. He thought she had fallen asleep again already
when she whispered softly, "Just you, don't be frightened!" she said. "I should be absolutely terrified."

"Why is that?"

She shook her head. Her eyes closed.

He carried her to the bedroom, pulled back the spread, then laid her on the sheets, still wrapped in the towel. He rolled her, freeing the towel from beneath her. She lay on her stomach. Her eyes opened and closed again.

Her back was still damp. He moved the terrycloth towel gently over her, then tossed it aside. He pressed his lips against her spine and felt her slight shift of movement. She tried to open her eyes but her lashes fell softly over them once again.

He smiled, rose and brought the covers over her, then turned off the light as he left the room.

In the living room he sat before the fireplace and drank his wine. Sam pushed his nose onto Brent's lap and Brent idly patted the dog. "You don't understand any of it, do you, boy? Neither do I," Brent assured him.

He leaned back. He shouldn't be here. He shouldn't have let her talk him into anything. He should have put her on a plane.

But it was good to be here. With her.

"She came back for me, Sam. I left her on a sailboat, heading away with friends, and she came back. What do you think of that? Actually, it was pretty humiliating. Here I am thinking I can still hear a pin drop in the dark, and she crawled right on that boat without my even realizing it. I'm slipping, Sam. Her fault. I was thinking about her. I haven't been able to stop thinking about her for a minute."

He stroked the dog's ears a few minutes longer,

then sighed and rose. "Out, Sam. I need you outside. To watch for bad guys. Don't let me down, boy."

With Sam out, Brent finished his wine. He was feeling the slime himself, and chose to shower in the hallway bathroom rather than take a chance on waking her up.

The heat and the steam felt great. He came out with a towel wrapped around his hips and made one last tour of the place. Robert had already made sure the alarm was working, and the cop was outside somewhere. And he did have a lot of faith in Sam.

He picked up the gun and carried it with him into the bedroom. The lights were always left on in the pool area, and he could see from the bathroom window that nothing seemed to be disturbing the peace of the yard.

Satisfied, he started for the bedroom. Then he saw her bikini on the floor.

He sniffed, bent to pick it up and tossed it into the trash can. Then he flicked off the bathroom light and silently walked into the bedroom. He slipped the gun beneath his pillow, discarded the towel and crawled in beside her.

He had no intention of waking her. He lay in the comfort of the bed, tired but not sleeping, feeling the luxury of the sheets after the night on the hard deck.

Then she started to move toward him. He turned. She came even closer.

He slipped an arm around her. He smelled the sweet scent of her shampoo in her still-damp hair, and the delicate, subtle scent of the perfumed soap she used. He wasn't going to wake her....

He stroked the softness of her upper arms. Her back fit provocatively against his chest, and her derriere was right up against a rapidly hardening part of his anatomy. He needed to push her away just a bit.

He set his palm upon her hip, but he didn't quite manage to push. Instead his palms tenderly cupped the curve, then stroked the rounded fullness there with a sensual appreciation. He heard her moan softly. She was still half asleep.... But she was also half awake.

He swept his hand from her hip to her breast. Slowly, he caressed the lushness of her flesh, the tempting hardness of the bud of her nipple. She moved slightly, adjusting her body more tightly against his. He swept his hand over her belly and laid his lips against the nape of her neck, then her earlobe, all the while moving his hands upon her.

He tossed the sheet aside and saw the gleam of her naked flesh in the night glow that touched the room. He groaned.

He stroked the rise of her hips once again, pushed her thigh forward, then thrust himself fully and deeply within her from behind. He heard the sharp intake of her breath and pulled her closer against him. Her scent was sweetly intoxicating. The movement of her body was subtle yet wildly erotic. He kept running his hands over her naked hips and buttocks, then slipped them to her belly, bringing her nearer to meet the force of his thrust. He lost all sense of finesse and thundered against her. The climax rose within him unbearably, his body constricted with the need, with the desire, with the pleasure and the anguish, then seemed to erupt. Shudder after shudder went through him, and he thrust and thrust until he was emptied within her. He heard her cry out softly, and even as he drifted down, he pulled her to him again, loathe to pull away. He stayed within her, just holding her gently.

She didn't speak, but she seemed content.

He smoothed her hair from beneath his nose. In time, he dozed.

Kathy awoke with a start when his hand landed with a not really gentle crack on her rear. She started up, sweeping the sheets around her and staring at him with daggers and reproach.

"What was that for?"

"You have to get up."

"You didn't have to slap me!"

"That was just a love tap," he said with a wave of his hand. He had been up for a while, she surmised. He was dressed in jeans and a red polo shirt. He had shaved and seemed in top form.

While she felt ancient, exhausted. She hadn't a speck of makeup on, and her hair was probably one big tangle.

"Rough night?" he asked her. "I didn't mean to wake you."

He seemed so damned cocky. She couldn't resist. "You didn't!" she told him innocently.

He cast her a warning, reproachful glare and pretended for a moment that he would get her with the towel he had just plucked from the floor. She had to laugh, and he smiled and turned away. Her laughter faded because she knew that once he would have tossed himself over her, warned her that he was going to be damned sure she was awake this time, and made love to her all over again.

But this wasn't the past, and he was only here because all their lives might be in danger.

"Robert is on his way over," he told her. "Coffee's on. I thought you could make the omelets this time. And they'd better be good. I'm starving. Some first mate you turned out to be. I didn't get a thing to eat all day."

She arched a brow, sitting up, pulling the sheets to her chest. "I don't remember inviting you to any meals."

"Well, if you want my performance to be the kind that really wakes you up," he drawled, "then you have to keep me well fed, keep my strength up and all that."

She threw a pillow at him.

He grinned. "Invite me to bed but not to dine!" He chastised from the door. "Unless, of course, you meant—"

He couldn't finish. She threw a second pillow at him and heard his laughter. Then the door closed.

She bit her bottom lip. How had they ever let this

end? There could be so much laughter between them, so much warmth. If only…

If only, if only. She had lived with "if only" forever, it seemed.

Swallowing hard, she got up and hurried into the bathroom. After a brisk shower, she put on a little makeup, then dressed in jeans and a knit pullover. She paused before opening the bedroom door.

Brent was at the piano. He was playing slowly, but she instantly recognized the tune.

"Forever My Love."

How could he? she wondered bitterly, then she heard the sound of his voice—husky, provocative, unique.

Tears rose to her eyes. She swung open the door, determined to ignore him.

She stalked past him into the kitchen. He didn't look up. He seemed perplexed.

She opened the refrigerator and nearly threw the eggs and ham and cheese on the counter. Then she realized he had stopped playing, he was staring at the keys.

"What are you doing?" she demanded harshly.

He looked at her. "What?"

"I said, what are you doing?"

"Oh, I was just thinking. Thinking about the tour."

The tour! He was thinking about the tour! He was playing a tune that had managed to rip her heart out, and he didn't seem to remember that the song had fallen into place because of her. She felt like throwing the carton of eggs on his head. She turned and started to chop ham. He didn't seem to notice.

He left the piano and wandered over. "I poured you a cup of coffee. Over there."

"Thanks," she said briefly. She didn't look at him. Boy, was their ham going to be well chopped.

"Why don't you just puree it?" he asked.

The knife was in her hands. She looked at him, the knife raised innocently, and demanded sweetly, "What?"

"Kathy, what did that ham ever do to you? Ah, never mind. I think that's really my body on that chopping block. What did I do?"

"Nothing," she said.

"Ah! I've got it. You really were awake, that's it!"

She groaned and turned to the refrigerator for the butter. He was behind her, taking the knife from her hand, spinning her around in his arms. He was frowning, perplexed.

"What is the matter?"

"Nothing."

"Kathy."

"Nothing, really. I—" Her eyes fell. "I just wish you wouldn't play that song."

His eyes softened instantly. He smiled, and it was a curious smile, filled with tenderness and with pain. "I know. It seems to embody years, doesn't it? Our entire youth."

No, our love! she wanted to say. But she didn't. She had already said too much.

"It just…hurts," she said.

He pulled her against him, cradling her very tenderly. And they seemed to stand there forever. She felt his touch as she hadn't felt it before. She felt the tenderness and the magic that had always been there. She felt the elusive bond that had held them so tightly for so long. She felt the love, all the years they had shared, everything that had ever been right and natural.

Then the knife slipped and fell to the floor with a clang and they stepped quickly away from each other. Kathy turned abruptly toward the refrigerator and Brent moved around the counter.

"I was thinking about the tour," he told her, "because Harry Robertson always seemed to be humming that tune. Nervously. And then sometimes I would catch him whistling it, and when I would look at him, he would always break off."

"Maybe he was afraid you'd think he was trying to steal your song," Kathy said.

Brent shook his head. "No, no, it wasn't anything like that. It was more like he absolutely hated the song."

"He couldn't have. No one hates that song. It's one of the most beautiful you've ever written. It hit the charts for months on end! It's almost twenty years old and little kids and teenagers still seem to know it."

"Well, Harry Robertson hated it," Brent said flatly.

Kathy beat the eggs and said curtly, "Want to do the toast, please?"

"Sure. We have to keep your strength up, too," he told her idly.

Then they both stopped because they heard Sam barking like crazy.

"Get down!" Brent snapped to Kathy. She saw that the gun was in his hand. He had been wearing it the whole time they had been talking.

"Brent—"

"Get on the floor, Kathy!"

He was heading toward the front door, wary, silent, alert. He leaned against the door frame and carefully stared out the peephole. He started to laugh.

"Brent, have you lost your mind?" Kathy demanded.

He turned to her, smiling. "No, just my instincts, I think. I guess you'd better throw on a few more eggs. It's just Robert. He's at the gate looking sadly perplexed. Poor Robert! Sam never did seem to take to him."

Brent grinned and opened the door to step out. Sighing with relief, Kathy reached for another egg. Then she heard the gunshot. For a single instant she froze with terror.

Then she screamed and raced for the door.

Chapter 7

Common sense didn't enter Kathy's thinking. She had heard the crack, and had horrified visions of Brent lying facedown in a pool of blood.

She didn't pause at the door; she didn't look through the peephole. She threw open the door, screaming his name. Then she pelted down the walkway with such speed that she flew into him as he stood before the gate. The two of them tumbled to the ground together.

"Brent!"

There was nothing on him, no blood, no injury. His eyes weren't closed in pain. Instead they were wide open, staring into hers as if she was dangerously insane. She was on top of him, then Sam was on them both, licking Brent's face.

"Sam, quit!" Brent insisted. "Kathy, what the hell is the matter with you?"

"The shot! I heard a shot!"

"You heard a shot so you came running out the door? You idiot! If there had been a shot, you should have stayed the hell inside!"

He wasn't injured, he wasn't even touched, and according to him, there hadn't even been a shot. But she'd heard it! She was here because of her fear for him.

Her eyes narrowed. "Fine! The next time I think you might be in trouble, I'll let you bleed to death!"

"It would be smarter than running out here to bleed to death along with me!" he swore.

"Children, children, children!"

Kathy realized that a pair of feet shod in black moccasins was planted by their side. She looked up slowly to find that Robert McGregor had come in through the gate while the two of them sat entwined, arguing. "Getting along the same as usual, I see."

"Kathy, get off me," Brent groaned.

"Oh, Kathy, get off me, yourself!" she spat out. "You never oblige when I ask you to get off me."

"Ah, the plot thickens," Robert commented.

Kathy flushed. How could she have said what she said with Robert standing right there? It was Brent's fault; he was always goading her, it seemed. Whether he meant to or not.

Brent rose, then with hands planted firmly on her waist, he helped her up. She smiled sweetly at Robert. "The plot isn't doing a darn thing, Lieutenant McGregor, I assure you."

"Oh, I think it's wonderfully thick," Brent muttered darkly. "Kathy was going to save me from bullets with a shield of human flesh. Great idea, huh?"

"Bullets!" Robert said, then smiled at Kathy.

"Kath, no bullets. An old car going down the street backfired, that was all."

She smiled over clenched teeth. "Wonderful."

"Maybe we shouldn't be standing here like this, though," Robert said. "Not that I think that anything is going to happen here. Let's go inside."

Kathy led the way in. Robert followed Brent. She ignored them both and went into the kitchen. She heard Brent telling Robert about Shanna, then she heard him go into an explanation of everything he had known or suspected when Harry Robertson had been arrested.

"You're sure that that's what's going on?" Robert asked him.

Kathy picked up an egg as she watched Brent shrug. "What else? Why, do you think—"

"I think what you think," Robert said. "It's just we've got no leads, no clues. The bombing that killed Johnny was a very professional job. Whoever did it knew exactly what he was doing. And I'm sure you weren't meant to be in the explosion. I think someone thinks you know something."

"Well, I don't," Brent assured him. "I don't know a damned thing."

Kathy added another egg to her mixture, watching the two men intently. She knew Brent well enough to believe his exasperated statement.

Robert ran his fingers through his short, dark hair. "What are you going to do about the benefit Friday night?"

Kathy reached into a cabinet beneath the counter for a frying pan. She set it on the counter.

"Robert—" Brent warned.

"What benefit?" Kathy demanded, leaning over the counter to challenge them both, pan in hand.

Robert arched a brow to Brent and looked at Kathy uneasily. "Kathy, it's been in the paper—"

"What benefit?" she repeated.

"It's not a concert or anything. Just a big party out on Star Island. To raise money for the homeless," Brent told her.

"Well, you can't do it," Kathy said. "Obviously. Robert, tell him he can't do it. It would be idiotic."

"Kathy, I'm doing the damned benefit," Brent stated irritably.

"Robert, tell him—"

"I think he might need to do it more than ever now, Kathy."

"Don't you see, Kath? It might be the only way to talk to people involved, to try to figure out—"

"Are you both crazy?" Kathy exploded. "Brent, you wanted me out of town. You didn't think that my house was safe! Now you want to go out to somebody else's place and be surrounded by all those people—"

"People I've worked with," Brent reminded her.

She stared at them incredulously. They thought Brent should go.

"Robert!" she wailed furiously. "How can you let him do this?"

"Kathy, we've got nothing! And he's not going to

stay in a closet for the rest of his life, you know that! The place will be crawling with police and security."

"It will probably be the safest place in the world for me to be," Brent assured her.

"You're not a detective!" Kathy exploded.

She watched the stubborn set of his jaw and his voice went low, which tended to mean he was very angry. "Kathy, I need to go. What the hell are you doing with those eggs? Aren't they ready yet?"

"What?" she snapped.

"I said, what about—"

"The eggs, yes, well, they're right here, you all enjoy them!" She strode out of the kitchen, the frying pan still in her hand. Frightened and infuriated, she thrust it at Brent, catching him soundly in the stomach with it. She heard him grunt as she hurried down the hallway to her room.

Brent held the pan, gritting his teeth around the pain. Then he smiled at Robert. "She really loves me, you can tell," he said.

Robert laughed, then sobered quickly. "I can give you a lot of protection but no guarantees, Brent. Do you really think doing the benefit is such a good idea? Maybe you should just disappear for a while."

Brent shook his head. "What am I going to do, Robert, run for the rest of my life? I have to try to find out what this is all about."

He walked around the counter into the kitchen with the frying pan. "Eggs?" he asked.

Robert winced. "I think I'll just take some coffee."

"Oh, come on. My omelets are better than hers anyway."

"Maybe she'll join us in time, huh?" Robert said.

"Oh, I don't know. She has a heck of a temper."

"Well, so do you."

Brent lowered his head. "I know that. Yeah, hell, I know that!" he replied wearily.

"She came running out of the house like that because she was concerned."

"I know that, too. It's just she scared the damn hell out of me, that's all. Hey, Robert, get out of my personal life and be useful, won't you? Throw in some toast."

Brent finished the omelets. As the two of them ate, Robert went over every little thing one more time and Brent answered as slowly and carefully as he could.

Brent gave Robert the number where he could reach the Brennans, explaining that he didn't want to call from the house in case there was some kind of a tap on the phone. Robert promised to make sure that Shanna and everyone else had arrived safely on the island.

Then Robert went to the door to leave. "I've people up at the state prison, trying to find out what they can from any of the inmates who were associated with Harry Robertson. Maybe we'll come up with something from that angle. I've talked to Keith Montgomery, and I've talked to the Hicks brothers. They don't seem to know anything, either. I've got twenty-four-hour security going for them, too. Maybe you should talk among yourselves."

"I was planning to do just that, at the benefit."

"They're going to bury Johnny this afternoon," Robert said.

Brent glanced toward the bedroom. "Yeah, I know, I picked it up on the news."

"You were planning on going?"

"Yeah, I didn't want to say anything. Hey, Johnny was a real pill sometimes. We didn't often see eye to eye, and we didn't get along that great. But I worked with him enough over the years. I wouldn't feel right if I didn't go."

"What!" came a sharp exclamation. Brent spun around. Kathy was out of the bedroom. "Now you're going to go running around to funerals, too!"

"Kathy, I have to go."

"Then I'm going."

"The hell you are!"

"Hey, hey, hey!" Robert protested. "Kathy, listen to this. Brent, you listen, too. I'll come for you both in time for the services, all right?"

"She shouldn't—" Brent began.

"*I* shouldn't! What about you?"

"You're starting to sound married again," Robert warned them.

It worked. They fell silent. Robert smiled and waved. "The funeral could be interesting, too, you know," he told Brent.

Kathy turned to go to the bedroom. Brent saw Robert out. He paused by his car, looking at the house. "This is a good setup here. The gate, the fence, the dog, the fact that the peninsula is private and a getaway would be almost impossible. No one's coming after you here, not even a professional. It couldn't be a clean enough job."

"Thanks," Brent said wryly.

"Seriously—"

"I know."

"I'll be back."

Inside Brent picked up the dishes. Kathy hadn't come out to eat. Almost two hours later she still hadn't appeared.

Brent watched the news, then sat at the piano. He picked out notes and played rhythms and beats, until his fingers started to move over the keys to "Forever My Love." Then he hesitated, remembering she hadn't wanted to hear the song.

Brent closed his eyes, thinking. There had been something about Harry and that song....

He opened his eyes. Kathy was standing there in a handsome navy business suit, her hair pulled back and wound into an elegant knot at her nape. "Are you going like that?" she asked him, indicating his jeans.

He smiled. "That depends. I was waiting to crawl through the closet. What have I got to wear?"

She shrugged. "I don't remember. But you've waited pretty long. Robert should be back soon."

"I didn't wait on purpose. You were in the bedroom."

"I don't remember that stopping you from entering before," she said flatly.

His smile deepened. "I'll remember that," he told her.

She turned on her navy heels, leaving him at the piano. She was cold, very cold. Like ice. Anything he might have gained in their time together, he had now lost, he thought.

He left the piano, entered the bedroom and rummaged through the huge closet until he found a suit. By the time he had changed, Kathy was calling through the door that Robert had come.

When Brent came out, Kathy told him Robert had checked on Shanna and that their daughter was fine and safe and sent her love.

Brent nodded and thanked Robert.

They rode to the church in the police car. The church was filled to overflowing, and the curious and the fans spilled into the streets. Teenagers carried banners proclaiming, "We'll love you forever, Johnny Blondell!"

Services were brief, then they moved on to the cemetery. Brent spoke with Johnny's sister, who had made the arrangements and seemed to be the one person there who had really loved Johnny Blondell.

He looked around while the priest's words droned on at the grave site. Kathy stood at his side; Marla Harrington, sniffing into a handkerchief, stood not far away. Cops surrounded the area.

Keith Montgomery didn't make a showing; neither did either of the Hicks brothers.

When the service ended Brent felt a tap on his

arm. Then he was suddenly engulfed in a massive and emotional hug as Marla threw her arms around him. She kissed his cheek and held him tight and looked at him with her huge velvet-brown eyes. "Oh, Brent! Poor Johnny, how horrible. And I was so, so worried about you! I called and called, and I drove by the house, and I talked to Keith and the others and no one, absolutely no one, not your manager, not your press secretary, no one knew where you were or how you were!"

He disentangled himself carefully from her arms. "I've been fine, Marla, fine. And I've hardly been gone a long time."

"It's just that I wanted to be with you so badly when I heard!" she whispered. Brent could feel Kathy at his side. Feel her like a live firecracker. "I wanted to do what I could to take your mind off things."

"Marla—"

"Are you still doing the benefit on Friday? I thought they'd cancel, but everyone thought it was such a good cause, and Johnny wouldn't have wanted anyone to cancel it because of him. Brent, I really need to talk to you. Maybe we could go together." Marla did have her talents. The purr of her voice was so sensual she might have been stripping as she whispered her words. It didn't matter. If she knew something, he wanted to know what, and he didn't mind playing a few games to find out what.

"All right, Marla."

"I'm afraid that won't be possible."

Kathy, stepping around him, spoke at last. She wore a wonderfully sweet smile as she addressed the very startled Marla.

"Pardon!" Marla muttered, glancing from Brent to Kathy in confusion. Then she stared hard at Kathy and gasped. "You're her! You're his ex-wife."

"Yes, I'm her, all right," Kathy said sweetly with just a touch of sarcasm. "And I'm afraid he can't accompany you because I'm accompanying him."

"No, you're not," Brent muttered.

"Yes, I am," Kathy said. They were both smiling at Marla over clenched teeth.

Kathy smoothly offered Marla a hand. "And you're Marla Harrington. I've heard so much about you. It's a pleasure to meet you."

"Thanks. I, uh, I didn't know that you and Brent were still on friendly terms."

"Oh, very friendly, at the moment," Kathy said sweetly.

"Really?" Marla said awkwardly. Then the situation was eased as Kevin Terrill, Brent's manager, made a sudden appearance, along with Pat Lacey, his press secretary. Both men were demanding to know where Brent had been and why he hadn't contacted them. Then they both recognized Kathy, and it seemed there was a lot of confusion.

Johnny's sister was led away, sobbing, and the caretakers made it pretty obvious they wanted everyone to leave so they could fill the grave.

Marla made it back to Brent for a brief moment. "Brent, darlin', I've really got to talk to you!" she whispered huskily.

Did she know something? Brent wondered. Anything?

"Sure," he said, squeezing her hands. "Sure, we'll get some time alone together. I'll see you on Friday."

She turned and left him. He started to turn away only to find Kathy standing there, staring at him. She looked so sophisticated. Elegant, beautiful—and very cold. Her smile was glacial. For such a tiny person, she could appear very superior.

"Brent, darlin', are you ready to leave? I believe that Robert is waiting for us. And the police aren't staying around much longer so the fans will be free to attack you if someone more—or less—lethal doesn't decide to first."

"I'm ready, Ms. O'Hara." He took her hand and led her toward Robert's car, his strides purposely long so she had to run on her high heels to keep up with him.

She was silent during the drive home while Robert quizzed Brent about the funeral. "I didn't find out anything," Brent said. "Well, I did find someone willing to talk, but Kathy rather nicely put an end to that."

"Oh, darlin', I don't think talking was what she had in mind."

"I have to find out."

"That's your prerogative," she told him innocently.

By then they had reached the house. She thanked

Robert sweetly and in a matter of seconds, she was out of the car, through the gate and hurrying up the walk to the front door.

"She? Marla Harrington?" Robert asked.

Brent nodded, watching as Kathy disappeared inside. "Yeah, I'll try to get through to her on Friday. I've got to talk Kathy out of going."

"You want to borrow some handcuffs? That might be your only chance," Robert warned him.

"Thanks." Robert got out of the car with Brent, but refused his invitation to come in. Brent locked the gate and patted Sam, then wondered if he wasn't being a little ridiculous with the security.

No. He'd just left Johnny's funeral and he wanted to stay alive. Life had become exceptionally intriguing once again.

He went into the house. Kathy was in the bedroom; the door was closed. He could hear her, though. She was on the telephone, setting up a date for a photo shoot in two weeks. Then she was on the phone again, easily hedging questions about him, making sure she had the studio time and the photographer she wanted.

He'd almost forgotten she had her own business.

"Brent?" she said on the phone. He shouldn't be eavesdropping, even if she was talking about him. Especially if she was talking about him and suddenly sounding very casual.

"Yes, well, I've heard from him, of course. He was concerned about Shanna. I'm sure he's fine. I don't really know. We are divorced."

Ah, divorced... But on very friendly terms, that was what she had told Marla.

He smiled and tried the door. It wasn't locked. He pushed it open and went into the room. She was stretched out on the bed. Her feet bare, she was lying there in her tailored white blouse and form-hugging linen skirt. She had freed her hair and it fell in soft tendrils and waves around her shoulders.

She glanced at him and rather quickly ended her conversation.

He cast off his jacket and stretched beside her. "Busy?" he inquired politely.

"Well, Patty is great, but she really handles the house and my time more than anything else," she said casually. "I had a few things to catch up with."

"Oh." Leaning on an elbow, Brent asked politely, "Any repercussions from all this hitting you?"

"No, no, not really. Well, of course, people are curious about you. I guess our past association is fairly well-known."

"Our past association?" he echoed genially.

"Yes."

"Just our past association?"

"What are you talking about?" she asked irritably.

"Well, gee, Ms. O'Hara, I just got the impression we were dating again."

"Dating?"

"Friday night. You're accompanying me, right?"

"If you're going to go—"

"But I could have had a date!" he protested.

Her eyes flashed dangerously. "If you're going to stay in this house and make demands, then you don't get to date, too. Not while—"

"Not while what?"

"Not while you're…you're sleeping with me."

"Oh?"

The telephone started to ring, breaking the tension rising between them. Kathy quickly picked up the receiver, her eyes a crystal fire of warning. "Hello?"

Brent could hear that the voice on the other end of the wire was male. Kathy listened uncomfortably for several seconds. She looked a little pale. She glanced at him uneasily, then tried to glance away. She slipped a hand over the receiver and smiled at him pleasantly. "Brent, this is personal. I don't suppose you'd—"

She broke off as he slowly shook his head, his refusal brooking no argument. She flashed him a glance of pure fury and tried to resume her conversation.

"I'm sorry, I should have called you. It's just that things moved so swiftly. I'm fine, I'm really fine. Shanna is away. Well, yes, I'm back now. No, I'm sorry, anything this weekend is really not feasible. I—"

She gasped as Brent suddenly pulled the phone out of her hands.

"Axel? Hi, Brent McQueen here."

"McQueen, what are you doing there?"

"Oh, just stretched out, resting for the moment. Kathy can't see you this weekend. She forgot to mention that she and I are on, er—what did you call it, Kath?—very friendly terms at the moment."

Kathy lunged at him. He swept an arm around her quickly, sliding his hand over her mouth as she tried to grind out a few rugged expletives. "Ooh! What was that, sweetheart?" he murmured loudly.

"What the hell is going on? What are you talking about?" Axel demanded. "Put Kathy on the phone this instant. Where is she now?"

"She's right here, lying in bed with me. But she can't talk right now. Her, uh, mouth is occupied, you know what I mean?"

A burst of rage from Kathy was spilling through his fingers. "Can't talk any longer, Axel. Boy, is she a tiger, huh? Talk to you soon." He slammed down the receiver, rather uselessly, he thought. For Kathy kicked and rolled and sent the phone flying to the floor with a loud clang. His hand slipped from her mouth and she managed to get on top of him.

"How could you? How dare you? I don't believe—"

"Hey!" he interrupted loudly, catching her flying fists and quickly flipping her beneath him. She was absolutely seething, her eyes pools of liquid blue fire, her hair a blond tempest flying all around her in an erotic tangle. She lay beneath him, hotter than flame, her breasts rising fascinatingly with each angry breath. She started to swear at him again and he smiled slowly.

"You had no right—"

"I had every right!" he retorted.

"You did not!"

"No, no!" he protested. "You called these shots, sweetheart. As long as I was sleeping with you, I couldn't date, right? Well, the same holds true for you, too."

"But I didn't—"

"You split up a date I was making with Marla."

"I didn't try to tell her what I was doing with you! I didn't say—"

"That my mouth was occupied?" he demanded, interrupting her.

"You bas—"

"Hey, Kath, don't make a liar out of me, huh?" He couldn't resist. He lowered his head and kissed her while her mouth was open. Kissed her with heat and fever and just a little bit of fury and the sudden explosion of passion that had come to him when he had heard her talking to another man.

She tried to wrench away from him, tried to shove his chest away. He didn't let her. His body sprawled over hers. He caught her cheeks with his hands, and he kept her mouth open, filling it with his tongue. She twisted and protested, and he knew that he could never let her go because the fires rising inside him were coming to combustible heights.

And then suddenly, she was kissing him back. Her fingers were almost painful as they threaded his hair; her nails raked down his back.

He broke away from her, his lips traveling down her throat, his touch opening her tailored shirt and baring the rise of her breasts. He drew out her fullness, his thumbs running over her nipples. The areolae were nearly aflame, swollen, hard, puckered, ripe to his touch, to his tongue.

"I hate you!" she whispered. And he froze. But she moved against him and her head tossed on the pillow and she whispered, "I want you, Brent! I…want you."

He shoved up her skirt and rubbed his body down the length of hers. He ran his touch over the texture of her garters and stockings, and over the soft bare flesh of her thigh. He lifted her hips and nipped and licked the flesh at the heart of her desire over the erotic lace barrier of her panties. Then he rose and stripped them away in a frenzy and barely managed to rip open his buckle and zipper before lifting her thighs around him and plunging into her and filling her with the rage of desire that obsessed him.

He heard his ragged cries, heard the tumult of her heart with her every breath, and he rose even higher with the sounds of her whispers. Then her cries and pleas came moist and sweet against his ear.

When they reached their climax, her words were incoherent. He held her while she shuddered. His fingers curled tightly in her hair and he kissed her forehead gently, his lips trembling. "Damn… Kathy…" he murmured with anguish. Then he groaned and staggered to his feet. He zipped his pants and left her.

Kathy lay there, still and startled, for long, miserable moments, wondering how such ecstasy could bring such loss and such pain. She bit the back of her hands, tears forming in her eyes. She had said she hated him.

She leaped up and started to smooth down her skirt. Then she paused and stripped off all her clothing and donned a terry robe instead. She walked out and found him at the piano. He wasn't touching the keys. He was leaning over it, his palms pressed against his eyes.

She sat next to him. Startled, he glanced at her, then stared at the keys again.

"Brent! I didn't mean it!" she said urgently.

He looked at her again. "What?"

"I—I didn't mean that I hated you."

He smiled slowly, ruefully. "I didn't think you did," he said very softly. Then he really looked at her and saw all the hurt in her eyes. He slipped his arm around her and pulled her against him. "It isn't you, Kathy. It's me."

"I don't understand—"

"I don't want to hurt you."

"You didn't hurt me, Brent. You've never hurt me, don't you understand? I—I wanted you." She paused, then whispered softly, "Desperately. Passionately. Deeply. You've never hurt me."

He stood suddenly, his back to her.

"Never?"

"Never." Again she paused. "Except when you left me," she admitted.

"I had to leave you," he said softly. Then he turned and came to her and gently massaged her temples.

"Why?" she whispered.

"I couldn't stay after what happened."

"But you didn't do it, Brent, you didn't."

His hands went still. "I wish I could believe that," he said quietly. He turned away from her and she knew he had ended the conversation, and that she hadn't reached him at all. She stood up to follow him, determined to get through.

"Brent—"

"I saw some steaks in the freezer earlier. Want to do them on the grill? They come out best half frozen."

"Sure. Fine. Brent—"

"Kathy," he said curtly, "we've barely been back together at all, and already we're fighting like cats and dogs."

"Well, hell, it's not that bad!" she protested. "You started it."

"I did not."

"You definitely did. You snatched the phone away from me and said really horrible and crude things to Axel. I don't think I'll ever be able to talk to him again."

Brent took the steaks out of the freezer. "Good."

"Good? You and I are just playing house, re-member. What happens to my life when this is over? Assuming we have lives left, of course."

"Well, you don't date Axel again."

"He's a very nice man."

"Yes, yes, he's fine. But I told you, Kathy. You deserve someone wonderful."

"Do I? What about you and the lady of the draping body?"

"There's nothing between Marla and me. I told you that."

"And I told you that Marla doesn't know that."

"Yes, you dealt with Marla very well."

"At least I wasn't crude."

"Ah! The difference between us!" he exclaimed.

She threw up her hands in exasperation. Then she smiled, because at least he was smiling again. She walked into the kitchen and stood on her toes to kiss him lightly on the lips. "Steaks sound great. I'm going to take a shower and change. A bloody Mary would be great, too, if you wouldn't mind fixing me one. I'll be out in a few minutes. Okay?"

He nodded. "One bloody Mary."

She started toward the bedroom. At the door she paused and called to him. "Brent?"

"Yeah?" He stood by the counter and watched her. His hair was ruffled and a little long over the collar. His shirt was in slight disarray, but he still looked great with his tall, lean, broad-shouldered physique, strong, handsome features and piercing, whiskey-colored eyes.

"You know what?" she asked him huskily.

"What?"

"You are wonderful," she said quietly. "Really wonderful." She grinned. "Even if you do say so yourself."

Then she slipped into the bedroom and closed the door. It might be good to let him think about the precise meaning of her words.

The phone was giving off a dull buzz from where it lay on the floor. She picked it up and set it on the night-stand. Then she smiled again and hurried to the shower.

Chapter 8

After she'd showered, Kathy pulled back the curtains on the bathroom door and looked out. Brent had the barbecue going. He'd changed to a pair of cutoffs and was stoking up the coals.

She started out of the room, then noticed the bathing suit in the little wicker trash basket. The basket was clean; the two pieces of the bikini were the only things in it. It was Shanna's bathing suit. Kathy couldn't let him throw it away. And she was really in the mood to torture him—just a little bit.

She rinsed the bikini, wrung it out and slipped into it. After grabbing a towel, she casually sauntered onto the patio.

He was no longer standing by the barbecue; he had moved closer to the pool to stretch out on one of the redwood deck chairs. From this position, he could see all of the forty-by-sixty pool, the screened dome enclosure and the patio plants within it, and the yard and the wall beyond. It was very private.

He was wearing sunglasses and sitting with a can of beer and the sports section from the newspaper. But as soon as Kathy stepped out, he swung around so swiftly that she cried out, startled. He might be sitting casually, she thought. But he was ready for anything.

"It's just me," she said. She couldn't see his eyes because of the sunglasses but she felt he was staring at her. "You were out here, so I was assuming you felt it was safe."

He still didn't say anything. She strolled over to the next deck chair and tossed down her towel. "Did you make my bloody Mary?" she asked him.

He gestured toward the round, glass-covered, wrought-iron patio table by the barbecue. She thanked him sweetly.

When she turned to take a seat, she found he was still watching her. He spoke at last. "I thought I had trashed that suit."

She arched a brow delicately over the rim of her glass and took a bite out of her stalk of celery before replying. "Trashed it? Oh, well, I did find it in the wicker basket. I thought it must have fallen there accidentally."

"It wasn't an accident."

"Oh? You don't like the suit?"

"Not on you."

"Thanks a lot."

"I didn't mean that," Brent said flatly. "What I mean is that it…it displays too much."

"Brent, really, no more than any other bikini—"

"All right. It's the way it displays what it does, then. Kathy, the damned thing is provocative as hell. You want old geezers jumping off their boats with their tongues stuck to the decks?"

She leaned back, smiling. "Only the old ones?"

"Kathy, you know something? There are times when you're a real little witch."

She sipped her drink, hiding a smile. "No, I'm really not. I'm just trying to plan ahead. For the future, you know."

He slipped his glasses down his nose and stared at her. "What future?"

"Mine. Well, you've absolutely destroyed whatever I might have had with Axel."

"You should thank me for that."

She ignored his comment. "So I'm going to have to go out looking, you know, so I might as well be as prepared as possible, right?" She was trying to goad him. Into what, she wasn't certain, but it didn't seem to be working.

He smiled. "I promise to cut that thing to ribbons before I leave."

"But when you leave is exactly when I'll need it. Just how long do you think you'll be staying, anyway?"

"That's hard to tell, isn't it?"

"You really had no right to do that to poor Axel. I'm being an extremely understanding ex-wife. I'm doing my very best while you destroy my life—"

"I'm trying to preserve your life, remember. And you haven't really given me the impression I'm destroying your life. Damned if I didn't think you were having, er, fun at various times along the way."

"Oh, yes, you can be mildly entertaining."

"Mildly entertaining?" he asked pleasantly.

She smiled, set down her drink, walked to the far end of the pool and dived in cleanly. The water was just the right temperature, cool against the heat of the day.

Seconds later, she heard a splash behind her. She quickened her strokes and moved to the side of the pool. Seconds later, Brent emerged from the depths before her. With a hand on either side of her he held on to the side. He asked again, "Mildly entertaining?"

She tried to slip below the surface and swim around his legs. In a second he had her by the foot and he was dragging her up. This time, his sleek bronze body pinned her against the side.

She didn't speak. He kissed her and their lips were damp and cool from the water, but when his mouth parted hers, all the warmth rushed in. He kissed her throat and she wound her arms around him as he nibbled her shoulders, biting her flesh lightly, running the hot liquid of his tongue over the spot to soothe away the erotic little hurt. She leaned her head back as he teased her throat again, as breath dampened and warmed her earlobe and collarbone. Then she felt his thumb and fingers running along the band of the bikini. "Let's see, what is it that you want to hear? This thing is incredible on you, sexy as all hell, provocative, evocative, titillating. Old men, young men, in-between men would all be drooling at the sight. I love it on you. Here. In private. And I am going to cut the damn thing to ribbons before I leave."

"You can't do that. It belongs to Shanna."

"Shanna! You mean you let her wear that thing?"

"She'll be eighteen soon. I can't stop her from using her own judgment. Besides, she looks absolutely dynamite in it. David loves it on her."

Brent leaned back, groaning. "This is getting worse and worse."

"Don't you remember being that young?"

"I remember you being that young. And I remember a few of your outfits, too. And I remember—"

"What?" Kathy demanded as he broke off.

He started to laugh. "I remember a few of your father's comments about them, too. It's frightening, 'cause I know exactly what David feels."

"What do *you* feel?" Kathy whispered.

His fingers moved below the waistband, erotically, intimately, against her flesh. If he wasn't holding her, she would sink. She leaned her face on his shoulder while he replied huskily, "This."

He pulled her closer against him, and she felt the mound beneath the fabric of his jeans, flush against her own sexuality.

She closed her eyes. But they flew open again as she heard a loud explosion. Like a gunshot. Then she heard the ferocious, deep, snapping growl of Sam's bark.

Brent swore. Kathy's eyes widened. "It's probably just that car backfiring again," she said.

"Kathy, that was a damned gunshot, and the bullet ripped into the water somewhere!"

"Oh!"

By now, Sam was sounding like a wild thing. The Doberman had rushed around the dome enclosure to the back wall.

Brent let out a loud expletive, grabbed her hand and dragged her to the steps. "Stay the hell down!" he warned her. Dripping, he raced across the patio, dragging her behind him. He paused briefly at the table that held the steaks and swept up a kitchen towel.

She realized his pistol was beneath the towel. Her heart started to hammer even more ferociously as they entered the house through the sunroom that led to the living room. Brent shoved Kathy toward the kitchen. "Get down and stay there!" he warned her briefly.

"Wait! Where the hell are you going?" she demanded.

"Get down, Kathy! I am not playing duck shoot for anyone!"

She grabbed for his arm, but he was gone. "Brent!" Terrified for him, she raced through the sunroom. Through the French doors, she could see that he had already reached the back wall, that Sam was barking like crazy as Brent scaled it. He disappeared over the wall, and there wasn't anything she could do.

Call the police.

But even before she had taken two steps toward the phone in the kitchen, Sam started barking again. Kathy froze, watching the Doberman tear around from the back of the house to the front. She held still, paralyzed, then she tore to the front door and stared through the peephole.

It was Robert. Worn, tired, in his rumpled business suit, he stood there, waiting, keeping as far away as he could from Sam.

She gasped with relief, leaning against the door for a second. Then she remembered that Brent was out there, and she threw open the door as quickly as possible. She set the alarm code to Off and raced to the gate, swinging it open desperately.

"Get down, Sam! Robert! There was a shot. We were at the pool. Someone took a shot at us and then Brent went after him!"

"Where?" Robert said tensely.

"To Mrs. Fenniman's. The neighbor's yard. Around that way."

"Keep that damned dog with you, Kathy. Get back in. I'll go around."

He shut the gate, pulled his gun from his shoulder holster and went off. Kathy bit her lip, wishing she was with them instead of being left alone.

She gripped Sam by the collar. "Come on, Sam. You come in with me. You're the only male I really trust." She remembered how he hadn't let out a peep while Brent silently broke into the bathroom. "Never mind. You're a traitor, too, but you're all I've got for the moment."

She brought the dog into the house. The air-conditioning made it cool. She was wet and shivering, but she couldn't bring herself to move. She felt numb. Brent was out there. He had gone tearing after a killer, so it seemed. He shouldn't have done that, he should have stayed in the house. He could get himself killed.

He had to do it. She knew Brent so well, and she knew he would never sit still while others took crack shots at him. He would never wait this thing out. He couldn't live that way.

They couldn't live that way.

She sat on a bar stool and leaned her head against the counter. It was solid and soothing. She realized that Brent wasn't going to stay. No matter what she said, no matter how she teased, no matter how she tried to tell him the truth, he wasn't going to stay. It was all over.

And now he was out there....

She really couldn't bear it if he died. No matter what happened, she didn't want him hurt. She did love him, very much, and she needed to know he was alive somewhere.

"Kathy!"

At the harsh sound of his voice, she turned, so startled that she nearly fell off the chair.

He was covered with dirt, his eyes bright against the smudges on his face. She didn't know how he had gotten into the house so quietly. He hadn't come through the gate. Then she remembered the back alarms were off because they'd been at the pool.

And that damned Sam. He never would warn her when Brent was coming.

"I told you to get into that kitchen and get down!" he told her harshly.

She arched her brows at him. "I asked you not to go running out there!"

"I had a gun—you didn't."

"What happened?"

"When I tell you to stay down from now on, stay down!"

"Brent, what happened?"

He set the gun on the counter and walked into the kitchen, then turned on the water at the sink and scrubbed his face. "Nothing happened. I chased him through the dirt and trees and bracken but he had a little motorboat out there waiting." He paused. "I think I winged him. In the shoulder."

"You shot him?"

"Kathy, he was shooting at us. Yes, I shot him. I wasn't trying to kill him, though. I wanted to talk to him."

He froze, grabbing the gun, as Sam started to go wild again, running for the front door, slamming his paws against it, whining furiously.

"What the hell—" Brent began.

"It's just Robert."

"Robert?"

"He came to the front—"

"And you answered the damn door? After I told you to stay down?"

"I could see that it was him through the peephole."

"Kathy, I ought to blacken your hide!"

"Brent, this is my life you're in, remember! I was careful, I—"

"You're going to listen to me from now on!" he muttered fiercely, striding quickly by her. He keyed off the alarm again and went to the gate to meet Robert. Kathy followed him to the door. She watched as the two men talked for a moment, then Robert walked to his car. He must be using the radio.

Then the two men walked up to the house. Robert was still asking Brent to describe the man, but there was nothing much Brent could tell him. The man had been about medium height, medium build, thirty to forty years old, dark hair. He had disappeared into the bay in a motorboat.

"Well, we may get him," Robert said. "Even if we do, sounds like a hired job to me. I don't know what we'll get out of him. I do think I've got something for you, though."

"What?" Brent demanded. He opened the refrigerator and pulled out a pitcher of tea. He held the cold container against his face for a moment before walking across to the cabinet for glasses. "Anyone want to join me?"

Kathy shook her head, Robert accepted. He sipped the tea, then leaned over the counter. "We found a few guys at the state prison who were willing to talk about Harry Robertson."

"And?" Brent demanded.

"Seems like Harry was always saying he was going to be okay once he got out. That he had the real prize stashed away somewhere. He'd had a partner, the guy who had gotten him into the smuggling to begin with. He felt that the partner had ruined his life, then let him take the rap all by himself. But he was going to get even with the partner. He was never going to let the guy find the real treasure. The one guy, Harry's cell mate, seemed to think that there's a warehouse vault in Miami somewhere with Harry's treasure in it."

"What does that have to do with Brent?" Kathy asked.

"Someone in the band knew the combination to the lock on the warehouse vault. And it has something to do with Brent. Harry said so."

"What?" Brent demanded.

"You've got the number somehow, someway. You're the one who's got it."

"So why try to kill Brent? Why kill Johnny?"

Robert shrugged. "Johnny had a reputation. Maybe Harry's partner thought Johnny knew something. And knowing Johnny, he might have kept his mouth shut but told this guy—the partner—to kiss off. Maybe the partner didn't give warnings. I don't know. But at least you know a little more about what's going on, Brent."

Sure, they knew a little more, Kathy thought bitterly, but what good was it? They couldn't even go outside without someone taking shots at them. And Brent was still insisting on going to the benefit on Star Island.

She heard sirens. "There are the patrol cars," Robert said. Kathy looked at him with alarm and he smiled. "It's all right, Kathy. They're going to look through the woods out back, down to the water, to see if they can find something. Then we'll need to fish the bullet out of the pool. Ballistics might help, you never know."

Kathy nodded. Brent had disappeared into the bedroom and reappeared with her terry robe. He tossed it at her with a scowl. "Put that on, will you, please?" he demanded fiercely, then started out the door, holding Sam by the collar. Robert shrugged at Kathy and followed Brent to meet his officers.

Kathy checked the barbecue grill. The coals had died, so she brought the steaks in and threw them into the refrigerator.

Darkness came. Eventually Brent and Robert returned with other officers, and Kathy sat and answered what seemed like ridiculous questions while Brent went with one of the men into the pool to look for the bullet.

At midnight she made coffee and sandwiches. They found the bullet, then checked the grounds again. The officers left.

Brent and Robert sat on bar stools, talking. Brent was clean again; the water in the pool had washed away the dirt and grime from his skin. Robert was insisting that Brent think, and Brent was growing irritable, telling Robert he didn't have any damned solutions. It was going to go on for a while, Kathy decided.

"I'm calling it a night, guys," she told them. They looked at her blankly and she started down the hall for the bedroom.

Robert called after her. "Kathy?"

"What?"

"You should be thinking, too. You were on that tour with everyone else. You might know what Brent knows."

"I don't know anything!" Brent flared.

"All right. So the killer may think Kathy knows whatever he may think you know. So anything, anything at all, you call me, Kathy."

"Sure, Robert. Good night."

In the bedroom she stripped off the robe and the bikini and crawled into an oversize tailored shirt and slipped beneath the covers. She wanted to wait for Brent, but as she lay there, her eyes closed. He would wake her, she thought. If he wanted, he would wake her.

But he wasn't coming in that night. Somehow she knew it.

She dozed. She awoke a few hours later and saw that it was almost three. He hadn't come in. She closed her eyes and slept again, and when she next awoke, sunlight was filtering through the curtains and bathing the room in a golden glow. She rose and washed her face, brushed her teeth and combed her hair. Then she walked to the living room.

He was on the couch. He hadn't changed. He was still in his cutoffs, his arms crossed over his bare chest. His eyes flew open as she stared at him.

He sat up, startled. "Morning, huh? Already?"

She nodded. "I'll start the coffee. Want anything to eat?"

He nodded and stood. "Yeah, toast and bacon and eggs, sunny-side up. You feel like doing it?"

She nodded. "Well, it seems that the rest of my activities have been curtailed. I might as well."

"Thanks." He stared down the hallway. The phone began to ring. "I'll get it," he called to her.

Kathy went into the kitchen and started the coffee.

Brent picked up the receiver in the bedroom and after his initial "Hello?" went rigid.

"McQueen. You've got something of mine and I want it. You understand?"

"Who is this?" Brent demanded heatedly.

"No, McQueen, no way. I know that there's a tap on this phone and I'm not staying on long enough for a trace. You just find what I want. Your wife will go first. Then your daughter. And don't ever kid yourself. I can get to her. You just can't hide from me. Find what I want."

"What the hell is it you want?"

"The number. I want the number. Soon. I'll give you until the benefit, then I want that number!"

"You sure as hell aren't going to get it if I'm dead. And someone was shooting at me."

"Warning shots. Next time, it won't be a warning. Next time, we'll take your wife. And if you don't give us what we want, you won't get her back. You understand?"

The phone line went dead. Brent jiggled the phone, then called Robert's office. Robert wasn't in, so Brent talked to one of the detectives, who apologized. They had gotten the husky, sexless whisper of the caller on tape, but they hadn't had time to run a trace. Brent thanked the man and hung up.

His hands were covered in a cold sweat. The caller couldn't get Kathy. No one could, not here. It was just that the thought of it...

And he had said he could get Shanna, too, that they couldn't hide.

He slammed his fist against his hand in raw, helpless fury. He had to find out what the hell was going on. None of them was safe if he didn't.

He picked up the phone and called the police station again. Robert had come in by then. He agreed to send a few plainclothesmen to stay with Kathy while the two of them set out together.

Brent rose and showered and dressed quickly. He went into the kitchen. Kathy had coffee poured for him and the scent of the sizzling bacon was delicious. He sat, wondering how to tell her casually what he was doing. He didn't want her to know about the call.

The phone started to ring again. He made a leap for it but the wall phone was right next to the refrigerator and Kathy picked it up. She looked at him, startled, when he nearly crawled over her.

"I'll get it," he said.

"I've already gotten it," she said to him. Her eyes remained on the receiver while she said, "Hello?"

She listened for a moment, her smile growing plastic. "Yes," she said at last. Then she thrust the phone at him.

"Who is it?"

"Marla Harrington. I was going to tell her that your mouth was occupied but I don't think she would have cared. She's insisting on talking to you. She's terribly sweet. She told me that she'd see me Friday, too, but I'd have to understand that there were things between you two and she needed some time alone."

Her plastic smile remaining in place, she thrust the receiver into his hands. He watched the rigid squaring of her shoulders as she walked away.

"Hello?" he said to Marla.

He didn't hear her answer at first. Kathy had turned around, and as he watched her, the voice on the phone seemed to fade. In the long tailored shirt that reached down to her upper thighs, her hair pulled back in a loose ponytail, her makeup all scrubbed away, and with her back nearly arched and her claws just about showing, she was a picture of dangerous appeal. Her eyes flashed at him, beautiful deep blue, and little tendrils of her hair curled around her classic features, framing them.

"Brent, are you listening to me?" Marla was saying.

"Uh, yes, yes, I heard you." What the hell had she said?

"I'll talk to you more at the benefit, but I know Johnny thought you knew something, too. I think Johnny knew exactly what was going on, but he didn't believe what the consequences would be until it was too late. Brent, I do think you have the key somewhere."

She wasn't telling him anything, Brent thought wearily. Just the same old stuff.

"Yeah, sure, thanks. I'll see you Friday," he said, then told her goodbye and hung up. Kathy had laid out the plates. He sat down and sipped his coffee, watching her.

"There really isn't anything between Marla and me, you know."

"Hey, what's it to me?" she said sweetly. She took a delicate bite of egg, then smiled at him. "But if you touch that bathing suit, I'll break your arms."

He smiled and set down his fork. "When I leave, it's coming with me."

"A present for Marla? Not on your life."

He groaned and bit into a piece of bacon. They heard Sam start to bark, and the bell out by the gate began to ring.

Brent leaped up. Kathy looked at him, her eyes widening suspiciously.

"I've got to go," he said.

"Where?"

"It's all right. Someone is coming to stay with you, and I'm going to my place and to my studio with Robert. I'm going to go through every damn thing I have and try to find out whatever this number is that's causing all of this."

"If you find a number, what good will it do you? There are numbers on everything. What good is a number?"

"Kathy, I've got to go. I'll be back later."

She thought he was going to kiss her, but he didn't. He paused, then walked to the door.

A few minutes later, there were two young men in jeans and T-shirts at the door with Brent. One was working very hard on getting to know Sam. The other offered her his hand and a grin.

Then Brent was there, behind the two. "Kathy, these are Detectives Clinton and Barker—"

"Jerry," the darker of the two said.

"Steve," the second told her, reaching out a hand. They were both young and friendly and smiling with open admiration.

Kathy realized she was barely dressed. Brent was less than subtle about it. "Kathy, will you please go put something on?"

She flashed him a furious gaze. "I wasn't expecting company, remember?" she asked sweetly.

She stared at him then turned. His gaze remained implanted in her mind—the condemning, hard gold in his eyes, the tightness in his features. She strode into her bedroom and pulled out shorts and a tank top. Then she sat on the bed, a tempest of emotions roiling within her.

Damn him! He didn't want her, but it seemed he didn't want anyone else to have her, either. She should call Axel and apologize.

But she didn't want to apologize. And even as she wondered just what the relationship was between Marla and Brent, she knew she really didn't care about Axel. Oh, she did, as a friend. He was a very nice man, a good man. He just wasn't…wonderful.

And Brent was.

She rose and dressed, and when she came out, she offered the plainclothesmen coffee and breakfast, but they had just eaten. They were both great guys, easy, relaxed. Still, they were making her a nervous wreck.

She tried to work. She did manage to plan a few layouts. She talked to Patty and found out her picture had been in the paper. She had been standing next to Brent at the funeral and people were speculating.

There was nothing to speculate about, Kathy assured her. She asked Patty to sit tight. The police wanted them under guard for a while, that was all.

She hung up and tried to work again. She wanted to talk to Shanna, but she knew she couldn't.

She was sitting there, still trying to work, when

the phone rang. She answered it and was surprised to find that the caller was Marla Harrington again.

"Kathy, is he around anywhere?" Marla asked her.

"Uh, no, not now. Why? What is it?"

"I just wanted you to know…" The other woman hesitated.

"Know what?" Kathy demanded, exasperated.

Then Marla started to talk in a rush. "I care about him, you know, I really care about him. I'm not trying to cause trouble or anything like that. It's just that…you hurt him. You're bad for him. He was just starting to get a new life. You should…you should leave him alone!"

"Marla, I'm sorry, I don't know what to say to you. I didn't come to Brent. Brent came to me."

"You don't understand. I don't know what he's said to you, but it may not be the truth. He's trying to protect you, but…he's going to marry me. He asked me to marry him. We weren't exactly living together, but we were together most nights. Don't get involved. You'll hurt everyone."

"Marla—"

The phone went dead. Kathy hung up.

The woman was lying. Kathy was certain of it. Brent had said he wasn't sleeping with her. He had said he had *never* slept with her. Hadn't he? Or had he evaded the question? She couldn't remember.

She pressed her head between her hands. Someone was lying. It wasn't Brent. He didn't lie to her.

Or did he? He had never pretended he was staying. He was trying to protect her. If she loved him, she should believe in him.

She loved him. She had always loved him. That didn't mean he loved her, and it didn't mean he was sworn to tell the truth.

"Hey, Mrs. McQueen." It was Steve, tapping on the door to her bedroom. "Are you a poker player?"

She smiled at him. "Sure."

She played poker with Jerry and Steve. She made lunch, dug out *Casablanca* and her colorized version of *King Kong* and they argued over the merits of both.

The day passed. She thought about calling Brent's house and his studio, but every time she picked up the receiver, she put it down again.

In the evening Jerry went out for pizza and they agreed on everything but anchovies and cold beer. At one o'clock she thanked them both and said she was going to bed. They both assured her it was one of the nicest assignments they had had.

She went to bed and lay awake for a very long time. Then she closed her eyes and dozed restlessly at last.

He wasn't coming back.

But he did. Sometime in the night, he returned. Though he didn't touch her as he had before. He didn't try to make love to her.

He lay on his back, looking at the ceiling. She opened her eyes and saw him there. She didn't know if she wanted him to touch her, or if she was afraid that he would. She wanted to ask him the truth about Marla, but couldn't quite bring herself to do so.

His eyes closed. She turned her back on him. A few minutes later she felt his arms around her, pulling her close.

He didn't make love to her. He simply held her in the curve of his body, and she could feel the heat and security of his naked body wrapped around her.

She lay awake for a very long time.

Chapter 9

Kathy awoke in the morning to music.

She was alone in bed. Brent was at the piano playing the chords to "Forever My Love." She got up, showered and dressed, hoping that he would have quit playing the tune by the time she reached the living room.

He had. When she came down the hallway, he was still sitting at the piano, but he did so silently, his hands idle on the keys.

"Hi," he told her morosely.

"Hi."

"Coffee is already on."

She nodded and walked by him into the kitchen. She poured herself a cup and came out. She wanted to talk to him, really talk to him. She wanted to tell him about Marla's call and demand to know the truth.

And of course, she wanted him to tell her that Marla was behaving like a child, trying to destroy things for them.

Destroy what? Could anything be more broken

and shattered than their relationship? These few days were just an interlude. No one had ever pretended they were anything else.

No. They were pretending that these days would pass, and then nothing more would follow. She had to talk to him.

But it didn't seem to be the time. She didn't have his attention. "So you didn't find anything at your place? Or at the studio?"

He shook his head. "Robert seems to think that I must have a paper or something stashed away. Something Harry gave me. And there's nothing." He hesitated. "I just keep coming back to the song." He shrugged. "Tomorrow's the benefit. Maybe something will come from that."

"Maybe," she agreed. She shrugged. "If you want, I'll play around with the song, too."

"I thought you hated it."

"Yes, well, it seems to be all our skins that we're dealing with here, doesn't it? And I never hated the song. I just hate to hear it now."

It seemed that she had his attention at last. He was watching her, his eyes gold and curious and his smile wry and crooked. "Why is that?"

She started to answer him, but they were startled by the sound of Sam's ferocious barking.

Kathy arched a brow at Brent. "Robert?"

He nodded. "One more day of searching through records and notes and all. Kathy, I've got to figure out what the hell it is that I supposedly know."

She nodded. He rose and came toward her. He pulled her into his arms.

For a moment, she stiffened. For a moment she could see Marla Harrington with him in that video, and she could hear the woman's voice coming to her urgently over the phone. Maybe she was just hurting Brent and herself. Maybe this was insane.

But he was touching her. And she seemed to melt in his arms. They were hard and secure around her and his lips were achingly tender when they touched hers. He kissed her slowly, lingeringly, then he stepped back and brushed the moisture from her lips with his thumb. "I'll be back."

"Will you?" she asked him softly.

He frowned. "Of course. Why?"

She shook her head. "No reason. I'll…I'll play with the song."

"Your two little friends are back, you know."

Her lips curled into a smile. "Little?" Detectives Jerry Clinton and Steve Barker were both over six feet tall.

Brent shrugged. "Well, they're just kids, you know."

"Mmm," she agreed. "Very attractive ones. And actually, I imagine that they're both at least in their mid to late twenties. Mature, responsible—"

"And duly impressed with your charms. Behave," he warned her. "I heard all about that poker game."

"Hey, I won."

"Yes, that's what I heard. They were having problems concentrating."

She smiled. "Bye. Have a nice day. And you behave, too."

"I don't have much choice. Poring through drawers with Robert doesn't give me many opportunities to practice my wicked ways."

"Ah, but is Robert the only one around?"

He frowned. "Kathy, what are you talking about?"

She shook her head. "Never mind. We'll talk later."

"Yes, we will," he said flatly. His eyes remained on hers. They could hear Sam going into a frenzy. Brent sighed and turned. "It'll probably be late," he said.

Something about the tone of his voice bothered her. There was a weariness to it, and a desperation. Maybe something more. She felt a cold hand squeeze her heart. Was it because of the things going on between them? Passion had risen so quickly, and now it seemed that the embers were cooling as fast.

"Brent, there's something you're not telling me," she said flatly.

He swung around, staring at her, and she knew she was right.

"My God, it's true!" she whispered, backing away from him.

"What's true?" he demanded, following her.

"The phone call—"

"How the hell do you know about the phone call?" he demanded brusquely.

"Because she called me!" Kathy flared. "That's why!"

"She!" He stopped dead in his tracks. "How do you know it's a she?"

"Oh, come on, Brent! Are you trying to tell me now she isn't a woman? Oh, my God! This is getting worse and worse. Just go. Go and—"

"Kathy!" He caught her shoulders, pinning her against the wall. "Kathy, what the hell are you talking about?"

"Marla."

"Marla is the one killing people and making all these threats?"

"What?" Kathy gasped.

He shook his head. "Wait, wait, we've got to start all over again. Who called you? What call are you talking about?"

"What call are *you* talking about?" she challenged him.

"Kathy, what—"

"Marla. She said you'd been having a really hot and heavy affair and that you were going to marry her."

He groaned and released her shoulders. Then he leaned against the wall, laughing.

"Brent!" Kathy snapped furiously.

"I'm not marrying Marla, all right? And any hot and heavy affair I've had with her is in her mind. She was a friend. I worked with her. She's usually a nice kid. Actually, I thought she was after Johnny. I've been places with her, yes. But she called you and said I was going to marry her?" he said incredulously.

Kathy nodded.

"And you believed her?"

She shrugged. "I was going to ask you about it."

"Well," he said softly, "that was good of you. If she calls back, hang up on her." He paused. "No, don't. She thinks she knows something. Talk to her. See what she says, all right? I've got to go."

He started to leave, then stopped, came back and kissed her. "Actually, I'm not supposed to owe you an explanation like that. I'm only supposed to behave while I'm actually sleeping with you," he said huskily.

"Well, it's just that you did so well in destroying my relationship with Axel," she said sweetly. "I'd hate to see you walk away from this untarnished."

He laughed. "But we've agreed. Axel isn't wonderful."

"Mmm. And I suppose we've agreed that you are?"

"Hey, you said so," he reminded her. He started to kiss her again. Sam was going crazy outside and the bell was ringing away but they ignored both. After a few moments, he finally pulled away regretfully.

"I've got to—"

"Wait!" she said swiftly, holding tight to his arms so he couldn't walk away. "What phone call were you talking about?"

A little shield seemed to fall over his golden orbs. "What?"

"Brent, what phone call—"

"We'll talk later. I've really got to go."

"No! Not until you tell me!"

He hesitated. "The killer called," he said with a sigh. "He wanted the numbers I supposedly have. He wants them by tomorrow night."

"Oh, my God! You can't mean—"

"I think it was a man. The call was very quick. The police weren't able to trace it."

"Brent—"

"I have to find the numbers, or whatever it is this maniac wants. Not to give to him, but to use to stop him. I have to, Kathy. Can you understand?"

"I understand that I'm scared," she whispered. "Maybe he gave Johnny a call just like the one he gave you. Brent, you shouldn't be out. You shouldn't go to that benefit."

"I have to go. You don't."

"If you're going, I am, too."

He swore softly.

Outside, it seemed that someone was sitting on the bell. Sam was barking himself into a spasm.

"We'll talk about it later," Brent said gruffly.

Seconds later, he was gone. Kathy leaned against the wall, then sank slowly against it.

"Mrs. McQueen?"

It wasn't her name. The cops should have known it wasn't her name. It didn't matter. She looked up and saw that Steve had come into the hall. Sam was with him, his tail wagging. Brent had introduced Sam very properly to Steve, and it seemed that the two were the best of friends.

"Hi, Steve."

"Are you all right?"

"I'm fine, thanks."

She smiled at him and let him help her to her feet. She said hi to Jerry, then excused herself and sat at the piano.

She began to play the song, humming it softly. She didn't have Brent's voice, and she didn't have his magical touch with musical instruments. But she knew the song. She knew it backward and forward, and she sang it softly.

I will love you forever, forever, my love.
Longer than the heavens ride the sky up above.
Deeper than the depths of the darkest seas,
Stronger than the life that breathes within me,
Forever, into time eternal,
Forever, into light, and into dark,
Forever, my love, forever, my love.
She comes to me like the breeze in the night
A touch, a whisper, in the twilight
And her perfume fills the air,
I breathe her hair,
A brush of velvet, stroke of silk,
I reach, and she is there
Whenever I see her face,
Whenever I feel her smile,
I know that time can never erase
The visions all the while
I touch her skin

The sun rushes in
I sit alone by the dock on the bay
And I know that there will never come a day
When I do not love you forever, my love
Forever, my love, I will love you.
Forever my love, forever my love.

The last notes of the song softly died away. Kathy remained at the piano, silent, still.

It was supposed to have been forever. That had been the promise between them. Why had they let things fall apart?

She was going to grow nostalgic and drip all over the piano keys, she thought. She couldn't do that. Not now. She was supposed to be trying to figure out the secret behind the song. Before tomorrow. But there were no numbers in the song.

She got up and wrote the words on paper and stared at them that way, but no numbers came to her. There weren't even any references to any particular place.

She stared at the words a while longer, then smiled at Jerry when he said he was going for Chinese food. She gave him an order for shrimp with lobster sauce, then suddenly leaped up and raced into her room, to the cavernous closet.

She dragged out all the boxes from the back. She'd saved everything about Brent, everything that had been written. She'd kept a scrapbook, which she'd given Shanna after the divorce, but she still had a copy of every article ever written.

She flipped through newspaper clipping after magazine article after newspaper clipping and finally found what she wanted. It had been the first story about him in a major publication, written after "Forever My Love" had first been released. He'd liked the interviewer and he had given the woman a great deal of insight. Kathy had always loved the article. She scanned it quickly.

There'd been so much analyzing done over the song. Brent hadn't felt that the music was that startling or unusual, nor had he found the words to be anything more than a simple statement from the heart. The interviewer rather hit the nail on the head when she said the lyrics and music just came together in a really beautiful ballad that touched the heart. Brent would probably be known for it forever.

Kathy read on. He talked about writing on the dock near his house, and there was a wonderful picture of a very young Brent with his lazy smile. He said that it had just never come together for him until he'd met Kathryn, his wife. Maybe that was why the song worked. It wasn't just a song. It was everything he felt in his heart and his mind and his soul.

She set the article down. There wasn't a thing about numbers in the article.

She turned the page. There was a picture of her in her wedding gown. It was a traditional snow-white gown sewn in a Renaissance style. She wore a tiara of pearls, and the veil fell behind her in a cloud. If she had ever been beautiful in her life, it had been on that day. The picture caught the blue of her eyes, the soft blond of her hair. She might have been a fairy-tale princess with her knight at her side, except that her knight was incredibly handsome in a black tux, cummerbund and starched white shirt. And his eyes were heated, intoxicating gold as he smiled at her....

She closed the magazine. It was about to make her cry. And it hadn't told her anything at all.

A few seconds later, Jerry was at her door. "Shrimp with lobster sauce, at your service, Mrs. McQueen."

"Thanks!"

The day passed slowly. She couldn't remember hours ticking by so slowly. She thought about calling Brent to see how he was doing, but then she remembered that Brent had been called here. It was possible someone might manage to hear what they were saying, that she might lead someone to Brent.

She didn't call. She waited.

She tried to be lighthearted and relaxed and enjoy Steve and Jerry, but it was difficult. And then it was finally night, and she pretended she was exhausted. It seemed that she lay awake forever and ever, and when she finally fell asleep that night, it was as if she was dead. She didn't hear Brent when he came in.

In the morning, she awoke slowly, feeling more tired than she had when she went to bed. She could hear Brent in the living room talking to someone. She froze for a second, wondering if he was on the phone, if the killer had called. But then she heard Robert's voice and she knew their friend was already at the house.

It was Friday. The day of the benefit.

She showered, dressed and went into the living room. Brent was sitting at the piano. Robert was leaning across it, talking intently, his voice low.

They both looked up, startled, when she appeared. "All right, what is it now?" she demanded.

"Nothing. Nothing, really," Brent told her.

"Nothing," Robert echoed solemnly.

She rubbed Robert's shoulder. "Didn't anyone ever teach you that it's a sin to tell a lie?"

They exchanged glances. Brent shrugged. "Our mystery man called back. He's going to give me a few days. Maybe someone will trigger something in my mind tonight."

"A few more days," Kathy murmured. "That's good of this guy."

"Well, we've got tonight."

"Yes, of course. Tonight."

"And you behave!" Brent warned her.

"Me?" she inquired innocently. "Why, Mr. Mc-Queen, you just flirt your little heart out, anywhere you think it might do you some good. I'm just the ex-ball and chain, remember?"

He grinned at the tone of her voice, raising a fist in mock anger and warning. "There's so much I remember."

"And you behave. Who knows, I just might be able to flirt in the right direction, too."

It wouldn't hurt to keep him on his toes. Especially when she wanted to talk so badly. To sit down and say all the things she never managed to say all those years ago. He was still hers, but if they made their way through the clouds, he might just keep walking.

"Breakfast anyone? Or is it lunch? Thank God for the benefit. I'm starting to go mad in this house."

They agreed on lunch. It was almost a pleasant meal, almost an easy one. They decided to make pasta primavera. Brent and Kathy chopped and cooked and tripped over one another and Robert laughed and they talked over old times.

Robert stayed and stayed, and though Kathy knew that he, being a dear old friend, was guarding them, she really wished he would leave.

He wasn't leaving. He was coming to the benefit with them. He had his tux in the car. He'd be with Brent all night.

She was relieved, she supposed. She wanted Brent to be safe. But she was suddenly afraid. Something could happen, and she might never have the chance she wanted.

Her announcement that she was taking a bath failed to bring Brent into the bedroom. Men never appeared when you wanted them to, she thought mournfully, surrounded by bubbles. They only walked in by surprise, stealing away years of a woman's life, and nearly throttling her when she dared to scream at the intrusion.

She soaked until she was thoroughly pruned, gave up, dressed in sheer white stockings, white bikini panties and garter belt, and waist-hook white bra to accommodate her backless white cocktail gown. The soft, swirling skirt of the dress was studded with rhinestones. She applied her makeup, decided on gold stud earrings and her small gold cross as her only jewelry. She was slipping the dress over her head when Brent at last appeared in the room.

He paused in the doorway, watching her. "Wow," he said softly.

She smiled. "Want to help me?"

"Put it on or take it off?"

"Put it on. You talked out there way too long to contemplate taking it off. I need the hook done in the back."

"All right. But only if I get to take it off later."

She turned her back to him, sweeping her hair up to show him the hook at the nape. He walked behind her and obligingly did the hook, but his fingers lingered upon her shoulders and his lips touched her bare back.

"You bought this ensemble for Axel?" He seemed to growl.

She was glad he couldn't see her slow smile. "He has wonderful taste in clothing."

He muttered something she didn't quite understand. There was a knock on the door, and Robert asked if they were about ready. Brent swore and replied none too politely that he'd be ready in a damned minute. "Run out and grab my tux, will you, Kath? I'll be right out of the shower."

"Yes, sir!" she said, saluting. She ran out, smiled sweetly to Robert, who was uneasily pacing the living room, lifted the tux off the couch and came back into the bedroom. She laid the tux out on the bed. Brent appeared a second later, the steam of the shower rising from his flesh. Kathy watched him dress, admiring him, suddenly wishing that they could forget the benefit. She loved the sleekness and the muscles of his long body. She loved the relaxed way he moved. And she loved the way he seemed so easy with her, as if the years had never been.

"Is this straight?" he asked her. He was in a traditional tux with a black vest, bow tie and elegant, old-fashioned shirt with ruffs at the cuff and pleats down the breast. He was fooling with his tie.

She nodded, feeling a lump in her throat. Poised on her high heels by the door, she could suddenly find nothing to say.

He walked toward her, smiling. He paused when they should have been hurrying, and he touched her cheek, then picked up her hand and kissed it. "God, Kathy, you are beautiful. I've tried so many times not to remember just how beautiful."

"You're pretty beautiful, too," she said softly.

He groaned. "Oh, no. I knew the ruffs were too much."

She grinned. "No. Just beautiful. Not because of the ruffs." Her grin faded, and for a moment, there was no danger. Robert wasn't waiting for them, and there was no place they really had to be. The world had receded except for him. She whispered softly, "Brent, I love you. I love you so much."

An anguished looked appeared in his eyes. His features constricted and a shudder seemed to rip through him. Then he leaned his hands against the door on either side of her head and kissed her lips gently. The words that he whispered seemed to be torn from him. "I love you, too, Kathy. I've always loved you, I will always love you, no matter…no matter where we are, no matter how far apart, no matter how many years go by."

Her mouth went dry and she felt tears welling in her eyes. He loved her. He wanted her.

But he wasn't going to stay with her.

"Hey!" A fist thudded against the door. "What's taking the two of you so long? Hell, maybe I shouldn't be asking," Robert muttered. "Listen, you're going to have a nice long night after this event. You're divorced. You're not supposed to even like each other anymore, so will you please come on!"

Bless Robert. She managed to smile into Brent's eyes, and then she laughed, and he managed to laugh, too, though the sound was just a bit pained. He took her hand and swung open the door. Robert almost fell in on top of them. "Finally," he said. "If we're going to do this thing, let's do it!"

Kathy straightened Brent's tie. "You look great. Truly undercover."

"Oh, honey, there's going to be so much security there tonight nothing could possibly happen. I promise."

"Let's do it then," Robert said.

Thirty minutes later they were in the full swing of the party.

It was a massive event, held in a beautiful contemporary home with twenty-foot windows that looked straight out over a huge patio and pool and the bay. People in beautiful and garish and outlandish costumes were posed all around—on stairways, in hallways and on the patio. Kathy greeted old friends, shrugged off her appearance with Brent, tried to avoid those who were determined to pin her, and at the same time keep an eye on Brent.

They hadn't been there for five minutes when Marla found Brent. Kathy greeted her very sweetly and didn't let out a murmur when Marla led Brent away. After all, she just might say the right thing.

But still, Kathy didn't want him where she couldn't see him. Not because of Marla, but because she was worried. Even if Robert was following him like a leech.

A tuxedoed waiter swept by with champagne glasses. Just as Kathy reached for one, hands slipped around her waist and she felt a friendly kiss on her cheek. She managed not to drop the champagne, to thank the waiter and spin around all at once.

"Keith!" she said. She put her arms around him, still balancing the champagne, and hugged him tight. She had always liked him.

"Kathy, it's so good to see you. You know, Brent has never been the same. We've missed you. We've all missed you. But you're here tonight. Does this mean—"

"You know what this means," Kathy interrupted him. "Keith, I'm so sorry about your wife. And about Johnny."

"Johnny," Keith muttered. "Well, Johnny lived hard, and he died hard."

He sounded bitter, Kathy thought. He was a handsome man, with intelligent, dark brown eyes, dark hair, and the look of one of yesteryear's composers. Beethoven, perhaps. But tonight he looked haggard, drained.

"Kathy, want to talk, really talk?" he asked her suddenly.

"Sure."

He drew her outside. Workers were setting up for the bands and singers by the pool. Keith didn't want to be there. He drew her away from the house, into the trees. She followed him trustingly. He stopped at last, and he seemed to have difficulty breathing. "Kathy, do you know what's going on?"

She nodded. "Someone killed Johnny Blondell. Someone who grew angry. The same person who had Harry Robertson killed in jail. The same person—"

"Who probably killed my wife. Kathy, I was ill, I missed her so badly. But you know, this is terrible, I don't want to die myself. He's after a number.

There's something stashed somewhere. Something of incredible value. And it's here and it's close, and we should all know it. Kathy, it's in the song."

She shivered suddenly, feeling the coolness of the night breeze rake up her spine. "How do you know?" she said.

"Johnny called me up and said he had some of it figured out but he'd be damned if he was going to be double-crossed. He wanted to talk to Brent. He was all excited. I think Johnny might have been halfway in it with Harry."

"But Johnny is dead."

"Harry probably didn't trust Johnny. Oh, I don't think Johnny was in on the smuggling. But Harry told him something. Brent was the only one that Harry really trusted. That's why I think he stashed this thing somewhere purposely, using numbers that would mean something to Brent."

Kathy shook her head. "I've been through the song, Keith. I've been through it and through it and—"

"Brent has to come up with something! Or else we're all going to die, Kathy. We're all going to die."

"Kathy!"

Brent shouted her name, thrashing furiously through the trees. He snatched her by the shoulders, bringing her against his chest and staring furiously at Keith over her head. "What the hell are you doing, Keith?"

"Talking. I was just talking."

"So you dragged her out here."

Just then there was movement in the trees. Two

guns were suddenly beneath their noses, held by hands attached to the arms of Steve and Jerry.

"We were with her all the time, Mr. McQueen. Honestly," Steve said.

"Hey, what the hell—" Keith began.

"We were watching you, too, Mr. Montgomery," Jerry promised him solemnly.

"Yeah, hell, Miami's finest," Keith muttered. He looked at Brent. "You used to be my friend. Why don't you really try to keep us all alive, huh?" Then he swept past them.

"Sorry," Steve said. "I guess we should have stayed in the bushes."

Brent shook his head, looking after Keith. "No, no, it's all right." He slipped an arm around Kathy's shoulder. "Let's get back in, shall we?"

They walked along a trail to the patio. Robert was waiting for them, watching them emerge from the trees.

"Everything all right?" he asked Brent.

"Yeah, fine," Brent told him briefly.

"Good. I'll stay with Kathy. You're on stage in a few minutes."

Brent nodded and disappeared. Kathy stood by Robert as a group of English brothers who had made it very big and bought property in south Florida came on. Their harmonies were legendary, and they put on a wonderful show. Kathy applauded enthusiastically. Then someone tapped her on the shoulder and she turned to receive a sloppy kiss and hug from each of the Hicks brothers.

Larry, blond and blue-eyed, looked her over openly, then grinned. "Okay, Kathy. Looking good. So you're together again. We're real glad."

Thomas nodded. He was the more serious of the two. "It's good to see you, Kathy. Really good. I hope we see more of you. Although I don't know. We haven't had a chance to talk about doing anything else about the Highlanders."

"Aren't you playing tonight?" she asked him.

He nodded again. "Yeah, sure. We just saw you and we had to stop." He looked around her shoulder to Robert and nodded cordially, but he was wearing a small frown. "It's the fuzz, huh?" he muttered to Kathy.

She smiled and nodded. "Yeah, I guess, you could say that. Robert, this is Thomas Hicks, and his brother, Larry Hicks, and—"

"Oh, hey, man, it's you!" Thomas laughed, greeting Robert. "I didn't recognize you in the duds, man. Lieutenant McGregor! Nice to see you. And thanks for being so conscientious. Those guys of yours have been with us like a second skin."

Kathy was staring at them all curiously. "We met," Robert explained to her. "I had to question everyone after the explosion that…that killed Johnny," he said.

"Oh, of course," Kathy murmured.

"We'll get together," Larry said. "We'll all get together. Maybe we can solve it that way, huh?"

He waved to Kathy, then he and his brother were weaving their way to the stage. A few minutes later, after a pop female vocalist had done her number, Brent, Keith, Larry and Thomas were announced— as the Highlanders. Brent was at the mike saying in his husky voice that they were dedicating the night to Johnny Blondell. And then they were doing Highlander numbers, and the crowd was going crazy.

At the end, Brent announced that he was going to do an old favorite. And he sang "Forever My Love."

There didn't seem to be a sound, a rustle of movement, as he sang. The song was haunting, beautiful. As it ended, Kathy knew he had chosen to do the song as their finale on purpose. He wanted to goad someone with it, to stir up something.

But then she realized that he was singing the song to her. His eyes sought her out in the crowd, and he was singing to her. And she felt his eyes with the same quivering excitement she had known all those years ago.

The last notes hung in the air. Then there was an explosion of applause that lasted and lasted. The Highlanders tried to leave the stage, and Kathy knew he was heading toward her, but it seemed like forever before he reached her.

When he did, she suddenly realized something. "Brent!"

"What?"

"I've got it!"

"What?"

"Well, I haven't got all of it, but I've got some of it, I think."

"What are you talking about?" he demanded.

Robert was turning to them. She didn't want to share this with Robert. Not yet. Only with Brent.

"Can we go?" she asked.

"Now?"

She sighed with exasperation. "Well, you had your little chitchat with Marla, didn't you?"

"Yes—"

"Then let's go! Please, Brent, I think I've got something."

"All right, all right."

"What's all right?" Robert demanded.

"Kathy wants to go. She's—tired."

Robert nodded. He seemed disappointed. "Sure. Let's go."

When they reached the house Kathy warmly kissed Robert good night, then warned Brent with her eyes that she didn't want him to discuss the night's happenings with Robert forever.

Still it was almost thirty minutes before he came into the bedroom. "He wanted to know everything Marla had to say."

"What did she have to say?" Kathy demanded.

"Not much. Except that Johnny talked to her. And Johnny said Harry had told him I was the key to the whole thing, that the answer was in the song. But I'll still be damned if I see—"

"But I do!" Kathy exclaimed. "It's in the article." She pulled the article from the box. "Brent, only someone who knew you well could see it. I don't have the number yet, but I think I know where!"

"Where?" he demanded, puzzled.

"There's a line about the bay and a paragraph where you talked about the writing of the song. You mention your old house and how you could see the bay and—" She paused, staring into his eyes, waiting for him to remember. He did.

"The warehouses by the bay. They all have combination locks. And combination locks mean numbers."

Kathy shook her head emphatically. "Yes."

"I still don't have the number."

"It's in the music, Brent. It has to be in the music."

He nodded. Then he laughed and kissed her. He spun her off her feet, seeming to fly with her off the ground, and they landed on the mattress. He demanded excitedly, "Do you know what I'm going to do now?"

"Work on the music?" she suggested.

He shook his head. "No. Now I'm going to get to take this whisper of satin and shimmer off you, my love."

His eyes were gold and sparkling. His whisper was husky and provocative, and he had called her his love.

Suddenly she didn't care what the future might bring. She wanted only the magic of the night.

Chapter 10

She lay in a froth of white and satin and sparkle. He'd watched her from the time they'd reached the party that night, watched the material swirl around her, watched the rhinestones catch the light. He'd seen the easy sway of her walk and he'd listened to the sound of her laughter. He'd found himself praying just to have the night, no matter what came after. Just this night.

And it was his. Her eyes were eternally blue as they stared into his. Her smile was sensual, tempting. He should tease her lips, but he didn't. Instead he kissed her forehead, her cheeks and the lobe of her ear. He whispered against it, telling her just how wonderful she looked in the dress, and just what he intended to do to her and where. He lowered his lips to her shoulder and gloried in the satiny texture of her flesh there. He nuzzled the plunging cleavage of the gown, pressing his lips and tongue against the rise of her breasts.

Then he rose, anxious to rid himself of his constricting clothes. She was suddenly on her knees before him, working on the buttons of his shirt. He wrenched it off and tossed it carelessly to the floor as she kissed the planes of his belly. When her tongue moved into his navel, he drew her against him and his lips found hers at last. Hungrily, they met and meshed and parted, then met again, openmouthed and hungrier.

His fingers wound through her hair, found the hook at the back of the dress and released it. The white sparkling bodice fell forward and her breasts seem to burst from their confines. He buried his head against her, tasting the sweet-smelling flesh there, pressing her closer and closer against him and pushing down the lacy garment to close his mouth around the ripeness of her nipple.

Her head fell back and soft blond hair cascaded over his fingers. The sensual sound of her whimpers nearly drove him to a frenzy. With shaking fingers he tried to take off the bra. But she eluded him, moving away with a subtle smile. In a pool of light she dropped the lacy garment and stepped from the froth of glitter and white.

She stood arrayed in garter and panties and stockings that shimmered seductively down the length of her legs. She remained still for a moment, seeking his eyes, seeking something. Perhaps she discovered all that she really wanted in his eyes, because her kiss-dampened smile deepened and she whispered softly, "I love you, Brent."

He groaned. "I love you, too, Kathy." Then he sank at the foot of the bed, staring at the rounded beauty of her naked breasts and the erotic wonder of her legs. Just a part of her thighs was bared, and the thin wisp of her panties barely covered the exotic blond beauty of her deepest sexuality. He reached out his hands. "Come here," he commanded softly.

When she did, his hands wrapped around her waist and he pulled her against him. Her fingers went through his hair, then fell to his shoulders. He stroked the garters and brushed her thighs with the warm moisture of his kiss. He cupped his hands over her buttocks and pressed her closer against him. Tenderly he assaulted the apex of her thighs, the panties more of an enhancement than a barrier as he bathed her with fiery wet heat, delving, caressing and delving once again.

She trembled and shuddered and cried out and fell against him, and he crawled over her. He knotted his fingers around the panties and pulled them off, leaving her clad only in the stockings and garters. She moaned softly, and he kissed her lips and breasts, and once again fell against the heart of her desire, only now there was no barrier between them. She cried out sharply, releasing everything to him, her head thrashing on the pillow.

He shed his trousers and briefs, shaking with the desire to plunge within her. Still he controlled himself, for she was so alluring with her hair spread in wild disarray, her flesh sheened from his lovemaking, her lips parted, her eyes shaded by the fall of her lashes, and the garters and stockings framing the wet, welcoming beauty of her sex.

He held back no longer. A strangled cry tore from his lips as he plunged deep within her to find a welcoming warmth close around him. Her eyes widened with the force of his entry, then her thighs locked around his hips. It seemed that the spark of desire, dying within her just moments ago, rose to life again on a rampant breeze. She squeezed him tightly, and he stroked and thrust with an increasing rhythm that seemed to bring the promise of climax closer and closer.

She met his thrusts with the arch of her hips. He ground against her. She cried out softly and he kissed her lips and breasts. When he knew he could hold back no longer, he caught her lips once again and filled her mouth with the desire and frenzy of his tongue as he filled her with the last shuddering force of his body and the stream of his seed. He felt her writhing beneath him, and he held her tightly in his arms until the spasms were over.

He wondered how anything could be so good and stay so good, and how she could electrify him time and time again. He knew it wasn't the wanting, it was the love, and that desire grew from that love.

But if it was so good, why had it all turned on them so painfully?

He held her closely. The seconds ticked by. She didn't speak, and neither did he. And when she would have spoken, he pressed his fingers against her lips and silenced her with his kiss. He made love to her again.

Later, much later, he felt the dampness on her cheeks, and he knew that she had been silently crying, but he couldn't say anything to her.

They had to get through this. And then he had to leave. There would be no way for him to change the past, no way for them to go back. No way to pretend he hadn't hurt her. And for himself, no way to pretend he wouldn't do so again.

All he could do was hold her and pray that the night would never end.

He was up, wide-awake, leaning over her. She opened her eyes slowly—they didn't want to open. They hadn't slept at all. She hadn't minded, she hadn't wanted to sleep, she had wanted to touch him, to hold him, forever.

But the night had ended, and day had come.

His lips landed wetly and enthusiastically on hers, and then they were gone and his golden eyes were staring into hers. "You gave me the secret! Kathy, I think I've got it. I've got to get to my place and get the guitar. I've called Robert. He should be here any minute."

She groaned. "With Jerry and Steve, right?"

"Right. What's the matter with Jerry and Steve?"

"Nothing. They're real nice guys. Cute as buttons. You should worry about leaving me here alone with them."

"You're not coming with me. It could be dangerous for you to be out."

She groaned again. "Brent, if you're going out—"

"If I'm going out, I feel safer with you here."

The sheet fell from one of her breasts. His eyes slipped to the rise of her flesh, and he leaned over her to take her warmly into his mouth. Regretfully, he rose and smiled at her. "I'll be back."

"Promises, promises."

He was starting for the door. "Wait!" she cried. "You didn't tell me! What did you figure out?"

"I'm not sure yet."

"You think it's Keith, don't you? You were awfully rude to him last night."

"I don't think anything," he said coldly.

He turned and left. Kathy watched him and sighed. A few minutes later she heard the commotion at the door that meant Robert and his troops had arrived. She was exhausted but she knew she'd never be able to sleep. She felt exceptionally restless.

Because he knew something. He knew, but he wasn't sure, and so he wasn't going to tell her. But maybe someone else would think he knew.

The killer, perhaps…

She shot out of bed and hurried into the shower. Thirty minutes later she emerged from her bedroom to discover that Jerry and Steve had brought doughnuts and that they had gotten very good with her coffeemaker and were smiling and eager to greet her.

They were both very nice. Dedicated, all-

American. That morning she spent drawing them both out and trying not to think about Brent. Jerry was one of five children. He'd spent three years in the navy, had lived in Miami all his life and wanted to change the city's image of being a hotbed for the drug and smuggling trades.

Steve was from a very small town in Alabama. He had a wife and a two-month-old baby, and he simply loved the Miami area, the beautiful old homes and the foliage in Coconut Grove, the water that was always warm and always available. He even loved the action of the garish nightlife.

It was such a nice, easy conversation. Kathy didn't notice when it turned to her. There was nothing tricky or subtle about the change of subject. Jerry noticed a picture of Shanna and commented on what a truly stunning girl she was. And Kathy found herself laughing and agreeing and saying that yes, Shanna was their pride, both hers and Brent's. Then she was explaining how she had gotten into advertising, how she had worked while Brent struggled with music, how he had insisted they had everything, but that she should go back to school and take something that interested her. Sometimes her schedule had conflicted with his touring, but they had always worked something out.

Jerry was quiet, watching her. Then he blurted out, "It sounds so damned good. You were both courteous to one another. How the hell did you ever wind up divorced? No money problems, no religious differences. What happened?"

"Jerry," Steve groaned, sinking into his chair. "You gotta excuse my partner," he said.

"Oh!" Jerry said. "I forgot about your son—" He broke off, turning a mottled shade of red.

Kathy smiled gently, reached out and touched his hand. "It's all right. It wasn't Ryan, anyway."

"Then—" Jerry began.

"Stop!" Steve protested.

"It's just that—"

"Jerry!"

"It's all right!" Kathy laughed. "Jerry, I just can't really explain. It's too personal."

"You should still be married," Jerry said stubbornly.

"Well, you'll have to tell Brent that—" Kathy began but she broke off and they all stared at one another when Sam began to bark.

Then Jerry and Steve were up, both quiet and highly professional, guns drawn as they moved to see who was outside.

Jerry shoved his gun into his holster. "It's the lieutenant," he said.

"Oh. I'd better get Sam," Kathy said. She opened the door and called for the dog while Steve went to open the gate.

"Kathy, can you come with me?" Robert asked, watching Sam with distaste. "Brent needs to discuss something with you. I think he thinks he'll hit the last key to this thing if he has you with him."

"Of course!" Kathy agreed. "Let me grab my purse, and I'll be right with you."

She went into her room and dumped her wallet and brush and cosmetics from her evening bag into a big leather shoulder bag. She hurried to meet Robert, anxious to help Brent.

Why did she want to help Brent? she wondered. Once this was solved, he was going to walk out of her life. She was trying so hard with him, yet she wasn't getting anywhere. She had known that last night. She was going to start crying if she didn't hurry.

In the living room Robert was telling Jerry and Steve to hang around the house. He didn't know when he would bring Kathy back. With the phone ringing, he hurried her down the path and into his car.

"Think I ought to go back and get that?" Kathy asked. "It might be Brent." A cold finger of fear squeezed her heart. "You left him alone, Robert. Are you sure he's all right?"

"No, we don't need to get the phone, and yes, I'm sure he's all right," Robert assured her. "I left him all locked in where no one can get to him. Honestly."

He smiled at her. She smiled back.

Jerry picked up the phone. It was Keith Montgomery, and he seemed very agitated to discover that Kathy wasn't there. "What's the problem?" Jerry asked him.

"Well, I talked to Brent. He called from his house and he seemed upset. He wanted me to come over and stay with her, to make sure that she didn't leave the house for any reason. He had a hunch."

"He changed his mind," Jerry said. "He just sent the lieutenant to pick her up."

"That's not like Brent."

"The lieutenant's on the job, Mr. Montgomery. Just hold tight, and we'll get one of them in touch with you as soon as possible."

Jerry hung up. He looked at his partner and explained the call.

"Sounds like there's something wrong, doesn't it?" Steve said.

"Maybe we should get over to McQueen's place."

They looked at one another uneasily. Steve exhaled slowly. "Boy, our rumps could really be on the line here, you know."

"Yeah, I know."

Jerry shrugged. "What the hell. We can both go back to Alabama, right?"

"Yeah, sure, Alabama."

They left the house. At the last minute, Steve whistled to Sam.

Sam loved cars. He didn't hesitate a moment.

It wasn't long before Kathy realized they weren't heading toward Brent's house.

She'd never been in it. He'd bought it after the divorce, but she'd dropped Shanna off at the gate often enough, and she knew that though they were headed to the water, they weren't going to his house.

She frowned at Robert. "What's up?"

He shrugged. "We were down at the warehouses."

"By his old house, the small place," she breathed. "Where he wrote the song. So I was right."

"Yeah, yeah, you were right. And it had to do with that article you dug out, too. We're pretty damned sure. He was twenty-two when he finished the song, so he wanted to try the twenty-second storage unit. All he needed was the numbers to the vault."

"You're a cop, Robert!" Kathy laughed. "Can't you just blow it open?"

He shook his head. "I can't just go blowing up property of other citizens, can I? What if Brent is wrong about the numbers?"

"I guess you're right. But maybe you should get a unit down here or something—"

"Let's just see if Brent knows what he's doing first, huh?"

"Are you sure he's safe?"

"Oh, yeah. I'm sure."

They turned into the road that led to the warehouses. It was already twilight. The area was old and shabby-looking. Kathy didn't see a soul anywhere.

Robert pulled his car around back, close to the water. She looked at the docks. There were a few fishing boats pulled up to the pier and a few old motorboats. Darkness was falling quickly.

It seemed that no one had been to the warehouses

in years. The paint was peeling. The scrawny grass and trees that wrestled a hold through the rocky earth were overgrown and mixed with weed.

"Come on," Robert said.

Kathy shuddered. "Boy, I wouldn't want to be here alone on a dark night," she told him. She cast him a smile. "Thank God I'm here with a cop."

He grunted. "Come on. Around this way."

He took her arm and led her to a small door in the rear of the brick enclosure. There was a padlock on it, but he pulled out a key and opened it. Kathy frowned, wondering what good the padlock would have done to protect Brent.

But before she could comprehend anything, Robert pushed the door open. For a moment, all Kathy could see was darkness.

Then she realized that Brent was in the room, gagged and on the floor in handcuffs. His ankles were cuffed, too, and chained to the wall. Kathy let out a scream and started to run for him but Robert caught her arm and wrenched her back.

"I told you he was safe," Robert said. "And he can stay that way." She heard a click and realized that he had pulled back the safety on his gun and had it aimed at her temple. "It didn't have to go down this way. Brent has the numbers, you see, Kathy. I could have taken the diamonds and—"

"Diamonds!"

"Yeah, it's diamonds. I came up with a connection in South America. And Harry Robertson and I had a deal. It's a long story. It started with a bribe at least ten years ago. Of course, I never let scum like Harry or Johnny Blondell know who I was. I didn't dare. And you would have never known. Except that once we got here, Brent seemed to figure something out. He started playing innocent. Then I caught him at the radio so I shot him."

"Shot him!" Kathy gasped. He wrenched her closer, playing the cold muzzle of the gun over her cheek. "I grazed him. Had to knock him out. I couldn't risk a fight. He picked up too much about self-defense in the service. I just nicked his temple. He'll have a little bald spot for a while. But he'll be all right. If you can talk some sense into him."

Her eyes had grown accustomed to the darkness. She felt ill and terrified, aware that the loaded gun was against her head and that Brent was helpless on the floor. She didn't know if he was still breathing.

She couldn't comprehend that Robert... They'd gone to school together.

Then she realized that Brent was definitely alive. His eyes were open.

"He's awake," she said flatly. She had to stay calm. She couldn't panic. She had to reason with this man...when all she wanted to do was scream and scream and scream.

"Let him up. Uncuff him. I'll get him to give you what you want."

Robert kept the gun steady on her. He handed her a key. "You uncuff him. And remember, killing gets easier after the first. Not that I'd kill either one of you right away. A shattered kneecap can make lots of people talk really quickly."

Her fingers were shaking so badly she could barely undo the cuffs. Brent's eyes remained open, golden and warning on hers. She released his hands first, and he ripped off the gag and unlocked the steel cuffs on his feet. He staggered up and had to accept Kathy's help.

Blood trickled down his forehead from the gunshot wound. He faced Robert then, shoving Kathy behind him.

"I'll kill her. You know I'll kill her," Robert warned him.

"Yeah. And what guarantee do I have that you'll let us go once you have the diamonds?"

"None. But you know I'll blow you away if you don't."

"We're at a stalemate then, aren't we?" Brent said.

"No. Because I'm going to shoot Kathy somewhere within the next five minutes if we don't get the diamonds."

"All right. Let's go try warehouse number twenty-two," Brent said. "I don't have damned guarantees to give you, just an idea."

He started to stride by Robert, holding Kathy's hand tightly in his own, trying to keep her at his rear. Then he pushed her in front of them when Robert fell behind them.

It was almost completely dark. Shadows surrounded them. Kathy looked around Brent, still unable to comprehend that Robert could be at the root of all of this.

"Why?" she asked him incredulously.

"Why?" He smiled. "Have you ever taken a real good ride around here? Have you ever wondered how so many people can have so much money? Hell, the drug traders get off with good lawyers. The lawyers get rich on the drug money. Everybody's getting rich. I went so long without it, and then I just wanted a piece of it. There was a guy who needed to escape in the night. He gave me the location of some of his stash, and I took a chance. I let him go. And it was there, a whole cache of diamonds. And it was mine. Just for letting that thug go before the courts could do it instead. I learned a lot from that. But Harry Robertson turned out to be a pathetic little rat. And then he held out on me. I had to have him killed.

"But I want the diamonds. The game is up. They'll buy me a place and security for the rest of my life. I always liked you, Kathy. Always. I'm sorry. I wanted to keep you out of it. I didn't have any choice. Brent, open that damned door, now."

"You killed Keith's wife!" Kathy gasped, horrified.

"I thought Keith was the man at first. I needed to scare him. To get him off guard."

"So you killed her."

"And I'll kill Kathy," he reminded Brent.

Brent eyed him, then looked at the electronic combination lock. He played with some numbers. Nothing happened. Seconds ticked by.

Robert wrenched Kathy to his side and shoved the gun against her face. Tears stung her eyes. She could almost taste the metal.

"Now, Brent, now."

"Then what?" Brent demanded. "You've got the gun down her throat right now. What am I giving you the diamonds for?"

"All right, listen. You get me the diamonds. We leave Kathy here, and you come with me. She won't say a word to anyone because I won't let you go until we're far out at sea."

"Let her go now," Brent said.

Robert hesitated.

"Let her go," Brent repeated.

Robert shoved Kathy away. "Get down the walkway," Brent commanded her. "You stay away, you hear me?"

She nodded jerkily.

Brent pushed more numbers. The vault slid open.

Robert waved his gun in the air. "Get the diamonds."

Brent disappeared into the vault. Robert turned the gun on him. "Get over here, Kathy. Or I'll shoot him right now. He's too dangerous to take with me. It has to be you."

She stood still. He aimed his gun toward the vault. She cried out and raced toward him. A second later he had her in a hammerlock. "Give me the diamonds, Brent. And for every one that spills, she loses a finger. Push them along the ground."

Brent reappeared, staring at Kathy and Robert. He

bent down and slid the velvet sack of diamonds on the floor to Robert. Holding the gun to Kathy's face, Robert stooped with her to pick up the satchel. Then he started to back away. Brent followed. Robert aimed the gun at Brent's face. Brent followed anyway.

They moved across the stone and the earth to the docks. And still Brent followed, keeping his distance. Then Robert stopped in front of a motorboat.

"Give me back my wife. You've got the diamonds, and you're free."

"Can't trust you, Brent, sorry," Robert said. There was about a three-foot drop between the dock and the boat. Robert shoved Kathy off the dock, and she cried out, landing hard on the boat's deck. He leaped quickly behind her, untying the rope that looped the boat to the dock. He stepped forward, his gun aimed at Brent, while he pulled the cord on the engine.

The small motor seemed to cough and wheeze and leap to life. "Stay there. She'll come back to you," Robert said.

"Like hell!" Brent swore. "You'll shoot her out at sea and dump her body. You won't have any other choice."

Suddenly, they heard the sound of barking. It was enough to distract Robert, if only for a second. In that split second, Brent leaped from the dock to the boat, landing on top of Robert. The gun went flying. And the boat moved from the dock.

Kathy staggered up from beneath the fallen men. The motorboat was spinning in circles as the two men viciously battled at her feet. She tried to slam her fists against Robert's back, but the boat careened, and both men went overboard.

In the murky darkness, she couldn't see either of them. They could be anywhere, beneath the motor…

With a scream she lunged forward and cut the motor. The barking was suddenly very fierce and she noticed that Sam was on the dock, going crazy. Jerry and Steve were behind him, searching the water with a flashlight.

The boat pitched precariously, catching her off balance. She tumbled into the darkness of the water and sank into the dark green depths.

There were fingers in her hair. Her lungs burning, she twisted and tried to see. Robert had her. And he was dragging her down.

But he was wrenched away and she kicked furiously, desperate for air. She surfaced. "Brent!" she screamed. He didn't come up. Someone touched her and she tried to fight. "It's me—Steve. Let me help you."

"No, no. Brent—"

"You can't help him. Don't you see? The lieutenant keeps using you against him!"

She let Steve pull her away. Jerry dragged her onto the dock and Steve went into the water. She breathed heavily, trying not to panic.

"It's all right, it's all right," Jerry was saying.

No, it wasn't. Brent wasn't coming up.

But then there was a burst from the water. Straining to see, she made out Brent coming to her with strong strokes. Sobbing, she sank to her knees and reached for him. Jerry reached for him, too, then Brent was up and out of the water, lying flat on his back on the dock. For long moments he gasped for breath with his eyes closed and his heart thundering. She was still so afraid.

Then Sam was there, licking his face. Brent touched the dog and his eyes opened and saw Kathy.

"I would have done better. Honestly. It wouldn't have taken me so long except for this damned nick on my forehead."

She started to laugh with relief, then she was crying again. Then she was in his arms. Jerry was smiling, too, and Brent paused to put an arm around the anxious Sam. "You're a good old dog. With good instincts. He never did like Robert," he reminded Kathy.

No, Sam had never liked Robert.

Steve searched the water until the team Jerry had called for came with masks and diving equipment. Within an hour, they found Robert. He had become entangled in the seaweed beneath the dock.

By then Kathy was sitting in a car, sipping coffee, a blanket around her. Brent told her the news, and he explained to her that the numbers had been in the main chords to the song—C, G, E. All he'd had to do was count their place in the alphabet, and he had it.

"Why Harry did that to us…" Brent murmured.

"Maybe he thought it was his only chance to live and see justice come to his tormentor, too."

"But he died."

"How did he know he was going to die in prison?" Kathy said. Brent, hunkered down before her, shrugged, and she knew he understood.

Keith arrived on the scene, Jerry had remembered to call him. He and Brent embraced, and Brent apologized. Keith hugged Kathy. When she whispered again that she was so sorry, he told her it was all right. He had his little son, and they were going to make it.

Steve and Jerry drove Kathy, Brent and Sam to her place. Inside, Brent shook their hands and thanked them both. "We were lucky you came. After all, you had no reason to doubt Robert. He was your lieutenant."

Steve shrugged. "Yeah, well, it was hard. He turned bad. We had to stop him. But that isn't the norm, you know, it really isn't."

Kathy smiled and pushed past Brent. She kissed Steve on the cheek. "You guys are the best. And I'll always believe in you."

Steve smiled. "He kind of soiled the badge, you know."

"He tried to," Brent corrected. "And he tried to ruin the music, too."

"Yeah, well, that's why we figured you were probably all right in there with him. He was after your wife and, in a way, all the things you believed in. I'll never think badly of musicians if you promise never to think too harshly of cops."

"It's a deal," Brent promised with a grin.

Then they were gone, and Kathy and Brent were alone. They were both crusted with seaweed and dried salt water. Suddenly Kathy started to shiver. She whispered, "It was Robert. Oh, Brent, it was Robert all the time."

"Don't think about it," he told her, sweeping her into his arms. "Don't think about it."

He carried her into the bathroom and set her down, still shivering. He started a bath and filled it with bubbles. He peeled away her clothing and set her in the water. She leaned back, and when she opened her eyes, he was with her, holding two glasses of wine.

Naked, he joined her. They drank the wine as he held her against him. She was soon drowsy, and though the pain of a friend's betrayal and death did not disappear, it was banished to a corner of her mind.

After some time he picked her up, and he laid her out on the bed. He dried her naked flesh. Then he made love to her more tenderly than he had ever done before. She slept in his arms.

In the morning, she awoke and found him fully dressed, standing by the window. He seemed to sense that her eyes were on him because he turned to her, and she could see all the anguish in his face. He walked to the bed and sat beside her.

"I was…I was going to leave while you were sleeping," he told her. "But then I felt I had to say goodbye."

She didn't say anything. The tears were welling in her eyes. He kissed her, a light kiss. But it became a deeper kiss, long and lingering.

"Don't go," she breathed to him.

"Kathy, I have to. If I ever hurt you again—" He tore away from her. He was on his feet and heading out the door.

She paused, her heart hammering. Then she was up, slipping on a terry robe and running after him.

He was already out the front door, heading down the walk.

"You idiot!" she called after him, and he paused, his back stiff. "You dumb idiot! Brent, I swear it, the only way for you to hurt me is to leave me! I could stand anything, anything at all, if you're with me. Don't you understand that? Brent, I love you. For the love of God, don't walk away from me again. Brent, I need you." She paused, then added softly, "Forever, my love."

She waited, and it seemed that the earth spun full around the sun, and still he stood there.

Then he turned, and he was running to her. When he reached her, he was suddenly on his knees, and he was holding her against him, his face against her belly.

Her fingers lingered over his hair. Then she held his face up to her and she whispered, "Please, don't leave me again, please."

"Do you really think we can make it?"

"I know we can."

"My temper is horrible."

"So is mine. But that's okay, Brent, don't you see? Oh, Brent you were never out of control, never, never. It was just that with what happened, you thought…you lived with the belief— Brent, it just wasn't true! Oh, Brent…"

He was on his feet, lifting her into his arms. He stared into her eyes and said, "Kathy, I love you. Forever."

She smiled and touched his face. "Good. You can marry me again. And quickly. Okay? Enough of this living in sin. I'll even invite Marla to the wedding."

"And I'll let Axel come. Maybe we can introduce them to each other."

"Maybe," Kathy said.

He closed his eyes, then opened them. "Kathy, I'm scared."

Her eyes widened. He was never scared. She loved him for his honesty, for so many things. "I'm scared, too," she whispered. "But don't you see? It doesn't matter if we're together."

He walked with her slowly toward the house. "I hate that other place. It was always new and empty. We'll live here."

"Wonderful."

"We'll have to help Keith get back on his feet."

"Great. I'll love to take care of his baby."

"Baby! Shanna! We've got to reach her quickly."

"Soon," Kathy said, smiling. "It's just that right

now, well, you know, it's not that you haven't been just wonderful already, but, Brent, you're going to stay. We're engaged, right? We're going to be married. We—"

"We can go for a license right now. And head straight for a justice of the peace. The hell with the wedding. We'll invite Marla and Axel to a reception later."

Kathy smiled. "I love it. But first…"

"First?"

She grinned and whispered, "You know that awful temper of yours?"

"Mmm?"

"Well, please, ravish me, will you? Just this one last time in sin. Then we'll pick up the license and head to the justice of the peace."

"Ms. O'Hara, that's a last request I'm more than willing to fulfill," he promised her.

And proceeded to do just that.

Epilogue

They sat in the doctor's office. Kathy's hand was in Brent's, and he was listening intently to every word Doctor Langley was saying.

"Honestly, Mr. McQueen, miscarriage is a terrible thing because people blame themselves. Women always think they did something to injure the baby. And the truth of the matter is that women lose babies because something *is* wrong. But there is absolutely no reason to fear that anything will go wrong with this pregnancy."

Brent didn't even redden, Kathy thought with amazement. His eyes were gold and intense as he leaned forward and said, "Dr. Langley, I made love to my wife very passionately and—"

"Well, Mr. McQueen, most of us wouldn't be here if that didn't happen to our parents."

"She nearly bled to death."

"The placenta pulled away. It wasn't your fault. But if it will make you feel better, abstain from sex until she's finished with her first trimester. It's never been proven that sex has anything to do with miscarriages, though. And we'll see Mrs. McQueen every two weeks. At her age, I suggest an amniocentesis."

They talked a while longer. Brent seemed relaxed, and Kathy was delighted that she had made him come.

They'd been married for seven weeks. But she must have gotten pregnant the night he broke into the house. Of course, the moment she told him, he'd panicked. He'd wanted to know why she hadn't told him before, and she'd had to explain that she hadn't known. Then she'd grinned and told him that she was awfully glad she hadn't, because she definitely didn't want to think he'd married her because he'd had to. He hadn't laughed, so she had thought that taking him to Dr. Langley would be a great idea.

"Don't you even wink at me for the next few months, young lady," Brent warned her.

She laughed and promised him, "Okay, I won't!"

She did worry that he would try to stay away from her, but he didn't. Every night they slept closely together. Tightly, tenderly.

Then came the day for the amniocentesis. She was terrified at first, but it was all right. The echo sound showed them the baby's tiny hands and feet and ribs. The nurse pointed out the four chambers of the heart, the kidneys and the brain, and she told them that the baby looked wonderful. When the doctor came, he was so pleasant and easy that he quickly had them both relaxed. He was a music lover, who teased with the nurse that they had best be good, lest Brent write them up as bad guys in a song.

Brent didn't do so very well watching the needle going into her stomach, but he was fine after that. And as the days passed after the procedure and Kathy seemed fine, he began to be more at ease.

They'd agreed to find out the sex of the baby together. The lab called to tell them that the results were normal, that the baby looked fine. Brent asked them to send a letter with the sex of the baby.

He and Kathy were going to meet for an elegant dinner. She was in her fifth month, and they were going to celebrate with non-alcoholic champagne, a delicious meal, and...sex. After they learned that of their new offspring.

When the letter came, Kathy called him at Keith's where he was working on a new album. She had a few things to do, but she'd meet him at the restaurant at eight. She'd made the reservations. She'd ordered the champagne. Everything was set.

She was stunning, he thought when he entered the restaurant and saw her. She had a glow about her. The soft silk maternity gown molded her breasts and fell softly over her growing stomach. She smiled, rose and kissed him.

"Got the letter?" he asked her.

She raised it.

"You didn't steam it open, did you?"

"Of course not!" she protested.

He signaled the waiter, who came and poured

their special champagne. When he disappeared, they both took a sip then smiled at each other. "Go ahead."

Kathy shoved the letter over to him. "No, you."

"All right." He slit the envelope, looking at her. "Would you rather it be a boy or a girl?"

"I don't care, you know that. What would you rather it be?"

"A healthy baby."

"We've got that."

"I guess you'd like a son."

"I don't know. Shanna is wonderful."

"Hmm. Okay, so neither of us cares. Let's just open it and see."

Brent pulled out the letter and scanned it quickly. Then he began to laugh.

"Brent!" Kathy said. He was still laughing. "Brent, which sex is so damned funny?"

He shook his head. He was still laughing.

"Brent—"

"All right, all right. I see the blue fire in those eyes! Kathy, it's neither."

"What do you mean, it's neither? The baby has to be something!"

"That baby is, but Kathy, this isn't the letter. This is the bill for services rendered."

"Oh!" She snatched the letter and read it from top to bottom. Then she started to laugh, too. "Oh, Brent! The champagne, the dinner..."

"Well, they're not wasted," he said. "We'll still have them. And I'm still on for the sex part, too," he promised blithely.

She lowered her head and smiled. "Yeah, well, I'm rather into it myself."

"Excuse me," he told her. "I'll be right back."

She toyed with her glass. It was still going to be a great night. It was just that she had been so very set to know....

Brent came back and slid into the seat. He leaned over and kissed her.

"Guess what?" he asked.

"What?"

"Blue."

"What?"

"Start buying blue." He smiled. "Kathy, it's a boy."

"How do you know?"

"I called Langley and got him out of bed. The results were sent to him right away. It's a boy, Mrs. McQueen. Very definitely a healthy little boy. And we'll keep him that way, Kath. I promise. I won't be afraid, and I won't let you be afraid."

"A boy," she murmured, grinning. She sipped from her glass and leaned against him, content.

"Brent."

"What?"

"I really think we're going to live happily ever after. I believe everything is going to be all right. And I love you so very much."

He shushed her with a long, wet kiss and then his golden eyes looked into hers.

"Forever, my love," he whispered.

She smiled and kissed him. Because she knew it was true.

* * * * *

First I must thank Greyhound bus lines for the ride of our lives, and God for providing the snow that trapped us in Cleveland on our way to New York. Had I not been stuck on a bus with my partner-in-crime for thirty-one hours, this story might not have been born.

This book is dedicated to a dear friend and fellow writer. She is my partner-in-crime, just as Ethel was to Lucy. We began this journey together—may it always be as fun, exciting and "bizarre" as it was in the beginning when we couldn't wait for "the call." Cheers, Rhonda, we made it.

SOLITARY SOLDIER

Debra Webb

DEBRA WEBB

wrote her first story at age nine and her first romance at thirteen. It wasn't until she spent three years working for the military behind the Iron Curtain and within the confining political walls of Berlin, Germany, that she realized her true calling. A five-year stint with NASA on the space shuttle program reinforced her love of the endless possibilities within her grasp as a storyteller. A collision course between suspense and romance was set. Debra has been writing romantic suspense and action-packed romantic thrillers since. Visit her at www.DebraWebb.com or write to her at P.O. Box 4889, Huntsville, AL 35815.

Prologue

"I'll pay anything you ask," Rachel Larson insisted.

Victoria Colby regarded the woman across the wide expanse of her oak desk for a long moment before she responded. "Miss Larson, this is primarily an investigations agency. We accept clients who require personal protection on a case-by-case basis, and generally by referral only."

Disappointment shadowed Rachel's pale features. Dark circles beneath eyes that contained as much wariness as fear, and the ill fit of her clothing told Victoria that this young woman had not slept or eaten well in too many months. Her overall look of extreme fatigue signaled her proximity to the edge. The ability to size up a client had facilitated Victoria's climb to the top in this business. And right now, every instinct told her that this young woman was more than simply desperate.

"I'll need to know a great deal more before I can make a decision as to whether the Colby Agency will take your case," Victoria explained.

Rachel drew in a shaky breath and squared her shoulders. "Detective Clarence Taylor sent me. He was a police detective here in Chicago before moving to New Orleans."

Victoria considered the name for a moment. "Yes, I remember Detective Taylor. He left three or four years ago I believe."

Rachel nodded, hope kindled in those dark brown eyes. "That's right. He knows that I've exhausted every other possibility, including the police." Rachel leaned forward and clutched Victoria's desk like a lifeline against the violent waters churning her obviously troubled soul. "You have to help me, Mrs. Colby. He's going to take my little boy." A single tear slipped down her colorless cheek before she could swipe it away with the back of her hand. "I can't let him do that."

Sympathy tugged at Victoria's softer side—the side that hadn't hardened over the years in this cutthroat business. She knew all too well that kind of fear, that kind of pain. She blocked the memories. If Clarence Taylor had sent Miss Larson to her, Victoria would certainly do all she could to help her. "All right," she offered. "I will consider your case, but you have to tell me *everything,* Miss Larson."

"Thank you." Rachel's voice cracked with emotion.

Victoria opened her notepad and removed her gold pen from its holder. "I'll need to know as many details as possible about the stalker." She glanced up from her pad. "First, do you know his name?"

Rachel licked her lips, then swallowed visibly. "I believe your agency has worked on a case involving him before. His name is Gabriel DiCassi. They call him—"

"Angel," Victoria finished for her, the name barely more than a whisper. She shuddered with remembered dread. Several years, but not nearly enough, had passed since she heard that name. Not since… Sloan left.

"Detective Taylor thought that one of your investigators might have experience dealing with…him," she said uncertainly.

Taking her time, Victoria placed her pen on the blank notepad, then leveled her gaze on Rachel's. "Unfortunately, I do know him."

Despair reigned supreme in the young woman's features. "Then you know that this is no ordinary situation."

"Yes," Victoria agreed gravely. "Angel is a highly paid assassin whose reputation boasts a perfect record of kills. He's ruthless. If you're his target, he won't stop until you're dead."

"Please tell me you'll help me." Desperation weighed Rachel's weary tone. "I have to find a way to protect my son."

A frown tugged at Victoria. Somehow the part about the child didn't quite gel. "Why would Angel want to take your son?" Victoria thought briefly of the small dark-haired boy sitting in her outer office under her secretary Mildred's watchful eye.

Rachel looked away for a moment. "Because he's Josh's father." Her lips trembled with the effort it took to force her next words. "Five years ago, we were…involved."

"Involved?" Victoria heard the contempt in her own voice, and immediately regretted it. Humiliation clouded Rachel's expression.

"I was very young. It was a mistake." She squeezed her eyes shut and shook her head slowly from side to side. A soul-deep pain clouded her gaze when she opened her eyes once more. "He used me to get to my father."

"Yet you're still alive." Victoria arched a speculative brow. "That's not Angel's style. He never leaves loose ends."

"He would have killed me…" Rachel blinked furiously at the tears gathering, then shrugged. "I was lucky to escape. I've been running ever since. Later, he found out about Josh, and now Angel wants him."

If her story were true, Rachel Larson was as good as dead. Angel allowed nothing to stand between him and what he wanted. Anyone who tried to stop him was accepting a death sentence. Though Victoria employed the very finest in their fields, tracking down a man like Angel would take resources she simply could not risk. She had learned that lesson too well seven years ago.

Victoria braced herself for what she knew had to be said. "Regrettably, Miss Larson, the Colby Agency cannot provide the services you have requested."

Rachel stiffened. "You won't help me?"

"I don't mean that at all." Victoria pulled open her right desk drawer and flipped through her files. She removed a manila folder and scanned its contents. Satisfied with what she found, Victoria turned her attention back to Rachel. "There is only one man, to my knowledge, who knows Angel well enough to be of any assistance to you, and he doesn't work for me anymore." Victoria copied the name and address from the folder onto the back of her business card. "I can't guarantee that he'll be willing to take your case, but he's your only possible hope at succeeding. Tell him I sent you."

Rachel accepted the offered card. "Who is he?"

"Someone who used to work for this agency." Victoria leveled her gaze on Rachel's. "Someone I would trust with my own life. His name is Trevor Sloan."

"He must be the investigator Detective Taylor mentioned."

Victoria dipped her head in acknowledgment. "Sloan was the best investigator the Colby Agency has ever had the privilege of employing." Regret trickled through her. "As I said, he doesn't work for me anymore. Although this agency has utilized his services from time to time over the past couple of years, Sloan is very selective in the offers he takes these days." Victoria paused before continuing. "Considering the circumstances, he might not want to take your case at all."

Rachel searched Victoria's gaze. "If he's willing, how can he help me?"

Memories Victoria would rather not have recalled played in the private theater of her mind. "He knows Angel. He knows how the man operates and what motivates him."

Frowning, Rachel hesitated at first, but then asked, "How is it that Sloan knows Angel so well?"

Victoria sighed her own hesitation. What would it hurt to tell her? If Sloan could help the woman, Victoria rationalized, understanding would make dealing with him somewhat easier. "Seven years ago Angel assassinated two very prominent business-men here in Chicago," she began. "The Colby Agency was called in to consult on the case." Victoria tamped down the guilt that quickly sur-faced. "I assigned Sloan to support them. He pos-sesses an uncanny ability to read people. He studied Angel's case, tracked him for months." Victoria met Rachel's unsuspecting gaze knowing that what she would say next would only add to her growing fear. "When Sloan got too close, Angel retaliated in a particularly ruthless manner. Recognizing the kind of man Sloan was and what would hurt him most, Angel murdered Sloan's wife and took his three-year-old son."

Rachel gasped and her eyes widened in horror. "Oh, God."

"The child's body wasn't discovered for a while, and during that time Angel taunted Sloan with telephone calls of his son's recorded cries for Daddy…" Her voice drifted off as the painful memories of that seemingly endless year of tracking Angel sifted through Victoria's thoughts. Sloan had pushed himself beyond any man's physical and mental limitations, and found nothing. Then, finally, they'd discovered the small body burned beyond recognition. Something had snapped inside Sloan then and he'd simply disappeared. Months later, Victoria learned that he'd resurfaced as a private contractor in Mexico. He hadn't allowed her close since. But he was still the best in the business of tracking and protection.

Rachel's complexion turned a whiter shade of pale. "How will I ever stop him?"

Victoria studied her a long moment before answering. Perhaps Angel had some sort of twisted reasoning for allowing Rachel to live just as he had when he spared Sloan's life. Living with the loss was much more difficult than dying. Gabriel DiCassi was evil incarnate.

Victoria pointed to the card in Rachel's hand. "Talk to Sloan." If even a small part of the man she once knew lived behind that hardened, go-to-hell armor he wore, Sloan would never be able to turn this woman and her child away. And maybe the opportunity would allow him to lay his own demons to rest. "And don't let his attitude scare you off," Victoria added. "If there is anyone who can help you, Sloan can."

* * *

Rachel stood on the street corner in downtown Chicago and stared at the card in her hand. Los Laureles Cantina in Florescitaf, Mexico. That's where she would find this man named Sloan. What sort of man used a cantina for his business office? Maybe she didn't want to know. Rachel shivered despite the August sun beating down from the clear blue sky. No amount of heat would ever make her feel warm inside knowing what lay ahead of her.

But she had no choice…she had to do something.

No matter how far and fast she ran, Angel always found her. He wanted her son. Angel only allowed her to take care of Josh for the time being because he felt the boy needed his mother. He had said those very words to her on more than one occasion. One day though, he intended to take Josh. Rachel shuddered at the thought. She had to do something before that day came.

"I'm hungry, Mommy."

Rachel's attention jerked back to the here and now. She smiled at the little boy whose hand she held tightly in her own. "I'm sorry, honey. We'll have lunch soon." Satisfied, Josh smiled back at her. Somehow she had to find Sloan and convince him to help her.

No matter what it took.

Chapter One

Thank God.

After searching all afternoon beneath the blistering August sun, Rachel Larson had finally found the place no one seemed to know about. Or perhaps it was her poor excuse for Spanish they didn't understand. Rachel surveyed the run-down building before her. Located in an unsavory part of an obscure little Mexican town called Florescitaf, the cantina known as Los Laureles looked even more forbidding than she had expected. Maybe that's why no one would admit to knowing its location.

Squaring her shoulders against the uneasiness skittering up her spine, Rachel reminded herself of why she was here. She had to do this. There was no other alternative. Besides, the place was named after some sort of flower, surely it couldn't be so bad.

Instinctively Rachel tightened her hold on Josh's hand when he peeked around her skirt to watch the children playing in the alley between the cantina and the equally run-down, open-air meat market next door. Rachel glanced down at her son and smiled when his eyes widened in wonder at the goats the children appeared to be tending. Barefoot, and faces bright with smiles, the local children stared back at Josh with that same wonder in their dark eyes.

Josh seldom played with other children. They were never in one place long enough to make friends, and even if they were, ties to anyone was just another risk Rachel and Josh couldn't afford. Rachel sighed. Would their lives never be normal?

Rachel stole one last, lingering moment to savor the children's innocent faces, the warmth of the merciless sun, and the pungent smells of raw, drying and roasting meat from the nearby market. After today, one way or another, her life would never be the same.

Today things were going to change.

Drawing in a deep, bolstering breath, Rachel took the first step toward that end. The stench of stale tobacco, alcohol and sweat enveloped her as she entered the disreputable-looking cantina. Overhead ancient fans slowly stirred the fetid air. Before her eyes adjusted to the dim, smoky interior, Rachel felt one narrowed gaze after the other scrutinize her as if she were the latest addition to the menu. Uncertainty warred with the desperation that was her constant companion.

You can do this, Rach, she reminded the part of her that wanted to run as far away from here as possible. Angel had warned her that he was growing impatient with her useless measures to elude him. What would he do when he discovered that she had come to this man named Sloan? Rachel shivered, and pushed away the thought. She couldn't think about that now.

This was the only way.

Still holding Josh's hand in her left and with her right clenched tightly around the strap of her over-stuffed shoulder bag, Rachel weaved her way between the tables and to the bar that extended half the length of the room. She hated to bring her four-year-old son into a place like this, but what else could she do? She didn't dare allow him out of her sight. And she had to find Sloan.

Their lives depended upon it.

"Excuse me," Rachel said as politely as possible with fear pounding through her veins. "Do you speak English?"

"*Sí.* What is your pleasure, *señora?*" Propped against the worn smooth counter, the bartender's examining gaze lingered on Rachel's breasts before he looked up and smiled.

Heavyset, with thick dark hair and a wide mustache, the man oozed what he likely considered charm. Rachel swallowed the fear clawing at her throat and manufactured a tight smile of her own. "I'm looking for a man called Sloan."

One bushy eyebrow quirked the slightest bit, but the smile stayed in place. "And why would such a pretty lady look for such a dangerous man?" he asked in that heavily accented voice, putting emphasis on the words *pretty lady.*

"A friend sent me." What if he wouldn't tell her where Sloan was? What if Sloan wasn't even here? He could be working some other case in God knows where. What would she do then? Rachel's heart pounded so hard she felt sure the man behind the counter could hear it.

"It's very important that I find him," she forged ahead, her voice faltering despite her best efforts to keep it firm. Rachel moistened her lips and held her ground as he took his time considering her request.

"El solitario." With a jerk of his head, the bartender gestured toward the darkest corner of the establishment. "The one who sits all alone."

Rachel nodded stiffly. "Thank you."

Before she could turn, his next words stopped her. "Do not thank me, *señora.* It is not my habit to send sheep to slaughter, but you asked." He picked up a grimy cloth and absently wiped the counter, his gaze still leveled on hers.

Rachel stared at him, uncertain what to do with his offhanded warning. Should she run now and cut her losses? Her hand tightened around Josh's. Maybe Victoria had been wrong about Sloan.

"It's very important."

The bartender shrugged. "Perhaps, pretty lady, you should come back later." He darted a look at the faded plastic clock on the wall. "It is just four o'clock, his mood will be nasty for a while yet."

"I'll…" Rachel backed up a step. "Thank you," she said hesitantly. She glanced down at Josh and said another quick prayer before starting in the direction the bartender had indicated. Surely the bartender was exaggerating. Sloan couldn't be as fearsome as all that. Victoria Colby had recommended him. He was a former employee of hers. The Colby Agency had come highly recommended to Rachel. She trusted Detective Taylor's judgment implicitly.

Ignoring what were most likely lewd Spanish remarks tossed in her direction, Rachel walked straight to the far end of the room. She would show no fear. She was not afraid, she chanted like a mantra with each step she took. Rachel paused a few feet away from her destination and pulled out a chair from an unoccupied table. After settling Josh into the seat, she crouched in front of him and forced a wide smile she didn't in any way feel.

"Josh, I want you to stay right here until Mommy speaks to the man just over there." Rachel pointed out the table only a few feet away. "Okay, sweetie?"

Josh bobbed his head up and down, his eyes wide with uncertainty, and even a little fear. Rachel's heart squeezed in her chest. Josh would start school next year. How many of his classmates will have experienced a place such as this? Then again, how many of them could claim the devil himself as a father?

Rachel pushed aside the painful thoughts and ruffled her son's dark hair. She pulled a coloring book and small box of crayons from her bag and placed them on the scarred tabletop. "I want you to color Mommy a pretty picture and I'll only be a minute."

Josh nodded once and flipped the coloring book to a fresh page. Satisfied, Rachel stood. She forced herself to turn away from the child she loved more than life itself. She looked back twice as she took the few remaining steps, each time hoping to comfort Josh with the halfhearted smile her trembling lips managed to maintain.

Her son waved shyly and Rachel felt a real smile spread across her lips then. Yes, she could do this. She would do it for Josh. Confident in her decision, Rachel turned back to her objective.

The man sat alone, an empty tequila bottle on the table before him. *El solitario* reverberated through Rachel. A solitary soldier. A mercenary for hire. Just the kind of man she needed. He didn't look up when she stopped an arm's length away. He seemed fascinated with the gold liquid in the glass he was turning between his thumb and forefinger.

Rachel's first up close impression of the man was *dangerous,* just like the bartender said. Sloan looked like he would be tall, and he was definitely solidly built. His too-long tawny hair brushed his broad shoulders. The sleeves had been cut from the faded shirt he wore, displaying muscled arms. He looked very strong, and for one fleeting moment Rachel felt a little safer in the knowledge that this was the man who could help her.

But then he spoke….

"Unless you're selling your wares, I'm not interested."

Rachel shivered at the husky sound of his deep voice. Disregarding his crude remark, she summoned her waning courage and asked, "Are you Sloan?"

He lifted his gaze to hers then, and Rachel's breath caught. Icy, translucent blue eyes cut a hole straight to her soul. His square, beard-shadowed jaw reaffirmed her first impression. *Dangerous.*

"Unfortunately—" He tossed back the last of the tequila in his glass without taking that piercing gaze from hers. Rachel jumped when the glass clunked down onto the table. "I haven't had enough to drink to be anyone else." He licked the taste of liquor from his lips. "But it's still early."

Mustering her scattered courage, Rachel forced herself to speak. "I've come a long way and—"

"You do know," he interrupted as if she hadn't spoken at all, "that this is no place for children." His gaze darted past her to where she had left her son.

Rachel glanced over her shoulder to make sure Josh was okay. She swallowed back the mushrooming uncertainty. "I know," she replied slowly, her resolve crumbling beneath his stony, emotionless glare. "My name is Rachel Larson. I…I need your help."

In one fluid motion he stood and towered over her. She battled the urge to flee. Absolute silence screamed around them for the space of two heartbeats before he responded.

"Then you've wasted your time, Miss Larson."

Her heart lurched. "Please, you have to hear me out."

One side of his mouth quirked upward. "The only thing I have to do is die. And between now and then, all I plan to do is drink tequila and get laid. Anything else is uncertain." He cocked his head and made a sound, more growl than laugh. "So unless you plan to help me with one of those two things, I would suggest that you don't waste any more of your time or mine."

A new surge of fear shot through Rachel's veins. She could not allow him to dismiss her so easily. He was her only chance. "Victoria Colby sent me," Rachel announced in a stronger voice than she had thought herself capable. "She said you could help me."

Something flickered in that cold, remote gaze, then vanished as quickly as it came. "Victoria made a mistake."

Before Rachel could protest, he turned and started toward the bar, his smooth stride unhurried and making her think of a panther as it stalked its prey.

Watching her only hope slip through her fingers, desperation tightened Rachel's chest. She had to do or say something to convince him to help her.

Now!

"Angel intends to kill me," she blurted. "If you won't help me, what am I supposed to do?"

Sloan stopped and turned to face her. He stared at Rachel for a long moment with those pale, empty eyes, his unrevealing expression unchanged. What felt like a lifetime later, he spoke, "Get your affairs in order."

Stunned by his indifference, and frightened beyond reason by his refusal, Rachel watched him walk to the bar and order another drink. The bartender filled a clean glass with tequila, the sound echoing around her, drowning her last shred of hope with its golden appeal.

Desperation exploded inside Rachel. She glanced at Josh to see that he was still occupied with his coloring, then she strode straight up to the bar, anger and frustration building almost as fast as the fear. She glared at Sloan's unyielding profile and summoned the courage to defy his dismissal.

"I know what he did to you," Rachel told him, her voice quaking with emotion she could no more hide than she could stop breathing. "I know about your wife and son."

He stilled, the drink almost to his lips. A muscle flexed in his rigid jaw and his knuckles whitened around the glass. Slowly, with exacting precision, Sloan placed the untouched liquor back on the counter. He turned and stared at her, the full impact of his size slamming into Rachel for the first time. He was tall, with massive shoulders. He was more man than she had ever been this close to before. A new kind of tension zipped through her, adding to her already unbearable apprehension.

"Since you seem to know so much about my experience with Angel," Sloan suggested with equal measures sarcasm and contempt, "why don't you tell me what fascination you hold for the son of a bitch."

Rachel's throat constricted. She swallowed, but it didn't help. "He wants my son."

Sloan glanced at Josh. Josh was busy selecting another crayon from the well-worn box. Rachel's heart threatened to burst from her chest. Would this man help her when she told him the rest? *Please God,* she prayed, *please don't let him turn us away.* Not now. They had come so far.

Distrust or maybe disbelief flickered in Sloan's otherwise emotionless eyes. "Why would he want your son?"

Everything inside Rachel stilled as she stared into the eyes of the only man on earth who could help her. And what she was about to tell him would likely be the very reason he would not.

"Because Josh is Angel's son, too."

It took a full ten seconds for the words Rachel Larson uttered to fully assimilate in Sloan's brain. His gaze shifted to the dark-haired boy seated a couple of tables away. As if feeling Sloan's gaze on him, the boy looked up. Wide, curious eyes stared back at Sloan. The same black eyes that haunted Sloan whenever he tried to sleep without getting half wasted first. A tremor started someplace deep inside him, like an earthquake before it reaches the surface of the earth. Sloan's right hand shook and he curled his fingers into a tight fist. Something dark and ugly filtered through Sloan's mind, but he pushed it away.

This was Angel's son. Sloan didn't need to see a birth certificate; the proof was written all over the boy's face. He was a mirror image of his father. Sloan averted his gaze and blinked to dispel the image that somehow evolved into a full-grown version of Angel. Sloan reminded himself that this was only a child, innocent of his father's heinous crimes.

"What do you want?" Sloan heard himself say, his voice so cold and hard that he barely recognized it as his own.

"I need your help," she repeated, her tone low and pleading.

Sloan blew out a breath. "Yeah, well, you said that already." He leveled his gaze on huge brown eyes that made his gut clench with an old feeling that was familiar yet alien to the man he had become. He squashed the protective instincts that rose automatically at the sight of this needy young woman and her son.... Angel's son.

Sloan swallowed. Hard.

"Exactly what kind of help is it that you think you need from me, Miss…"

"Rachel Larson," she told him again.

Sloan studied the woman as she worked up the nerve to spell out what she wanted from him. She was a real looker if a guy liked his woman a little on the skinny side. From the dark circles under her eyes though, Sloan would lay odds that she didn't sleep long or often. But all that thick brown hair hanging around her shoulders was her saving grace…and the lips. She had those full, kissable lips that any man breathing would lust after. The blouse and long flowing skirt were too loose and concealing to determine if there were any curves at all hidden beneath them. Strappy sandals with sensible heels adorned her feet. It wasn't until his gaze collided with hers again that Sloan realized she hadn't spoken yet because she was too busy fighting the urge to turn tail and run. His blatant appraisal had seriously disturbed her shaky bravado.

"No matter where we go," she finally burst out, then caught herself. She took a calming breath. A combination of frustration and fear danced across her pretty face. "Or how many times we move, he always finds us." She clasped the shoulder strap of her bag more tightly. "The last time he found us he told me that he was tired of my running and that very soon he was going to take Josh…and…and then he would have no further use for me." She blinked furiously to hold back the tears threatening. "I don't know what else to do. You're our only hope."

Sloan mentally stepped back from what every instinct urged him to feel. He refused to feel any of this. It was a hell of a sad story but it had nothing to do with him. Angel's former lovers held no interest for Sloan. Besides, this sounded too good to be true. That someone Angel might care about, with his son in tow, would waltz into Los Laureles looking for

Sloan's help seemed a bit too pat. This had setup written all over it. Still, she had said that Victoria sent her.

"Sounds like a domestic problem to me, Miss Larson," he suggested, testing the waters of sincerity. Sloan pressed her with a steely glare intended to intimidate. "And I'm no social worker." She faltered, but didn't scurry away as he fully expected.

"I don't need a social worker," she said with determination, and a hefty dose of bitterness. "I need someone who can protect my son from Angel."

Still skeptical, Sloan cocked his head and eyed her speculatively. "Call a cop," he offered.

The flash of anger that brightened her eyes took Sloan by surprise. He almost smiled, but he was too busy watching the metamorphosis in Rachel Larson.

"You know the police can't help me," she returned with barely controlled fury.

"Then tell me, Miss Larson," he goaded. "What is it you think I can do that the police can't."

The look that passed between them proved immensely more telling than the words that followed. "Angel will come for his son. I want you to do whatever it takes to stop him."

A long silence followed, but her fiery gaze never wavered. She was dead serious, Sloan realized then. Rachel Larson wanted him to do the one thing he had longed to have the opportunity to do for seven endless years. She wanted him to kill Gabriel DiCassi.

Time had not dulled his fierce desire for vengeance, only the urgency of it. His wife and son were dead. Nothing could change that. Sloan set his jaw hard against the paralyzing emotions that wanted to surface even now, after all this time. The finality had crashed down around him long ago, after almost a year of nonstop searching for Angel. Grief and the need to avenge his wife and son had kept him looking when everyone else had given up. The realization that nothing he did would matter, it sure as hell wouldn't bring them back, hit him eventually. Then there was nothing. He stopped feeling anything at all.

But now anticipation surged anew through Sloan's veins. The mere notion of killing Angel made him almost giddy. His gaze traveled back to the boy. The woman was even providing the perfect bait. How far would a piece of crap like Angel be willing to go for his own son? A strange calm settled over Sloan then. He knew just how far any man would go. And he wouldn't have to do anything but wait Angel out. Long buried sensations bombarded Sloan. A dozen snippets of memory flashed through his mind. He closed his eyes in overwhelming despair when the sound of his son's cries echoed through his soul. Sloan wanted to kill Angel more than he wanted to draw in his next breath. For the first time, Sloan had the perfect means by which to lure him.

Sloan opened his eyes to the woman standing before him. Self-disgust abruptly made him sick to his stomach. Uncharacteristic moisture stung his eyes. Had he fallen so very far? He shook his head. What kind of man would use a woman and child to assuage his own savage thirst for revenge? Sloan swallowed the answer that welled in his throat, the answer he didn't want to acknowledge. But it was there, it had always been there. The urge was so strong that Sloan could taste it. Not one doubt had ever existed in his mind that, if given the opportunity, he would do anything, give anything, within his power to make Angel pay for what he had done.

But not this.

He would not use a child. He could not. Not even Angel's child.

He leveled his gaze on Rachel's and with his next words affirmed his decision, "I'm not the man you need for the job."

Sloan walked away without looking back.

He pushed through the swinging doors and into the harsh light of day. He lifted his face to the sun's warm kiss and drew in a ragged breath. No point wasting any effort on regret. There would be a day of reckoning, he had no doubt. He would take Angel down, Sloan had made that vow long ago. But he would never stoop to Angel's level to do it. Sloan could not—would not—use a child.

Cool, soft fingers touched Sloan's arm. He pivoted and glowered down at the woman who had followed him from the cantina.

"I told you I'm not the man for the job," he growled. The little boy cowered behind his mother now, cautiously peeking past her skirt. Sloan swore under his breath. Now he was scaring small children.

Rachel held her ground, meeting his lethal glare with lead in her own. "You're the only man for the job," she insisted with quiet strength.

"Lady, you've got a hell of a lot of nerve coming to a place like this." He gestured at all that surrounded them. "Do you have a clue the kind of men you walked past in there?" He stepped closer to her, putting himself in her personal space now and forcing her to acknowledge his superior physical strength. "Florescitaf is the bottom of the barrel down here. There are sleazebags here that would sell their own mother for their next drink. Any one of them could eat you alive and not blink. I'm surprised you made it this far."

She opened her mouth to speak, then hesitated. "I had to come here," she said finally. "This is where you are. And I need you."

Sloan shook his head. Victoria had no business sending this woman and her son to him. He wasn't a do-gooder anymore. Sloan took the jobs no one else wanted to take. The ones too dangerous for a man who cared whether he lived or died.

"I'm no knight in shining armor, Miss Larson. In fact, I'm so far from it that most women who know my reputation wouldn't consider themselves safe this close." He allowed his gaze to rove the length of her once more for good measure. "You're sure it's me you're looking for?"

Uncertain now, she shifted nervously. "Victoria said you're the best. She said you know Angel." She licked her full lips. To Sloan's irritation, he followed the movement with growing interest. "She said," Rachel continued, "that if there was anyone who could help me, it was you."

"Like I told you before, Victoria made a mistake." He started to turn away, but something in those big, pleading eyes stayed him.

"You know what he'll do," she murmured. Tears slipped past those long lashes and streamed down her cheeks. "Can you turn your back on us knowing what he'll do?"

Sloan looked away. He didn't want to see or hear any of this. He wanted to go back into the cantina and finish off that bottle he left on the bar. He wanted to forget the name Gabriel DiCassi. He wanted to erase the image of this woman and her son from his mind. But he could never do either of those things.

"Josh!"

Sloan jerked his attention back to Rachel. She whirled around, calling her son's name. Josh was nowhere in sight.

"Oh, God, where can he be?" Rachel rushed forward, then hesitated as if unsure which way to go. "He was right behind me…. Josh!"

Sloan's heart pumped hard in his chest. The vivid memory of endless days and nights of searching for his own son broadsided him with the force of a runaway train. The first moment of realization that his little boy was not at home…not at the neighbor's… not anywhere. A cold sweat coated Sloan's skin. The final gut-wrenching instant when he had to admit defeat. His son was dead…murdered. Sloan shuddered, then trembled with remembered pain so sharp that nausea burned the back of his throat.

"Josh!" Rachel cried out, her voice riddled with hysteria and the panic no doubt tightening like a steel band around her chest. She zigzagged in and out of the throngs of people milling from shop to shop.

Siesta had long passed and the streets were filled with shoppers and peddlers going about their business as the heat of the day slowly subsided with the retreating sun. Children played in the alleys and the streets. Dogs barked and sniffed about, looking for handouts. The occasional car horn honked to clear the way as it inched past on the cluttered cobblestone street.

Sloan scanned face after face, each distracted with his or her own agenda. Another handful of children skipped past, chattering and laughing. But none proved to be the one he was searching for.

Josh was gone.

Sloan moved toward Rachel, then caught her by the elbow and pulled her around to face him. He pinned her with a steady gaze, hoping to calm the fear dancing in hers. "Stay right here, out in the open where Josh can see you." Another tear streaked downward. Before he could stop himself Sloan reached up and swiped that tear from her soft cheek with the pad of his thumb. "I will find him," he promised, then turned away.

Josh couldn't have gone far on his own….

Chapter Two

Rachel's frantic search stalled in the middle of the street. Sloan's warning to stay where Josh could see her belatedly echoed in her ears. She watched in utter despair as Sloan came out of the last shop empty-handed. Her heart pounded so hard that her chest ached with each heavy thud. She wanted to run through the streets screaming her agony, but her arms and legs felt like useless wooden clubs. This couldn't be happening. The nightmare she feared most had reached long bony fingers from the blackest depths of her subconscious and climbed into her reality.

Josh was gone.

They had looked everywhere.

Sloan paused near a group of children and spoke to them in fluent Spanish. All other sound except his voice faded into insignificance. The children shook their heads in a sort of surreal harmony. No, they had not seen an American boy. Rachel blinked, once, twice. This was her fault. She had taken her eyes off Josh for just one moment and—

A horn blasted behind her. Strong hands jerked her forward and against a hard wall of muscle.

"Dammit, woman, you're going to get yourself killed," Sloan growled, the sound rumbling from his massive chest.

Beyond caring whose strong arms were around her, Rachel wilted against him. The tears she could no longer restrain flowed from her, bleeding out the last of her resolve in salty rivulets. She fisted her fingers into the soft cotton of Sloan's faded shirt and fought to hold on to consciousness. She could not give in to the relief her exhausted body propelled her toward. She had to find Josh. She couldn't live without her son. She had to find him…to protect him.

With renewed determination Rachel pushed away from Sloan, oddly bereft without his powerful arms around her now. But she had to do something. She couldn't just stand here. She swiped the moisture from her cheeks and stared up into those piercing blue eyes. "He has to be here…."

"I told you I would find him and I will. But I can't look for him and keep you out of trouble at the same time." The irritation in his voice manifested itself in a line between his eyebrows.

The look of concern that emanated from Sloan's gaze frightened Rachel all the more. If a man like Sloan was worried, then the situation must look pretty hopeless. A tremor shook her. No. She wouldn't believe that. Josh couldn't have gone far.

He was just curious, that's all. Sloan was right. He was probably exploring and had wandered out of sight. The goats had captured his attention earlier. And the children…

"I have to look for him, too." Dragging in an uneven breath, Rachel averted her gaze from the one watching her so very intently. She dug furiously through her bag until she found a recent snapshot of her son. Armed with the only weapon she possessed, her determination, she hurried to catch up with the children who were slowly meandering down the street. With both of them looking they could cover more ground.

"Excuse me." Rachel displayed Josh's picture. Maybe they would remember seeing him if they knew what he looked like. A half-dozen sets of dark expectant eyes looked first at Rachel then at the picture she held in her trembling hand. "My son… my *niño* is lost." Rachel moistened her lips and forced herself to take a breath. The blood roared in her ears. She wanted to cry again. Her mind whirled, making concentration difficult, but she had to focus on finding Josh. The children only looked at each other, then at her and shook their heads. Frustration twisted inside Rachel. Surely someone had seen him.

He couldn't have simply disappeared into thin air.

Unless…Angel was here already. Overwhelming dread pooled in Rachel's stomach. No…he couldn't have known she was coming here. He couldn't have found her so quickly.

Rachel felt strangely detached from her surroundings. She squeezed her eyes shut to chase away the black spots and to slow the spinning in her head.

"Mommy!"

Sloan was the first to spot the boy. Josh stood on the other side of the street. To Sloan it looked as if someone had just left him there. Instinct pricked him. This didn't feel right. Sloan waited for a rusty old truck to chug past then he ran to the boy. He crouched in front of him and surveyed him for injury. Profound relief raced through Sloan's veins, chasing away the suspicions niggling at him. The kid was fine.

Josh's lips protruded into a pout. "I want my mommy," he muttered, tears welling in his dark eyes.

Rachel was suddenly on her knees next to Sloan. She hugged her son so close Sloan was sure the kid couldn't possibly be breathing. Rachel was crying and kissing Josh and telling him how much she loved him.

Sloan stood and looked away.

What the hell was he doing with this woman and her child? They aren't your problem, he told himself firmly. It wasn't his fault that Rachel Larson had herself in a no-win situation. Sloan would just send them back to Victoria on the next flight out of Chihuahua. The last thing he needed or wanted was complications. And this lady and her kid were definitely complicated. They reminded him too much of the past…of what he had lost. And even if Angel did care enough about his kid to come for him, Sloan had no desire to start a war with a woman and child caught in the middle.

No way.

"Josh," Rachel said hesitantly. "Where did you get this bear?"

Sloan's gaze swung back to the boy. Rachel pulled Josh's hand from behind his back. He quickly hugged what appeared to be a small brown bear to his chest.

"It's s'posed t'be a secret, Mommy," the boy whispered too loudly. His doubtful gaze darted up to Sloan, then widened with distrust.

"Look at me, Josh." Rachel held him firmly by both shoulders. "Where did you get the bear?"

Josh huffed a big breath. "It's a present from my daddy." He turned the bear to his mother then so that she could see his prize. "See."

Recognition slammed into Sloan. The bear with its big button eyes and red ribbon tied neatly around the neck mocked him. Sloan's son had cherished a bear very much like this one. The bear had been found with his…*body.* Sloan had buried the toy with his child. Sloan tugged the bear from Josh's grasp and inspected it more closely.

Josh wailed his protests. Rachel pulled him to her and tried to quiet him, her face stricken with a mixture of fear and desperation. She was thinking the same thing Sloan was. He could see it in her eyes.

As if in slow motion, Sloan turned all the way around, his gaze searching every face, every shop window, every shadow.

Could Angel be this close?

Anticipation ignited the adrenaline already flowing with the wild hammering in his chest. His attention still tracking every move around them, Sloan passed the bear back to Rachel.

"Let's go."

Rachel stood, Josh clutched tightly in her arms. "What do you mean?" Hope flashed in her eyes.

Sloan shot her a look that quelled any other questions she might have asked, "You're coming with me." A new kind of evil just rolled into town, he didn't add.

Rachel felt completely drained. She glanced over the seat at Josh who was preoccupied with his new bear. Fear twisted inside her each time she recalled Josh's words. It's a present from my daddy. The more distance they put between them and the town the calmer Rachel felt.

Once Sloan had ushered them into his Jeep the interrogation had begun. Sloan wanted to know every detail of every moment Josh had been out of their sight. It didn't seem to matter to Sloan that a four-year-old had no concept of time. Josh explained that he had followed one of the children who was chasing a dog and had gotten lost. When he couldn't find his mommy he simply sat down and cried. A nice dark-haired lady, according to Josh, had come along and told him not to cry and that she had a gift for him from his daddy. Then she had led Josh to where he could find his mommy.

The lady's description matched most every woman in this country, including Rachel's. She consoled herself with the belief that perhaps some kind lady had offered comfort to a lost child and then helped him find his way back to his mother. Maybe the woman hadn't had time for pleasantries, or didn't care about being thanked.

Sloan was far more skeptical of Josh's story. He had his own theory, though he hadn't felt compelled to share his thoughts as of yet. But Rachel knew he was convinced Angel had something to do with it. Whatever motivated him, Rachel was grateful that he had changed his mind and decided to help them. The concern he had shown when she couldn't find Josh warmed her, and gave her hope that Sloan wasn't really as bad as he pretended to be.

But then, Rachel was a die-hard optimist.

She stared out at the passing landscape. The desert seemed to swallow them up almost as soon as they left Florescitaf. The sun was dropping even lower now, casting purple and pink hues like a halo around the descending ball of fire. And with it went the oppressive heat. Rachel shivered and chafed her bare arms with her hands to warm them against the cooler wind whipping through the open Jeep now.

"There's a jacket in the backseat if you're cold."

Rachel glanced at Sloan's unyielding profile. He could have been carved right out of the rugged Sierra Madre Mountains that jutted skyward before them. How odd that he would show concern for her comfort when he had scarcely spoken a word since they left town except to question Josh. She couldn't decide which persona she liked best. The Sloan who defined indifference, or the fleeting moments of the other man who obviously lay beneath all that bitterness and attitude. He hadn't even named his price for the services he apparently intended to render. Now that Rachel thought about it, the fact of the matter was she had no idea where they were headed. His home, she assumed. A rustic cabin or a tent were the first images to pop into her mind. Sloan didn't appear the type to put much stock in personal possessions.

"Thanks, but I'm fine," she said, in response to his offer of the jacket. Rachel focused her attention on the dusty road in front of them and asked, "Where are we going?"

"My place." The answer was curt, and spoken grudgingly.

Iceman was back. Instinct told her that Sloan didn't want anyone close to him. It would behoove her to keep her distance. His momentary lapse of concern had obviously passed.

"Our things are at the hotel," Rachel realized aloud, only now remembering that they had checked into a hotel when they arrived the day before. With no idea how long it would take her to find Sloan or to persuade him to take her case, it had seemed like the right thing to do. But with Josh getting lost, sensible thinking had gone out the window.

"I'll take care of it tomorrow."

"Thank you." He said nothing. Determined to ignore his lack of social grace and to listen to her own instincts, Rachel leaned back into her seat and tried to relax. After two days without sleep, she was spent physically. She had no idea when she had eaten last either. In all honesty, food no longer held any appeal for her. Eating equated to survival. She survived for one reason and one reason only, to protect her son. Nothing else mattered at this point.

Sloan slowed and took a left, heading directly into the more rugged terrain that led to the foothills of the Sierra Madre. The Jeep bumped over the rough road for another mile or so before Sloan slowed once more. The mountains loomed in the distance, their jagged peaks rising to the clouds to greet the darkening sky. The landscape that lay ahead sharply contrasted the sprawling desert land they had covered so far. Desert scrub and cacti eventually gave way to trees that sprouted up from the towering mountainous terrain.

Rachel saw the wall first, then the roof of the house that lay beyond it. She bent forward slightly, and stifled a gasp. The place looked like a modern-day fortress. A towering wall, at least ten or twelve feet high, surrounded the house. A huge iron gate stood before them when Sloan stopped the Jeep. He pressed a series of buttons on a keypad by the gate. The massive iron gates opened immediately, then closed automatically behind them. Rachel watched in a sort of surprised bewilderment as they drove away from the intimidating entrance.

Sloan parked before the double doors at the front of the Southwestern-style house. The exterior was a stucco finish, painted a pinkish-tan like the wall surrounding the property. The roof was a rustic-red tile. One of the front doors suddenly opened and a short, thin man stepped out to meet them.

"This is where you live?" Rachel asked, then winced. God, what a stupid question. Of course this was where he lived.

"Ever since I ran off the local drug lord," he said before hopping out of the Jeep.

Rachel frowned. Was that supposed to be a joke? Did she really want to know? Too tired to consider the remark any further, Rachel unfastened her seat belt and leaned between the bucket seats and released Josh's. The boy, teddy bear in tow, scrambled out of the seat and into his mother's arms. Rachel settled Josh onto the ground once they were out of the Jeep. Sloan was speaking to the other man in Spanish. Rachel couldn't quite get the gist of the conversation. Something about a room, and trouble.

She and Josh were the trouble, of course.

"Good evening, Señora Larson," the man said, his smile wide and pleasant. "I am Pablo. I am very sure that you are hungry. Come in and I will prepare a proper feast for such honored guests."

Rachel took an instant liking to the man. She returned Pablo's smile and followed as he led the way into the house. Rachel could feel Sloan behind her. She didn't have to look, his formidable presence was unmistakable. There was an aura about the man that entailed much more than his air of danger.

Details flooded her senses. Muted colors, thick upholstered furnishings. Rachel had to admit that she had been way off base about the man's taste in accommodations. Sloan's home was elegant in an understated sort of way. Her artist's eye was drawn to the clean lines and sparse but inviting furnishings of each large room she passed. The expansive hall cut through the middle of the house, flowing both left and right about midway. Pablo turned right and continued until they reached the third room on the left.

He gestured for Rachel to enter before him. "If there is anything you need, *señora,* do not hesitate to ask."

"Thank you, Pablo," she said tiredly.

"I'm hungry!" Josh piped up.

Heat scalded Rachel's cheeks. Josh was always hungry. "Josh," she scolded.

"The boy needs to eat," Pablo agreed. "Come with Pablo, little man, and we will prepare the feast together." Pablo winked when Josh eyed him hesitantly. "You may taste as we go."

Josh was ready to go then. He took Pablo's offered hand and told him about his new bear as they disappeared down the hall. Rachel was amazed at how easily Josh befriended the strangers he met. She thought of the woman and the bear and decided that a long talk with her son was in order.

With Josh and Pablo gone, Rachel had no choice but to acknowledge her host's brooding presence. She turned hesitantly to face him.

"I don't know why you changed your mind," Rachel began, trying hard not to allow that icy blue gaze to undo her. "But I—"

"You should eat and get some rest," he said, his words an order rather than a suggestion.

He turned to go but Rachel stopped him with a hand on his arm. He stared first at her hand then at her, as if her touch were somehow offensive to him. But the feel of his skin beneath her fingertips was anything but offensive to Rachel. She jerked her hand back when a mild shock radiated through her, but caught herself before she frowned.

"I'd like to discuss your plans," she managed in a surprisingly even voice. "I don't want to be left in the dark. I need to know what you have in mind."

For one long moment his gaze held hers and something intense passed between them. For Rachel, it felt all too much like sexual awareness. Sloan was handsome, in a fierce, rugged way. He was big and muscular and with eyes that could unsettle her with just a look. He frightened her, yet drew her on some level that Rachel could never hope to explain. Maybe it was simply the need to feel protected by someone who was strong enough to go up against Angel.

"I don't have a plan." His gaze remained unreadable, as seemed customary for him. "I'll let you know when we have anything to discuss." He brushed past Rachel and sauntered in the direction into which Josh and Pablo had disappeared.

Rachel leaned against the door frame, crossed her arms over her chest and sighed wearily. The man's attitude infuriated her. How on earth would she ever tolerate his rude indifference? Rachel was too tired to contemplate the issue any further at the moment. She was so tired she wasn't even sure she would make it through dinner. For Josh's sake she would have to muster up the energy to at least show up, then see to her son's bath and to get him tucked into bed. And just maybe, she could manage a leisurely bath of her own.

She glanced around the spacious room she and Josh were to share. She thought of the property's elaborate security system, and then of Sloan himself. Despite her enigmatic protector's personality, or lack thereof, Rachel felt safe for the first time in nearly five years.

Sloan stared at the bottle of tequila on the table before him. He knew there would be no sleep for him tonight, no matter how much he drank. His mind was reeling with bits of information he didn't want to remember. Faces he didn't want to see. Voices he didn't want to hear. But there were certain points he had to allow himself to recall. He had waited too long, planned too often for this very moment, yet feared it would never come. Not once since pulling himself from the gutter pain and depression had hurled him into had he allowed a glimmer of real hope. Anticipation was one thing, but hope entirely another. He'd learned the hard way that hope was only for those too weak to acknowledge defeat when it had them by the throat.

Sloan had faced defeat, but he hadn't wallowed in it, at least not for long. He couldn't change history, but he sure as hell had some say in the future. And he would make Angel pay. Very soon.

To Sloan's supreme irritation the vivid mental image of Rachel Larson suddenly loomed large in his mind. He could still hear the fear and panic in her voice when she called out for Josh. That same desperation had haunted his own voice seven years ago. The euphoria still lingered from the profound relief he had felt this evening when Josh was in his mother's arms once more. The relief he had been denied seven years ago. Then the realization that Angel might be close by.

Too close.

Sloan shook off the feelings nagging him, but he couldn't completely shake the picture of Rachel. The fear in those big brown eyes, the way her lips quivered with uncertainty. If anyone he had met in this business had ever needed protecting, she sure as hell did. But Sloan wanted to do more than protect her, he wanted to know her as a woman. That simple touch this evening in her room had sent fire raging through his veins. For the first time in more years than he cared to admit, Sloan yearned for more than mere physical release.

Ire burned in his gut. He couldn't feel this way.

It was nothing more than his exaggerated instinct to protect. That's all, he assured himself.

Angel flickered amid the other tangle of images and thoughts involving Rachel Larson. Sloan swore. His attraction to a woman who had once been involved with Angel made Sloan's gut clench. Those feelings were a betrayal to the memory of his wife and son. He must be losing his mind to entertain such a fantasy. Hell, he had already lost his mind. He had brought Angel's son into his own home.

Sloan swore repeatedly.

He hated himself for what he was doing. But it was the ultimate goal that made it all worthwhile. Angel would come for his son. It was the basic concept of possession. The kid belonged to him. Angel would want him back, so he had to come. When he did, Sloan would be ready.

And Angel would die.

Then Rachel and Josh would be safe.

That wasn't supposed to be what counted to Sloan…but somehow it was. Somehow their welfare already meant entirely too much to him. And that didn't sit well with him. But he would not let either of them any closer. He would stay in control—no matter what it took. All these jumbled feelings were nothing more than his deeply entrenched need to protect those weaker than him.

The way he couldn't protect his own wife and son.

"Excuse me."

Sloan's head shot up at the softly uttered greeting. Rachel Larson hovered near the door. Hesitantly she stepped out onto the patio and approached him, her bare feet soundless on the cool tile. His gaze followed her movements, his body automatically responding and he silently cursed himself again. He was a fool. Sloan leaned back in his chair and leveled an impatient gaze in her direction.

"I prefer drinking alone, Miss Larson," Sloan said tersely. "So if you're looking for company, you'll find Pablo's more to your liking."

Rachel hesitated a few feet away from the table. "I…I just wanted to thank you for helping us. I realized after I put Josh to bed that I hadn't properly thanked you for allowing us refuge in your home."

Sloan tossed back the tequila in his shot glass and set the empty glass down next to the bottle. The last thing he needed was her gratitude distorting the already fuzzy scenario taking shape in his head. "Don't thank me, *Miss Larson,* I'm not doing it for you." He poured himself another shot. "I'm doing it for me."

Rachel nodded mutely. "Of course," she murmured. "Well, good night then."

Before she could turn away, and to Sloan's royal irritation, he stopped her. "There is one thing you can do for me," he said, his words dripping contempt, his senses already piqued in anticipation of her response. "You can tell me how you managed to get yourself *intimately* involved with a lowlife scumbag like Angel."

Rachel visibly faltered. She seemed to struggle with her answer for so long that Sloan felt certain she didn't plan to tell him. She shoved a handful of that thick dark hair behind her ear and drew in a deep breath. When her gaze finally connected with his again, her eyes were suspiciously bright. His gut clenched. Sloan swore another silent oath.

"I was very young, just nineteen," she began slowly. "He tricked me into believing he was someone he wasn't." She swallowed, the effort required displayed along the delicate column of her pale throat. "My father died because of what I allowed to happen. If I hadn't..." She fell silent, her eyes downcast.

Sloan's chair scraped across the tile as he pushed back from the table and stood. Her head snapped up and she shivered as he walked deliberately toward her. When he stopped, he stood only inches from her. She tensed, and her breath caught with a little hitch. Damn him, he wanted to touch her. Anger swirled around him, inside him. He didn't need this.

"You allowed yourself to be seduced by the bastard while he was plotting to kill your own father?" Sloan hurled the words at her like missiles intended to wound, intended to push her away. Hadn't he done the same damned thing? Seduced by the challenge of the hunt, he had dogged Angel's every step until the animal retaliated. Years of pent-up rage unleashed inside Sloan at the thought.

He leaned closer to Rachel, directing that unforgiving energy at her, widening the emotional gap between them. "I guess that makes us both pretty stupid, huh? Neither one of us were smart enough to know what we were up against until it was too late."

She trembled, but held her ground. "He tricked me. I didn't know—"

"Yeah, well that was a tough break for your old man, wasn't it?"

Her anger flared finally, however faintly. "I don't want to discuss this anymore." She pivoted and started toward the door.

Sloan snagged her by the arm and swung her around to face him. He ignored the electricity that crackled where his hand closed around her bare skin. "You screwed up, just like I did." He pulled her closer, his body's response to hers only fueling his building anger. She glared up at him, her own anger taking belated shape. "You've come all this way looking for a miracle. And what do you know? I'm fresh out. Maybe you'd better rethink your strategy."

"You're our only hope." Her sweet, desperate breath fanned his lips.

Sloan clenched his teeth and shook his head, every muscle in his body growing harder by the moment. "Maybe you think coming here is the answer to your prayers, but you're wrong. I'm just a man, Rachel Larson. I'll take Angel down, but that won't change what he took from you or me. I'm no superhero, and I'm sure as hell no saint. But if you hang around long enough the one thing I can guarantee you is that you'll end up in my bed."

Sloan saw it coming, but he didn't try to stop her. Her right palm connected with his jaw. He took the blow, because he deserved it. The pain was somehow cleansing. Pain he could handle, these other feelings he couldn't.

Rachel jerked weakly at his fierce hold on her left arm. "Let me go."

"You went to a lot of trouble to track me down," he rasped as he snaked his arm around her waist and hauled her up against him. "Don't you want to find out if I'm half the man you seem to think I am?"

The dam broke loose then, tears trickled down her face. She pushed uselessly against his chest. "I already know all I need to know." She was shaking uncontrollably now. "I saw how you reacted when you thought Josh was lost. You're a good man. I know you are."

Sloan had no comeback for that allegation. He could only stare into those deep brown eyes, watery with the kind of pain he understood all too well. Just when he felt certain that he would have to kiss her…kiss her or die, she wilted in his fierce hold. Startled, Sloan scooped her slight body into his arms.

Damn.

She had been through too much. He had pushed her too hard. All because he couldn't control his own sadistic impulses.

Sloan considered the sweet, innocent-looking woman lying unconscious in his arms for a long moment. He shook his head in self-disgust.

"I told you I was no knight in shining armor." He let go a mighty breath. "What am I supposed to do with you now?"

Chapter Three

Rachel moaned contentedly and snuggled into her pillow. Her lids slowly opened to the realization that it was now daylight. The last vestiges of sleep retreated bringing awareness one degree at a time. The fluffy pillow beneath her cheek, the cool sheet over her body, and the slight breeze whispering across her face. She inhaled deeply of a scent that was at once alien and soothing. A pleasant masculine scent, musk and leather.

Sloan.

Rachel's eyes opened wide. She surveyed the part of the room readily viewable without having to move. This was not the same room Pablo had shown her and Josh to last evening. Her heart pounded in her chest as last night's heated words with Sloan replayed in her head. She remembered collapsing…

Her attention suddenly lit on the puddle of clothing a few feet away on the carpeted floor. Her blouse, her skirt and sandals. The fact that being on the small side in the bust allowed her to go braless most of the time slammed into her. She sat bolt upright on the side of the bed and looked down at herself. She wore what appeared to be a man's T-shirt. Too large for Pablo's. She swallowed tightly. Sloan's. She looked around the room and realization dawned with unnerving clarity.

She was in Sloan's room. In his bed.

Rachel spun around to look on the other side of the bed. It was empty.

Where was Josh?

Fear rushed through her limbs to lodge in her chest. She had tucked him into bed in the other room. She blinked, forcing herself to concentrate rather than losing herself to the panic. Maybe he was having breakfast already. What time was it? Her gaze sought out the nearest clock. The LED display on the bedside table read 10:00 a.m. Rachel shot to her feet. How could she have slept so long?

Where was her son?

Laughter floated through the open window. *Josh.* Rachel bounded over to the generous windows. She peered out into the backyard. Sheer, gauzy drapes fluttered around her in the gentle breeze. With Pablo watching, Josh chased a bright red ball. His delighted squeals and laughter brought the first relaxed smile to her lips in too long to remember. It felt so good to see her son play without worry that someone would snatch him away from her. Pablo tossed the ball again, and Josh's enthusiastic race for the brightly colored, bouncing object gladdened her heart. This was all she had ever wanted for her son…for him to feel happy and safe.

Taking stock of the area for the first time in daylight, Rachel amended her earlier impression. This was not a backyard, this was a courtyard. As beautiful as any she had ever seen. And she had seen a few while growing up. Rachel's smile faded as she considered the bittersweet memories of growing up with her father. Her mother had died when she was only a small child. But her father had made up for the loss many times over. He took Rachel everywhere with him. A well-respected figure in the State Department, they had traveled frequently, abroad mostly. The hotels were always luxurious. But she had yet to view a courtyard any more spectacular than Sloan's.

Elegant tile or cobblestone pavers covered what was most likely a sandy yard. The house surrounded the courtyard on all sides, adding to the feeling of security. Numerous sets of French doors opened onto the courtyard from the rooms facing it, including the one in which she now stood. Lush foliage, mostly tropical, probably native to the area, nearly camouflaged a sparkling pool. Beyond the house, a water tank towered, supplying the residence with water despite the sprawling desert that surrounded it. The word fortress flitted through Rachel's mind again. She wondered if there were generators and a bountiful food supply stored somewhere on the grounds, making the place self-sufficient despite the desolation and its remoteness.

Relieved that Josh was safe, Rachel pushed her other curiosities from her mind. She would ask Sloan more questions when the opportunity presented itself. For now, she should get dressed and join her son outside. She had a feeling that Sloan would let her know what he wanted from her, monetarily and otherwise, when he made up his mind or developed some plan. He didn't strike her as the sort of man one could hurry.

Finding her reluctant host watching from the open doorway, Rachel gasped. That unreadable blue gaze traveled down the length of her, then back to connect with hers. Her state of undress sent a flush of heat up her neck and across her cheeks. She edged closer to the sheer material hanging around her for some sense of protection from his all-seeing gaze.

The sound that rumbled from his chest was more growl than laugh. "Don't be shy, Miss Larson, I've already seen all there is to see."

He had undressed her last night, then again just now with his eyes. On some level she had already known that Sloan was the one. Though she preferred to undress herself, Pablo having done so would have been a great deal less humiliating alternative. To her chagrin, her nipples tightened at the thought that Sloan had looked at her so intimately. That was not an appropriate reaction, she reminded herself with rising indignation.

"I'd like to get dressed now," she announced, hoping he would take the hint and leave.

"Your suitcase is in your room. Pablo picked it up this morning, along with a few other things I told him you would need." A holster, complete with sleek black gun, was strapped to one broad shoulder. He crossed his arms over his mile-wide chest and leaned against the door frame.

Rachel tried not to follow the distracting movement of powerful muscle. She moistened her lips and asked the question that tightened the back of her throat. "Why did you bring me to your…in here?" Surely she would remember if anything happened. She couldn't have been that far out of it. She shivered at the thought of those strong hands touching her bare skin.

"The boy was asleep. I didn't want to wake him."

Somehow she sensed that there was more to it than that. He hadn't wanted to be in the same room with Josh—even for a few minutes, she suddenly realized. "I don't usually…react like that," she began in explanation of what he probably considered weakness. She squared her shoulders and stepped away from the meager protection the drapes provided. Somehow she had to learn to hold her own in the man's presence. "Despite how it may look to you now, I am a strong person."

He straightened. Rachel jumped, instantly making a liar out of herself. Sloan crossed the room to stand directly in front of her. He stared down at her for a long moment before he spoke. Rachel had the distinct impression he was trying to read her mind.

The same scent that lingered on the crisp white sheets of his bed emanated from his big, powerful body. The T-shirt he wore molded to his chest, outlining every ripple and contour. The sweatpants concealed little of his masculine assets.

"Strong willed, yes," he finally said. "That's probably what has kept you alive until now." His gaze slid slowly over her body once more. Rachel shivered. "But," he continued, "physically you're weak. That makes all that willpower useless in the end."

She knew without analyzing his words that she had just been insulted. But Rachel also knew full well that he was right. "That's why I came to you. You have the strength and the know-how to protect us."

"When Angel comes—" Sloan glanced out the window, his gaze tracking Josh's energetic romp, then quickly moving to something else "—it won't be for me." His gaze returned to Rachel's. "He'll come for you and the boy. You have to be prepared to protect yourself."

Rachel swallowed at the lump of uncertainty clogging her throat. "Isn't that the service you're supposed to provide?"

He made a sound of distaste in his throat. "Lady, I'm not about to get myself killed trying to help someone who isn't willing to help herself."

Irritation grated her nerves. "I do the best I can. Fighting and eluding madmen weren't choices on the curriculum in any of the schools I attended."

Anger flickered in his steely gaze then. "Well, maybe it should have been, and just maybe you wouldn't be in this predicament now."

"What's that supposed to mean?"

"It means," he growled, his expression fierce, "that there's no time like the present to get your act together." He stopped her with a look when she would have interrupted to argue with his summation. "You and your son need protection. I can give you that temporarily, but long term you need to be prepared to deal with what life throws your way. This ain't a perfect world, lady."

Rachel exhaled, forcing her frustration back to a controllable level. "Fine," she acquiesced. "You're right. I need to know how to defend myself and Josh." She lifted her gaze to his. "You can teach me how to do that while we're here?"

He shrugged. "You wanted a plan. That's the plan."

Annoyed by his attitude, she glowered at him. "Is this going to cost extra?"

"I'll throw this part in for free." Sloan turned and walked toward the door. "You'll find what you need to wear for today's lesson in the other room." He paused at the door. "Put the swimsuit on under your clothes and be in the kitchen in twenty minutes."

The man might be barbaric in his manners, but Rachel refused to forget hers. He was doing her a tremendous favor, and she owed him her gratitude, even if she momentarily forgot at times when he made her so angry. Taking care of her the way he did last night wasn't part of the bargain. "Thank you," she offered before he could disappear through the door.

Sloan turned back to her. "For what?"

Rachel moistened her lips and summoned the courage to say what needed to be said. "For taking care of me last night. That was above and beyond the call of duty. I appreciate that you didn't take advantage of me."

Something changed in his eyes. Something Rachel couldn't quite identify.

"You were exhausted, not to mention out of it," he explained. "When I have you, you'll be very much aware of what's happening."

When, not if. Anger washed over Rachel. "That's comforting," she retorted, her irritation building once more. She wouldn't bother to tell him that he could wait until hell froze over and she still wouldn't allow him to seduce her. She had been a fool once. And it would never happen again. Dangerous men—men in general truthfully—were not to be trusted. "After that remark about my ending up in your bed," she added quickly, "I only meant that when I woke up I wasn't sure if…" Her voice trailed off at the renewed intensity in those fierce blue eyes.

The barest hint of a smile tilted one corner of his mouth. "Last night isn't what I meant when I said you would end up in my bed."

With that warning he disappeared down the hall.

Rachel fumed. She would just see about that. Maybe Sloan was accustomed to having any woman he decided he wanted, but she wasn't *any* woman. She had a son to think of. This was a business deal, nothing more.

Never again would she fall victim to any man's charm, no matter if this particular man stirred some restless feeling deep inside her. She had come here for Josh's sake. If she was lucky, when she returned to New Orleans, Angel would be dead. She knew with complete certainty that Sloan understood what she wanted. She wanted Angel out of Josh's life forever.

She wanted him dead.

In that crystalline moment, Rachel acknowledged mentally that she would do anything necessary to ensure her son's future safety. She considered the man in whose home she now resided, then the wide inviting bed which belonged to him. She drew in a shaky breath and released it slowly. Could she do that if he pressed the issue? Angel had been her first, and there hadn't been anyone since. Her judgment was obviously flawed. How could she trust her instincts? How could she bring herself to allow another man's touch?

Rachel frowned when an old memory filtered through her thoughts. There had been a man once who seemed awfully nice, but, of course, she hadn't been interested. Not really. It was about a year and a half ago, before she and Josh had moved to New Orleans. The man had been their neighbor. He was a widower, and seemed as lonely as Rachel. He had dropped by a couple of times and brought fresh bread from the bakery he owned in town. And she had enjoyed the companionship of his short visits. Her frown deepened. But he died only a couple of months after she and Josh moved there. A car accident of some sort.

A chill raced up Rachel's spine. Not once in all this time had she considered that Angel might have had something to do with his death. But now, out of nowhere, the revelation broadsided her. And she knew as surely as she knew her own name, that it was so. Angel watched every move she made.

Just like now.

And, just like Sloan said, he would come. For her. And for Josh.

None of them were safe.

Sloan glanced at the clock on the wall once more as he poured the freshly brewed coffee into a mug. Rachel Larson's twenty minutes were up. Where the hell was she? He placed the carafe back onto the warming plate, and then the mug onto the table. Patience was not one of his virtues. He hated to wait. Especially unnecessarily. This woman had come to him for help. She would have to learn that it was his way or no way.

Irritated beyond reason, he strode out of the kitchen and in the direction of his bedroom. He slowed in the hall long enough to check and adjust the thermostat as he passed. The previous night's unseasonably cool temperatures had waned, and the wilting August heat had taken its place.

His bedroom was empty. Sloan crossed the room to close the windows since the air-conditioning had just kicked on. He had already closed the other windows Pablo had raised last night to allow the cool desert air to filter through the house. But he had left these open to keep from disturbing Rachel this morning. She had needed the rest.

The bed was made, he noticed when he turned around. His T-shirt was neatly folded and lying atop one pillow. The one she had slept against last night. He picked up the T-shirt and held it to his face to inhale her scent. His groin tightened when her sweet fragrance filled his nostrils. He closed his eyes and allowed the memory of holding her in his arms while he sat on the bedside undressing her to replay. The sandals had been the first to go. After releasing the button and lowering the zipper, he had dragged the long, silky skirt from under her and then down her legs. Her skin had felt like satin beneath his callused palms.

By the time he released the final button of her blouse, he was painfully aroused. Sloan opened his eyes and stared out the window, seeing nothing but the image of the woman who had been in his arms last night. Even now the memory of seeing her small breasts made him hard. It had taken almost more restraint than he possessed not to touch her. Her nipples had tightened into tempting, rose-colored peaks, as if even in sleep her body responded to his touch.

He hadn't wanted to cover her, but he had. His

fingers fisted in the soft cotton of the T-shirt that had just minutes ago covered her slim body. He could have carried her to the bed where her son slept, but he hadn't wanted to see the child. He had watched his own son sleep so many nights after a long day at the Colby Agency. Those moments alone with his son had been one of his favorite times. So much innocence. How could anything bad ever touch that sweetness?

But it had. Sloan had brought that evil into their lives.

He repressed the painful memory. That was a long time ago. He would not think about the past today.

The images beyond the window slowly came into focus, bringing Sloan back to the here and now. Rachel needed him and he couldn't turn his back on her. No matter that each time he looked at her son the agony he had spent seven long years burying was resurrected. As Sloan watched, Rachel, wearing the T-shirt and sweats Pablo had selected, knelt before her son and threw her arms around him and hugged him tight. She drew back and brushed the tousled hair from his face and kissed his nose. Sloan turned away.

He had to keep the past out of the present. Remaining focused would be impossible if he allowed those demons to escape the tightly compartmentalized place he had banished them to all those years ago. Sloan thought briefly of Victoria. His life then, his work with the agency seemed so far away. Almost like someone else's history. Victoria had sent this woman to him, Sloan owed it to Victoria to do what he could. She, of all people, understood this level of urgency.

He owed it to himself to take Angel down.

The concept of intense physical training during Rachel's stay here had been borne of necessity. In her current condition, Rachel was as helpless as Josh when it came to defending herself. She needed to build up her strength and endurance, otherwise she would only be a liability when Angel showed up. That wasn't really the issue here. Sloan would deal with Angel.

But until that time came Sloan needed a distraction, or else he would lose what was left of his mind, then he would be a liability....

Just like before.

Sloan was waiting in the kitchen leaning against the counter when Rachel, breathless from a few minutes of play with Josh, rushed through the door a full fifteen minutes later than he had instructed.

"Ten-thirty means ten-thirty, Miss Larson. This isn't Club Med, and playtime with the kiddies is not on the agenda."

He was PO'd. Impatience and irritation radiated from him like heat rising off that long stretch of desert highway she had traveled by bus from Chihuahua to Florescitaf. He clearly resented her choosing Josh over his orders. His sandy-colored hair was pulled back, revealing the lines and angles of his handsome face.

"I'm sorry," she offered. "I wanted to check on Josh."

"Pablo will see to your son while you're training."

Rachel started to argue, then thought better of it. No point in antagonizing the man the first day. "I'll remember that," she promised. "But *you* will have to remember that I can't pretend my son isn't here," she added, intending to make her point whether she argued or not.

Ignoring her last statement, Sloan gestured to the table. "Coffee or water." Both sat on the table, ready to be consumed. "You can eat after this morning's workout. Tomorrow we'll start at six in the morning."

Six o'clock? Trying not to grimace, she pulled out a chair and sat down. Choosing the water over the coffee, Rachel took a long sip. "What're we going to do first?" she asked in hopes of making conversation. Anything was better than his brooding silence.

His gaze intent on hers, he pulled out the chair directly across from her and straddled it, then propped his arms across its back. "We'll do some stretches, run a couple of miles, then do laps in the pool. Maybe throw in some strength training."

Rachel's eyes widened in disbelief. "Anything else?" At least she now knew why he'd insisted she wear the swimsuit beneath her clothes.

"Not until this afternoon." He eyed her skeptically, no doubt watching for some sign of surrender to the challenge he lay before her.

She mustered a smile. "Sounds doable." She

downed the last of her water and pushed out of her chair, the legs scraping across the floor with her movement. "I'm ready." She tried desperately to remember if she had ever purposely run two miles in her life. She didn't think so. But she would never let him suspect.

Sloan stood in one fluid motion, drawing her attention. He turned the chair around and pushed it beneath the table. A little hitch interrupted her breathing. How could a man as tall and solidly built move so effortlessly? And why did she have to notice?

"Let's get started."

Rachel followed him outside. She waved to Josh who was helping Pablo attend to the pool. "He can't swim!" she called out nervously. Though she felt sure Josh was in good hands, still, he had been to a pool only a few times in his short life, and never without her to watch him.

"Don't worry, *señora*. We'll have him swimming in no time at all."

Josh punctuated the statement with enthusiastic whoops. Rachel smiled in spite of her misgivings. Her son was enjoying himself and that was all that mattered. She had been so afraid that coming here would be hard on him. Pablo was a blessing.

When she directed her attention back to Sloan he was already on the other side of the courtyard, leaving her behind. She hurried to catch up with him, but he didn't seem to notice. He led the way to an atrium that made up a large portion of the west side of the house. The room and plants were gorgeous. Rachel thought again how out of character this house was when compared to its owner. She suddenly recalled his words when she had asked him if he lived here. *Ever since I ran off the local drug lord.* Was it possible that Sloan had been serious?

Now that she thought about it, the place did look like the kind of luxurious setup a drug lord would flaunt, not to mention the elaborate security system.

"How long did you say you had lived here?" She hastened her step to match his.

"I didn't." He kept walking without sparing her so much as a glance.

"Did you design the house yourself?" she persisted. "The layout is spectacular."

He shot her a sideways glance and exhaled impatiently. "No."

So much for small talk. Rachel huffed a sigh of her own. She supposed she would simply have to get used to his ways. Lord knew she was definitely at his mercy.

He passed through another door and Rachel found herself in a room filled with workout equipment. Through the windows on the other side of the room she could see the water tower that stood midway between the house and the protective wall a hundred or so feet away. This was the first time she had seen the back of the property, though she really couldn't see that much. Beyond the wall the beautiful mountains stood proudly in the distance.

"There won't be any distractions here," he said, drawing her attention back to him.

His comment had nothing to do with the view she had been admiring. He meant Josh. He didn't want her son around. Rachel wished she could say something that would make things less difficult. But she couldn't. Josh was Angel's son. Angel murdered Sloan's son. There was no way to paint a pretty picture. Sloan would merely tolerate Josh while they were here.

She met his watchful gaze. "I'm ready. What do you want me to do first?"

Sloan dragged two large blue workout mats to the far side of the room. He stepped onto one and waited until Rachel moved to the other.

"Warm-ups."

Rachel watched his sinuous moves, then mimicked each as best she could. She repeated each step until he went on to something else and she followed suit. They set into a routine of exercises, some involving the elaborate equipment that quickly stole her breath. Refusing to give up, she completed the same amount of repetitions as Sloan. But she was pretty sure he had noticed and was adjusting his usual routine to accommodate her.

The two-mile run came next. Rachel couldn't begin to keep up with Sloan's long legs. She was grateful when he slowed his pace so that she didn't lag so far behind. The sun had risen high in the sky by the time they headed back into the house. She had long since lost count of the number of times they had circled the huge compound. Her legs felt like limp noodles. The only scenery was the incredible view of the mountains in the distance beyond Sloan's property.

Sweat rolled down between her breasts as they slowed to a walk when they neared the rear entrance. Sloan wasn't even winded. Rachel huffed like she had run twenty miles instead of two. Sloan continued in silence as he led her back through the atrium and into the inner courtyard. He hadn't paid much attention to her since they started, unless it was to bark an order or to point out a snake basking in the sun on a nearby rock. Rachel wasn't sure if he had done so to warn her or simply to keep her close. No way was she falling far behind when snakes and lizards abounded in the area. Too bad the gate didn't keep them out too.

Just one more thing to worry about Josh coming into contact with. Snakes. She shuddered. She would be sure and mention her worry to Pablo.

Josh and Pablo were having lunch on the patio. Rachel gave her son a quick pat on the head before following Sloan to the pool. Her pulse tripped when Sloan peeled off his T-shirt, tossed it aside, then stripped off his sweats. His running shoes and socks lay next to his discarded shirt. Rachel's mouth went dry as her eyes took in his sculpted body in the swimwear. She blinked and he was gone. The water barely splashed as he cut through the sparkling surface.

Rachel quickly toed off her shoes and dispatched her clothes. Rather than diving in as Sloan had, she took the steps. The water felt wonderful closing in around her heated body.

Sloan stopped long enough to push the damp hair from his eyes. "See if you can manage ten." He turned into his second lap without waiting for her reply.

She couldn't remember the last time she had been swimming, but she had every intention of giving his demand her best effort. Rachel dived into the water and swam half the length of the pool beneath its refreshing surface to cool off. It felt wonderful. How nice it was, she decided as she cut through the water, to have such an amenity in the middle of the desert.

By the time she managed lap number nine, Rachel felt certain she would die right then and there.

Sloan sat on the edge, his damp hair slicked back and curling around his nape. The golden hair sprinkled on his chest glistening in the sun. "You can stop anytime, you know," he offered, obviously reading the strain on her face. "Ten laps was only a suggestion."

"One more," she said between gritted teeth. Her arms moved awkwardly now. But she had to make just one more lap. She would not show weakness. She had to do it.

"Mommy, Mommy, can I swim, too?"

Rachel kicked harder to make it the last few feet. She stopped in the waist-deep water and held on to the side of the pool to stay upright. Her muscles quivered in protest of the workout they had gotten.

"Hey, sweetie." She smiled wanly at her little boy. She glanced at Sloan then, who was busy ignoring the whole situation. "Do you mind?" she asked cautiously.

He stood. "Why should I?" He gave Rachel his back and stalked away.

Rachel watched him disappear inside the house. How could she feel sympathy for such a cold, hard man? But she did. He had lost so much. She and Josh were vivid reminders of just how much. Rachel produced a smile for her son and put thoughts of Sloan out of her weary mind. Nothing was more important than her son.

Chapter Four

"Spread your feet shoulder-width apart."

Rachel moved her feet farther apart and took aim once more. "Like this?"

Sloan walked slowly around her, surveying her stance. If his irritable expression was any indication, she wasn't doing anything right.

"Lock your elbow," he ordered.

She stiffened her arm, her left hand supporting her right at the wrist.

"Now." He moved up beside her. "Close your left eye and look straight down the barrel with your right until you've sighted your target."

She did exactly as he told her. The circles on the silhouette blurred then cleared as she focused on the innermost ring—the bull's-eye.

"Take a deep breath and let it out slowly," he said near her ear.

Rachel shivered and lost her aim on the target. She swore silently, and refocused.

"You can't let anything break your concentration," he warned, noting the subtle change. "Losing focus for one second can mean the difference between living and dying."

She drew in a long breath and let it out a little at a time, forcing her tense muscles to relax.

"Fire!"

Without taking time to think, she pressed the trigger just like he had demonstrated before. The recoil forced her hands upward. Rachel staggered back a step. The explosion echoed against the mountains in the distance.

She turned to her instructor and waited for his appraisal. Sloan stared at the target she had missed entirely and made a dismissive sound.

"Let's try that again."

"I've never fired a gun before," she offered quickly in explanation of her lack of skill.

"I noticed."

Rachel steamed at his indifference. The man could be such a jerk. He had disappeared after this morning's workout. Of course, that wasn't so hard to conceive of when you considered the size of his house. She had played in the pool a while with Josh, then put him down for his nap. She smiled as she considered her son's playful antics in the water. He loved it. Pablo was right. It wouldn't take long to teach him to swim. He took to the water like a little fish.

Sloan hadn't reappeared until Josh was out of the way. It worried Rachel that he harbored such negative feelings toward her son. Maybe negative wasn't the right word. He just didn't want to be around Josh. Though she understood to some extent how he felt, it was difficult. She loved Josh. None of this was his fault. He was innocent. Yet, she supposed looking at him was painful for Sloan. Unfair as that was.

"Your feet still aren't far enough apart," he said gruffly.

Startled back to the present, Rachel gasped when his left arm closed around her waist. He tucked her hard against his muscular body. His right hand covered her left in support of her firing arm. Still holding her firmly against him, his jaw pressed to her temple, he thrust one jean-clad thigh between her legs and forced her feet farther apart.

"Sight your weapon."

Rachel felt the words rumble from his chest. She tried to slow the pounding in her own chest. She moistened her lips and took another of those slow, deep breaths—for all the good it did. She knew he could feel the rapid rise and fall of her breasts, but she couldn't slow her body's reaction to his nearness.

"Relax, I don't bite," he murmured.

"Do you have to hold me so close?"

"Sight your weapon and fire," he ordered, ignoring her question.

Summoning her determination, Rachel tuned out the many ways he affected her one by one. First, the feel of his hard, male body spooned against hers.

Second, the whisper of his breath on her cheek. And then the unmistakable scent that belonged uniquely to him. A fine line of perspiration formed on her forehead as she closed her left eye and focused intently on the silhouette hanging in the distance.

She pulled the trigger. Sloan's strong arm controlled the effect of the recoil, his powerfully built body absorbed the force that rocked her hard against him. Each stimulus she had worked so laboriously to disregard flooded her senses once more.

He released her and started toward the target. "Much better," he allowed.

Lowering her weapon, Rachel swayed, this time from the loss of his arms around her. She attempted without success to rationalize her physical reaction to the man. Obviously her tremendous gratitude for his help was spilling over into other emotions she wasn't prepared to deal with and certainly shouldn't feel. She hadn't allowed herself this close to anyone in more than five years. She swiped her forehead with the back of her hand and pulled in another of those calming breaths. Maybe it was need, pure and simple.

Sloan held the silhouette out for her inspection. "Let's see if you can do that again."

Rachel studied the figure and smiled at the small hole she had made on the edge of the outermost circle. Now, if she could just learn to do that without his arms around her.

"Next time just think about Angel when you set your sights on that faceless silhouette."

She lifted her gaze to meet his and tried to decipher the hint of emotion in his eyes. She considered the way he had emptied the weapon into the first silhouette, each shot a near perfect bull's-eye.

"Is that what you do?"

That strange understanding passed between them again. Just like before, in the cantina. He didn't have to say yes. Rachel read the response in his eyes. He turned away and made the return journey to the stand. She watched as he placed the target back into position in preparation for her next shot. With complete clarity Rachel knew precisely what drew her to Sloan. It wasn't just the fact that he could protect Josh and her. It wasn't even the knowledge that he knew Angel better than anyone, thus offering the best hope at beating him. No, that wasn't it at all. The single thread that bound them even now, so early in their new alliance, was their mutual hatred for Angel. The desire to make him pay for the pain he had inflicted in their lives.

And he would pay, Rachel felt confident for the first time in five long years.

Sloan sat in the near darkness on the patio. The lights from the pool cast just a hint of light in his direction, but not enough to disturb his sense of concealment. He stared at the bottle on the table and wondered why he even bothered. Hell, it didn't do him any good, no matter how much he drank. The damn nine millimeter lying next to it would do a much better job of putting him out of his misery, but he hadn't been able to do that seven years ago and he couldn't do it now. He moved through each day, doing his job and caring about nothing. But now he had the opportunity to take down the son of a bitch who had destroyed his family. And suddenly everything changed.

His ability to take the edge off his waking nightmare had evidently grown impotent with the arrival of his guests. He clenched his jaw hard against the bitter words he wanted to shout into the dark night. Rachel Larson had waltzed into his life hardly more than twenty-four hours ago and already nothing was the same. He couldn't drown the demons from his past. He couldn't sleep and didn't really care to eat. He only forced himself to do so because it was necessary for survival.

Survival.

He laughed at his misnomer. He wasn't surviving, he was existing. He reached for the bottle, but hesitated. What was the point? Whenever he closed his eyes Rachel would still haunt his dreams, waking as well as sleeping. And then the other memories would creep in. The betrayal would stab at his battered heart for allowing the son of Gabriel DiCassi into his home. For allowing the woman who had once been Angel's lover to enter his dreams at all.

Sloan knew better than to direct any of his rage at the kid. The kid was innocent, a victim just like him. He closed his eyes and forced the boy's image from his mind. He didn't want to know this child, didn't want to care about him.

Sloan swore under his breath. He was pathetic. His *existence* was pathetic. But something so deep inside him that he couldn't touch it, and he sure as hell couldn't name it, urged him to keep going... wouldn't let him quit.

He picked up the tequila bottle with the intention of giving those demons a run for their money anyway when something in his peripheral vision snagged his attention. A movement near the pool. Adrenaline surged through his veins, sending every nerve ending on alert. Sloan slowly placed the unopened bottle back on the table. He picked up the Beretta as he silently stood and started in the direction of the pool. He stayed near the edge of the light's reach, cloaking himself in the concealing darkness.

Taking the weapon off safety, Sloan prepared to move around the wall of foliage. He listened intently for any sound. Nothing. He considered only for one moment the possibility that he had imagined the movement. He had seen it all right. Someone or something was out there. It wouldn't be Pablo, he was gone for the evening. Rachel and her son had gone to bed an hour ago.

Sloan slipped between two large potted plants. The lights shimmered off the water at the shallow end of the pool. He inched closer, then swung around the palm tree into the open area around the pool, his weapon leveled on the first thing that made a move.

Josh.

Sloan's hand shook as he lowered the weapon. His body weak with receding adrenaline, he set the safety. It wasn't until that definitive click that Josh looked up from his position near the edge of the pool.

"I founded my bear." He displayed the stuffed animal to back up his announcement, then smiled unsuspectingly up at Sloan. "He was lost."

A harsh breath shuddered from Sloan's lungs. Dammit, he could have—

He forced the thought away.

"What are you doing out here, kid?" He forced his body to relax from its battle-ready posture.

Those big dark eyes blinked at his brusque tone. "I waked up and couldn't find my bear." He hugged the toy close. "My mommy was in the baf'tub…so I comed to look for my bear."

Sloan glanced at the French doors leading to the room Rachel and her son occupied, one door stood open. He swore. Josh's eyes grew even rounder.

"Mommy'll wash your mouth with soap." He nodded knowingly.

Sloan heaved another heavy breath. He motioned for the kid to stand up. "Come on, I'll take you to your mother."

Josh gazed longingly at the pool, then back up at Sloan. "We can't go swimmin'?"

Sloan shook his head. "You can talk to your mother about that. Let's go."

Josh scrambled to his feet, his bear wrapped in one arm. He looked at the weapon in Sloan's hand, then at Sloan. "You want t'play army? I could play wif your gun."

"This isn't a toy," he explained. Sloan nodded toward the house. "Come on, kid, it's late."

Josh obeyed. Sloan scrubbed a hand over his face and tried to calm his racing heart. The thought of what could have happened throbbed inside his head. He had never once fired a weapon without identifying the target first, but he was edgy. It could happen. It wasn't impossible. The woman would just have to keep a better watch on her kid. Sloan glanced at the boy. Wearing nothing but a T-shirt and his underwear, it was obvious he had been in bed. Why the hell didn't Rachel have the door locked?

The kid suddenly stopped and peered up at Sloan. "If you had a little boy, mister, then I could play army wif him."

A chunk of ice formed in Sloan's stomach. If he had a little boy...

Rachel towel-dried her hair and then studied her reflection as she brushed it. The huge tub full of hot water had felt great to her sore muscles. She would be surprised if she could move come morning. Sloan had really pushed her hard today.

Or maybe she had pushed herself. She examined the details of her reflection in the mirror. Not failing was extremely important to her, especially where he was concerned. She wanted to please him, and she couldn't fully understand that. His approval shouldn't mean nearly so much to her.

Rachel's gaze lowered to her nude body. He had undressed her last night. She swallowed, and couldn't help but wonder what he thought of her body. Were her small breasts a disappointment to him? Men like him probably liked full, voluptuous breasts. And she was too skinny, even she recognized that. She was fairly tall, about five-seven. She wasn't blond, she wasn't beautiful or big breasted. Then there was the cesarean scar.

Rachel sighed.

What the man thought of her in that respect shouldn't matter to her. She wasn't here to improve her social life.

Rachel laughed at that one. What social life? She hadn't had one in nearly half a decade. Hadn't been kissed, or touched intimately, by a man in the same. Her body trembled at the sudden memory of Sloan's powerful arms around her. She closed her eyes and enjoyed the warmth that being near him usually elicited. She had to be losing her mind to allow a man so dangerous to make her feel so…needy.

"Enough, Rachel," she scolded. She snatched up her panties and tugged them on. The only thing she should feel for Sloan was fear. And respect, she amended. It took a great deal of courage for him to face this nightmare again, and she knew that. She would have to be a fool not to. But no amount of admiration or gratitude should send her hormones into hyperactivity.

She slipped into her gown. The cool, silky material felt heavenly against her skin. Rachel took a deep breath and stared at her reflection in the mirror. "Sloan is not the kind of man you fall in love with. This is a business arrangement…not a lovers' liaison."

With that declaration firmly resounding in her ears, she padded back into the bedroom to check on her sleeping child. Josh had worn himself out chasing Pablo's shiny red ball this evening. The man's patience was never ending.

The bed was empty. Rachel's heart slammed against her rib cage. "Josh?" The sound leaked out of her with the air in her lungs. She turned all the way around in the room. "Josh!" Was he hiding? Had he awakened and decided to play—

The door to the courtyard stood open. Fear snaked around her chest and squeezed.

The pool.

Her feet had taken her out the door before the rest of her realized she was moving. "Josh!"

How could she have been so careless? Did she forget to lock the door? What if…

Rachel trembled, then dragged in a gulp of air. He had to be here. He had to be all right. "Josh!" she screamed again.

"Mommy!"

She raced in the direction of her son's voice. He

was hugging his bear, walking toward her from the direction of the pool. Sloan was with him, his gun in his hand.

A new kind of fear saturated her senses. He would never harm her son…would he? Rachel's gaze locked on Josh. Those dark eyes, the dark hair, the shape of his face. He looked so very much like his father. Rage boiled up inside her.

Without another hesitation she flew to her child and scooped him up in her arms. "What are you doing?" she demanded, her fury aimed at Sloan. The idea that he would go near her son with a gun in his hand shook her to the very core of her being. He was still wearing the shoulder holster. Why wasn't the gun holstered? "Are you insane? Why do you have that gun in your hand?"

Clearly confused, Sloan looked from her to his gun and back. "What the hell are you talking about? Why weren't you watching your kid?" he countered as he holstered the weapon.

Rachel held Josh closer to her chest. "I don't want to talk about this now." She glowered up at Sloan. "I'll be back in two minutes, and then we'll talk."

"Fine." Fury snapping in his eyes, Sloan pivoted and strode away. Rachel took Josh back to their room and tucked him into bed. She tamped down the anger Sloan's actions fueled. She would not allow her son to be touched by her irritation with the man.

"Why on earth did you go outside, sweetie?" She smoothed the hair from his cherub face. "You should never go outside without Mommy or Mr. Pablo. I couldn't bear it if anything happened to you."

"I'm a big boy," he insisted. "I hadda find my bear. I forgotted him by the pool." His little lips curled down into a frown. "I couldn't play army. I didn't have a gun." He sighed a sleepy sound. "He wouldn't let me go swimmin' or play wif his gun. He said I hadda ask you first."

Ire rushed through Rachel, but she restrained the outburst that threatened. She would finish her business with Sloan shortly. "He's right," she told her son. Though she hated to admit it. "I don't want you playing with guns and you should never go to the pool without my permission. Promise Mommy that you will never do that again."

He sniffed. "Promise," he murmured.

She smiled and gave him a quick peck on the soft cheek. "Good. Now, it's way past time for little boys—and big boys," she amended, "to be asleep."

"Night, Mommy." Josh turned on his side and hugged his bear to his chest.

The memory of where the bear had come from still stirred uneasiness within her. But Josh had made the stuffed animal his new favorite toy. Rachel patted him softly and murmured, "Good night, sweetie." She watched him a moment longer, then pushed to her feet. Her anger renewed itself as she walked as quietly as possible to the door. She closed it carefully behind her and then stormed across the courtyard to where Sloan waited.

Sloan leaned casually against an ornate column that supported the part of the roof that canopied a large area near the French doors leading into the main hall. His expression revealed nothing. Right now Rachel was too annoyed to care what he thought.

"What do you mean carrying an unholstered weapon around Josh?" she demanded, hands on hips.

He straightened. Rachel resisted the urge to take a step back. He cocked one eyebrow and glared down at her. "You should keep closer tabs on your kid. If I hadn't seen him, he'd be facedown in the pool about now."

Anxiety tightened in Rachel's chest at the image his words evoked, but did little to assuage her fury. "What were you doing with the gun?" she insisted.

"I thought we'd been invaded by aliens and I went to check it out. What the hell do you think I was doing with it when I saw movement in the dark?"

A new kind of terror swelled inside her. "You…" She shook her head, unable to voice the unthinkable. She gathered her courage around her and fixed her gaze on his. "Don't ever take that gun out around my son again."

"It's pretty difficult to protect someone without a weapon." He straightened. "What did you come here for, *Miss Larson,* a protector or a babysitter? I'm no nanny."

She blinked back the tears stinging her eyes. God, she hated to cry, but she always cried when she was angry. "Surely you can tell the difference between an intruder and a child!"

"I never discharge my weapon unless I have the target in sight. When I realized it was the kid, I lowered my weapon." He stepped intimidatingly closer. "Contrary to what you appear to believe, I know what I'm doing."

"You actually pointed that thing at my son?" The mixture of fear and anger overwhelmed her then, made her tremble. All other thought ceased. "Just stay away from him." Her voice didn't waver, despite the trembling rampant in her body now.

Renewed anger kindled in that cold blue gaze. "Keep the kid out of my way and we won't have a problem."

"His name is Josh." Rachel took the step of aggression this time. "Little boys are naturally curious. I can't promise you that he'll stay quiet and out of the way. Children play, children explore," she argued, her voice growing higher with each word.

He was truly furious now. His eyes shone with it, his posture shouted it. "I'm surprised you haven't lost him already the way you let him run around here. There are a dozen hazards for kids around this place, besides the damned pool. What were you thinking leaving the door unlocked like that? You can lose your kid in the blink of an eye."

"The way you lost yours?"

The moment the words left her mouth Rachel knew she had made a mistake. Overstepped her bounds. Her anger died an instant death. All emotion drained from Sloan's expression, from his eyes. The look of devastation that remained ripped her heart into shreds.

"Yes," he said, the word an expression of pain. "Exactly like that."

A tear rolled past Rachel's lashes and trickled down her cheek before she could swipe it away. "I'm sorry," she said tautly. "That was uncalled for. What happened to your son wasn't your fault."

"That's where you're wrong. It was entirely my fault. I made a mistake." His gaze leveled on hers. "Don't make the same one I did."

He turned from her then. More tears trekked down her cheeks, but she didn't care. She was wrong. She had no right to say such hurtful words.

"Wait." Rachel touched his arm, he hesitated, but didn't look back. "You can't believe what happened was your fault." Her fingers tightened on his muscular arm to relay the sincerity of her words. "It was Angel—not you. You didn't do anything wrong."

He turned back to her then, his eyes on fire with some emotion she couldn't quite define. His fingers encircled her wrist and pulled her close. He glared down at her. "You don't have a clue what I've done wrong in my life. All your misguided sympathy isn't going to change the past, so don't waste it on me." His grip tightened. "I don't need your pity, lady. If that's all you've got to offer you'd better go inside and see after your kid."

Rachel jerked free of his hold and glared at him. "Go to hell, Sloan," she snapped.

"I'm already there, or hadn't you noticed?"

Knowing the truth in his words, but unable to bear his indifference, Rachel hurried back to her room.

To Josh.

Chapter Five

Time proved no ally to Sloan in the matter of his houseguests, or his work. By Thursday he still had no leads on Angel's current whereabouts. Sloan could not connect him to any recent assassinations in the States. Things had apparently gotten too hot for him since the Larson hit to risk high-profile assignments in the good old U.S. of A. The bastard was probably doing most of his dirty work abroad these days.

Sloan blew out a breath of frustration. As was now his habit, the house was quiet for a long time before he came inside for the night. Even in this twenty thousand square foot home he felt crowded with Rachel and her son scurrying about. They had only been here three days and four nights, and it felt far too long already. Their presence disturbed him in ways he couldn't or didn't want to name. Pablo appeared determined to make an affair of preparing and serving dinner to the two. So Sloan ate alone, after the others had left the kitchen. Tonight he had skipped the affair altogether. Instead, he sat in his office, staring at a blank computer screen.

He glanced at the near empty bottle on the desk and released a disgusted breath. It was a sad state of existence when that much tequila couldn't even begin to put him out of his misery. He had attempted to methodically numb himself to the desires of his body and the memories he'd just as soon not recall. When that failed, he decided on something else with which to occupy his rambling mind. Research. He needed to know how Angel always found her so easily. Rachel wasn't a stupid person. She had likely taken steps to elude the bastard.

Anything was better than allowing the words she had said to him the other night to replay in his head. *The way you lost yours…? What happened to your son wasn't your fault.*

But it was.

And nothing could change that.

Pushing all else aside, Sloan entered Rachel Larson's name and social security number, which he easily found in her purse, into the Colby Agency system and waited. Victoria continued to authorize his use of her data banks. Hell, he had helped put it together. It wasn't like she could have kept him out. He smiled when he considered his longtime friend. Maybe when he had his head on a little straighter he would give her a call.

Sloan quickly dismissed that idea. His days at the agency were just another part of his past he had worked hard to forget. No point in digging up bones better left alone.

A few minutes later Rachel Larson's life story appeared on the screen before him. The agency ran a thorough background search on all prospective clients. Though Victoria had sent Rachel to him, she would still be investigated. If anything suspicious had been discovered, Sloan would have gotten a call immediately, alerting him before Rachel's arrival in Florescitaf.

His attention focused on the details emanating from the screen. Twenty-four now, Rachel had dropped out of college at nineteen and disappeared from public life. Her father, Colin Larson of the State Department, had been assassinated in his own home a few weeks prior to her disappearance. Sloan could well imagine Angel's motivation for that one. With the kind of security Larson no doubt had, someone on the inside was almost a must. Rachel had been the key to Angel's success. Her statement and alibi had been thoroughly investigated during the weeks following the murder. The case was listed as unsolved. Since her disappearance she apparently supported herself with the huge estate left by her independently wealthy father.

"Bingo," he muttered. That's how Angel kept such close tabs on her all these years. Shaking his head, Sloan stared at Rachel Larson's five-year-old driver's license photo on his computer screen. No matter how careful she had been in her efforts to elude

Angel, she had dipped into that bank account whenever necessary and Angel had her. She couldn't have been any less subtle if she had sent him a Christmas card from each new location. Angel had that account wired, and she never suspected a thing.

Still too sober and restless to sleep, Sloan picked up her purse and prowled through it again. A curse hissed past his lips when he found a transaction slip from the International Bank of Mexico in Chihuahua. Rachel had withdrawn a fairly large sum of money the day she arrived. No wonder Angel had found her down here so quickly.

Next, Sloan opened a plain, unmarked envelope that looked a little worse for wear. He withdrew a handful of dog-eared snapshots and shuffled through them. Rachel and an older man. Her father, he decided on closer inspection. He couldn't reconcile the woman at home in sweats and a T-shirt with this younger version decked out in sequins and pearls at some ritzy social function. In the pictures her smile was wide and mischievous. Those big brown eyes glittered with happiness, as did the matching ones belonging to her father. Her full lips were rosy and so were her cheeks.

Sloan frowned. Now those eyes were weary and underscored with dark circles. Her lips and cheeks were no longer so rosy. Fatigue and fear had long since robbed Rachel Larson of the happiness that once glittered in her eyes. Sloan tucked the pictures back into the envelope, then shoved the contents back into the purse and tossed it aside. Now she was here, in his home, with Angel's son. Her life had taken a terrible twist five years ago. He glanced back at the screen. Josh had been born in St. Luke's Hospital in Arizona. According to the hospital records, there had been complications and a cesarean section had been necessary.

"I'm thirsty."

As if somehow his ruminations had summoned him, Sloan swiveled in his chair to find the boy hovering near his office door. His own son had been able to sneak up on him like that. Their innocence somehow slipped under his acute detection skills. Sloan fought the emotions that warred inside him each time confronted with Rachel's son.

"Where's your mother?"

The boy rubbed his eyes with his fist. "She's too sleepy, she can't wake up."

Perpetually wary, Sloan pushed to his feet and made the trip from his office to Rachel's room. The kid followed. Sloan paused to check the alarm. It was armed. No way had anyone gotten in without alerting him.

The glow from the adjoining bathroom light cast a slight halo over Rachel's still form when he entered the guest room. She was sleeping soundly. Sloan supposed that today's additional laps in the pool had done her in. Regret trickled through him before he could stop it. He did what he had to do. Aggression wasn't in her nature. He needed her pissed off so she would work harder. If she hated him, that was all the better. This ill-fated attraction he could feel building between them had to be kept under control.

"See," the kid whispered.

Sloan glanced at his expectant face. "You should be asleep, too."

The kid shook his head adamantly. "I'm thirsty."

Sloan sighed in frustration. Why couldn't the kid sleep like his mother? He swore under his breath. "Fine," he relented. "I'll get you a drink."

Sloan stalked through the house, flipping lights on as necessary to illuminate the way. He didn't have to look back to know the boy followed him. He flipped one more switch as he passed through the doorway and the kitchen's overhead lights blinked on. He pulled a glass from the cupboard and filled it half full with tap water. He made a mental note to add disposable cups for the bathroom to Pablo's shopping list. Then the kid could get his own drink when he woke up in the middle of the night like this.

He thrust the glass at the boy. "Here."

"Milk, please." Those big, dark eyes full of unhurried expectation mocked Sloan's impatience.

He dashed the water into the sink and plopped the glass onto the counter. He gritted his teeth against the emotions churning inside him as he reached into the fridge and snagged the container of milk. Holding the door open with his hip, he poured the milk into the glass, then chunked the container back onto a shelf. He kneed the fridge door closed as he held the glass out to the boy waiting patiently less than three feet away.

The kid turned the glass up and gulped down half the contents, leaving a picture-perfect milk mustache.

"Go back to bed when you're finished," Sloan ordered as he left the room. Irritated beyond reason and with his gut tied in a thousand knots, he dropped back into the chair at his desk. He glared at the image of Rachel on the computer screen. "Why the hell did you come looking for me?" he muttered. "I told you I wasn't the right man for this job."

Resigned to his fate, Sloan focused his full attention on the string of words displayed before him.

"That's my mommy."

Sloan jerked at the sound of the kid's voice. Josh walked right up to Sloan and pointed at the image on the screen.

"How'd she get in there?"

"You're supposed—"

"I wanna see," Josh interrupted as he climbed onto Sloan's lap.

Startled, Sloan stared at the kid, unsure what he should do. His first thought was to run like hell. He blinked. But he was a grown man. He wasn't about to run from a kid.

"Mom-mee," he pronounced slowly, pointing to the name printed beneath the picture. "What does that say?" he demanded then, tugging on Sloan's shirt when he failed to answer quickly enough.

"Hair color, brown," Sloan said crossly. What was he supposed to do now?

"Read Mommy's story to me," the child insisted as he settled against Sloan's chest.

At the feel of the small body resting against him, something stirred beneath Sloan's sternum, an unfamiliar tightening making it hard to breathe. "I don't think—"

"Read it to me," he repeated sleepily.

Sloan swallowed hard. One instinct warred with the other. Push him away, hold him closer. He didn't know what to feel.

"'Kay?" The plea was hardly a whisper.

Sloan began to read the words on the screen, leaving out the parts not intended for small ears. He lost himself to the detailed summary that was Rachel Larson's life. Josh snuggled more closely against him, curling into a fetal position, as the information he wouldn't understand or even remember tomorrow unfolded regarding his mother.

Finally, there were no more words to read. An odd silence filled the room. Too many emotions to sort strummed through Sloan. Reluctantly, he lowered his head and looked at the sleeping child in his lap. The memory of holding his own son exactly like this when he would be working late in his home office played through his mind. The sound of his son's young voice, his rambunctious laughter. The smile that could make the worst day feel like the best. Sloan closed his eyes to fight the tears that burned there. He swallowed against the ache building at the back of his throat. His arms instinctively tightened around the small boy cuddled so close to him.

He would gladly give his life for just one more moment with his son. How could God be so unmerciful as to allow his child to die, then sentence Sloan to life? He clenched his jaw as a single tear slipped past his restraint. He sucked in a harsh breath and blinked rapidly to slow the emotion still brewing, threatening to make a bigger fool of him than he already was. His son was dead. He couldn't change that. Couldn't go back.

He stood, cradling Josh gently against his chest. Without making a sound he took the child back to his room and placed him in the bed with his mother. Sloan stared down at him for a long while after that. He would not care about this child, he promised himself. No attachments, no bonds. Sloan would do the only thing he could for him—he would destroy the evil that threatened him and his mother. If it was the last thing he ever did, he would kill Angel.

Their routine had fallen into a rhythm of sorts the past couple of days, in Rachel's opinion. She worked hard to follow Sloan's instructions to the letter. She rarely spoke to him unless she needed to question some instruction she didn't quite understand. Each day when the morning workout session was complete, Sloan disappeared while Rachel played in the pool with Josh. Each afternoon she honed her fledgling marksmanship skills. After the first couple of shots at each session, Sloan insisted she wear ear protection. He wanted her to become accustomed to the sound, thus a couple of shots without the headset.

Rachel was proud of her progress so far. She hadn't made that bull's-eye yet, but she always hit within the circles. She could control the recoil better, and her balance. Sloan was right about one thing, it was all in the way you held yourself. *Think of the weapon as an extension of your body,* he would say. And he was right, technique was everything. She felt tremendously more confident now. It felt good to be able to protect herself, at least to some extent. A few days ago she hadn't even known how to fire a weapon, much less load one.

There had been no indication other than the bear the day she found Sloan that Angel knew her whereabouts. But Rachel knew his method of operation; he would strike when she least expected it. He would come. And she had to be ready.

After dinner each evening Josh watched television for a while, and Rachel sketched with a pencil and plain pad of paper. It kept her occupied. Fortunately Sloan had a satellite which picked up Josh's favorite cartoons. Bedtime came early, however. She needed all the rest she could get to keep up with Sloan's demands. He wasn't an easy taskmaster. Especially if he felt she wasn't giving her all. She had already swam at least a dozen extra laps in the pool each day because he wasn't satisfied.

She sighed when she thought of his refusal to join

them for dinner. But Pablo made things a great deal more pleasant. His patience with Josh never seemed to end. Each time Rachel considered how strained the atmosphere would be without Pablo, she thanked her lucky stars he was here most of the time. She wondered if he disappeared to his own home late at night.

Rachel sat down on the side of the bed and watched her son sleep. His rosy cheeks and newly tanned skin made her yearn to hug him and kiss him from head to toe just like she did when he was a baby, but that would only wake him. Josh was always ready for naptime after his energetic romp in the pool and leisurely lunch in the kitchen. Considering this morning's rigorous workout, Rachel felt ready for a nap herself. She yawned. It was Friday, surely Sloan would cut her some slack.

Maybe she would rest her eyes for just a few minutes anyway. She was an adult, she didn't have to ask for permission. She had thirty more minutes before she was to meet Sloan in the *gym*, as he called it. She eased down beside her son and snuggled close to his warm little body. She loved him so very much. She couldn't possibly live without him. Her last thought before she drifted off was of how unbearable it must be for Sloan living with the loss of his son.

Hell. He'd said it was hell.

"Señora."
Rachel's eyes fluttered opened as Pablo gently shook her shoulder.

"Señora Larson, Señor Sloan is waiting for you."

Rachel sat up quickly. She checked the clock on the bedside table. 3:00 p.m. She had slept for an entire hour. She raked her fingers through her mussed hair, pushing it back from her face and met Pablo's concerned gaze. Sloan would be royally PO'd. Why hadn't he sent for her sooner?

"I'll be right there," she assured Pablo.

He nodded and scurried away to deliver her message. Rachel scooted off the bed and padded to the adjoining bathroom. She felt groggy after her unintentional power nap. She hadn't slept that long, or that soundly in the middle of the afternoon in ages. After taking care of essential business, she quickly brushed out her hair and straightened her sleep-tousled clothes. She dropped a quick kiss on her still sleeping child's sweet head and hurried from the room.

She had to admit that Sloan had been right about the soreness as she made her way down the long hall. She had worked most of it out. She felt stronger already. When Angel came, and she knew he would, she wanted to be ready. She felt certain that it would take all the courage and strength she could muster to face him. He would be out for blood this time.

Her blood.

And probably Sloan's.

Pablo and Sloan were talking quietly when she reached the great room. They stopped abruptly when she walked in. Rachel felt certain that she and Josh had been the subject of their hushed discussion.

"Josh is still sleeping," she informed Pablo, then looked from one man to the next. Pablo looked downright embarrassed, Sloan looked like he always did—indifferent. They'd been talking about her all right.

"Not to worry, *señora,* I will take very good care of him."

Pablo made her the same promise each day, and he always did just as he said he would. Rachel was immensely grateful for all that he did for her son. Pablo made life with Sloan tolerable.

Rachel smiled her thanks, then turned to Sloan. "I'm ready."

"Today we're going to do something a little different," he said without preamble. Evidently not deeming clarification necessary, he led the way from the room.

Uncertain whether his announcement was good or bad, Rachel followed. She noted again what a strong man Sloan was. Tall, muscular build. Broad, broad shoulders and a lean waist. Cute butt, she thought with a tiny smile. The way his jeans hugged him was…inspiring. Heat flagged her cheeks. She was acting like a silly schoolgirl. She tried to look anywhere but at his well-formed behind as they continued toward the workout room. She never had this kind of reaction to a man. Not even all those years ago to—

Rachel forced that thought away.

A rare, pleasant breeze shifted her hair around her shoulders. The temperature was hot, but not as unbearably so as yesterday, she decided. What kind of woman would it take to please a man like Sloan, she suddenly wondered? Rachel scolded herself mentally for allowing her musings to wander in that direction again, but somehow she simply could not help herself. She had already decided that she wasn't his type—not that she wanted to be. But she felt certain that skinny brunettes were not his playmates of choice. He would be an aggressive lover, she decided. One who would please his partner over and over before he took pleasure himself.

Her pulse reacted to the vivid fantasy that leaped to mind with the thought. Startled by her own musings, Rachel banished the forbidden thoughts and images of the man in front of her. She needed him rightly enough, but not for anything other than the job she had hired him to do.

Rachel frowned as she considered that he still had not named a price to her. She would have to ask him about that later. If she could get him to talk to her. The only words that had passed between them thus far were the orders he snapped.

Sloan paused near the large blue mats where they usually began their morning workout. She hoped he didn't have more of the same planned. She had flexed and contracted every muscle in her body too many times already.

Well maybe not every muscle, she amended as her gaze swept over Sloan's masculine frame once more. The new thought disrupted Rachel's equilibrium.

How could she be thinking like that about this man? About any man?

He shrugged off the holster and laid it aside. "Starting today we're going to alternate between weapons training and hand-to-hand defense tactics," he told her in his usual, indifferent tone.

Rachel's frown deepened. She chewed her lower lip a moment as he slid the two mats closer together. "You mean like karate moves or something?" she asked hesitantly.

He studied her for a moment, those piercing blue eyes trying doubly hard to see inside her head. "Do you have a problem with hand-to-hand?"

Yes, she wanted to shout. She didn't need to touch him, or have him touch her any more than was necessary. Her imagination was already in overdrive.

"No," she said instead. "I just wanted to be sure we were talking about the same thing."

"Good." Sloan braced his legs wide apart and motioned with one long-fingered hand for her to come to him. "Charge me," he instructed.

"W-what?" she stammered. Rachel smoothed her palms over her loose T-shirt. She didn't want to charge him. The outcome surely would not be good. For her.

"Is there something wrong with your hearing today?" he demanded. "I said *charge me.*"

What had put a burr under his saddle? She had noticed his more uncivil than usual mood this morning, but she had hoped it would have worn off by now. She moistened her lips and took a small step, then stalled. "I'm not sure if I understand exactly what you mean," she hedged.

He walked straight up to her, too close. So close she had to back up to keep from being nose to chest with him. Her traitorous body responded immediately to his nearness.

"What's to understand?" He glared down at her. "What do you do when a man comes at you like this?"

She attempted a shrug, but his fierce gaze stopped her. "Run?"

"I would catch you before you got halfway across the room." Sloan blew out a breath of frustration. "You need to know how to put a man down."

Rachel laughed nervously. "I couldn't possibly put you down. You're much…much stronger than me." And bigger, with far too many bulging muscles, she didn't add.

"If you want to learn," he growled, "you'll do what I tell you." He moved back to the far side of the mat and assumed a readied stance. "Now, come at me."

Afraid to comply, but even more afraid not to, for fear of disappointing him, Rachel marched straight up to him as he had done her. "Okay," she began nervously, "What now?"

He rolled his eyes. Impatience evidenced itself in every angle of his face. "Hit me."

Dismayed, it took a moment for words to form. "I can't do that."

He pinned her with that icy gaze. "Do it."

Rachel blinked, uncertain. "Do we really need to

do this? Isn't there another way?" Fury blazed in his eyes, sending her back a step.

"Do you want me to help you, or not? You need to know how to defend yourself. It might save your life sometime. Or maybe your kid's. This isn't a game. Now, *do it*."

Exasperated, Rachel shoved a handful of hair behind her ear and nodded. "All right." He looked ready to pounce on her if she didn't obey. "Where should I hit you?"

"Just swing at me," he growled.

Rachel drew back and aimed her fist at his taut abdomen. Just before she made contact with her target he moved. The next thing Rachel knew she was lying flat on her back on the mat, the wind emptied from her lungs.

He extended his hand toward her. "You've already had your nap." One corner of his grim mouth hitched up in a facsimile of a smile. "Try to stay on your feet this time."

She accepted his hand and pulled up. He'd done that on purpose. She was sure of it. He knew she wasn't ready for a move like that. "I can do better," she said crossly. "You surprised me, that's all." She lifted her chin a notch when doubt clouded his expression. "Shall we try it again?"

"It might help if you acted like you mean it." He cocked his tawny head and studied her stature. "I've seen smaller women than you take down a man larger than me."

Rachel planted her hands on her hips and studied him just as he had her. "You know what they say, the bigger they are the harder they fall."

He stepped intimidatingly nearer. "Put your money where your mouth is, baby," he rasped.

Anger boiled up inside her. "I'm not your baby."

"Your choice." He readied for the next round. "Hit me with your best shot, *Miss Larson*."

Rachel aimed for his belligerent face this time. He snagged her arm and flipped her onto her back once more. She grimaced as if in real pain from the fall. A flash of concern flitted through his gaze as he offered his hand. Furious, she grabbed his hand with both hers and jerked with all her might. He stumbled, then went down as she rolled in the opposite direction. One muscular leg snagged her before she could move far enough away. She struggled, but he was on top of her too fast.

"Get off me," she ordered, breathless.

He pinned her arms above her head. His glare was deadly. "Make me."

She squirmed in his hold. His heavy body covered hers, trapping her and making her aware of every male contour. "How am I supposed to do that?" Her heart pounded so hard she was sure he could hear it. "I can't imagine how you stay in business with the way you treat your clients," she huffed. "Whatever happened to customer satisfaction?"

"I haven't had an unsatisfied customer yet," he

said huskily, something new kindling to life in his eyes, which he promptly blinked away.

Awareness shivered through her, and Rachel had the strangest feeling that his words were more promise than fact. Or threat, depending on how one looked at it.

"Are you going to do something or are we going to lie here all day?"

A new blast of anger shot through her as she considered her limited options. She was trapped, there was nothing she could do. Anxiety suddenly coursed through her veins, adding to the uncertainty mushrooming inside her. She had to do something.

He shifted his weight slightly, Rachel tensed, then reacted. She jerked her right knee up, aiming for his crotch. He twisted his lower body in a protective move, his attention diverted briefly from her face. Rachel bit his left shoulder as hard as she could.

Swearing hotly, he tried to pull away, she followed. He rolled, Rachel in tow. She fought hard, kicking at every opportunity. One hand slipped free of his hold. She grabbed a handful of his hair. Another ear-scorching curse echoed around them. He was on top of her again. This time he was madder than hell. His breath, as ragged as hers, fanned her face. Rage glittered in his eyes, he trembled with the force of it. She could feel it radiating from his tense muscles, especially those that marked him male. Fear, more real than any she had ever felt in his presence, washed over her.

"Let me up," she demanded, her voice quivering with the fear manifesting itself in every fiber of her being.

He shook with the effort of restraint. The battle taking place in his eyes frightened her beyond anything he could have said.

"Please," she whispered when he didn't move. "You're scaring me."

He blinked, clearly rattled. He released her and pushed to his knees. Rachel scooted away from him then, to the other side of the mat.

He swallowed hard, her gaze followed the stiff movement, before the feel of his eyes on her summoned her gaze to his.

"Are you all right?"

She nodded and scrambled to her feet. "If that's all," she said, going for calm, but falling well short, "I think I'll just go back…" She gestured toward the door, as she backed in that direction. Whatever had just happened, she didn't want to hang around and analyze it.

He stood as she reached the door. Before he could speak again, Rachel spun away and hurried back to the house.

He had lost control there for a minute. Allowed some emotion she couldn't fully analyze to push him too close to the edge. Was his hatred for her growing rather than diminishing? Maybe she had made a mistake in coming here.

Distressed and certain she didn't want to be alone,

Rachel went in search of Josh and Pablo. Maybe Sloan was dangerous, she contemplated. Maybe Victoria Colby didn't know him anymore. After what he had been through, Rachel was surprised he hadn't lost his mind long ago.

She slowed to catch her breath. Maybe he had.

She closed her eyes and allowed the last of the fear to drain away. When it was gone, all that remained was the desire elicited by the feel of his body pressed against hers.

Rachel shook her head in defeat. Obviously she was at least a little crazy, too.

How could she be drawn to Sloan when he so clearly despised her? *Hormones, Rach,* she told herself. Nothing but proximity and hormones. *You'll get over it.*

Chapter Six

Sloan glanced at his watch, 6:00 a.m. What the hell was she doing up so early on a Sunday morning? His gaze shifted back to the courtyard, to Rachel. As he stood quietly in the open doorway leading from the hall, he studied the movements of her hands. She sat at the patio table several feet away, her profile turned toward him. She appeared so deep in concentration that she hadn't noticed his presence.

She was drawing. She had been an art major in school, he remembered from reading her bio. He ruthlessly squashed the other memories that wanted to surface from two nights ago. The feel of Josh in his arms. He shook his head. He wasn't going there again.

Rachel looked so intent. Her right hand moved quickly, but with a light touch. Her hair was pulled up into some sort of loose bundle on top of her head, leaving her down-turned face unobscured. The delicate features of her profile were achingly feminine. Her lips were very full, and with much more color than when she had first arrived almost a week ago. The sun, as well as the feeling of security she had gained since her arrival had brought that same rosy color back to her cheeks. Though tanned slightly, her skin looked as smooth and soft as satin. He knew from experience that it would feel very much like satin.

She sat with those unbelievably long legs propped on the table. She wore shorts today, which displayed a fair amount of toned thighs. Sloan licked his dry lips as his gaze traveled from bare feet to the hem of khaki shorts. The tank top hugged her body well. He wondered if her small breasts were unrestrained today as they usually were. He had noticed on more than one occasion the tight peaks, had felt the firm swell against him when their bodies touched during training. For the life of him he couldn't explain why he found those small breasts so damned intriguing. There was absolutely nothing extraordinary about them, except the intense desire with which he wanted to taste them.

Rachel had gained a couple of pounds, which was good. She was eating right. Probably for the first time in a long while. She was still too thin for his liking. But she was strong, emotionally and physically. He had gotten a glimpse of her fierce determination more than once. She wouldn't say die, no matter how hard he pushed her. He had the distinct impression that she would pass out from exhaustion before she would admit defeat. He admired that quality. Hell, truth be told, he admired a lot more than that. He shifted, his jeans suddenly tight with his growing arousal. He cursed himself again. To his infinite irritation he had lost count of the number of times he had been unable to control his thoughts in that direction where she was concerned.

His behavior day before yesterday shamed him still. How could he have gone so far out of control? So many emotions had gotten all twisted inside him. Josh. Rachel. His murdered wife and son. Angel. He couldn't think, he could only react. He knew he hadn't physically hurt her, but he had frightened her. He had wanted to kiss her so badly. Hell, he hadn't wanted simply to kiss her, he had wanted to take her, whether she wanted him or not. The effort required to force himself back under control had been monumental. He let go a heavy breath. There was no excuse for his behavior. He owed her an apology. No, he owed her much more than that.

They had hardly spoken since. She kept her distance. And he hadn't touched her again. Isn't that what he'd wanted?

Suddenly, she looked up, then turned to him. Her breath caught, he saw the quick movement of her breasts as she inhaled sharply. Her tongue darted out to trace the fullness of her slightly parted lips. It was his turn to have difficulty breathing then. He straightened and started toward her. Her gaze traced his body, making him that much harder. He could almost feel the touch of her eyes as she slowly examined his bare chest where his shirt fell open.

"You're up early," he remarked with more non-chalance than he felt as he sat down across the table from her.

She blinked, clearly startled. By his presence or her own wayward thoughts, he couldn't be sure. But there was no way to ignore the way she had looked at him a moment ago or the flush on her cheeks now. The table shook with her sudden move to get her feet off, then underneath it.

When she was settled, her shuttered gaze met his. "I wanted to work on my drawings without any distraction," she admitted hesitantly.

Sloan took a deep resolute breath and leveled his gaze on her wary one. He wasn't a man to mince words. "I owe you an apology. There's no excuse for the way I behaved the past couple of days, especially Friday afternoon. It won't happen again."

Her mouth dropped open, but she quickly snapped it shut. She nodded slowly as if considering his statement. "All right."

"Good." Sloan held out his hand then and her eyes rounded with uncertainty. He wiggled his fingers. "Don't be shy, Miss Larson, let me have a look."

She rubbed at her neck as if only just realizing it ached from staring down at her work for so long. "It's nothing. Just some drawings I started the other night. You wouldn't be interested." She refused to look at him now.

He leaned forward and tugged the pad from her fingers. "Why don't you let me be the judge of that?"

She started to run her fingers through her hair, thought better of it, obviously remembering the way she had it stacked atop her head, then crossed her arms over her tight little breasts. Damn, he wanted to touch her. The desire swelled so swiftly inside him that it overwhelmed all other thought for the space of two beats. Sloan forced his gaze to the pad of paper in his hand. It was a writing tablet. A frown lined his forehead. Definitely not the right kind of pad for drawing.

"I lost my sketch pad on the trip down," she explained quickly as if reading his mind. "I hope you don't mind my using that notebook. Pablo said it would be okay…."

The fear in her eyes annoyed him. Why did she always look at him that way? Except when she thought he was unaware. It was different then. He had seen a glimpse of her own want. But always, always when he looked directly at her, fear replaced all else in those velvety brown depths. Sloan let go the breath he hadn't realized until just then that he'd been holding. He knew he was a hard man, that his words and actions incited fear in most women and men. But after nearly a week with him, she should know that he would never harm her. Well, he supposed his most recent actions had probably lessened her fledgling trust.

"It's fine," he assured her quietly, then lowered his gaze to the pad in his hand. The drawing she had been working on was of Pablo and Josh. She was very good. Her detailing was actually quite excellent. Given the proper tools he was certain she would be a phenomenal artist. He turned back a page. The courtyard. Then another page was her son sleeping. Sloan peered down at the drawing, long and hard. The image of the child sleeping in his arms transposed itself over the image on the page. He hastily turned another page and stared down at the likeness of himself.

"It's not quite finished," she put in quickly, her cheeks flaming redder.

Did she see him that way? he wondered. The grim set of his mouth, the hard expression on his face. Hell, he supposed she did, that was the way he was.

He tossed the pad onto the table. "You're very good." His gaze connected with hers, pride glimmered there.

"Thank you," she murmured. "When I was a little girl, I used to dream about being a famous artist." She smiled, embarrassed that she had said as much out loud.

Sloan could still see the little girl in her now. She was young, too young for an old man much closer to forty than thirty to be looking at her this way. But he wasn't dead, and she tripped way more of his triggers than she should.

"You still could be. You're only twenty-four. Lots of people go back to school after having a child."

She moistened those full lips, his groin reacted. "I wanted to...but I could never leave Josh. I couldn't trust anyone." She shook her head. "It was just a dream."

"It's not too late, Rachel." With much hesitation, she met his gaze. "You could still do it. Don't let one mistake hold you back from living the rest of your life."

She shook her head. "I was a fool. My actions cost my father his life."

The picture of her, dressed in sequins and pearls, smiling and hugging her father, loomed large in his mind. "Angel is a professional. He's honed his talent over the years. You couldn't have known his intent. If he hadn't gotten to your father through you, he would have found another way." Sloan leaned forward again, needing to touch her. He wanted her to believe in herself again. "He wouldn't have stopped until he finished the job one way or another."

She closed her eyes and bowed her head. "Why would anyone have hired Angel to kill my father? He never hurt a soul. He was a good man."

"There's your answer." Unable to help himself, he reached across the table and covered her hand with his own. She started to pull away, but didn't. The feel of her skin beneath his fingers made him ache to feel more. "You've heard the saying Good Men Are Hard To Find? There's a reason for that. The bad guys keep taking them down. Your father stood for something or supported something someone else was at odds with, so they took care of the obstacle he represented."

"He spent days seducing me," she said so softly that he barely heard her, her face still down turned.

She was talking about Angel. Sloan squeezed her hand, urging her to go on.

"He was the most handsome man I had ever seen. I knew he was much too old for me, but that was part of the appeal." She drew in a heavy breath. "He did everything right, as if he knew just what it would take to win me over."

"He did know," Sloan said quietly. "He probably watched you for weeks. He set you up to get what he wanted. What he took from you personally was just a perk."

She looked up then, tears glistening in those wide brown eyes. "How can I ever trust my own judgment again? He didn't just take my innocence—" she swallowed tightly "—he took my trust, my confidence, everything."

He had been right, Sloan thought grimly. Angel had been her first lover. The son of a bitch. "You can get those things back," he assured her. "But you have to earn them. You'll trust yourself again, when you learn to trust others. The same goes for the confidence. It isn't gone, Rachel, it's only cowering behind the fear."

She pushed back from the table and stood abruptly. She shook her head again. "I made a terrible mistake." A tear slid down her cheek. "The sad thing about it is that I can't regret it the way I know I should." She looked at him, emotions warring in her eyes. "If I regret what happened, that means I regret Josh. And I don't." She turned her back, unable to hold his gaze any longer.

Sloan pushed his own chair back and stood. He moved up behind her, trying to comfort her with his nearness. "You're not a bad person for loving your son," he said softly. He closed his eyes against the need to touch her. "Lots of women end up with the wrong man, but they love their children anyway."

She whirled around and glared up at him. "Angel isn't just the wrong man. He's a killer." Her lips trembled. "Look what he did to you. He…he…" She looked away.

Slowly, in spite of his own emotions waging a battle inside him, he reached with both hands and swiped the tears from her cheeks with the pads of his thumbs. She tilted her face to him then, those sweet lips trembled once more. "How can you stand to look at me, knowing what I did?"

Need so strong welled inside him that he felt certain his heart would fail in his chest. He wanted simultaneously to hold her comfortingly and to take her ruthlessly. Sloan tried to restrain the desire whirling out of control, but he couldn't. He had to taste her. "Because I can't help myself," he murmured. He leaned toward her, his lips yearning to meld with hers. She touched him then. Her soft hands splayed across his bare chest. And he was lost to the fight.

Her lips felt every bit as soft as he had known they

would. Her taste was sweet and so very warm. He cradled her head and deepened the kiss. His want was so strong that he had to restrain his savage desire, for fear of hurting her. She moaned beneath his assault, the sound only urging him on. He touched the seam of her lips with the tip of his tongue and she opened. He thrust inside, his body shuddered with need. Her fingers found their way to the sides of his shirt and fisted there, drawing him nearer. He slid one hand down her back and over the swell of her bottom. He pulled her against him, a useless attempt at easing the ache of his throbbing arousal. The feel of her made him crazy to be inside her.

She tried to pull away. Her small palms flattened against his chest and pushed. "Wait," she said between his forceful kisses.

He pulled her mouth back to his and took it hard. She squirmed in his arms. The feel of her body against him only fueling his raging lust. He would not deny himself this pleasure. The need had been building for days. Her body would soon be on fire just like his. The taste of her salty tears jerked him back to reality.

Sloan pulled back as if she had slapped him. She was crying. And he was a bastard. No better than the man who had taken her the first time. He licked the taste of her from his lips and set her safely away from him.

Her hand shook as she wiped her eyes with the back of it. Her mouth was kiss swollen, nearly bruised from his aggression. "I'm sorry, I shouldn't have…"

Just like before, she thought this was her fault. The realization sickened him. He reached to comfort her, but she staggered out of his reach. His entire body hummed with desire. He wanted her, still, so badly he could barely take a breath. She was wrong, she wasn't the fool. He was.

"I have to check on Josh." She pivoted and ran away from him.

Sloan's fists clenched at his sides. Anger and bitterness, fierce and hot filled him, replacing those forbidden feelings. What was he thinking? How could he have allowed himself to kiss her? He had upset her twice now. He had betrayed the memory of his wife and son twofold. Destroyed any trust Rachel might have developed in him or herself. And for what? To satisfy his own selfish needs.

It wouldn't happen again. This was a business arrangement. And, by God, he intended to keep it that way from this point forward.

Rachel twisted the faucet's handles, then quickly closed the shower door to wait for the water to get hot enough to suit her. Distracted with thoughts of the man who consumed her entire existence now, she peeled off her swimsuit top and dropped it to the floor. She tugged her shorts down and kicked them aside, then did the same with her swimsuit bottom.

Despite the fact that it was Sunday, Sloan had insisted that she run the two miles and do as many laps as she could in the pool. He hadn't mentioned working on the hand-to-hand self-defense training again. She wondered as she took a couple of towels from the linen cabinet if it was because of what happened on Friday.

She stepped into the shower and moaned softly as the hot spray of water pelted her skin. It disturbed her immensely that she couldn't choose between the dangerous man who inspired fear in her and the one who had listened with such care this morning. She moistened her lips. And who had kissed her so passionately. Her heart fluttered at the memory. She had known on some level that his kiss would be like that. His touch made her tremble, but his kiss stole through her every defense.

Rachel slowly massaged the shampoo into her hair, then rinsed. As the foamy water slid over her skin she considered the gentle way he had assured her that it wasn't too late for her dreams to come true. She could still go back to school, he had insisted. But there had been nothing gentle at all about his kiss. He had possessed her with such intensity that she had been mindless with her own need. The horrifying memories from the past had shattered the haze in one heart-wrenching instant. She had made a mistake once, could she risk herself again?

She shivered even now, with the hot, soothing water sluicing over her body. Still, the memory of Sloan's kiss sent heat swirling inside her, made her feel that strange restless sensation again. But she shouldn't feel that way. How could she ever trust any man enough to share her body with him? No matter that she trusted Sloan completely with her life—or as completely as one could—she could never trust him with that part of her. Or, perhaps she simply could not trust herself. His words echoed through her. *You'll trust yourself again when you learn to trust others.* But she couldn't do that, not yet.

Not on that level.

Steam billowed around her as she stepped out of the shower. She wrapped her wet hair in a towel, then used the other to methodically dry her skin. She slipped on a T-shirt and panties and padded back into the quiet bedroom. She smiled at her son, sleeping soundly in their bed. He didn't have a care in the world, and that's the way it should be. She wanted to keep him safe and happy for as long as possible. Careful not to wake him, she sat down on the edge of the bed and worked the towel over her hair to dry it more quickly.

Sloan had hardly spoken two words to her since the incident in the workout room. Then suddenly, this morning he had been so giving emotionally as well as physically, she had been caught off guard. Rachel's hands slowed in their work. Could it be that so much time had passed with her avoiding men in general that her time spent with Sloan was waking her long-slumbering feminine senses? Had she played mother and protector for so long that she had forgotten how it felt to be protected? She sighed, confused. She forced herself to examine the time she had spent with Angel. The mere image of him sickened her. She winced and glanced at her cherished son. At least something good had come of all the loss.

Angel had been attentive, making her feel special that such a handsome, mysterious man would take interest in a naive college girl. Her friends had been envious. She and Angel had only been together twice, both times had proven more experimental for her than passionate. At the time she had wondered what all the fuss was about. Admittedly, though it grieved her now, she had felt attraction and a measure of excitement during their time together. She drew in a deep breath and confessed what she knew to be the truth. The feelings Angel had evoked in her were nothing to compare with what she experienced with Sloan's mere touch.

His kiss had robbed her of her senses, at least momentarily. Fear had made her hesitate. Fear of trusting him so fully. Fear of trusting herself that much. What if she made another mistake. What would it cost her this time?

Was she willing to pay the price? Things were different now. She was older and she had Josh to consider. There would be no more foolish love affairs for Rachel. Her son had suffered enough for her mistake. She would not risk making another one of such proportions.

A light rap on the door startled her from her confusing thoughts. She hurried across the room to open the door before another knock sounded. Not properly dressed for company, she peeked around the edge of the door. It was Pablo.

"*Señora*, you must come to the kitchen," he said quietly. His eyes did not reflect the hushed quality of his words.

"Is something wrong?" Her heart reacted to the concern and fear she saw in his dark eyes.

"I'm afraid so. Señor Sloan says you must come right away."

"I have to change." She started to close the door.

"No, *señora*," he insisted. "You must come *now*."

Fear chilled her insides.

"What about Josh?"

"I'll stay with the boy."

She nodded mutely and opened the door wider for him to enter. Please, God, she prayed, please don't let Angel be here. She wasn't ready.

Sloan reread the typewritten note in his hand once more. The son of a bitch was playing his game. A note had been left at the front gate. Tied there with a yellow ribbon. The same kind the entire city of Chicago had tied around trees, mailboxes, and lampposts to signify their prayers for Sloan's missing child. Adrenaline rushed through his body again, awakening the demons so that they roared inside him. He clenched his jaw against the explosion of emotions.

He pushed off the counter and plowed his fingers through his hair. He wasn't concerned about going up against Angel. Sloan would win this time. Angel was going to die, one way or another. It was Rachel that worried him. She needed more time. Hell, maybe the time would never be right for her. She wanted Angel dead, yet he was the father of her child. How would she ever explain that to the kid?

As if on cue, she burst into the room. The pale look of dread claiming her features was reason enough to incite him to murderous thoughts where Angel was concerned.

"What's wrong? Pablo said you had to see me right away." She searched his face, his eyes for some forewarning of what he was about to say.

Sloan handed her the note. It was the only explanation she would need. He waited silently, knowing her devastation would be complete when the impact of the words he had memorized absorbed into her brain.

Rachel,
You have two days to leave Mexico or I'm coming for my son.

Angel

"My, God," she choked out. "He's coming."

"It looks that way." Sloan took the note from her trembling hand.

"Where did it come from?"

Sloan shrugged. "It was left at the gate. The vehicle was dark, maybe black, a sedan. Probably a rental. I didn't get the plate number."

"You're sure whoever it was is gone."

"Positive."

Rachel's fearful gaze locked on his. "He knows we're here. What are we going to do? We can't let him take Josh."

Anger twisted in Sloan's gut at the intensity of her fear. "He isn't going to take Josh."

"How can we stop him?" she demanded, the pitch of her voice rising with the hysteria clearly building inside her.

"He won't win this time, Rachel." Sloan grasped her arms and shook her gently. "I won't allow him to harm you or Josh."

Her head swung from side to side in denial. "He'll kill you." She swallowed tightly. "And he'll kill me, then he'll take Josh."

"We have time to react. Trust me."

"You don't understand," she argued. "He's here. How else could he know how to find me? He's coming for my son."

Sloan struggled for calm. "Listen to me, Rachel." He willed her to look at him. She complied. "If Angel were close, he would simply strike. Sending warning messages is not his style. Someone else sent this message. Someone who's doing Angel's babysitting."

"I don't understand," she said haltingly. "Who?"

He let go a mighty breath. "That I don't know. A girlfriend maybe. As far as I know, Angel has never had a partner." Sloan considered the events in town the afternoon Rachel tracked him down. "Maybe the woman who gave Josh the bear. Whoever it is, he or she is watching you. They've probably kept Angel up to speed."

She frowned, tears threatening. "Are you saying that the note might be a hoax?"

"I wouldn't risk it. Angel may have instructed his messenger to send it in hopes of avoiding a confrontation with me. He'd rather have you back in New Orleans where it would be just the two of you."

Rachel blinked furiously, but a tear trickled down anyway. "We can't let him find my son," she whispered, her ability to stay vertical in serious jeopardy now.

Sloan pulled her close, sliding his arms protectively around her. "Don't worry, we're going to make sure he doesn't find Josh."

"How can we do that?" Her voice was muffled by his shirt.

"We're going to take him someplace Angel will never think to look."

She drew away from Sloan, searching his eyes once more. "Where?"

"Someplace the rest of the world has forgotten."

Chapter Seven

Following Sloan's instructions, Rachel quickly shoved clothes into the dark, canvas backpack. Satisfied that she had everything she and Josh would need for a couple of days, she dropped the pack to the floor and dressed in the darkest clothing she owned. She rarely wore black. The color was Angel's calling card. He always wore black.

Rachel shivered. Her chest felt so tight she could hardly draw in a breath. But now wasn't the time to think about Angel. His warning echoed inside her head. He was coming for his son very soon. They had to hide some place safe. Sloan would take care of Angel. The prospects of Sloan having to face the man worried her, but it was the only way. To kill a man one had to be willing to face him. And Sloan was willing.

She released a shaky breath. Never in her life had she wanted so badly for someone to die. She prayed Sloan could do the job without getting hurt…or worse. Unless Angel died, she and Josh would never be free. Somewhere beneath all her fear and hatred for the father of her child, Rachel knew it was morally wrong to wish for his death. But, God help her, she just couldn't stop herself,

She tugged on the navy blue tank top, then the black shirt Pablo had provided in case she didn't have anything dark enough. The shirt belonged to Sloan. It was much too large for Pablo's small, thin frame. Rachel smoothed her hand over the soft cotton material. Need welled inside her so fast it made her knees weak. She willed the unbidden yearning back into submission. The unfamiliar feelings he evoked in her confused her as well as frightened her. She shouldn't be experiencing these kinds of feelings. Sloan was not the sort of man a woman fell in love with unless she wanted to get her heart broken. Rachel didn't need any more damage to her heart. The only thing she needed from him was his protection.

After tying her shoes, she gave herself a final once-over in the mirror. The big shirt hung on her like a tent, but it would do the trick. She was as ready as she would ever be. All she had to do now was get Josh ready. Her eyes sought the child sleeping soundly in the rumpled bed. Rachel released a heavy breath. Josh was all that really mattered in all this insanity.

Please, God, she prayed, protect my baby.

She grabbed the dark clothes she had selected for Josh and crossed to the bed. She sat down on the edge of the mattress and gently roused her little boy.

"Josh," she murmured. "Wake up, sweetie, we're going to play hide-and-seek." That was what she always told him. Whenever they had to run, whether it was the middle of the night or straight up noon, she always made it a game. "Come on, sweetie," she encouraged when he curled into a little ball beneath the covers. "We have to hurry. Mr. Sloan is going to play, too. He's waiting for us."

Her son's eyes popped open. He rubbed one with his fist. "'Kay." Josh scrambled from under the cover. "Can my bear play, too?" He hugged the stuffed animal to his chest.

"Of course your bear can play." Rachel produced a smile. She refused to consider that the damned thing likely came from Angel or whomever he had watching them. She couldn't really be sure, and Josh loved the fuzzy stuffed animal. There was no reason she could think of to make him leave it behind.

Once bathroom necessities were out of the way, she dressed her son as hastily as she had herself. Rachel pulled on the backpack, then reached for Josh. He hugged his arms around her neck and rested his little head against his mommy's chest. She inhaled deeply of his sweet scent and sent up one final silent prayer. Rachel was halfway to the door when the anticipated knock came.

Dressed completely in black, Pablo waited in the hall. "We must hurry, *señora*. I will carry the boy."

Rachel shook her head. "I'll carry him," she insisted. Though she trusted Pablo, she wanted Josh with her.

He nodded reluctantly before turning away. Rachel followed him through the house, then across the quiet courtyard. In the atrium, they took the door leading to the rear of the property as she and Sloan did each day for their run and target practice. Her heart pounded harder with each passing moment. She didn't ask the questions tightening her chest. She had to trust Sloan. Where he was taking them didn't matter. All that mattered now was keeping Josh safe. Pablo paused at the towering wall and entered the code required to open the massive gate. She wondered then where Sloan was. Had he gone ahead of them? That notion unsettled her further. Though Pablo was a good man, Rachel felt much safer with Sloan—at least as far as personal protection went.

A quarter moon provided enough illumination for Rachel to see fairly well. Pablo's short legs ate up the ground before them. Rachel hurried to catch up for fear of losing his wiry frame in the darkness. The order to dress in her darkest clothing was crystal clear to her now. They were less likely to be seen in the dark of night by anyone watching the house.

Rachel suddenly slowed. Why hadn't Sloan joined them? Was he waiting up ahead? She peered at the dark terrain that stretched before her. She could see nothing. She strained to listen. Nothing. Pablo moved forward soundlessly, leaving her behind. She supposed she had better catch up again. But where was Sloan?

"Keep moving."

The quiet order came from right behind her. Rachel spun around to find Sloan only inches away.

"I didn't know you were behind me." She struggled to capture the breath that had escaped her. "I was afraid to go on without you." Her arms tightened instinctively around her son, who had fallen back to sleep the moment he settled into her hold. "Where are we going?"

Even in the sparse light she could see Sloan's vivid eyes. Such a translucent blue, and unnervingly intent. The pounding in her chest increased, but it had nothing to do with what might lay before them. It was Sloan. His presence surrounded her. Though she feared her reaction to him on many levels, anytime he was near, Rachel felt safe. She almost shook her head at the absurdity of her other feelings, but they were there just the same. She felt bewildered by her body's response to him. There simply was no explanation. He was fiercely demanding and forever indifferent to even his own feelings. He defined dangerous. But every part of her longed to know him intimately.

He touched her arm, sending heat rushing through her traitorous body. "Pablo is waiting. I'll carry Josh now."

"I'm fine." Rachel didn't give him a chance to argue the point. The urgency she'd heard in his voice propelled her feet, about the only part of her that was not affected by his nearness, back into action. She hurried in the direction she had last seen Pablo. She squinted, hoping to get a glimpse of movement. Rachel tried not to think about the snakes, or the lizards she knew resided in the area. Goose bumps raised on her skin and she moved a little faster. As scared as she was of the reptiles that might be slithering around her feet, she knew without a doubt that there was nothing in this desert that posed as deadly a threat to her and her son as Angel did. And standing around lusting after Sloan wasn't going to help.

"This way, *señora*."

Startled after several long minutes of total silence, Rachel took a calming breath, then followed the soft sound of Pablo's voice as he repeated his instructions. Sloan was somewhere behind her. Though she didn't look back, she could feel him. She had the impression that he moved around them frequently. Sometimes way ahead, sometimes lagging behind. He was scouting for Angel or his helper, she realized after further consideration. Rachel's skin crawled at the thought that Angel might be out there somewhere. But Sloan had assured her that whoever left the note was gone. She forced the worry away and focused on keeping up with Pablo.

"You must stay very close, *señora*," Pablo warned as she all but collided with him. "The path grows treacherous now."

They had reached the base of the mountains. The rugged peaks that looked so beautiful in the light of day loomed ominously in the darkness, half hiding the moon. Rachel could feel the change in the terrain beneath her feet. Though still sandy, the ground was more uneven now, the clumps of scrubby grass much thicker and more prevalent.

"I won't fall behind again," Rachel assured Pablo. She didn't want to take any chances that if anyone were out there, they might catch up to them.

"The higher up we go, the more narrow the path becomes," Pablo explained. "Keep to the right, hug the cliffs."

Rachel followed his gesture as he pointed to the vertical terrain rising before them. "Okay." Her voice reflected the anxiety she couldn't restrain. Among her numerous other firsts since her arrival, she had never climbed mountains before. That her first expedition was with only the moon to light her path didn't help.

Sloan's hand was at the small of her back then, urging her forward. She obeyed, moving cautiously. Pablo matched his pace to hers, speeding up when Rachel moved faster, then slowing down as she did. The trail climbed upward, winding around the cliffs, its width cut right out of the face of the mountain. The oak and pine trees that soared amid the mountainous terrain cast long shadows around her, completely darkening the path in places. She couldn't slow long enough to consider the sharp contrast between the forests of the mountains and the meager desert scrub surrounding Sloan's house not so far away.

Rachel kept her gaze steady on her path. She didn't dare look beyond the narrow ledge for fear she would stall dead in her tracks. Her stomach knotted against the butterflies flapping their tiny wings inside her. The skin on the back of her neck prickled against the unseen threat. How much higher would they climb before they started their descent?

Rachel shifted Josh's weight in her arms. She couldn't be sure how long it had been since they left the house, but her arms ached and her legs felt like rubber. One way or another she had to keep going. Pablo was very far ahead of her now. Hastening her step, she stumbled but caught herself before she hit the ground. Josh whimpered and tightened his hold around her neck. Once her heart had slid back down into her chest, she soothed her baby with soft cooing sounds. Trembling with her own unmanageable fears, Rachel forced one foot in front of the other. She couldn't stop now. They had to get as far away as possible. Angel was coming.

Pablo paused until she came up beside him, he reached for Josh then. "Let me carry the boy now, *señora*. You grow weary." Josh resisted, snuggling closer to his mother.

"It's okay," Rachel returned. "I'll manage." Though Josh loved Pablo for a playmate, at naptime or bedtime he wanted his mother.

"He's slowing you down too much," Sloan growled next to her.

Rachel shifted to peer up at him. His posture reflected the impatience in his tone. Pablo reached for Josh again, but he would have no part of it.

"Come on, sweetie," Rachel urged. "Pablo wants to carry you for a while. Mommy will be right behind you."

"No!" Josh clung to her.

"I'm sorry," she began, hoping the two men would understand the fears of a child. Though she wanted to comply with Sloan's demands, her son's comfort came first. "He—"

Sloan took Josh from her arms before she could finish her sentence. A wail of protest burst from her son's mouth. Rachel reached for him, but Sloan backed away.

"Keep moving," he ordered.

Josh stared up at him as he spoke. Suddenly, as if only then realizing who held him, he snuggled against Sloan's chest. Stunned, but immensely relieved, Rachel resumed her trek behind Pablo. Her entire body shook with weariness now. Her arms trembled after having carried Josh for so long. But she would have carried him until she dropped from exhaustion if necessary. She glanced over her shoulder once more. Her son clung to Sloan as he had clung to her minutes before. The image warmed her.

"No slowing down, Rachel."

She shivered at the sound of her name on Sloan's lips. He hadn't called her by her first name before. Rachel shook off the foreign sensations and trudged after Pablo. Why should it make her tremble so to hear him call her name? She was tired. That's all. She had no idea what time it was, but she felt certain that physical exhaustion was her problem at the moment.

But what about the rest of the time?

His every touch, every look affected her deeply. She knew it. There was no point in denying the truth. He was her protector, her hero. That's all, she decided. It wasn't personal, it was chemical. As soon as Angel was out of her life and she and Josh returned home, Sloan would be nothing but a distant memory.

One last look over her shoulder was all it took to make a liar out of her. Her gaze connected with his in the moon's silvery glow and fire surged through her veins. Rachel wondered if he felt it, too?

She almost laughed out loud at that one. Men like Sloan didn't come undone over a silly hero-worshipping female. She was most likely nothing but a nuisance to him.

"Get the lead out," he barked, confirming her musing.

Rachel sighed and quickened her pace. Just because he had kissed her didn't mean anything… except that she was even more pathetic than she thought.

By the time they started their descent, Sloan had grown accustomed to the little body clinging to him like a choking vine. This, he thought with self-deprecation, was the very reason he hadn't wanted to take this case. He didn't want to feel anything for Rachel Larson or her son. Despite his best efforts,

Sloan was drawn to the boy in a way over which he had no control. The memory of him falling asleep in Sloan's lap the other night haunted him even now. He didn't want to be reminded of how a child's warm little body felt in his arms. Or of the way they slept so innocently, so trustingly. But it was too late now, the deed was done. He cared for the child with the basic human compassion he thought he had buried long ago. And, God forgive him, he hated himself for it. This was not his child…this was Angel's son.

No matter. Sloan had failed to protect his own son, but he would not fail Josh. Angel would not take Josh from his mother, nor would he harm either of them. Sloan intended to kill the bastard. Very soon. He clenched his jaw against the rage that threatened to overwhelm him. Now was not the time to allow those emotions. Right now he had to concentrate on hiding Josh away from the game that had begun. Sloan's gaze traveled over Rachel as she picked her way downward. Convincing her to leave the boy would not be easy. But it was necessary to the child's safety.

Rachel stumbled again. Sloan tracked her progress as she pulled herself up and continued the difficult journey. Pablo reminded her again to stay to the right. If Rachel paused and took detailed note of the dizzying drop that lay to the left of the goat trail they now descended she would likely faint with fear.

Sloan tightened his hold on Josh and navigated a particularly treacherous, twisting drop. Rousing enough to recognize that he was no longer in his mother's arms, Josh whimpered.

"It's all right," Sloan murmured against his head. He tried not to notice the scent of baby shampoo, but it was impossible. The memory of holding his own son so close when he was frightened exploded into his consciousness. Climbing the big tree in the middle of their backyard with his son zoomed into vivid 3-D focus. They had sat there for hours on end just to watch the birds go about their business. Mark had jabbered about the adventure for days.

Mark.

Sloan hesitated. *His son.* Pain so fierce that his breath ripped through him. He hadn't consciously allowed that name to enter his thoughts in years. Stalling, he closed his eyes and tried to repress the images of his son's sweet face. The thick curls that were more blond than brown. Laughing blue eyes. And a big toothy smile.

Rachel's shriek jerked Sloan from his painful reverie. His heart slammed hard against his sternum. She had stumbled again. The momentum as she slipped to the ground, then slid forward took her the last few feet of the downward trek before Sloan could reach her.

"You okay?"

She stood and dusted herself off. "Yeah. I tripped over something," she said, her voice shaking. "I was trying to catch up with Pablo."

"He went on ahead to announce our arrival."

A brittle laugh slipped from her lips. "No wonder

I couldn't catch up with him." She paused, belatedly absorbing his words. "Announce our arrival?"

Sloan ushered her forward. The trail wound to the right and off through the trees now. In fifteen or twenty minutes they would arrive at the small village where Pablo's people lived. The group was reclusive and distrustful of strangers. It was important that Pablo explained their arrival in advance.

"There's a village not far from here," he explained. "Pablo's family lives there."

"Is that where we're going?"

"Yeah." He pushed onward, hoping she would follow without asking any more questions.

There was no need to explain the rest right now. Sloan scanned the sky. He felt a storm brewing. The wind kicked up, making him all the more aware of nature's restlessness around them. There would be no time to waste once Pablo had paved the way for Sloan's plan. He glanced down at the boy sleeping in his arms. The sooner this was done the better off they would all be.

Twenty minutes later a welcoming campfire came into view. Sloan breathed a bit easier upon seeing the dancing flames. The fire was a sign that Pablo's people welcomed the strangers into their village. Had they not been welcome, there would have been darkness and silence. Three figures stood within the light of the flames—Pablo, a woman Sloan recognized as Pablo's elderly mother, and the village leader, Camilo.

Sloan turned to Rachel before they entered the perimeter of the village and lowered Josh into her arms. Later she would have regretted not having held him those final minutes. He hoped she wasn't going to make this any tougher than it needed to be. There was no other way to ensure his safety. Sloan scanned their surroundings as he moved toward the waiting group. The numerous sod huts and primitive cabins fanned out from the village center like the spokes of a wheel. The small party waited in the center, the place of honor, to greet their guests.

A rough male voice uttered a simple phrase that Sloan recognized as a greeting of welcome.

Sloan bowed slightly in deference to the man's village title. *"Gracias."* Though he understood some of the native language used by these people, he spoke none. Pablo would translate.

"Camilo says yes to your request," Pablo said as they approached. "My mother has also agreed."

"Muchas gracias, Señor Camilo," Sloan offered, *"y* Señora Vecino." He placed his hand over his heart to emphasize the depth of his gratitude. Spanish was not lost on these people, and Sloan was aware that any attempt at direct communication would be appreciated.

The elderly woman spouted a short monologue in her primitive language, much too quickly for Sloan to grasp the complete meaning. He turned to Pablo who quickly translated for both Sloan's and Rachel's benefit.

"Mother says that a child is a treasure from God and all measures must be taken to cherish and nurture such a gift."

Sloan nodded his agreement. *"Sí, señora,"* he bowed again to the elderly woman.

Señora Vecino lifted a small stick of wood from the fire to use as a torch and gestured for them to follow. Sloan guided a hesitant Rachel forward. The woman led them to a nearby hut, somewhat smaller than the others. A dim light marked the low entrance. With a sweep of her hand she indicated that Rachel should enter before her. Rachel's uncertain gaze collided with Sloan's. He nodded for her to obey. Looking entirely too much like a lost child herself, she ducked through the open doorway. Señora Vecino scurried in next. Sloan followed.

Two thick pallets of animal pelts covered most of the available floor space in the main room. Señora Vecino motioned for Rachel to place Josh on one of them. Again Rachel looked to Sloan for assurance. He nodded.

Rachel knelt next to the nearest pallet and carefully laid Josh in the center of it. His lids fluttered open, but quickly closed once more. When it was clear that Josh would continue to sleep, the elderly woman made an urgent sweeping motion with her gnarled hands. She wanted them to leave. Rachel hadn't missed the meaning, either. She looked startled and completely bewildered. When Rachel didn't move swiftly enough the woman mumbled crossly, the words spoken too quickly and gruffly for Sloan to catch the meaning.

"What is she saying?" Rachel held her ground next to Josh.

Sloan closed one hand around Rachel's arm and pulled her to her feet. "Let's talk outside," he whispered near her ear.

She shook her head adamantly. "No. I'm not leaving Josh."

The old woman grumbled something that sounded very much like, *"away with you, the devil is on your heels."* If she only knew how close to right she was. Too damned close.

"Don't make this anymore difficult than it needs to be, Rachel," he warned in a low, lethal tone he hoped relayed the seriousness of the situation.

Tears brimming in her big brown eyes, she followed him outside. "What do you think you're doing?" She jerked free of his hold and glared at him. Fear and worry radiated from those velvety depths.

"He'll be safer here. We have to go back."

She shook her head again. "No way. I won't leave him." Her chest rose and fell too rapidly. Hysteria would set in any second now.

She was afraid she would never see her son again. Of all people, Sloan could sympathize with that heart-wrenching fear, but there was no alternative.

"Listen to me." He took her by the shoulders and gave her a little shake to bring her to her senses.

"Angel is coming. Maybe not tonight or tomorrow, but soon. We don't want Josh anywhere around when that happens. He'll be safer here."

Rachel pounded her fists against his chest as a sob shook her. She knew he was right, but the pain of leaving her son behind was more than she could bear. "How can you be sure he'll be safe here?" she demanded. Tears rolled down her cheeks, twisting the knot in his gut that much tighter.

"He'll be safe." He wanted to take her in his arms more than he wanted to take his next breath, but that wasn't what she needed now. She needed to think rationally. "These people will hide Josh among their own children. With his coloring no one will ever suspect that he doesn't belong here—even if anyone came looking, which is highly unlikely." Her lower lip trembled and his whole body reacted. He pulled her close and held her in spite of the warnings sounding in his head.

"We've never been apart before," she sobbed against his chest. "I'm not sure I can do it."

The fingers of his right hand threaded into the silky length of her hair as the left splayed on her slender back, holding her body to his. The need he felt could be contained no more. Sloan kissed her temple, then lower, next to her ear. She shivered. "Don't cry," he murmured. "I swear he'll be safe here. Pablo will protect him with his own life."

She tilted her head back, searching out his gaze in the sparse light. "And if we can't come back for him?" She blinked back the fresh wave of tears he heard in her voice. "What happens then?"

He clenched his jaw against the flood of emotions that washed over him. When he had composed himself he leveled his gaze on hers and said the words tightening his throat. "You will be back for him," he promised. "This battle is mine."

She searched his eyes for the truth in his words. "I have your word on that?"

"You have my word."

She swiped the tears from her cheeks with the backs of her hands and drew in a heavy breath. "All right." She pulled out of his arms. "I just need to kiss him goodbye."

Sloan stepped back for her to pass.

Rachel struggled to pull herself together while Sloan said something in Spanish to the old woman who hovered near the door. Rachel's chest ached with every beat of her heart. She held her breath and fought a new rush of tears. She had to be strong. Josh's life depended upon her strength right now. She had Sloan's word that everything would be all right, and she had to trust that. Victoria Colby's statement resounded in her ears. *Someone I would trust with my own life.*

"Don't wake him," Sloan said, drawing Rachel's attention back to him. "There's no point in upsetting the kid. Pablo will be with him when he wakes."

"Sí, señora."

Rachel turned to Pablo who had stepped from the

shadows. This all felt too surreal. This place—*a place the rest of the world has forgotten,* Sloan had said—felt too surreal.

"Hurry, Rachel." Sloan ushered her toward the small door. "We have to get back."

Rachel felt confused. Why did they have to hurry? Why couldn't they stay until morning and then she could explain things to Josh. She swallowed with monumental difficulty. Because Angel was coming. He might be there by morning.

The old woman blurted something in the alien language that definitely wasn't entirely Spanish. Another plea for her to hurry, Rachel supposed. Suffering that strange detached feeling again, she ducked her head and stepped back into the rustic hut.

Josh slept soundly, completely oblivious to the life-altering circumstances happening around him. Tears welled in her eyes once more and Rachel cursed herself for being so weak. She knelt beside her baby and kissed his smooth cheek. She brushed the dark hair from his face and smiled, committing to memory once more just how beautiful her child was.

"I love you, Josh," she whispered. Her hand trembled as she caressed his baby soft hair. "Mommy'll be back for you soon. I promise." She kissed him one more time then pushed to her feet and rushed out the door without looking back.

She stood only a few feet from where her baby lay

sleeping while Sloan gave Pablo his final instructions. Rachel wanted to scream her agony. She shuddered with the need of it. She scrubbed the tears from her eyes and battled the rampant trembling in her body. She had to do this, she repeated silently. When Angel was dead, she would be back. Sloan had promised.

And Angel would die.

"It's time to go." Sloan took her by the arm and propelled her forward.

Rachel glanced back one last time at the tiny primitive hut where her son slept. No force on earth would keep her from her son.

She would be back.

Chapter Eight

"We need to move quickly, a storm is coming."

Rachel felt numb. Why didn't he just leave her? She faltered in her forward movement, hoping he would do just that. Her feet felt too heavy to lift for the next step. She wanted to go back to the village and cradle her son in her arms.

"We don't want to be caught in the open when it hits," he added, his words meaningless to her.

Not really caring, but knowing that he wanted her to heed his words, Rachel surveyed the sky. As she watched, a dark mass of clouds moved across the moon. The wind was stronger now. Maybe Sloan was right about the weather. She knew little of the weather changes here, and cared even less at the moment. She was too heartsick to worry about trivial issues like the weather. She swallowed, fighting the renewed urge to cry.

How could she leave Josh like that? Reason told her that Sloan was right, he would be safest with Pablo and his people. But reason had never controlled her heart.

"Rachel—" Sloan's deep voice resonated around her, summoning her attention to him once more "—we have to move faster."

Reaching way down deep inside, Rachel found the grit to take another step, then another. When she had reached Sloan, she pushed harder, forcing her feet to cooperate…to take her farther away from her son. Her stomach roiled. Josh would cry when he woke and found her gone. He wouldn't understand that his mommy had left him there for his own good. Tears welled in her eyes, a stinging reminder that she had no choice.

Rachel inhaled deeply of the cool night air. The scent was fresh, earthy. She listened to the sounds around her as she trudged onward. The hoot of an owl, the rustle of the leaves and branches in the wind. She pushed herself to climb more swiftly up the rugged path. Maybe if she ran as fast as she could, pushed her body harder than ever before, maybe then those awful, heart-twisting feelings wouldn't catch up with her again.

Rachel had never left her son before. Not once in his life had she been separated from him. Not even in the hospital when he was born. His bassinet had been in the room with her. Except, she amended, for those few minutes the day she found Sloan. But that was the only time she and Josh had been apart. Would Pablo hold him when he cried? Would he understand the fear that would fill her little boy? Her heart banged painfully, keeping a rhythm of sorts with the words throbbing inside her head. Sloan's rational words joined the others whirling there. Angel would never find Josh. An odd relief flooded her with that last thought. Even if the bastard killed her and Sloan, which was very possible, he would never find Josh.

A smile tugged at the corners of her mouth. Josh would be better off with Pablo's people and their primitive culture than with the devil who was his father. Curiously, the thought of Angel searching high and low for his son without success gave Rachel perverse pleasure.

The dangerous path curved with the face of the cliffs then dipped downward. They were starting their descent already. With her thoughts so preoccupied, she hadn't realized they had traveled so far. Rachel slowed as clouds once more concealed the moon. Sloan was behind her now. She didn't have to look, and she sure couldn't hear him, but he was there. She could feel him, just like always. She shivered with awareness. He moved with a stealth that was more animal-like than human. The image of his muscular body moving over hers suddenly filled her mind. She shook her head to shatter the unbidden fantasy.

The feelings he elicited confused her—fear and desire; trust and danger. How could she desire a man she feared so completely? She couldn't understand it. She trusted him, yet she knew from his words and the intensity in those piercing blue eyes that he personified danger. Her feelings softened at the memory of how he had held Josh in his arms tonight. And Josh had let him, even snuggled close to Sloan's massive chest.

Holding her son that way was surely painful for Sloan. He had likely relived holding his own son in such a manner. But he hadn't complained. Sloan suffered in silence. She remembered the story Victoria Colby had told her. How could any man, no matter how strong, survive such a devastating loss? But Sloan had. He drank too much, put himself in harm's way every chance he got, but he survived. God surely had good things in store for a man who had suffered so very much and managed to survive day after day when a lesser man would have given up long ago. Sloan was a man of infinite courage.

Rachel considered Sloan's usual indifference toward her and life in general, then his hot kisses. He tried so hard not to care, but like her, he couldn't help himself. Not even where she was concerned. And he hated that fault, she realized with sudden clarity. He didn't want to feel anything for her, and she could scarcely blame him. She had slept with the enemy. She shuddered at the memory of Angel's touch. What a fool she had been. And yet, Sloan took her and Josh in, protected them. She had no doubt that he would give his own life to protect either of them. She hoped someday she would understand what made a man like Sloan give so very much for so little. He'd already given more than most.

Rachel hugged her arms around her middle. Could she do one thing for Sloan in repayment for all that he did for her and Josh? Sure she would pay his fee. Of course she had to nail him down to an amount before she could even do that. But that wasn't enough. She shook her head. Not nearly enough. Could she somehow show him that it was safe to trust his feelings again? That life wasn't only for those who had never been touched by the evil that had ripped his life apart? He deserved so much...she had to find a way to make him see that.

She would try. The decision made her almost giddy. If she could manage that one thing during the time she had left with Sloan, she would feel some sense of accomplishment. He needed to trust his heart again, to allow himself to feel. Rachel would give him that if it was within her power.

Distracted with her thoughts, her right foot slipped on the loose rocks. She lost her balance. Ice slid through her veins as she struggled to stay vertical. Her bottom hit the ground hard, her full body weight thrown into the downward momentum now. She slid precariously close to the ledge. Rachel grabbed at anything in her reach to slow her slide. There was nothing to hang on to. She twisted her body, clawed at the rocky earth beneath her.

Her legs went over the edge. Fear paralyzed her throat. Her fingers locked around something...a limb or protruding root. *Dangling.* Her body dangled in the air. She refused to look down, though she was certain she could see nothing anyway. Sloan was calling her name, but she couldn't look up, either. She couldn't move. All she could do was hang on to the limb that somehow protruded from the cliff.

"Dammit, Rachel, look at me."

She was going to die. A laugh bubbled up in her tightly constricted throat. Fate apparently planned to save Angel the trouble of killing her. *Josh.* He would miss her so much. He'd never had anyone but her… this would be so hard for him.

A strong hand suddenly gripped her right forearm. Rachel frowned and stared at the wide hand. *Sloan.* What was he doing? Her brow pleated in worry. He needed to stay back, he was only going to make her situation worse. Or get hurt himself.

"If you want to live you're going to have to help me out here," he growled, jerking Rachel from her haze of shock.

"I…I can't," she stammered. Terror washed through her again. Her hold on the limb slipped. She grasped it more tightly. Her palms were sweating. Damn. "I can't move."

He pulled on her arm. Rachel shrieked. "You're going to make me fall!"

"Damn it, you're going to fall anyway. Now grab on to my arm!"

Rachel gulped a ragged breath. She commanded her left hand to release its death grip on the limb and reach for Sloan. Her arm trembling, she reached for him. Her right hand shook with the added effort of holding on, supporting her full weight. She latched onto Sloan's shirtsleeve.

"I'm going to haul you up." His voice was strained. "But you're going to have to turn loose of the limb you're holding first."

The blood rushing through her body drowned out all sound but his voice. *Turn loose of the limb,* he had said. He wanted her to let go. But what if she fell? Or pulled him over the edge? The clouds parted, allowing the moon to spotlight her precarious situation. Her gaze connected with his fierce blue one. Her brain acknowledged the promise in those eyes.

"You have to trust me, Rachel," he urged.

"Don't drop me," she cried with his same urgency.

"Never."

Her body trembling, Rachel focused on the powerful hand gripping her forearm. She had to trust him or she was going to die. He wouldn't let her fall. Her eyes met his again and understanding passed between them. Rachel released the limb. Her weight sagged in Sloan's hold. Then he was pulling her upward. Over the ledge. Into his arms as he sat back on the ground.

"You scared the hell out of me." His hands were moving over her body. Checking for injury, assuring himself that she was unharmed.

Rachel slumped in his arms. She felt weak with relief. Her arms felt like overcooked noodles. She had almost fallen to her death, but Sloan had saved her. Now, as she sat safe in his arms, the pain of leaving Josh enshrouded her once more. She wanted to cry.

"You're okay now," he murmured near her cheek. The firm, warmth of his mouth caressed her skin.

Rachel didn't want to move. But he was lifting her. She wanted to close her eyes and forget this whole night.

"We have to hurry," he soothed as if feeling the need to explain why he couldn't keep holding her that way.

Somehow she was on her feet, his right arm around her waist, supporting her. She leaned against him and wrapped her arms around his lean waist. After all she had been through tonight she needed that simple pleasure.

Rachel couldn't be sure how much time passed, but she felt the change in the terrain beneath her feet. They had descended the mountain and were back on level ground, she decided. At least as level as the sandy earth and occasional clump of desert scrub got around here.

The wind whipped angrily against them, making their forward progress slow. Rachel huddled close to Sloan's big body for protection. They were walking directly into the wind, its force making each step a challenge now. Surely it wasn't far to the house. Rachel had no idea how far they had traveled or for how long.

"Wait."

Rachel looked up at Sloan, his face lost in the

darkness created by the thickening clouds. He withdrew something from his pocket. A handkerchief. He folded it into a triangle and tied it around her mouth and nose. Before she could ask why, the wind slashed them, sand stung her eyes.

"Keep your head down," he shouted above nature's fury.

She lowered her head and pressed closer to his body as they started forward again. He shielded her as best he could from the angry wind and blinding sand. His body was warm and inviting. He felt hard and amazingly male. Despite everything, her own body responded to his. The warmth and protection he offered had been sorely lacking in her life for so very long that Rachel couldn't help but want it when she finally found it.

What felt like hours later, but was probably only minutes, they reached the gate. Sloan entered the code and the huge iron bars opened. They stumbled through it and moved toward the house. The gate closed behind them with a teeth-rattling clang. The wind roared like a ferocious beast. Rachel shivered, thankful they were nearing the safety of the house.

Once they were inside Sloan ushered her to her room. "Get out of those clothes and get in the shower. Rinse your eyes," he ordered.

His tawny hair was tousled and sand clung to his skin wherever it was bare. His eyes were red. He had told her to keep her head down, but he'd had to watch where they were going.

"You need something for your eyes." A doctor was her first thought. The sand could damage his eyes permanently. She touched his cheek. "Is there a doctor we can call?"

He backed away from her touch. "I have eyedrops." He nodded toward the bathroom door. "Take a shower."

He turned away before she could answer and strode out the door. Exhaustion weighed down on her then. Every step she had taken crossing that mountain manifested itself in her trembling limbs. Determined to follow his orders before she collapsed, Rachel trudged to the bathroom and turned on the shower. While the water heated she stripped off her sandy clothes. She caught a glimpse of herself in the mirror and grimaced. Though her eyes weren't as red as Sloan's, she looked a fright. She blinked, noticing the gritty feel for the first time. Her hair was a mess. Sand added new texture to her scalp and skin.

She stepped into the shower and allowed the warm water to work its magic. She had a feeling it would take plenty of soap and shampoo to wash away the layer of grit. But nothing would erase the dizzying emotions whirling inside her. Leaving Josh behind. Touching Sloan. Needing his touch.

She sagged against the tiled wall. She was hopeless.

Sloan towel-dried his body. Pain radiated through his right shoulder and he grimaced. He twisted at the waist to see in the mirror what he'd done to himself. It wasn't that bad. Just a scrape. He'd live. He tugged on clean jeans, but didn't bother to fully fasten them. Instead, he reached for the drops that would hopefully provide some relief for the fire in his eyes. He tilted his head back and dispensed two drops in each eye. His eyes squeezed shut, he waited for the medicine to do its job and for the new kind of burn to subside.

He tossed the drops on the counter and blinked to adjust his blurred vision. He threaded his fingers through his hair, pushing the damp mass away from his face. Muttering a curse, he flexed his right shoulder. Though Rachel was a featherweight, pulling her up with one arm while holding on with the other had taken its toll. He slung the holstered weapon over his left shoulder. Angel or his watcher could show up anytime.

And this time Sloan would be ready.

Leaving the pile of sandy clothes on the bathroom floor, he padded barefoot into his bedroom. He needed a shirt, then he would check on Rachel. She'd gotten a little sand in her eyes, it wouldn't hurt for her to use the drops, as well. The thought of her falling into that canyon still ignited fear inside him. The call had been too close for comfort. A soft knock jerked his gaze to the open doorway.

Looking uncertain and entirely too vulnerable, Rachel moistened her lips. To Sloan's irritation, his body responded instantly.

"I wanted to make sure you're okay," she said hesitantly.

He closed his eyes for a second and let go a weary breath. Maybe he had imagined her. When his eyes opened again, she was still there. What the hell was she concerned about him for? He didn't need her concern or anything else she had to offer. The arousal growing in his unfastened jeans defied his mental declaration.

"I'm fine." Sloan gave her his back and strode to the closet. He blocked the image of her standing in his doorway wearing only a T-shirt. Heat rushed through him at the memory of what lay beneath that thin cotton. Her pink nipples would bud at his slightest touch. He clenched his jaw and squashed the thought.

"You're hurt."

She was across the room and right behind him before he could turn around. "It's nothing." He faced her, denying her access to his injured shoulder.

Her gaze narrowed in challenge. "If it's nothing, then let me see."

"I said—" he leaned intimidatingly nearer "—it's nothing."

"Liar," she retorted with a defiant lift of her chin. "I'm not leaving this room until you let me check it out."

Sloan breathed a four-letter word that made her eyes go wide. He abandoned the shirt he'd started to take from its hanger and turned his back to her.

"Damn." Her soft fingers traced the area near his right shoulder blade and down to his side beneath his arm. "This is a good deal more than nothing."

"It's just a scrape," he growled. Why the hell didn't she go to sleep? She had to be exhausted. The feel of her warm fingers was playing havoc with his ability to think clearly. "It'll heal without any help."

"Where's your first aid kit?" she insisted, ignoring his argument.

Slowly, deliberately, Sloan turned to face her. He glowered down at her, unable to completely mask the desire mushrooming inside him. His defense cracked when faced with the naive desire staring back at him from her big brown eyes. "Look," he began bluntly, "maybe you haven't noticed, but I'm as horny as hell. And you're only making things *harder.*"

The startled look that claimed her expression told him he had hit his mark. She visibly faltered. But his triumph was short lived when her gaze slid slowly down his body, paused at his half-open fly, then widened as a little hitch disrupted her breathing.

Sloan swore, another four-letter word that jerked her gaze back up to his. "Go back to your room, Rachel, before you get more than you came in here for." Lust thickened his voice, but that couldn't be prevented. In about five seconds he was going to be beyond reasoning.

She danced back a step. Crimson bloomed on her cheeks. "The first aid kit," she mumbled. "If you'll just tell me where it is I'll get it."

He had to face the fact that she wasn't going to give up on playing doctor. Sloan heaved a disgusted breath. He supposed she felt some sort of compulsion to attend to his injury since he'd kept her from falling to her death.

"Fine." He planted his hands at his waist and allowed his gaze to travel slowly over her scantily clad body. "The first aid kit's in the kitchen under the sink." She turned to scurry away. "But—" she glanced back "—don't say I didn't warn you about keeping your distance."

She blinked, uncertain, then hurried from the room. Sloan shook his head. He was an idiot. He wanted her. He raked his fingers through his hair. He would have her if she set foot back in his bedroom tonight.

And tomorrow they would both regret it.

Chapter Nine

He had warned her.

Rachel hesitated outside Sloan's bedroom door. She shifted from one foot to the other, an attack of second thoughts throwing a damper on her enthusiasm. Gripping the first aid kit like a shield in both hands, she blew out a shaky breath. He meant what he said. She hadn't missed the fire in his eyes. A fire that burned for her. She chewed her lower lip. God help her, she wanted him, too.

She wasn't supposed to, she knew that. Sloan frightened her beyond reason on a level that had nothing to do with her physical safety, yet he drew her on so many other levels that she simply could not ignore the need. With each day that passed the desire to know him fully grew stronger.

She had to be crazy.

If she walked back into that room… This was insane. Rachel turned to go, but hesitated. The memory of the intensity in his eyes halted her. The promise that he would keep her safe when he reached for her as she hung on for her life, her legs dangling in thin air. The understanding in his eyes when she spoke of how Angel had seduced her…Sloan understood as no one else could. The pain in those same eyes each time he looked at Josh, but Sloan protected him just the same. Rachel had never known a man as selfless. She admired and respected him…as much as she had the only other man who had made her feel safe, her father.

But this man wanted the woman in her.

Just like she wanted the man in him.

If she never did anything else right in her entire life, she would do this. She knew deep in her heart that it was right. He needed her…much more so than even he knew. She understood that. The bitter indifference was nothing but a suit of armor he wore to protect his heart from further damage. Though Rachel was well aware that they had no future together, because of Josh…and what Angel had done, she could give Sloan the only thing she had to give. Her complete trust in the most intimate way a man and woman could come together. If that one act could make him feel again, could make him see that he could care, that he could give himself that way, then it would be worth it.

Rachel almost laughed at herself. What was she thinking? She was no savior. Hell, she had been too busy running for her life to even be a Good Samaritan these past five years. Besides, she reminded that part of her that wanted to reach out to him, Sloan had never once said he wanted to be saved. She drew in a deep, bolstering breath and released it slowly. But he did want her, physically anyway.

Before she totally lost her courage, Rachel squared her shoulders and strode through the still open door. Across the room the French doors were open. Sloan stood, his back to her, staring out at the dark night. His long, tawny hair, still not completely dry, fell around his broad shoulders, curled around his nape. Her mouth parched as her gaze slid over that perfect butt she had admired on more than one occasion the past few days. She honestly could not recall ever having fixated on a man's butt. Not until Sloan.

He turned around and Rachel's heart leaped. His gaze skimmed her body, making her feel suddenly naked and entirely too warm. Electricity flowed beneath her skin when her own gaze moved over that beautifully sculpted torso. He took one step toward her. Just one, then waited.

Could he possibly feel a glimmer of the trepidation she felt right now?

"I found it." Rachel displayed the first aid kit like a prize. It was her acceptable excuse for entering his room again despite his warning. "It…it was right where you said it would be," she rushed on when he took another step.

His gaze never deviated from her. He simply watched while she mentally squirmed.

And she burned because of it. Burned for his touch, for the sound of his voice…

She gestured to one of the chairs flanking a table in the center of the room. "Sit down and I'll—" she blinked at the intensity now aimed directly into her eyes "—I'll tend that…nasty abrasion."

Unable to hold his gaze a moment longer she crossed to the table and opened the first aid kit. Its contents spilled across the shiny mahogany surface. Her cheeks flaming, she picked through the items as if contemplating the selection. At least this way she wouldn't have to look at him, and she would have something to do with her hands. He was closer now. Maybe this wasn't such a good idea after all. What did she know about reaching out to a man like Sloan?

He moved up behind her and Rachel could not prevent the shiver that raced up her spine. His wide hand closed over hers, stilling the fingers fishing through the scattered contents of the well-stocked kit. His thumb caressed her palm making her heart lurch.

"You're not afraid I'll make good on my warning." The fingers of his other hand threaded into her hair, then allowed the length of it to slip through them.

Rachel closed her eyes and savored the sensations that washed over her from his slightest touch. She shook her head in answer to his question. She was many things—unsure of her fate, unprepared for his impact to her heart, not certain of her ability to please him—but she was not afraid of him in that way. Not anymore. Maybe she never was.

He released her hand only to wrap his arm around her waist and pull her close. The feel of his hard male body against her buttocks was almost more than she could bear. Her breath fled her lungs when he moved her hair aside to kiss her neck. Firm and hot, his lips teased her neck, made a path to her ear.

"Is this what you want?" He pressed her more firmly against his undeniable arousal.

Rachel couldn't contain the little sound that escaped her, half moan, half gasp.

He inhaled deeply against her hair, then hummed a note of pleasure. "You smell nice." His fingers splayed on her abdomen, pressing her closer still. His tongue traced the shell of her ear, she shivered. "But, I have to tell you," he rasped, then nipped her earlobe, "I've never been overly fond of virgins."

Rachel whipped around in his hold. She stared at him, stunned that he would say such a thing. "You know that's not true." Why was he doing this? Was he trying to push her away? Or simply playing some sort of game?

A wicked smile tilted one side of his full mouth, making her pulse skip. "I've read your file. I know everything there is to know. Not to mention that I undressed you."

Her cesarean section scar. She'd been in labor too long, Josh had gone into distress. But that didn't lend credit to his calling her a virgin.

"But Angel and I—"

His expression turned savage so fast that Rachel

drew back from the fierceness of it. "I have my doubts as to whether he did the job right."

She shook her head, suddenly uneasy. Nothing he said made sense. "I don't understand."

He lowered his head, his gaze intent on hers. That fiery desire was back in his eyes again. "You will," he murmured before taking her mouth.

His kiss was greedy. He left no question as to what he wanted. The heat of it filled her so fast that she felt light-headed. Her arms found their way around his neck. He lifted her against him and want arrowed straight to her feminine core. The feel of his chest against her breasts even through the thin cotton of her T-shirt made her weak with desire. His tongue slid over the seam of her lips, urging her to open for him. She opened instantly, unable to do otherwise. He thrust his tongue into her mouth and her thighs quivered. His hands moved beneath the hem of her T-shirt and squeezed her bottom, lifted her more firmly into him.

The groan that sounded could have come from either of them. Rachel didn't know nor did she care, she only wanted to feel more of him. Her fingers tunneled into his long hair, and she reveled in the silkiness of it. She had known it would feel like that. The rigid angle of his jaw, the corded length of his neck, then the smooth contours of his awesome chest. Her fingers learned them all. The taut ridges of his abdomen, his lean hips, the tight feel of his butt. Anticipation zipped through her, urging her seeking hands over his bare back, down his muscular sides. She wanted to touch him all over.

He ushered her into the chair behind her, then dropped to his knees between her thighs. His mouth left hers only long enough to drag the T-shirt over her head. Then he kissed her even harder, his tongue delving, touching, teasing, his hands circling her waist. He showered a trail of kisses down her throat, lingering at the pulse points, tasting her, making her crave more.

"Sloan," she whimpered.

His mouth closed over her breast and her inner muscles convulsed. She cried out, wanting to encourage him, but unsure how. The exquisite torture continued. He nibbled, licked, then suckled until she wanted to scream with the need building inside her. She wanted more, needed more, but more would only make the sweet agony last longer.

He worked the same magic on her other breast, while the long fingers of one hand plucked and kneaded the one he had abandoned. She plunged her fingers into his hair and urged him on. The feel of his tongue, his teeth, his lips against her sensitized nipple drove her mad. She wanted to touch him in the same way, but could not bring herself to put an end to the feel of his mouth on her.

His mouth moved to hers again, his hands cradled her face. He kissed her so thoroughly she wanted to weep. He stood, pulling her up as he went. He lifted her into his arms and carried her to his bed, his lips teasing her skin mercilessly as he lay her there.

With painstaking slowness, he dragged her panties down her legs, his palm skimming her flesh, making her burn for more of his touch. So many sensations whirled inside her, her body felt ready to explode. He moved from the bed and Rachel reached for him, her desperation palpable when confronted with the possible loss of his touch. He shed his jeans, then lowered his long frame next to hers. Her pulse quickened as her gaze roved the length of him. Rachel's whole body sighed at having him next to her again, but quickly burst into renewed flames at the look of need in his eyes.

His palm flattened on her abdomen, then slid lower until he cradled her intimately. Rachel's breath caught, but he pressed a soothing kiss to her parted lips. One long finger parted her feminine folds, teased her. She made a tiny, startled sound, he shushed her with his attentive lips. That same finger slipped inside her, making her quiver with a new rush of pleasure. Then another finger moved inside her, increasing the friction. She arched against his hand, her body aching for something she couldn't name. Her eyes closed with the need of it. He moved those two fingers rhythmically until she wanted to scream. Her body writhed uncontrollably. Her hips undulated beneath his assault. But it wasn't enough.

He stopped. Rachel clutched at him, needing him. She searched his face, her body burning to have him inside her, he only smiled as if he knew the secret and wasn't sure he intended to share it with her just yet.

"Please." She tugged him nearer. She had never been on fire like this before. He had to do something before she lost her mind.

He covered her throbbing body with his own. His arousal pressed against her belly and for the first time Rachel felt a twinge of fear. She closed her eyes and arched upward, no longer caring, only needing. He moved between her thighs, which she spread in frantic invitation. His tip nudged her and she cried out his name.

He brushed a gentle kiss across her lips. "Open your eyes."

She obeyed and what she saw in his took her breath away. His need was every bit as desperate as hers. He took her hand and placed it on his heavy arousal. A surge of power rushed through her at the satiny feel of him. He was big and hard for her, because he wanted her. Her heart thudded, rushing her heated blood through her veins, fueling the desire vibrating her senses. With his help, she guided him to the part of her that ached to be filled by him.

He thrust his hips, entering her by slow, agonizing degrees. She couldn't breathe. She couldn't move. She could only stare into those searing blue eyes and take what he offered. The hot, stretching sensation sent waves of unexpected pleasure cascading over her like a waterfall. Those same muscles stretching to accommodate him, clenched tightly around him. Sloan groaned a savage sound. She had to close her eyes against the intensity of sensations she had never before experienced. Lights pulsed behind her lids. Her body tensed and wave after wave of pure sensation exploded around her. Somehow, in that state of elation just before she could take a breath, she realized that this was her climax.

And Sloan had been her first.

He thrust fully, filling her completely. Rachel gasped at the feel of him so deeply inside her. His ragged breath fanned her hungry lips as he stilled. He searched her face for a long moment, as if wanting to commit this moment to memory. He caressed her cheek with gentle fingers. He throbbed inside her, her own body already speeding toward the next peak she now recognized. The scent of their lovemaking filled her nostrils, warming her from the inside out. His skin felt hot where it melded with hers. She wanted to hold him forever, to make him feel what she was feeling right now.

She would have given her soul at that moment to read the indefinable emotion in his eyes. He shifted, burying himself deeper still, if that was possible. Just when she thought she would die if he looked at her that way one second longer, he lowered his mouth to hers. The kiss started out slow and tender, but quickly turned wild and frantic. He flexed his powerful hips. Rachel cried out, the sound lost to his kisses. Again and again, he thrust until release claimed her again, the rush even stronger this time. Then he came, too. His groan of release loud and savage. He thrust one last time, filling her so completely that she knew precisely what he had meant earlier.

She had not been taken thoroughly by a man until tonight. And Sloan had been the one to take her fully. No man, not even Angel, had touched that place inside her.

Rachel closed her eyes so Sloan wouldn't see what she now knew. She had made a mistake. She had just given Sloan much more than she intended. And there was no way to take it back.

Her heart belonged to him.

Rachel was more than a little certain that he did not want her for more than what they had just shared, and he would certainly never want her heart.

He didn't even want his own.

Sloan stood beneath the spray of hot water, his head pressed against the moist, tile wall, the water sluicing over his back. What had he done? He clutched at the slick walls and fought the pain knotting inside him. He was a fool. The act he and Rachel had just shared was not sex, and he knew it. He'd had sex plenty of times over the years. Sex could be just as hot, just as frantic, but sex brought physical satiation, not complete emotional turmoil.

They had made love.

He swore crudely. It was supposed to be about sex. He wasn't supposed to care. He damned sure wasn't supposed to feel like someone had taken a meat cleaver to his chest.

And he'd been right about her virginity. Angel, the sick bastard, might have tried to take it, but he'd failed. She had allowed Sloan inside—all the way inside. He breathed another curse between his clenched teeth. They had connected on some level that transcended the physical. He had known that kind of feeling only once before....

And look what it had cost him.

He was a damned bastard himself. He had taken everything she offered. He could have held back. He could have refused. But he hadn't.

He shut off the water with a violent twist. "Stupid bastard," he muttered as he stepped out of the shower. He had royally screwed up this time. Rachel Larson was as fragile as glass. Angel had seduced her, killed her father and plagued her life like a recurring nightmare. And what had he done? Taken her trust. She had reached out to him and he'd latched on with both hands, taking. Only taking.

Sloan swabbed at his body with a towel, too disgusted with himself to do the job right. He wanted to wash away the feel of her, the smell of her. He tossed the towel aside. A shaky breath sighed out of him as he stared at his reflection.

"So much for not getting involved," he muttered. "You're an idiot, Sloan."

He pulled on his pants, then his T-shirt. Well, he might be an idiot, but he wasn't stupid. Rachel Larson might think she cared about him—hell, she might even think that she loved him. But she couldn't, he assured himself once more. Not really. Whatever she might think she felt, he knew just how to diffuse any silly notions she might be harboring. All he needed was a couple of days and she would be back at square one. She would see the error of her ways and go back to believing him to be an even meaner bastard than she first thought.

Sunlight streamed into the bedroom by the time Sloan stalked out of the bathroom. Rachel slept trustingly in his bed. He swallowed tightly, refusing to relive even one moment of their lovemaking. And that's what it had been, no matter how he denied it. Her dark hair spilled across the white pillowcase, making him ache to run his fingers through it. Her creamy shoulders were bare, as was the rest of her sweet body beneath the sheet. He drew in a deep breath and released it slowly to fight the need rising inside him already.

Gritting his teeth against the response he knew touching her would stir, he shook her none too gently. "Wake up, sleepyhead. We have work to do."

Her lids slowly fluttered open. She smiled, her face aglow with satiation. She stretched like a cat. "What time is it?" she asked sleepily.

He fixed her with the coldest look he could summon. "Time to work. You have twenty minutes." He turned away from the confusion that clouded her innocent face. He didn't need to see it to know he had just hurt her. Hell, he could feel it.

"Don't be late," he warned as he strode out of the

room. He was a bastard all right. No better than the piece of crap who had raped her emotionally five years ago. Right now he had to focus on the confrontation with Angel. He couldn't afford the distraction Rachel represented. Just maybe if he kept her busy enough, exhausted enough and angry enough, she would keep her distance.

And he knew just how to do that.

"Hit it again, harder this time," Sloan commanded.

He watched as Rachel slammed her gloved fist into the punching bag once more.

"That's better. Now, back off and kick it like you mean it." He circled her position and watched her perform the little kickboxing routine he had taught her. "Not too shabby, for a girl."

She glared at him. Then kicked the bag like the move was intended for him.

Sloan winced dramatically, then resisted the urge to grin. Perfect, he thought. He wanted her pissed off. He wanted her to hate him. He might not be able to put the fear in her anymore, but he could sure as hell make her hate him.

Her damp T-shirt clung to her body, outlining those gorgeous little breasts. Sloan averted his gaze. He had worked her hard and his overbearing tactics seemed to be doing the trick if those drop-dead looks she kept directing his way were any indication. He had to rebuild that wall between them.

It was for her own good.

Not to mention his.

"Five more minutes," he told her. "Then do twenty laps in the pool and you can call it a day."

She stopped, midswing, and gaped at him. "Twenty laps! I've already done fifteen."

He quirked an eyebrow. "Twenty-five?"

She muttered a very unladylike curse. Sloan didn't even try to prevent his grin this time. She was too busy beating the hell out of the punching bag to notice anyway.

Whatever it takes, he reminded that part of him that wanted to take her in his arms and kiss the hell out of her. He set his jaw so hard his teeth were in danger of cracking. She was a client, nothing more. When this was over, she and her son would go back to their lives north of the border. Sloan had nothing to offer her.

And he…well, he would return to his usual existence. A few hours of passion couldn't change anything.

Nearly an hour later, her clothes tucked under one arm, a towel wrapped around her slender body, Rachel trudged across the courtyard after her laps. She looked beat. Sloan turned his attention back to the tequila in his glass. She couldn't have had more than two hours sleep this morning. And after the harrowing trip back from the village and having to leave Josh behind…

He caught himself. He would not feel any sympathy. No way. This course of action was best. He had to rebuild that mutual dislike that had first stood between them. Whatever it took to ensure she kept her distance.

"Hungry?" he asked as she neared. He propped his feet on the table and turned up his glass. The liquor's burn promised something he knew from recent experience it would not deliver—escape.

"No," she returned coldly. She paused only long enough to glare at him.

"Good." He deposited his empty glass on the table. "Cooking isn't one of my finer attributes. Maybe you could whip up something later," he suggested with a nonchalance that stiffened her spine. That last remark really ticked her off.

"Don't hold your breath," she snapped, then strode away, anger radiating from every beautiful inch of her.

The time moved at a snail's pace. He had no idea what time it was, he could only judge the passage of time by the empty bottle before him. And, as he suspected, it did nothing for him. Drinking had never kept him from performing well, on the job or in the sack, but it generally helped him not give a damn about much. He swore at his new run of bad luck. Hell, it didn't even do that anymore.

Sloan was reasonably sure whatever time it was, that Rachel had retired to her own room by now. With that in mind, he finally went inside.

The house was quiet. No television noise, no

sweet feminine laughter. No pitter-patter of little feet. He forced the unbidden yearning away. Already he missed the kid's questions, his ceaseless energy. And Rachel's singsong voice as she played with her child. Her laughter whenever Josh did something funny. Dammit, this wasn't supposed to happen. He had sworn that no one would ever get this close to him again. And look at him. Brooding like he'd lost something that belonged to him.

When Sloan passed the great room something in his peripheral vision brought him up short. Rachel, asleep on the couch. He frowned. She was still wearing the damned wet swimsuit and towel. With a heavy breath he moved silently to the couch and sat down on the table in front of it. She was exhausted. Mentally and physically—and totally vulnerable to him.

And it was Sloan's fault.

He closed his eyes and tamped down the regret that rose inside him. He summoned the image of his wife and son and tried to remember how it felt to be with them. His son was no problem. He could feel the child in his arms, hear his voice. But he couldn't do the same with his wife. Each time he attempted to visualize some moment they had shared, Rachel invaded his senses. The feel of her hair slipping through his fingers, the taste of her lips, the smell of her skin.

Sloan shook off the desire already tightening his groin. He opened his eyes and watched her sleep as if that would help. Beneath all that beauty and vulnerability lay more determination than he had ever known in any woman. That combination of fire and fragility drew him when he wanted to push away. The courage it must have taken for her to come all this way to track down a stranger. And then to endure his treatment with hardly a fuss. How in the world had this woman and her son—Angel's son—crashed into his life and made such an unwanted impact?

"You're losing your touch, old man," he mumbled. Sloan settled his gaze on her pretty face. Maybe he was getting old, and soft…or plain stupid. Whatever the case, his was not the kind of business one could risk such lapses in judgment. He had to do something to speed things up before he made any more mistakes. They both needed this over.

He had his head on straight now. What happened last night would not happen again. He owed it to Rachel to save her from the real threat—him. Angel was no longer a threat to her or Josh.

Angel was a dead man.

He just didn't know it yet.

Chapter Ten

Rachel awoke to sunlight reaching across the room. She blinked to adjust to the brightness and then stared at the alarm clock on the bedside table. 9:00 a.m. Why hadn't Sloan come for her? They started at 6:00 a.m. every morning. She threw the cover back and sat up. Why had he allowed her to oversleep? She frowned at the thought that something might be wrong. He certainly hadn't mentioned foregoing the morning workout when he rousted her off the couch last night and forced her to eat the eggs he scrambled. Eggs and toast were his specialty, he had insisted. Rachel felt relatively certain that he had simply wanted to make sure she kept her strength up.

She pushed to her feet and padded to the bathroom. She had fallen asleep on the couch, wet swimsuit and all. The now dry garment hung across the shower door. And who wouldn't have fallen asleep? Sloan had pushed her harder than he ever had before. Had her supremely annoyed as a matter of fact. She still wanted to punch him instead of that damned bag.

She'd had hardly any sleep the night before with taking Josh to the village.

Josh.

Her heart squeezed at the thought of her little boy. She missed him so much. She blinked back the tears and forced herself to go through the motions of preparing for the day. Maybe that was the reason Sloan had kept her so busy yesterday. He had purposely made her angry with his little remarks and unnecessary physical torture. Her arms felt weak from all the laps in the pool. Giving him grace, he probably realized she needed the distraction and then the exhaustion of last night to keep her mind off her son.

And the lovemaking? Had she needed that, too? She moistened her lips and swallowed at the dryness in her throat. Her body tingled even now at the thought of Sloan's lovemaking. She could not regret the act. It had touched her far too deeply. She had been right about Sloan. He had pleasured her to the point of madness before allowing himself the pleasure of release. He had been right, as well. Though Angel had been her first sexual experience, he had not made love to her the way Sloan had. Not by a long shot.

Rachel closed her eyes and quaked with revulsion at the thought of Angel. There was no comparison between the men. Not in the intimate act she and Sloan had shared, nor in any other way. Angel was a selfish, greedy bastard who killed people for a living. She clenched her jaw against the outrage that instantly filled her at the thought of the man. He didn't just kill people, he relished making an art of it. He stole into people's lives, then snatched that life away.

By contrast, Sloan was a good man. Despite the bitterness and indifference he radiated, worn as a shield about him, there was a good heart beating in that awesome chest. Even with the knowledge that Angel was Josh's father, Sloan still reached out to her son. Grudgingly maybe, but he had done it just the same. He would protect them with his life. There was no question in Rachel's mind. Sloan would do whatever it took to protect her and Josh. She closed her eyes and prayed fervently that it wouldn't come down to that. Sloan deserved to live and be happy again. Really happy.

But that happiness wouldn't be found with her. No matter how sweetly and tenderly he had made love to her, there was Josh. Even a good man would hesitate about loving the son of the man who had murdered his wife and child. This thing she felt for Sloan would never work out. Rachel had to think about Josh. His happiness was vastly more important than hers.

She made a mirthless sound and shook her head at the confused woman in the mirror. What was she thinking? Sloan made love to her once and already she's thinking about forever? *Get real, Rachel. The man doesn't want forever with you or anyone else. He just wants to be.* Disgusted with herself, she stamped back into the bedroom and jerked a drawer open to find something to wear. How could she be so naive? Sex, that's all it had been to Sloan. She had to face that fact and get on with it. How adolescent could she get? This was no hot romance. Sex. She shivered. Great sex, but nothing more.

A knock at the door made her jump. She pressed her hand to her chest and let go a breath. This was ridiculous. Sloan would have warned her if there was any immediate danger. The thought that Angel could show up at any time streaked across her mind, and panic detonated inside her once more.

"I hope you're up," came his gruff greeting.

She relaxed. "Come in." She held the jeans she had pulled from her drawer against her chest as if the faded cotton would provide some sort of protection against his too-seeing eyes. What was she so worried about? It wasn't as if he hadn't seen her already, and she was wearing a T-shirt.

The door swung open and Sloan filled the doorway, but didn't step into the room. Rachel breathed a sigh of relief. He hadn't burst into the room with news that Angel was here, and he didn't appear to want to come any closer. She wasn't sure she could handle an up close encounter with him just yet. Her emotions were still too near the surface. The ever-present weapon strapped to his shoulder reminded her that anything could happen in the blink of an eye. Complacency was dangerous.

"Get dressed, we're going into town," he said curtly.

A frown tugged at her lips. "Why are we going into town?"

He shrugged one broad shoulder. "To do what most people do—to shop."

He couldn't be serious. "What?" She moved closer to get a better look at his eyes. The stubble that shadowed his jaw added to the ominous look radiating from those cold blue eyes. Iceman was back.

"Be ready in twenty minutes." He turned to leave.

"Have you lost your mind?" she demanded, effectively halting him.

The look he sent her way went right through her— cold, hard. "You have a problem with going into town?"

She flung her free arm heavenward, still clutching her jeans with the other. "Angel sent word two days ago that he was coming. You know he will. He could be here now, watching and waiting. Going to town isn't safe, it's insane!"

He studied her for a few seconds, his gaze considering. "Angel's kills are always intimate. One on one, with no question as to why. Even if he is here, he won't make a move in public. He'll wait until he can make it personal." He paused, his gaze still searching hers. "Do you trust me, Rachel?"

She blinked, taken aback. Her outrage deflated like a spent party balloon. Of course, she trusted him. That was the one thing she could be absolutely certain of. "Yes."

"Be ready in twenty minutes."

She watched him walk away. Her chest tightened

with the need to go after him, to touch him and hold him close. But he didn't want that, not from her, not now. All day yesterday he had acted as if their lovemaking had not happened. Obviously, it had not affected him as it had her. Rachel shook her head slowly from side to side. It was clear to her that she was more than simply inexperienced, she was completely without any relationship savvy at all. An emotional teenager trapped in a woman's body, with a child who needed her to be a lot smarter than this.

Twenty minutes later, Rachel was ready. She had forgone her jeans and decided to wear her skirt and blouse. She hadn't worn the outfit since the day she arrived and it was her favorite. The long, silky skirt made her feel feminine. And it would be cooler than the jeans, she rationalized. She had braided her hair and dug around in her bag until she found her sunglasses. The eyewear would afford her some protection from Sloan's piercing gaze.

She went in search of Sloan before he could come looking for her. No point in antagonizing him further. He was back to his old self again, and Rachel had learned the lesson that it was his way or no way.

"I'm ready," she announced upon finding him in the kitchen. "I hope I didn't keep you waiting."

"You usually do, so why change now?" He gestured to the coffeepot and shot her an unreadable look. "Coffee?"

Ignoring his terse remark, she shook her head to the offer of coffee, then followed him outside. He walked her to the passenger side of his Jeep and offered his hand in assistance.

"I think I can manage," she refused with a feigned smile.

"Suit yourself." He rounded the hood and settled behind the steering wheel before she could climb in and fasten her seat belt.

Careful not to let him catch her, Rachel studied Sloan's grim profile as he drove toward town. His own sunglasses shielded his eyes from her, but she could tell from the tightening of his jaw when to look away. Whenever Sloan decided to glance at her, his jaw tightened and the set of his mouth grew grimmer. Rachel sighed. She couldn't possibly hope to figure out what was going through his mind.

She stared out at the passing landscape and sadness engulfed her. She missed Josh so much. Her arms ached to hold him. She closed her eyes and allowed his image to envelop her. Was Pablo playing with him? Did he ask where his mommy was? Tears pooled in her eyes. Would this never be over so they could be together without worry?

"Don't think about it." Sloan's deep voice was gentle, soothing and totally unexpected.

Rachel opened her eyes, then blinked to hold back the tears. "I miss him."

His fingers tightened on the steering wheel, and she wondered if he wanted to reach out to her but restrained himself.

"He's safe. That's the important thing."

Sloan glanced at her, though she couldn't see his eyes she saw the change in the set of his rigid jaw. He had feelings for her, if nothing more than basic human compassion, which she had first thought him completely devoid of. Maybe their lovemaking had affected him to some extent.

"Think about something else," he suggested after turning his attention back to the road.

He was right. She had to think about something else or she would lose her mind. Josh was safe and that was the bottom line. Something Sloan had said to her that first day skittered into her fragmented thoughts.

"Were you serious when you said that you took your house from a drug lord?" The question sounded foolish, she realized, but she had to know the answer.

A hint of a smile played about his lips as he considered her question a moment before answering. "He owed me. When I collected he offered me anything he possessed as payment." A heart-stunning smile claimed those full lips then. "I told him I'd settle for the house. He agreed."

Disbelief widened her eyes. "What on earth did you do that would compel the man to give you his home?"

He shot her an assessing sideways glance from behind his sunglasses.

Maybe she didn't want to know.

"I brought his daughter home to him."

His voice had changed. Somber now.

"Where was she?" Rachel asked hesitantly.

The answer was long in coming, finally he spoke. "One of his competitors had kidnapped her. He planned to use her as leverage in a territorial dispute. When he was finished he would have killed her either way."

"How did you get her back?"

He cut her another of those quick looks. "I don't think you want to know."

Rachel shivered at the lethal quality in that simple statement. "So he gave you his house in return?"

"It wasn't that big a deal. He owns several others. He rarely stayed at this one."

"His daughter," Rachel began, "she wasn't harmed?"

"Not a hair on her pretty little head."

Another thought struck her. "This drug lord, surely he had men who worked for him that do…this sort of work."

"None he trusted with his daughter's life." Sloan slowed as they reached the edge of town. He looked at her again, she didn't have to see his eyes to know that he looked straight into hers. She felt him. "None as good as me."

If anyone can help you, Sloan can. She recalled Victoria Colby's words again. This was no ordinary man. She had known it the moment she laid eyes on him. She felt it in his every touch. And for all he gave in this life, fate had taken everything from him.

The harsh reality grieved her. She wanted to reach out to him, make him believe that it could be different. But nothing she could say or do would ever change the past…or reach his fiercely guarded heart.

By lunchtime Rachel had seen yet another side of Sloan. All morning, he made a production of their shopping. He was more than simply attentive. He opened doors for her, touched her reassuringly at all the right times. Not once had she felt vulnerable under his watchful care. But what possessed him to bring her to town? To buy her clothes? And even toys for Josh? It didn't make sense. Especially considering yesterday's die-hard tactics.

The busy streets of Chihuahua teemed with excitement. Vendors peddling their wares, shoppers haggling in the marketplace. The open-air shops beckoned to passersby. Weavers and potters produced their goods right before her amazed eyes. The vibrancy and contrast excited Rachel. The city was colorful and noisy, and, quite frankly, exhilarating.

Or perhaps it was the man who led her through the streets who stole her breath. He held her hand, kept her close. Each time he whispered near her ear, desire sung through her veins. She used every possible excuse to touch him. Just looking at him in those body-hugging jeans and the open chambray shirt over a tight-fitting T-shirt made her tingle, made her want him. The bulge of his holstered weapon beneath his shirt made her feel secure in spite of the danger that might lurk nearby.

She had been right in her first impression of Sloan. He was more man than she had ever known, and he was dangerous.

A definite danger to her heart.

"One more stop before lunch okay with you?"

Rachel blinked away her worrisome thoughts and manufactured a smile. Sloan had tucked his sunglasses into his shirt pocket, those clear blue eyes analyzed her now, expectant and ever watchful.

"Sure, that's fine." *As long as I'm with you it doesn't matter,* she didn't add. God, she was pathetic.

He slid his arm around her waist and ushered her into a more modern shop. Shelves were chock-full of trinkets and assorted items she couldn't readily identify. There was hardly any room to walk around the abundance of merchandise stacked around the floor of the small shop.

"Wait here." Sloan left her near the door, but out of sight of those passing on the street.

Maybe he knew the owner, she considered, as he huddled at the counter with the heavyset man. The man glanced past Sloan's shoulder, smiling a secret smile. Rachel's forehead creased with curiosity. What was Sloan up to? Heaving a beleaguered sigh, she looked away. No point in trying to figure it out. If he wanted her to know, he would tell her.

A wrapped package under his left arm, Sloan rejoined her and hurried her through the door back onto the noisy street. He paused on the sidewalk, out of the path of the passing pedestrians and handed the package to her.

"This is for you." His eyes fairly sparkled with mischief, but his tone was oddly serious.

"But you've already bought too much for me and Josh," she protested.

"This is different." He gestured to the package. "Open it."

Resigned, Rachel tore the recycled brown paper from the rectangular object. What she found beneath the wrapping stunned her. A sketch pad and set of drawing pencils.

She lifted her gaze to his. "I don't know what to say." God, she didn't want to cry, but it seemed a definite possibility at the moment. No one since her father died had done anything this nice for her.

He shrugged. "Don't say anything. Draw something for me. A picture is worth a thousand words."

He wasn't nearly fast enough to mask the emotions in his gaze this time. Rachel saw the need there, saw the desire. He might try to pretend he was unaffected by her, but he wasn't. And now she knew for sure. Unable to stop herself, she threw her arms around his neck and hugged him, his unexpected gift clutched in her right hand.

"Thank you," she murmured. "This is the nicest thing anyone has ever done for me."

His arms tightened around her waist, holding her lower body firmly against his own, but he drew back slightly to peer down at her. "I'm glad you like it." Something sad flickered in his eyes, followed by a yearning that spoke to her more loudly than any words he could have said.

She couldn't say what possessed her at that

moment, but all other thought flew from her head. She kissed him. She needed to kiss him. He needed to be kissed.

The noisy marketplace, the cars moving slowly by, the haggling of buyers and sellers all faded into insignificance. There was only Sloan and the way he was kissing her. His mouth moved tenderly over hers. His hands stoked the flames raging in her heated body. She tiptoed, wanting more of him, but he drew back. He looked as dazed as she felt, his ragged breath fanned her freshly kissed lips, kindling a new fire within her.

"Lunch," he reminded, the one word breathless with a raspy quality that oozed sexuality.

She nodded. "Lunch."

But food would never be enough to fill her hunger.

Sloan kicked a small stone, sending it skittering across the sand. He checked the weapon in his holster as he paused long enough to survey the rear gate and the lighted area that lay beyond it. Satisfied with what he found, he proceeded around the east end of the house, scanning the windows as he went. He knew the grounds were secure. Fernando, his export business never taken lightly, had spared no expense when installing his elaborate security system. No code, no entrance. Any movement within six feet of the wall tripped the alarm. You had to enter by a gate, and you could only do that with the code. If you attempted to climb over, the alarm tripped.

He entered the front door, then locked it and reset

the alarm to night mode. Rachel had retired to her room with her prizes. He doubted he would see her again tonight. At least he hoped like hell he wouldn't see her again tonight.

He cursed himself all the way to the great room. He snagged his half-empty tequila bottle from the bar and didn't stop until he was outside on the patio. He didn't want to risk running into her if she decided she needed a drink of water, or simply wanted to say good-night. He kicked a chair from beneath the table and dropped into it.

Another curse hissed past his lips when he realized he had forgotten a glass. "Screw it," he muttered, then turned up the bottle for a long drink. When he came up for air, he sat the bottle on the table and closed his eyes. He propped his elbows on the table and massaged his aching temples.

He could kick himself if it would do any good. But it wouldn't, it was too frigging late. He had crossed the line and now Rachel would pay for his mistake. He swore and took another long pull from the bottle. It would have taken a blind man not to see the way she looked at him today. The foolish admiration and respect. And the other.

Dammit to hell. The woman was in love with him. He had screwed up royally. He was nothing now. A shell of a man. His life was bargain basement, all the best stuff was long gone. He was good at his job and nothing else. The only thing he had to offer her was Angel's head.

The woman deserved better than him. She was selling herself way too short. A muscle jerked in his jaw as he grabbed the bottle and turned it up once more. He swallowed long and hard. He scrubbed a hand over his face and leaned back in his chair. He had seduced her…or hell, maybe she had seduced him with her innocence. Whatever. He had known better. She didn't have enough experience to be wary of a man like him. He had warned her, but she came anyway. She just didn't realize what she was getting herself into.

He closed his eyes and tortured himself with the memories of making love to her. Her sweet responses. The taste of her skin. The feel of her snug body as she sheathed him. So damned tight. So hot. His loins grew heavy just thinking about being inside her. Her sweet lips tempted him beyond reason. Those big brown eyes, full of trust and vulnerability, made him ache to hold her. He had been furious with himself yesterday, his anger had protected him. Kept him from screwing up again. But watching her sleep last night had dissolved any rage he had tried desperately to hang on to.

He had tried to keep his perspective today. He had planned every step, careful to carry through with each. Whoever Angel had watching them had gotten an eyeful. Sloan was certain that Angel knew by now that the relationship between him and Rachel had gone beyond business. The son of a bitch would be seething. A smile tugged at Sloan's lips. He would move fast now.

The one thing Sloan had learned about Angel was to make the first move. He needed him off balance. Nothing got to Angel faster than someone moving in on his territory. Rachel and Josh were his, to Angel's way of thinking. The idea that Sloan now had them would be more than he could tolerate. He would be here soon. Very soon. And Sloan would be ready.

Sloan figured the woman who gave Josh the bear was Angel's watcher. She had either been with Angel long enough to know that little gift, and then the yellow ribbon, would send Sloan into a flashback or Angel had told her to give Josh that particular kind of bear. The tokens were meant to throw Sloan off balance. To remind him of what he had lost. It had worked, for a while anyway. But now he had the upper hand. Angel couldn't possibly know where Josh was. They had stolen across the mountain in the dead of night. The sandstorm had proved a blessing in disguise. It had blown away any tracks they left behind.

Josh was hidden safely away, and Sloan had Rachel. Angel would be irate. The bastard. Sloan took another long drink. The urge to kill the man was overwhelming. Then Rachel would be free. Free to raise Josh. To live her life. To marry and have more children.

For that reason Sloan would not touch her again. Even if she begged him, he would not touch her again. He hadn't meant for that one kiss today to turn so passionate. He had intended to stay in control. Too much was riding on this to make a mistake. He would not fail Rachel where Angel was concerned. And he would not allow this thing between them to go any further.

Rachel deserved a lifetime commitment and he had no life to offer. He stared at the bottle in his hand. Everything he was or dreamed of being died seven years ago. Even a woman as sweet and giving as Rachel couldn't resurrect the dead.

Chapter Eleven

A long hot soak in the tub had been just the ticket to relieve Rachel's aching muscles. Even with today's respite from Sloan's rigorous workout demands, the adventures of the last two days were tattooed onto every muscle of her body. Especially her feminine muscles. Her fingers stilled in their efforts to loosen her braided hair. Her heart quickened at the images that flashed before her eyes. Sloan's powerful body moving over hers, his skilled hands, the delicious torture of his equally skilled mouth.

She sighed. She shouldn't be feeling this way. Sloan didn't want her to want him, she knew that beyond a shadow of a doubt. He'd made that point crystal clear yesterday. Then today, he'd been more than a little reticent.

Except for that kiss. Heat shimmered through her at the memory. She had sneaked that one in on him. That stolen kiss. The beginnings of a smile teased her lips. He had held back at first, then he'd returned her kiss with the same fervor she felt. For just one fleeting instant afterward she had seen in his eyes what he wanted to hide, then it had been gone. Banished like the rest of the emotions he refused to feel.

He'd quickly reverted to the brooding man who confused and annoyed her so thoroughly. Rachel combed her fingers through her loosened hair. He didn't want this relationship. Why couldn't she get that concept through her thick skull? He didn't even want her, not really. He took what she offered, when she pushed the issue, but he didn't ask.

Exasperated, Rachel swore and stormed to her bedroom. Well, she couldn't help the way she felt. And she wasn't about to back off. She intended to show Sloan that it was okay to feel something, anything, for another human being. Somehow she would make him see. He had lost so much, he should have a future with a woman who would appreciate the kind of man he was. A rush of jealousy zapped her. She didn't want another woman to make him happy. She wanted to do it herself.

"Optimistic fool," she muttered. She glared at the new dress and the art supplies he had bought for her. Why did he do that? Was it his way of trying to be nice? Payback for what he obviously considered as nothing more than a sexual favor? She stared down at the short, silk gown she wore. He had picked it out, too. The way he'd caressed the fabric made her ache to feel his hands on her skin. Surely what they had shared touched him in some way. There had to be some reason why he spent the day so frivolously with her. The stuffed parrot and maracas he'd gotten for Josh waited on the dresser for his return. Josh would love them.

Rachel closed her eyes and resisted the urge to cry. She needed Josh back in her arms. She needed Pablo here to run interference. Then these out-of-control feelings would never have happened. She wouldn't have gotten caught up in this crazy need to make Sloan feel what he clearly did not want to.

Enough, she told herself. She'd started this, she would finish it. Sloan would not prevent her from reaching out to him. He didn't have to take what she offered, but she would offer just the same. She couldn't help herself. She cared too much to leave it this way. Her attempts, successful or not, might make all the difference. Decision made, she strode determinedly through the gigantic house looking for him. She would thank him again for his generosity and she would say good-night. It was the courteous thing to do. He might not care whether she was civil to him or not, but she did.

It didn't take her long to find him. An outside shower, open on three sides and designed for spraying off before or after swimming, had been built on the far end of the pool. Sloan stood beneath the spray of water, naked from the waist up. His shirt and holstered gun lay on a nearby bush. An almost empty tequila bottle hung from his right hand.

The water slid over his wet hair and down his chest to absorb into his already soaked jeans. While she watched he turned up the bottle and finished it off. He tossed it aside, it shattered where it fell. Rachel jerked at the sound. She moistened her lips and wondered if it would be wise to approach him in his present mood. She wasn't afraid of him, she reminded herself. He would never hurt her.

She moved closer, her eyes reveling in the way the wet jeans clung to his taut body. Her heart skipped a beat, then pounded in reaction. His broad shoulders and muscular chest drew her gaze upward. The water stopped and he pushed his hands over his face and hair, sweeping the wet length back. She thought of how few words he had spoken to her since that stolen kiss. Watching him now she recognized the thing most people missed when they looked at this fierce, almost hostile man—the pain. So very much pain.

He suffered in silence, with only the tequila for relief. It seemed impossible that such a strong and seemingly unfeeling man could be vulnerable to anything at all. But he definitely was. And somehow she intended to heal that deep hurt…just a little bit.

She moved closer still. His eyes opened as if he sensed her presence. Instinctively she knew he did. The pain in those clear blue depths made her breath catch, but he masked his feelings in an instant. The defiant set of his chin warned her not to waste her time.

"Are you all right?" she asked tentatively, venturing a step closer.

Ignoring her question, he banged his fist against the chrome control and the water showered over him once more. He shifted and lifted his face to the cold spray, and Rachel had no choice but to admire the perfect body displayed so enticingly in that wet denim. Lean, hard, and breath-stealingly male. When he turned back to her, his eyes still closed, she acknowledged the chiseled features of his face, and the blond stubble that glistened on his jaw. As handsome as sin, and every bit as seductive…and dangerous to her heart.

The water stopped and his eyes opened. His relaxed expression transformed into a glower with the realization that she hadn't left as he had silently ordered.

"What do you want?" The raspy growl skittered along her nerve endings.

"I…I wanted to say good night," she stammered, suddenly uncertain of herself beneath his fierce glare, "but then I found you like…like this and I was worried that maybe something was wrong."

"I'm just dandy," he said with a grimace. "Now go to bed." His gaze swept over her, and she didn't miss the glint of male hunger there.

Rachel crossed her arms over her chest. She should have worn something else. She was about as subtle as a sledgehammer between the eyes.

"I'm not going to bed," she informed him, defying his command, "until you tell me what's wrong. You've been acting strangely all afternoon." Though it was well past afternoon now, he knew what she meant.

He leaned against the shower wall and rubbed one wide palm over his tanned chest. "Coming out here dressed like that—" he nodded at her slinky attire "—is risky business, Rachel." He made a speculative sound in his throat. "It makes a guy wonder if you're really worried about him or not. Maybe there's something else you're looking for."

Ire prickled her. "You bought it for me—didn't you want me to wear it?"

He held her gaze for two beats before looking away. "Yeah." He plowed his fingers through his wet hair. "I did."

Resisting the urge to run back inside the house and lock the door behind her, she walked straight up to him. He watched, gauging her intent.

"What's going on, Sloan? Yesterday you had nothing to say to me other than to order me around. Today suddenly you take me shopping." She shook her head. "I don't understand." She swallowed the lump of emotion rising in her throat. "We made love—" he flinched as if she'd slapped him, her heart sank, he didn't want to talk about it, but she went on anyway "—and suddenly we're back to barely speaking."

He leveled his unreadable gaze on hers for emphasis. "Today had nothing to do with…the sex."

She trembled with the anger mounting inside her. Sex. Was that all it was to him? Of course it was. She blinked twice, three times. She would not cry.

"Then what was today all about?" she demanded, erasing as much hurt as she could from her voice.

"Today was for Angel's benefit," he said bluntly, those emotionless eyes still fixed firmly on hers.

Dread pooled in her stomach, temporarily slowing her outrage. "What do you mean it was for Angel's benefit?"

He cocked his head belligerently. "What do you want me to do, draw you a picture?"

Another surge of fury stiffened her spine. "I want you to answer the damned question."

"I wanted to make him jealous, so I escorted you around town like we were—" a humorless smile hitched up one corner of his mouth "—a couple. I'm sure his little friend couldn't get word to him fast enough."

He straightened, too close now. She held her ground in spite of the pulse-pounding adrenaline roaring through her. She would not back off. She needed to understand what he was getting at. Instinct warned that she wasn't going to like it.

He heaved a disinterested breath. "To Angel's way of thinking, you and the kid belong to him. So if I were you, I'd go back in the house and stay there, 'cause when he gets here he's gonna be pissed."

Rage more deadly than she had ever experienced before exploded inside her. None of the attention he had spared her was real. The gifts, the kisses, the lovemaking. It was all about revenge. Baiting the enemy. Drawing a line in the sand. She struggled to maintain her composure as she demanded calmly, "It was all about antagonizing Angel?" She knew the answer, but she wanted to hear him say the words. "Everything?" she pressed.

"Today was about Angel," he said flatly. "The sex was about giving you what you thought you wanted."

Tears welled in her eyes, betraying her. She wanted to rant at him. She was furious. She didn't want to cry. "I wasn't the only one who wanted it."

"I warned you to stay away." He captured a handful of her hair and allowed it to slip through his fingers. "What did you expect from a guy like me?"

One lone tear trickled past her hold. "I needed you," she said softly, her voice trembling.

Her words slammed into Sloan's middle like a sucker punch. This was the one thing he had wanted to avoid at all cost. Another tear rolled down her cheek, his gut clenched. He didn't want to hurt her. But she needed him to be something he just couldn't be, not for her, not for anyone.

"I told you in the beginning that I wasn't the man you think I am." *I'm nothing,* he didn't add. He shoved the damp hair back from his face. Dammit, why didn't she just go to bed and leave him be?

She moistened those full lips and let go a heavy breath. "And I told you," she argued, then paused as another shudder trembled through her, "that you're the man I need."

His desire kindling already, there was no way to ignore the desperation filling those big brown eyes.

He swore softly. "You don't need me," he repeated, his voice losing some of its conviction.

She shook her head in denial, then whispered, "More than you can know."

His need to hold her overrode his caution. He pulled her against him, his arms going around her as if it were the most natural thing in the world. She trembled in his hold. Sloan blocked any response to the hurt he knew would come next, but he couldn't let this happen.

He tipped her chin up so that he could look directly into her eyes. "What you need right now has nothing to do with me." Before she could protest, he shifted, pressing her back against the damp wall. He turned on the water. She gasped as the cool water sprinkled over her heated skin. The silk gown plastered to her skin, outlining her breasts, her thighs and that sweet place that lay between them. He devoured her with his eyes, every muscle in his body hardening so fast that his breath stalled in his chest. The spray of water stopped. He watched the rivulets slip down her bare skin, then disappear into the green silk.

Her nipples pebbled before his eyes. He licked his lips, restraining the urge to taste them. The only sound around them was that of their uneven breath, hers as ragged as his.

"Please," she urged, reaching for him, drawing him nearer. "I know you need me, too."

She lifted her mouth for him to take. He wanted

her more than she could imagine. More than even he had dreamed possible. She had to understand that he couldn't be what she needed him to be. "That may be," he murmured, his lips so close to hers that he could feel their pull. Electricity fairly crackled between them. "But you don't need me."

He held her desire-clouded gaze in a kind of trance. He couldn't look away any more than he could let her. He braced his right arm against the wall above her head, trapping her with his body in the same way he imprisoned her eyes with his own. A tiny hitch in her breathing signaled her approval. Determined to prove his point, he encircled her wrist with the fingers of his left hand and drew it up to her breast. She gasped when he placed her hand over the sensitive swell. He squeezed and kneaded using her fingers. She closed her eyes and shook her head, denying the pleasure.

"Look at me, Rachel." The softly uttered command was more guttural than he'd intended, but his own need was rushing toward desperation. "Look at me." He pinched her nipple between her thumb and forefinger, rolling the tight peak, then tugging the way he would do with his mouth.

Her lids fluttered open on a startled moan. "Stop," she insisted.

"Shh," he soothed. He would make her see if it killed him.

She strained toward his mouth, pleading for his possession. He squeezed her breast again, then moved to the other, kneading, squeezing. Her breath came faster. He struggled to slow his. It would be a miracle if he didn't come before she did. Her hips began to undulate, arching toward his aching arousal. He dragged her hand down her delicate rib cage to that part of her that pleaded for attention. Her eyes went wide when he pressed her hand firmly against her mound. She gasped. He stroked her harder. The fingers of her free hand found their way to his waistband and tugged. He placed those needy fingers on her breast and squeezed.

"No," she resisted, her eyes closing again in the pleasure she could no longer deny.

He stroked her harder, faster, knowing she was close now. She fought it, but he knew just how to make her surrender. She tensed, her body quivering. She cried out, the sound a combination of agony and ecstasy. His groin jerked in response.

Her eyes slowly opened, her breath coming in short pants. He peered down at her shuttered gaze. "See," he rasped, "you don't need me at all." Releasing her before he lost the last flimsy remnants of his control, he turned, snagged up his weapon and walked away. His whole body throbbed. Need ached savagely in his loins.

"Maybe you're right," she called after him, her voice still unsteady.

He hesitated, and turned around slowly to face her as he tugged the holster over his shoulder. The sight of her threatened his composure. Wet, her hair wild, her skin flushed from her recent climax, he wanted her like nothing or no one he had ever wanted before.

She lifted her chin and stared at him in magnificent defiance. She was gorgeous. "Maybe I don't need you," she agreed, her voice still husky. "But I want you." Her bare feet soundless on the tile, she moved toward him, a sensual vision in exotic green silk.

His pulse tripped. "Then you're a fool."

"Probably." She pushed the damp tendrils of hair from her cheek and met his gaze with steel in her own. "But I'm not a coward."

Uneasiness slid through him. "I see," he said with sudden clarity. "The big, brave protector you came all this way to find is really a coward. Is that it?" He squashed the little voice screaming for his attention. He wasn't a coward. He wasn't afraid of anything, certainly not death.

"You're not brave," she said quietly. "You're hiding from the world." She flung her arms outward, her palms flared. "Look around you, Sloan," she ordered, her voice rising to match her anger. "Do you think these walls or your fancy security system is going to stop men like Angel?" She stabbed at his chest with her forefinger.

He flinched, not at her jab, but a delayed reaction to her words.

"Is all that bitterness and indifference you hide behind going to change the past?" She shook her head. "No. It won't bring your wife or your little boy back."

He swallowed, hard. Tears stung his eyes. "Just shut up," he said tightly. "You don't know what you're talking about."

"Losing your family wasn't enough," she continued, hammering at his defenses, "you had to lose yourself, too."

"You don't know anything about how I feel." Trembling inside, he turned away from her. He had to get out of here. He didn't want to hear this. He didn't want to feel any of this.

"You are a coward, Sloan."

He closed his eyes and struggled for control. The hurt, the need was almost more than he could bear. It swelled inside him, threatening to burst from him. She didn't understand. He couldn't take that chance again. Not ever again.

"You're afraid to take what you want—what you need—because you're afraid of losing again. So you pretend you don't care about anything or anyone. You *pretend*," she added, driving the last nail in the coffin of his restraint, "that you don't care or want, but you do."

He turned around and closed the distance between them with slow, deliberate steps. When he was toe to toe with her, he stared into those wide velvety eyes for three long beats before he could speak at a normal decibel level. "You're sure you're willing to give what I want to take." His voice sounded strange to his own ears, thick with the desire simmering just beneath the surface, but at the same time deadly with the other raw emotions churning wildly.

"Yes."

His fingers plunged into her hair and pulled her mouth hard against his. Want exploded inside him. He had to have her. Now. He kissed her savagely until she gasped for breath. He lifted her then, and carried her straight to his bed, kicking the door closed behind him. He shrugged off his weapon and lowered it to the floor.

Unable to slow the building momentum, they tumbled onto the bed together, a tangle of arms and legs. Hands everywhere, their hungry mouths seeking, torturing. The sound of their ragged breathing shattering the silence. He couldn't wait. Couldn't stop the plunge toward completion. Her fingers wrenched his jeans open and tugged desperately at the wet denim. They groaned simultaneously, the sound reverberating in the kiss they could not bear to end. She pushed harder on the confining fabric. And suddenly he was free. Sloan jerked the damp silk above her thighs, pushed aside the scrap of lace and shoved into her in one long thrust. She screamed her pleasure. He shuddered with the release that crashed down on him the instant he entered her.

Her long legs wrapped around his, pulling him more deeply inside her. She kissed his chin, his lips. Her hands slid over his bare skin until she held him tightly in her arms.

He braced his weight on his elbows and stared into her eyes. Just looking into those huge brown eyes made him ache for the rest of what she offered. But that could never be. He would not take the risk. She smiled tentatively when he continued to stare so intently.

Sloan wanted to look away, but he couldn't. She cradled him so tightly that renewed need stirred in him already, or maybe it had never completely died. The sweetness of her lips tempted him even now, begged for his possession.

She traced the line of his jaw, her expression suddenly somber. "You mean a great deal to me, Sloan." She leveled her too serious gaze on his. "Nothing will ever change that. No matter what happens, I want you to know that. You're the bravest man I know."

He brushed his lips across hers. "So I'm not a coward after all?"

She blushed. "I was angry."

He hummed a sound of approval. "I like it when you put me in my place."

"I'm serious," she protested. "I just wanted you to know that I won't let you or anything else change my mind about how I feel."

"Is that a threat?" he teased.

"No," she huffed. "It's a promise."

It was his turn to be somber. "Be careful what you promise, Rachel." He flexed his hips. Her breath caught. Desire barbed low in his gut, urging him to thrust again. But he had to say what needed to be said first. She had to understand. "You might have second thoughts later. Things change." He trailed a finger down her smooth cheek. "Right now you've got me up on this pedestal, thinking I'm some sort of hero."

She squeezed his buttocks. "I don't want to talk." She wiggled her hips to punctuate her statement. Those wicked hands trailed up his sides, then smoothed over his chest, stopping only long enough to tweak his nipples. "I want to make up for lost time."

He groaned and grabbed her hands to pin them above her head. He nibbled at her mouth, retreating when she would have kissed him.

"Just remember," he murmured thickly. "I won't hold you to any promises you make tonight."

The ringing telephone woke him from the sweetest dream he'd ever had. The realization that Rachel was in bed with him, in his arms made his lips curl into a smile. He was dreaming of her. The phone rang again, disrupting his smile and his good mood. He glanced at the clock on the bedside table. 1:00 a.m. Who the hell would be calling at this time of night? Rachel snuggled closer to him. He watched her sleep a moment longer. So trusting, so giving.

Another insistent ring shattered the pleasant silence. Sloan swore and reached across the woman in his arms and snagged up the receiver.

"Yeah," he snapped.

The only sound he heard was a kind of mechanical hum that assured him someone was on the other end of the line but refused to speak.

"Who the hell is it?"

A strange scratchy sound.

Sloan clenched his jaw and prepared to hang up. The next sound he heard stopped him cold.

"Daddy…"

Mark.

"Daddy!" his son cried.

Chapter Twelve

"It wasn't a local call," he said quietly. "A cell phone probably."

Rachel stood a few feet away, watching the agony manifest itself in the lines and angles of his strong body. He'd pulled on a pair of jeans and a shirt, but hadn't bothered to button either. The holstered weapon hung loosely over his left shoulder. Pain and weariness etched itself across his handsome face. What could she do or say that would make that kind of suffering tolerable?

"You're sure it was him?" she asked hesitantly. She had awakened to Sloan standing naked next to the bed staring down at the telephone. She had never seen that much devastation in anyone's eyes. When she touched him, he'd trembled as if unable to bear even that slight human contact.

Sloan stared at the small, framed photograph he held in his hand. It was the first and only picture of his son Rachel had seen anywhere in the house. He'd had it tucked away in the right bottom drawer of his desk.

"It was his voice." He caressed the smiling face beneath the glass with his thumb. "It was the same recording Angel used seven years ago."

Rachel shuddered with the sudden, overwhelming urge to strangle Angel with her bare hands. How could he do this? Hadn't Sloan suffered enough? She shook her head slowly. He had agreed to help her and Josh, that decision had put him back in the line of fire.

"I made a mistake," he murmured.

Rachel wasn't sure if he was speaking to her or to the little boy with the curly blond hair and big blue eyes in the photograph. She only knew she had to reach out to him, to comfort him somehow. She moved closer and placed her hand on his arm.

"It wasn't your fault."

He stared at her hand for a moment, then turned his attention back to the child in the photograph. "I should have stopped." He exhaled a shaky breath. "But I didn't. I wanted to bring Angel down. To do what no one else had been able to do." He squeezed his eyes shut and rubbed his forehead with the tips of his fingers. But nothing was going to make those haunting memories go away. "That mistake cost me everything."

"You were only doing your job." Rachel slid her arms around his waist and held him. His arm went automatically around her shoulders, pulling her closer. Hope bloomed in her chest at that simple gesture.

"It was supposed to be between him and me." He closed his eyes against the horrifying images Rachel knew were replaying in his head. "I was following another lead on Angel late that night when I got the call." He fell silent for several long seconds. "I should have been at home with my family. Cops were everywhere when I got there. I pushed my way into the house and she…she was dead."

"I'm sorry." Rachel pressed her face against his warm chest. Moisture spilled past her lashes. She didn't try to stop it, there was no point.

"The detective in charge wanted to know where our son was. He wasn't in the house. He wasn't at the neighbor's." Sloan swallowed hard. "He wasn't anywhere. Angel had taken him."

She felt him shudder, and she held him tighter.

"We searched for days, hoping we'd find him. Ran pictures of him in the newspaper and on the news. Somebody had to have seen something." His voice grew distant and lost all inflection. "No one came forward. Then the calls started. Every night." He laughed a mirthless sound. "At that point, I even prayed…but God wasn't listening. Or maybe I wasn't worthy of his ear." He exhaled a shaky breath. "For weeks we followed every lead, searched that damned city from top to bottom. While Angel continued to call and haunt me with my son's voice."

Rachel braced herself for what he would say next. The tension drained from his big body, leaving the hopelessness she knew had engulfed him seven years ago. She couldn't help imagining how she would feel if she lost Josh. She trembled beneath the immense anxiety of the mere thought.

"Two months, one week, and three days later we found his body," he continued. "For almost a year after that I searched for Angel," he said through gritted teeth. "I wanted him dead, but he'd vanished without a trace. I pushed harder and harder…until I lost it. And then there was nothing."

She swiped her eyes and struggled to keep her voice even. "Why is he doing this now? This is about my son, not yours."

"Payback for what I did today." Sloan placed the precious photograph on his desk and turned to her. "We've got his attention now. You can bet he'll be here soon."

Rachel thanked God that Josh was hidden safely away. At the same time, she worried that Angel might kill her and Sloan, leaving Josh alone. No, she affirmed. That wasn't going to happen. Fate couldn't be that cruel again. But, if the worst did occur, Pablo would care for Josh. Rachel was certain of that. He would keep him hidden away until Angel stopped looking.

She leveled her gaze on Sloan's. "What do we do?"

He brushed her cheek with his knuckles. Concern flickered in his gaze. "You should get some sleep."

She shook her head adamantly. "How can I sleep knowing he may show up at any moment?"

"There's no way anyone is getting in here without

me knowing it." He gifted her with a weary smile. "Trust me. I have a backup system for my backup system. He won't get in without setting off an alarm."

"I don't think I could sleep anyway." She shivered, suddenly cold wearing nothing but his shirt. "How about some coffee?"

Before Sloan could respond to her offer, a single chime sounded. His head went up. She recognized the tone as the warning that someone had opened an exterior door. "Stay right here," he ordered.

Fear gripped Rachel by the throat. She tunneled her fingers through her hair and tried to slow the pounding in her chest. She had to stay calm. Becoming hysterical would not help. She stood statue still as Sloan moved silently toward the door on the other side of the spacious office. He drew his weapon and paused before moving into the hall to listen. Pablo burst into the room, Josh in his arms.

"What's wrong?" Rachel flew to him, reaching for her child.

"Sorry, *señora,*" Pablo said breathlessly. "The fever started this afternoon. The healer could not bring it down. I had no choice but to bring him to you—"

"My God, he's burning up." Rachel touched his cheeks, his forehead. A new kind of fear twisted inside her. She took Josh into her arms. His body was on fire. Hysteria climbed into her throat and lodged there. "We have to do something."

"Run a cold bath," Sloan instructed Pablo. "I'll get the ice."

Sloan disappeared before Rachel could gather her wits and comment.

"This way." Pablo ushered her into the hall.

Rachel followed him, Josh cradled in her arms, to their room. While Pablo ran the bath, Rachel stripped Josh down to his underwear. He whimpered but didn't rouse from the heavy sleep. There was no sign of any kind of injury. A virus? Something from the water or maybe the food? Was there a doctor in Florescitaf? What if he—? Rachel slammed the door on that line of thinking. She had to stay calm. She couldn't help Josh if she became hysterical.

Sloan came with the ice. Rachel carried Josh to the bathroom and watched as the two men readied the water. This couldn't be happening, she argued. But it was. Nausea burned the back of her throat, her knees felt suddenly weak.

"Let me have him." Sloan scooped Josh from her arms before she could react.

Rachel didn't want to let him go, but Sloan was already crouched in front of the tub with her son in his arms. She knelt beside him as he lowered Josh into the icy water. Her baby cried out. Rachel's heart squeezed painfully and a new rush of tears streamed down her cheeks.

"Shh, baby, it's okay," she soothed. His thin little body trembled and he sobbed softly. Rachel prayed like she had never prayed before. Sloan's words echoed inside her head. *I even prayed...but God wasn't listening.* God would listen tonight. He had to.

"Pablo," Sloan said over her head. "Take the Jeep into town and roust Doc Hernandez from his bed. Bring him back here with you if you have to do it at gunpoint. We can't risk leaving the house with the boy. Angel may be close by."

Pablo placed a hand on her shoulder and squeezed reassuringly. "He will be fine, *señora*. I will bring the doctor."

Rachel nodded, she couldn't speak. She could only watch her baby fight Sloan's efforts to keep his little body submerged. His feeble cries ripped her heart to shreds.

Five minutes or maybe fifteen passed, she couldn't say which, before Sloan jerked her from her near catatonic state by asking for towels. Rachel grabbed two from the cabinet and quickly wrapped them around her son as Sloan lifted him from the icy water.

"We need to get plenty of water down him," he told her as he carried Josh to the bed. "Do you have any Tylenol or anything like that for him?"

Her responses sluggish, Rachel nodded and tried to remember what she had done with her bag. The closet. She hurried to the closet and grabbed the bag and immediately upended it. She fished through the items until she found what she needed. With the chewable Tylenol in hand, she sat down on the side of the bed next to her baby. Sloan had pulled a sheet over him. The wet towels and underwear lay in a heap on the floor.

"I'll get a pitcher of water and a glass."

Rachel opened the small, plastic bottle and tapped out tiny, pink tablets. Her baby's drawn, pale face made her want to cry all over again. But she had to be strong for him. He would be upset if he saw her crying.

"Josh, sweetie, Mommy needs you to take your medicine." His dark eyes fluttered open and she held one tablet close to his chapped lips. He made no move to take it. "Please, baby, you have to chew it up and swallow it. It'll help you get better."

He opened his mouth and took the tablet. Rachel waited until she was sure he had chewed and swallowed it before she offered the next one. By the time the tablets were ingested, Sloan appeared with the water.

Rachel coaxed Josh into drinking as much of the water as possible before he fell into another heavy sleep. His temperature felt much lower now. Sloan produced a digital thermometer and according to it, his temp was only slightly above normal. Rachel breathed a tremendous sigh of relief. Now, if they could only keep it that way. But he would still need to see the doctor. She wanted to be sure he was all right.

Sloan smoothed a comforting hand over her hair. "Get some sleep, Rachel, I'll check on the two of you in a little while. If Josh's temperature starts to rise again, I'll wake you."

Too drained to respond verbally, Rachel nodded. She climbed into bed next to Josh and closed her eyes. Sloan stayed in the room awhile before leaving. Though she was too exhausted to talk to him or even to open her eyes, she was glad he was there.

Just before she drifted off, she remembered to say another little prayer. This time to thank God for listening.

When Rachel woke again it was five in the morning. She smoothed her hand over Josh's face and was pleased to find his skin only slightly warmer than it should be. She sat up and reached for the medicine bottle on the night table. After tapping out more tablets, she roused Josh enough to chew and swallow them. She managed to get a few sips of water down him, as well.

Reaching to the night table again, she pulled his favorite pajamas from the top drawer. He wouldn't like it if he woke up naked. He loved his pj's. After slipping the soft cotton outfit on him, she kissed his cheek.

Easing off the bed, she stretched her neck and shoulders. She must have slept in an awkward position. She should probably get dressed and find Sloan. She frowned when she considered that Pablo should be back by now. It wasn't that far to town. Surely the doctor hadn't come into the room and checked Josh without her realizing it. She was tired rightly enough, but not that tired.

She licked her lips and cringed at the bad taste in her mouth. Noticing the water still standing in the tub as she entered the bathroom, Rachel flipped the lever to drain it. Those frantic moments whirled in her head. Sloan had taken charge of Josh's care. Surely that meant something. He had to feel something for the child, no matter who his father was. Grimacing, she raked the brush through her tousled hair and scowled at the dark circles under her eyes. She looked a mess.

After washing up and brushing her teeth, she dressed in jeans and a T-shirt. She needed to talk to Sloan and see what the plan was for hiding Josh. Though she was thrilled to have him with her again, this new turn of events definitely required a new strategy. Josh was not safe here. Maybe not anywhere. Before leaving the room, she smiled down at her son and switched off the lamp on the bedside table.

Her stomach rumbled and Rachel suddenly remembered that she hadn't eaten dinner last night. Warmth glowed inside her when she considered what she had been doing. She hadn't been hungry earlier, by the time she decided she could eat she had been otherwise occupied. Sloan had attempted to prove that she didn't need him. Heat flushed her cheeks when she thought of the way he'd given her physical satisfaction without actually touching her himself. But he was wrong, it was his nearness, the sound of his voice that had pushed her over the edge. She closed her eyes and relived that moment when he filled her. She had thought she would surely die from the pleasure of it.

Rachel scolded herself for getting sidetracked.

She checked on Josh once more then padded down the long hall in search of Sloan. She smiled when the scent of fresh-brewed coffee tickled her nose. She found him in the kitchen staring out the window at the lingering predawn darkness.

For one long moment she could only stand there and look at him. His arms crossed over his chest, one lean hip propped against the counter. Her body responded to him instantly, growing warm and moist. His hair was loose around his shoulders, the tawny length tempting her fingers. He turned to look at her and her pulse skipped when that mesmerizing blue gaze collided with hers.

The hint of a smile that touched his lips melted her bones. She was so in love with him. If she could spend the rest of her life right here with him, she would. All he would have to do is ask. But he wouldn't do that. Though she had seen with her own eyes the tender moments he shared with Josh, he could never love him the way she loved him. Josh was Angel's son, that was the cold hard fact. Rachel closed her eyes and turned away from what she knew would never truly be hers.

"Is Josh okay?"

Rachel jerked back to attention and produced a smile. She focused on his mouth, his hair, anything but his eyes. "Yes. His temp's still at a safe level."

"Good." He sounded distracted.

The frown that claimed his features snapped her gaze to his. "Is something wrong?" she asked.

He sighed as if contemplating whether to worry her with his concerns. "It's Pablo. He should have been back long before now. There's always the possibility that the Jeep broke down, but that's not likely. He would have walked back or into town. He has a sister there that he could have gone to for transportation."

Rachel stilled. The hunger she had felt only minutes ago fled. "You think something has happened to him?"

He leveled his gaze on hers. "I don't think it, I know it. The only thing that would keep Pablo from coming back is someone putting him out of commission."

No further explanation was required. He thought Pablo was dead. The realization hardened like a rock in her stomach. Despair swooped down and tore at her chest.

"What can we do?"

Resignation clouded his angular features. "Nothing, but wait."

Rachel suddenly needed to be with her son. "I think I'll…I'll check on Josh."

Angel was close.

She couldn't be sure why she abruptly sensed that reality. But she could feel it. Some instinct that erupted out of nowhere. She had to get to Josh. The urge consumed her. When another of those odd chimes sounded she wondered if Sloan had gone outside to look for Pablo or if maybe he had finally arrived with the doctor.

She stepped quietly into the bedroom, not wanting to wake her son. The French doors standing wide open captured her attention. Ice filled her veins. She flipped on the overhead light with numb fingers.

"Surprise, Mommy!"

Josh sat on the edge of the bed with a stranger. A woman. The long, dark-haired woman.

"It's the lady who gave me the bear from my daddy," he explained happily. He frowned then. "But I forgotted him in the mountains."

The woman stood, her moves catlike, and expertly leveled her weapon on Rachel. "I think we should step outside, don't you agree?"

Josh looked from one to the other, his face still flushed with his fever. "Mommy?" Uncertainty filled his little voice.

"It's okay, sweetie," she assured him.

"Unless, of course," the woman continued, "you'd like to settle this in here."

The woman was taller than Rachel, and thin. She looked every bit as menacing as Angel. Forcing herself to comply, Rachel started toward the French doors. "Outside is fine," she urged. She had to keep Josh out of the line of fire. Whoever this woman was, she might be crazy enough to do anything.

"Good thinking," the woman cooed saccharinely.

Rachel paused at the door and gave her son what might be his final smile from her. "Josh, you stay right here and Mommy'll be back soon."

He nodded hesitantly.

The woman shoved Rachel through the open doors and into the night air. "Move," she snapped.

"Who are you?"

She shoved Rachel again, toward the center of the courtyard. "Shut up."

"Did Angel send you?" Rachel demanded, trying not to show her fear. She prayed Josh would not wander outside when she didn't return quickly enough.

"Oh, he sent me all right," she sneered.

Rachel turned around, making the woman pull up short. "Where is he?" Her anger kicked up, chasing away just a little bit of the fear. She was going to die anyway. "Was he afraid to come himself?"

The woman laughed dryly. "I think you know better than that, little Miss Goody Two-shoes."

"Then why are you here?" If she was going to die, she at least had a right to know the reason.

"Don't you know? I came to kill you," the woman said tartly.

Rachel blinked. "Is that what Angel ordered you to do?"

"Not quite." She smirked. "I'm supposed to keep an eye on you, like always."

"Like always?" Rachel had never seen this woman before in her life.

"Whenever Angel is on an overseas assignment, I keep an eye on you and the kid."

So that's how he kept up with Rachel's business and attempts to elude him, besides using the bank transactions Sloan had pointed out. "Are you his partner?" she wanted to know.

She laughed again. "He doesn't have a partner, honey. I'm Tanya." She quirked a brow. "His lover."

"I don't understand." If Tanya was supposed to be watching their every move, why was she holding a gun on Rachel now? "Where is Angel?" Rachel insisted. "He's not man enough to do the job himself?"

She gave Rachel a knowing look. "You know as well as I do how much man he is," she said pointedly. "That's the problem."

Tanya wasn't just his lover, she was his *jealous* lover. She wanted Rachel out of the way. This was crazy. Please, Rachel prayed, help Sloan keep Josh safe.

"Angel will be here soon enough, but it'll be too late for you, I'm afraid. I'm sick of hearing about sweet little Rachel," Tanya said vehemently. "I want you out of the picture."

Rachel shook her head in disbelief. "He doesn't want me, he wants Josh." How could she think that Angel wanted *her?*

"He wants you all right," she argued, "in some sadistic way. He could've killed you long ago. I'm not risking that he'll pick you over me when it gets down to the nitty-gritty."

"Then he doesn't know you're here?" The big picture cleared in Rachel's head.

Tanya waved her weapon. "I told you, I'm supposed to keep an eye on you until he gets here. But when he gets here I'll just tell him that Sloan offed you, and that I took care of Sloan to save him the trouble."

"He won't believe that," Rachel countered, renewed fear rising inside her. "Why would Sloan want to kill me?"

"Revenge, of course," she said triumphantly. "Angel was seething after I told him about your little escapade in town yesterday morning. He even cut his time in Europe short. He's coming in this morning, rather than later in the afternoon. I won't have any trouble convincing him that Sloan went ballistic and killed you. And that he would have killed the kid if I hadn't intervened. He knows how close to the edge Sloan is."

Rachel realized then she had overlooked one important detail. "How did you get in here?"

She made a disparaging sound. "Pablo has a sister who lives in town. It was simple. He didn't want to watch her die a slow and painful death so he gave me the code to get inside."

"Where is he?" Fury swept over Rachel, vanquishing her fear. This woman was just as evil as Angel.

"Don't worry your pretty little head about that," she patronized. "Pablo's beyond anybody's help now."

"You're making a mistake," Rachel warned. How long would it take Sloan to realize she was no longer in the house? Would Josh go to him? "Angel will figure out what you did."

"He'll be too busy grieving," she said with obvious disgust. "And raising his son." She smiled, enjoying Rachel's visible distress.

Anxiety hurdling through her, Rachel went for broke. "Why can't we come to some sort of mutually advantageous agreement?" There had to be some way to reach the woman.

Tanya rolled her eyes. "Don't be absurd. Why would I want to make a deal with you?"

"If you let me and Josh go, I swear we'll disappear and you'll never have to worry about us again." She mentally crossed her fingers. Surely the woman had a price. "I have money," she added quickly.

Tanya narrowed her gaze suspiciously. "I don't need your money. I have money." She shrugged. "Besides, Angel would only find you. You know that. You can't hide from him."

She knew that better than anyone. "Look, leave my son and Sloan out of it. Your problem is with me." The thought of Josh being taken by Angel and Sloan being hurt was more than Rachel could bear. She had already cost Pablo his life. She winced at the realization. "All you want is to get rid of me," she urged. "Leave Sloan and Josh out of this."

Tanya laughed. "Oh, this is rich. You're in love with the man. Did he tell you what Angel did to him?"

The phone call. "It was you," Rachel accused. "You played the recording."

"I'll bet that freaked out the poor bastard," she

said proudly. "I thought the bear and the ribbon were pretty ingenious, as well. The bear was an almost perfect match for the one his kid had."

"How could you do this?" Rachel searched the woman's face, her eyes, for some glimmer of goodness. Cold, calculating evil stared back at her.

"Easy. I had a good teacher. As soon as I discovered that you had come to Sloan, I rounded up Angel's bag of tricks designed specifically to trip this guy's trigger and followed you here."

Rachel felt sick to her stomach. Tanya actually derived pleasure from torturing Sloan. Would this woman be raising her son when Angel was off doing what he did? The thought made Rachel faint with panic.

"Please," Rachel pleaded, "there has to be a way to work this out."

"No more talking."

Tanya moved closer, she pressed the barrel of the weapon directly against Rachel's forehead. Rachel squeezed her eyes shut and braced herself for death.

"Time to send you where all good little girls go."

Chapter Thirteen

"Drop it."

Sloan pressed the barrel of his Beretta a little harder into the back of the woman's head. Everything inside him stilled in anticipation of her next move.

"Be careful, Sloan," Angel's lover warned, "I'd hate to splatter her brains all over the place."

Dawn rushed across the desert, spilling its golden glow around them as the tense seconds turned to one minute, then two. Sloan turned off his fledgling emotions and adopted the no-mercy attitude that had garnered his current hard-ass reputation.

"You have some reason to believe that she means something more to me than bait for Angel?"

Tanya stiffened. Uncertain. "I saw the two of you together. I *know* what she means to you."

Sloan eased closer in preparation of grabbing her by the throat. "You know what I showed you," he said softly, his voice lethal, purposely seductive.

She laughed a strained sound.

An unexpected weight slammed into Sloan's right leg, startling him. He jerked his gaze downward.

Josh.

Tanya picked that precise moment to act. She whirled around, Rachel clutched like a shield in front of her, the weapon pressed into her temple. Rachel's eyes rounded in horror when her gaze lit on Josh. Sloan swore silently and forced his attention on Tanya. He couldn't allow Rachel or anything she was feeling to distract him.

"Excellent," Tanya said with a sick smile in Josh's direction. "Nothing like a little family reunion."

"Let her go." A dead calm settled over Sloan. He took a bead right between Tanya's green eyes. His finger itched to pull the trigger.

"Back off, big boy, or she dies right in front of the kid," she hissed through clenched teeth. "I came here to do her, and I ain't leaving until it's done."

Josh clung more tightly to Sloan's leg. He could feel the child's heart thudding in his chest. Sloan clenched his jaw and took aim at Angel's whore.

"You'll die together then."

"No." Rachel held up her hand stop-sign fashion. "Get Josh out of here." She moistened her trembling lips. "Please, Sloan, keep my baby safe. Just go."

Sloan squashed the emotions threatening to tear him apart. He shook his head slowly from side to side. No way in hell was he leaving her. "Not a chance."

"How touching."

The abrupt sound of the male voice made Sloan's blood run cold.

Angel.

Sloan met that hellish black gaze. A flood of emotions hit him all at once, straining his hold on reality. Rage, pain, vengeance vied for his attention.

"Angel," Tanya said nervously. She released her death grip on Rachel. "I'm glad you're here. I was just—"

"Save it." Angel's weapon was trained on Rachel, but his gaze was focused on Sloan. "Drop your weapon or I'll end it now," he warned Sloan.

Reluctant but certain that Rachel's life depended on his cooperation, Sloan lowered his weapon. His eyes never leaving Angel, he crouched and placed it on the ground.

Fury streaked across Angel's face as Sloan stood, unarmed. "I've been on a damn plane all night." He made a production of straightening his suit jacket, then smoothed a hand over the expensive fabric. "While you were here, playing house."

The best-dressed assassin in the world, Sloan suddenly remembered putting that in his report as he searched for Angel all those years ago. A lady's man. A frigging madman. Hatred twisted in Sloan's gut. Now was his chance. All he had to do was drop, snatch his weapon, roll and take his shot. He could kill Angel where he stood before he had a chance to react. But he couldn't risk Rachel's life. Or Josh's. A ragged breath shuddered through Sloan.

"Imagine my surprise," Angel said angrily, his attention diverting to Tanya, "when I arrived earlier than planned to find you—" he glared at her briefly before shifting his wary gaze back to Sloan "—poised to kill the mother of my child."

"You don't understand," Tanya argued, desperation rising in her voice.

"Big mistake." Angel shot her. Rachel gasped. Tanya staggered back, then crumpled to the ground knocking Rachel down as she went. Rachel shrieked and scrambled away from her. "Don't move," Angel ordered. Rachel froze.

In that moment of distraction, Sloan snatched up his weapon and leveled it on Angel before he could regroup.

Angel smiled, acknowledging the smooth move. "Well. Looks like the proverbial Mexican standoff. How appropriate."

Sloan knew Angel was no fool. He kept his weapon trained on Rachel, knowing her life would mean a great deal more to Sloan than his own. The desire to kill the sick son of a bitch burst inside Sloan like shattering glass. He could taste the vengeance, the victory. His finger snugged around the trigger. The memory of his wife and his son rushed through him, weakening his restraint. The sound of Josh crying quietly, his little arms still tight around Sloan's leg invaded his senses, shoring up his resolve. He couldn't make a move with Josh in the line of fire, no matter how much he wanted to.

But the need to kill Angel pulled at him, like a powerful magnet. His body trembled with the effort of holding back the long awaited vengeance.

Angel's sinister smile widened. "Are you sure you want to do that?"

"Yes," Sloan rasped, his heart thundering in his ears. The desire was palpable, a physical ache.

Angel shrugged. "I only came here for my son." He flicked a disparaging glance at Rachel who hadn't moved a muscle. "I obviously can't trust her to keep him safe and away from losers like you." He leveled his confident black gaze on Sloan. "In fact, I'll sweeten the deal for you, old friend—"

"I'm not your friend," Sloan ground out, the urge to kill so strong now he couldn't draw in a decent breath. "I'm the man who's going to kill you if it's the last thing I ever do."

Angel laughed fearlessly. "No, I don't think so." He firmed his hold on the weapon aimed at Rachel. "It's quite clear to me that you've tasted what she has to offer, and I certainly have no use for her. It's ironic don't you think, that I've kept her from men all this time, and then you're the one to take her from me. But I'm a good sport. You keep the bitch, I'll take the boy, and we'll both be happy."

"Go to hell."

"Why don't you tell me what it's like there," Angel returned. "I'm quite certain that you're very familiar with the place."

"You're dead." Sloan braced himself for the recoil.

Angel sighed dramatically. "If you kill me then you'll never know what really happened to that sweet little boy of yours."

Sloan stiffened against the rage erupting inside him. "My son is dead."

Angel cocked his head and leveled a speculative gaze on him. "Are you certain of that?" He shrugged. "The body the police recovered could have been any child. After all, there wasn't much left to identify. I doubt DNA testing was even possible considering the condition of the…remains."

Sloan blinked back the remembered horror. He would not allow Angel to distract him with lies. "The teddy bear was my son's. And there were other details, other similarities."

"Well, now, that's true," Angel agreed. "But was the body your son's? It could have been one belonging to a child listed as a John Doe in a morgue in Los Angeles. The size and approximate age were right. But when a body is burned that badly, it's quite difficult to tell, don't you agree?"

Sloan trembled at the memory of demanding to see his child. The detective in charge of the investigation had warned him that it was pointless to put himself through it, but Sloan'd had to see for himself. There hadn't been any dental records. Mark had never been to the dentist. No way to really be sure.

"You know I'm right," Angel pressed. "You can't be sure."

Afraid to move for fear of causing some deadly

chain reaction, Rachel stood absolutely still, watching the scene play out before her. Every fiber of her being longed to run to Josh, to protect him. But she couldn't risk even the slightest movement. Her heart ached for Sloan as she listened to the verbal torture inflicted by Angel. She wished she had a gun so she could kill the bastard herself. She glanced at Tanya's motionless form. Her weapon was still clutched in her right hand.

"It's simple really," Angel explained, drawing her attention back to the deadly standoff. "You let me walk out of here with my son and I'll give you the location of *your* son." Angel tapped his temple as if suddenly remembering something. "In fact, he celebrated his tenth birthday just last month."

Rachel's heart raced with anticipation. Could he be telling the truth? She staggered beneath the impact of what his words insinuated. He wanted to trade information about Sloan's son for Josh. Rachel's frantic gaze flew to Sloan. The difficulty of holding back from the vengeance his soul screamed for was outlined in his posture and every feature of his face. The rigid set of his jaw, the grim line of his lips.

"An even trade," Angel urged when Sloan remained silent. "Your son for mine."

The slightest hint of a new kind of fear trickled through Rachel. No, she scolded mentally. Sloan would never do anything to harm Josh. Nothing could make him turn Josh over to Angel. She wouldn't believe that.

But what if Angel was telling the truth? What if Sloan's son was still alive? Would he trade her son for his own? Rachel looked at the man she loved with all her heart and she knew.

He would do the right thing.

Her breath caught as Sloan, his intent gaze never leaving Angel, reached down and pulled her son from behind him.

"He looks like you, you know," Angel badgered. "He even asks about his daddy from time to time," he added with a demented laugh.

A muscle flexed rhythmically in Sloan's rigid jaw. Angel had buried the knife deep in his chest, and then twisted. Rachel held her breath as the seconds ticked by before Sloan reacted. He pushed Josh in her direction. "Take him in the house," he ordered, the words raw, guttural.

"Don't move, Rachel," Angel warned. The slightest hint of desperation tinged his voice. "If you do, I will kill you. I should have done it a long time ago."

Rachel ushered Josh behind her. He clung to her as he had Sloan, burying his face against her hip in fear. She looked from Sloan to Angel. That satanic gaze latched onto hers and filled her with terror. He was on the edge now, poised to make a move. Adrenaline pumped through her veins, urging her to run, but at the same time nailing her to the spot.

"Go inside, Rachel," Sloan commanded, his fierce gaze reiterating the order. The savage sound of his words jerked her attention back to him. *"Now."*

But she couldn't leave him. From the corner of her eye, she saw Angel's aim swing from her to Sloan. Sloan realized his mistake instantly. Rachel saw the recognition that he had just traded his life for hers flicker across his face, then the determination that he would take Angel with him.

A shot rang out, shattering the tension. The look of utter surprise on Angel's face prevented his instinctive reaction to return fire. He stared down in disbelief at the hole in his chest as he dropped to his knees. The pale gray shirt he wore swiftly turned crimson with his blood.

"If I can't have you," Tanya mumbled, "no one can." Satisfied when Angel collapsed facedown, she dropped her weapon and slumped back to the ground.

Josh cried out in fear. Rachel fell to her knees and grabbed him in her arms. She pressed his face against her chest and made soft shushing sounds to comfort him.

Sirens blared in the distance. The police? Rachel wondered vaguely. Had Sloan called them before coming outside? Sloan walked over to Angel and rolled him onto his back with one foot to be sure he was good and dead. Then he stepped over to Tanya, kicked her weapon away and knelt next to her. She made a sound, more groan than word.

"Don't try to talk," he told her, his voice still cold and emotionless. He shouldered out of his shirt and quickly wadded it. He pressed it firmly down over the wound in her chest to staunch the flow of blood.

Hot tears rolled down Rachel's cheeks as she watched Sloan do what he could to help Tanya, though she didn't deserve it. The sirens were closer now.

"Mommy, hold me," Josh cried, tugging at her blouse.

Rachel held him tighter. "I love you, sweetie," she whispered against his hair. "Everything's going to be okay." She inhaled deeply of his sweet scent and thanked God again that he had answered her prayers tonight.

She opened her eyes and blinked to clear them. Angel was dead. Relief washed over her, making her weak and giddy at the same time.

Angel was dead.

She and Josh were free.

The medical attendants loaded Tanya into the ambulance and left, their siren screeching urgently. Rachel had long since collapsed into a chair, Josh asleep in her arms. One police officer was still questioning Sloan. Rachel had already answered their questions as best she could. Between their poor English and her nonexistent Spanish, Sloan'd had to act as translator.

Another officer covered Angel's body. Rachel closed her eyes against the image of blood pooling around him. The police seemed satisfied with Sloan's explanation of what happened.

Thank God, Pablo was not dead. The police had

found him in the Jeep on the edge of town. He had very nearly bled to death from Tanya's single shot to his midsection. He had managed to tell the police what was about to go down at Sloan's residence before passing out from his injury.

Rachel frowned as she realized that she had not thanked Sloan. He had been prepared to die for her. Had saved her life as well as Josh's. She had to thank him. To tell him she loved him. The thought warmed her. She loved him so much, she could hardly hold back from shouting it to anyone who would listen.

She scanned the courtyard for the man who made her tremble with just a look, but didn't see him. Holding Josh against her chest, Rachel pushed to her feet and went in search of either Sloan or the one officer who spoke pretty decent English. Maybe they were in the house, she decided as she headed in that direction.

The officer she hoped to find stepped through the French doors just as Rachel started inside.

He nodded. "*Señora,* we will take the body now."

Rachel's stomach roiled. He was talking about Angel. She blew out a breath in hopes of slowing the churning in her stomach. "I understand."

She stepped aside as two men pulling a gurney hustled past. She wished she could dredge up at least a little remorse that a life had been lost today, but she couldn't. Angel deserved to die. She shivered, remembering the sound of his voice, his touch. The urge to gag was overwhelming.

"You must sit down," the officer suggested.

Rachel felt the color drain from her face. She was dangerously close to fainting. She shook her head, clearing it of the hideous memories.

"No, I'm okay," she insisted. "Where's Sloan?"

"The hospital," he explained. "To see his amigo."

He'd left without saying goodbye. Rachel couldn't stop the hurt that accompanied that actuality. The sound of the gurney's wheels rattling over the tile tugged Rachel from her worrisome thoughts. Her arms tightened around Josh and she pressed his head against her shoulder, protecting him as the loaded gurney passed, as if even in death Angel might reach out for him.

But Angel was dead.

And Sloan would never know for sure if his son was alive or not. That comprehension shattered Rachel's newfound feeling of relief. In helping her, Sloan had faced his own personal nightmare all over again. Tears burned Rachel's eyes. A sob tore at her throat. God, it was true. Even in death, Angel reached out to haunt Sloan. He'd made sure of that. He'd left Sloan with a thread of hope that his son might still be alive somewhere. Sweet Jesus, how was he supposed to live with that?

The sob broke loose and Rachel clamped her hand over her mouth to hold back the next one. Her freedom had cost Sloan his. This new ray of hope would be like a prison around his heart, never allowing him to put the past behind him.

"*Señora,* you must say if there is something I can do," the kind officer urged gently.

Rachel sucked in a harsh breath and fought to hold onto some semblance of composure. "I need a ride to the hospital."

He nodded. "I am finished here. I will take you."

He led Rachel to his Jeep and held Josh while she climbed inside. Once Josh was settled on her lap she considered her plan. Angel was dead. He had taken the truth about Sloan's son with him, there was no changing that. However, Tanya was still alive, barely, but alive just the same.

Rachel prayed with all her heart that Tanya would know Angel's secret.

And that she would be willing to tell it to Rachel.

Josh giggled as the young doctor tickled him. A smile crept across Rachel's mouth. Josh bore no visible aftereffects from this morning's ordeal. She was immensely thankful for that. But later she would have him checked out by a psychologist just the same.

"Your son is fine, *señora,*" the doctor announced.

Rachel scooped Josh into her arms. "Thank you, Doctor. I wanted to be sure that there was nothing to worry about after that high fever."

"He is fine." The young man smiled at Josh. "Very fine."

"Where would I find surgery?" She needed to check on Tanya's condition.

The doctor pointed upward. "One floor up."

Rachel thanked him again, then wandered the halls

until she found the elevator. Once she found the nurses' desk, the next hurdle would be communicating.

The second-floor nurses' desk buzzed with activity. Rachel approached cautiously, surveying the busy faces for the one who looked the most sociable. The youngest one, she decided.

"Excuse me," Rachel said hesitantly. "Do you speak English?"

The young woman smiled. "Yes, may I help you?" Her long dark hair was smoothed into a neat bun. Her uniform was a crisp white against her olive skin.

"A woman, about thirty, was brought in a couple of hours ago with a gunshot wound. Is she still in surgery?"

The nurse nodded toward a set of double doors at the end of the long corridor. A policeman stood guard nearby. "She is still in surgery."

Rachel moistened her lips, her heart pounding within her rib cage. This was her only chance to help Sloan. Tanya had to make it. "Do you have any idea how she's doing?"

The nurse shook her head. "It will be many hours yet."

Rachel nodded, trying not to show her disappointment. "Thank you." Josh stirred restlessly in her arms. She turned to go, wondering what she should do now.

"If you would like to wait," the nurse suggested, "there is a small waiting room." She gestured to the other end of the floor. "I will let you know when your friend is in a room."

Rachel smiled and thanked her. She set Josh on his feet and led him to the room the nurse had indicated. She settled into one of the well-worn chairs, realizing for the first time how exhausted she was. She clasped her hands and rested her elbows on her knees. Rachel pressed her forehead to her hands and prayed once more that Tanya would survive. Though the woman was far from her friend, she was Rachel's only hope that Angel's secret had not gone with him to his grave.

Morning stretched into afternoon and Rachel grew restless. She and Josh had found the cafeteria and had lunch a couple of hours ago. She had worked up the nerve to stop by Pablo's room, as well. Sloan wasn't there. Pablo had been sleeping, but his nurse had assured Rachel that he was doing well and would fully recover. She tried not to think about why Sloan had disappeared so suddenly.

Rachel paced the length of the small waiting room once more. Josh was engrossed in a cartoon where all the characters spoke Spanish. Though she knew he didn't understand a single world, he laughed at all the appropriate times. She supposed cartoon antics were a universal language.

"Señora."

Rachel spun around at the sound of the young nurse's voice. "Yes."

"Your friend has left recovery and is in a room now," she said.

"Could you show me where?"

The nurse nodded. Rachel pulled a reluctant Josh into her arms and hurried after the nurse. Anticipation sped through her. Please let Tanya know about Sloan's son, she chanted. When they reached the room an officer was standing guard outside. Rachel eyed him with growing trepidation. What if he wouldn't let her see Tanya?

"Thank you," she told the nurse as she hastened back to her post.

The police officer eyed Rachel just as warily as she had him moments ago. "May I help you, *señora?*"

"Yes." She put Josh down. "Sweetie, I want you to sit down right here." She pointed to the floor next to the officer's chair. "And look at the book." He had carried one with him from the waiting room. Rachel would have to see that he replaced it before they left the hospital.

Josh settled on the floor and immediately began flipping through the pages. Rachel breathed a sigh of relief. He was still wearing his pajamas, and with no shoes. But there had been no time for thinking about clothes. She shook her head, then straightened to face the officer who stood between her and Tanya.

She took a calming breath and forced herself to speak slowly to ensure he understood. "I'm sorry but I don't speak Spanish."

"I speak English well," he assured her.

Rachel nodded her appreciation. "It's very, very important that I speak to the lady in the room."

He looked doubtful. "I am not sure that is a good idea, *señora*. This woman is a murder suspect."

"I know. But it's very important. You can leave the door open or you can come inside with me. I just have to ask her a couple of questions." Rachel aimed her most persuasive gaze at the young officer. "It's very important."

He shifted nervously. "All right," he finally relented. "But only for one moment. The door must be open."

"Thank you." She glanced at Josh.

"The boy can stay with me." The officer pushed the door open and stepped aside.

Rachel smiled, barely containing her tears of gratitude. The room was quiet except for the beeping monitor at Tanya's bedside. Everything was white from the walls to the floors. Tanya's long dark hair looked stark against the white sheets. She was pale. Two IVs hung above her head.

Tanya's eyes opened as Rachel paused near her bedside.

"What do you want?" she asked in a voice rusty with thirst.

"Would you like a drink?" Rachel offered.

Tanya nodded once. Rachel poured water from the pitcher into the cup. She removed the wrapper from a straw and placed it in the cup of water. She held the straw to Tanya's lips so that she could wet her dry throat.

Tanya stared up at her then, suspicion cluttering her expression. "What do you want?"

What if she wouldn't tell her the truth? What if she didn't know? "How long have you been with Angel?" she finally asked.

She barked a humorless laugh. "What do you care?"

"Please." Rachel grasped the bed rail. "It's important."

She huffed a disgusted breath. "Ten years, probably the same amount of time I'll do in prison for killing the bastard."

"Then you know about Sloan's son," Rachel suggested carefully.

"If you're expecting me to admit I had something to do with anything Angel has done, forget it." She swore hotly. "I ain't taking the rap for nothing he did."

"No, it's not that," Rachel explained quickly. "I need to know if you can tell me what really happened to the child."

Tanya smirked. "Damn, you've got it bad."

"Please." Rachel held her breath as she waited for her to answer.

"Well, I guess Sloan probably did save my life. I owe him that much." She fixed her gaze on Rachel's. "Listen up, 'cause I'm only going to admit this once."

Rachel leaned closer to hear the words about to be spoken for her ears only.

"He was going to kill the kid once he'd finished toying with Sloan."

Rachel's heart quivered in her chest.

"But Katrina, Angel's only sibling, begged him to let her have the kid. She couldn't have kids of her own. Some kind of disease. Anyway, Angel finally agreed."

Rachel's breath evaporated in her lungs. "So Sloan's son is alive." The words were a mere whisper…a thought spoken.

"Yeah. He lives with Katrina in Detroit."

"You have the address?"

Tanya breathed an exasperated breath.

"And you're sure," Rachel pressed. "You're sure the boy is Sloan's son?"

"I'm positive. Sloan's son is *alive.*"

Chapter Fourteen

"Mrs. Colby?"

"Yes."

Rachel clutched the pay phone's receiver to her ear. "This is Rachel Larson. Angel is dead."

A long moment of silence filled the staticky line. "And Sloan?"

"He's fine." *I think,* Rachel didn't add. She summoned her courage and forged ahead. "Does that offer to help still stand?"

"Of course," Victoria said without hesitation. "What do you need?"

Rachel held tightly to Josh's hand as she said the words aloud to another human being. "There's a strong possibility that Sloan's son is alive."

Another long silence echoed across the line. "How can that be? What about the body?"

"According to Angel's longtime girlfriend, he stole a body from a morgue in L.A. He set it up to look like Sloan's son, even made sure there would be no way to identify it."

"Why would he go to all that trouble?" Victoria asked, still suspect.

Rachel quickly explained about Angel's sister, and where she lived now according to Tanya.

"It'll take a couple of days to check it out, but I'll put Ric Martinez right on it."

"Thank you."

"Don't thank me," Victoria said quietly. "If there's any chance that Sloan's son is alive, I'll do whatever it takes to find him. I'll send Zach Ashton along, as well. He's our top legal advisor."

Rachel ended the call and decided she had one more stop before leaving the hospital.

Pablo was watching television when Rachel and Josh entered his room. A woman sat next to his bed.

"Señora Rachel, Josh! It is good to see you."

Rachel lifted Josh up so he could shake hands with Pablo. Rachel kissed the man's cheek in lieu of a handshake. Pablo blushed and patted her hand.

"This is my sister, Rosa."

"It's very nice to meet you, Rosa." Rachel beamed a smile at her. The resemblance between Rosa and her brother was easy to see. Same thin features. Same gentle smile.

The woman nodded and said something in Spanish.

"She's not much for the English," he explained.

Rachel shrugged. "That's okay. I'm not much for the Spanish." She placed her hand on his and squeezed affectionately. "You're doing okay?"

"Very fine. Yes." His gaze turned somber. "I'm glad the evil man is dead."

Rachel sighed. "Me, too."

"The woman who shot me, she is here in the hospital?"

"Yes, but she's under guard. She won't be going anywhere except to prison when she is well enough."

Pablo nodded. "Good."

"I haven't seen Sloan since I left the house." Rachel ventured.

"He had urgent business." Pablo took her hand in his this time. "Give him time."

"He left without saying anything, even goodbye," Rachel told him, unable to hide her hurt. "I'm sure he knows I've been at the hospital today, but he's avoided me. I don't understand."

"Don't doubt his heart, *señora,*" Pablo insisted. "But you must give him time. He is afraid to admit his feelings. He has lost so much in his life. It is difficult to risk such great pain again."

Rachel wished she could tell Pablo that Sloan's son might be alive, but she had to be sure first. It would be too painful to get Sloan's hopes up, and Pablo would surely tell Sloan about the investigation.

"I'm taking a room in the hotel across the street."

Pablo nodded. "I know the one."

"Would you please tell Sloan that if he wants to see me I'll be waiting there."

"Yes, I'll tell him. He will be back day after tomorrow."

Rachel hesitated before turning away. "Did he say or ask anything at all about me when he was here earlier?"

Pablo stared at his hands. "I'm sorry, Señora Rachel, but he did not. He was called away very suddenly."

"Well." Rachel blinked back the tears of disappointment. How convenient that he was called away so suddenly. She forced the bitter hurt away. "I should be going." She kissed Pablo's forehead, making him blush again, then smiled for Rosa. She had to get out of here. She needed time away from everyone to grieve for what she had hoped could be, but never would. Later, when Josh was fast asleep, Rachel would allow the soul-shaking tears to fall, but not now.

Two of the longest days and nights Rachel had ever lived dragged by. By noon on the third day she was sure she would lose her mind if she didn't hear from either Sloan or Victoria Colby soon.

Josh had colored in his new coloring book until he'd fallen asleep in the middle of the bed. They couldn't just keep staying here cooped up like this. This was ridiculous, she decided, she should just go to Sloan. She and Josh had left their things there. Though she'd bought a few clothes to get them through, she still had a legitimate excuse to go back to Sloan's house. But she couldn't do it. If he wanted her, he would come for her. She had known that this would be the way of it. Though she felt certain Sloan had feelings for her, for Josh even, they would never have a future together. Their combined pasts were too painful. Josh was still Angel's son, there was no changing that. She had to face the facts. Sloan didn't want her or her son in his life. She couldn't make him feel something that wasn't there.

The telephone rang and Rachel lunged for it. It had to be Sloan. "Yes," she answered, breathless.

"Miss Larson?"

It wasn't Sloan.

"Yes, this is Rachel Larson."

"This is Ric Martinez from the Colby Agency."

Rachel's heart sped into overdrive. This was the investigator Victoria had assigned to check into Tanya's story.

"Do you have news?" she demanded, impatient.

"Yes, ma'am, I do. But I would prefer to discuss the information in person. Could we meet?"

Rachel frowned. "Where are you?"

"In the lobby of your hotel."

"I'm in room 223."

"I'll be right up. And Mr. Ashton is with me."

Rachel placed the receiver back in its base and tried to slow her racing heart. It had to be good news. Why would Mr. Martinez and the Colby Agency attorney have come all this way otherwise? They wouldn't. Victoria would simply have called.

She opened the door on the first knock. A tall, lean man waited outside, a large envelope in his hand. As his name and accent suggested, Martinez was Latin.

He removed his designer sunglasses and tucked

them into his shirt as his throat. "Miss Larson, I'm Ric Martinez." He stepped inside her door. "And this is Zach Ashton."

Rachel's gaze shifted to the man who entered her room next. Older than Martinez, late thirties maybe, Mr. Ashton looked every bit the lawyer. Despite the heat, he wore a suit, the jacket draped over his left arm, his pristine white shirt remarkably devoid of wrinkles.

"Miss Larson, it's a pleasure to meet you." Ashton offered his hand. "We have some good news for you."

Rachel pushed the door shut, then took his hand. "Did you find him?"

Ashton gave her hand a quick shake. "Yes, we did." He turned to Martinez. "Ric will bring you up to speed on the case."

Hope mushroomed inside Rachel. She wanted to shout for joy but she contained herself until she heard the rest. "Would you like to sit down?" she offered, remembering her manners.

"That's all right, ma'am, we're fine," Ric Martinez assured her. "Katrina Renaldi lives just outside Detroit with a ten-year-old boy." He withdrew a hand full of eight-by-ten glossies from the envelope he held and passed them to Rachel. "She claims legal guardianship of the boy whom she says was orphaned by a distant relative seven years ago."

Rachel stared at the pictures in her hand. The boy

was tall for ten. His hair was blond, thick and slightly curly, with the same sky-blue eyes as Sloan. She had no doubt that this was his son.

"What name is he using?" she wanted to know.

"Mark Renaldi."

Mark. That was Sloan's son's name. It had to be him. "Is this enough proof?"

"Not quite," Ashton interjected. "We needed more conclusive evidence."

"Needed?" Rachel prodded.

Martinez grinned sheepishly. Rachel had to admit, when exposed to that brilliant smile, Ric Martinez was a true Latin hunk. Zach Ashton was every bit as handsome, in a more classic, sophisticated way. Rachel suddenly wondered if drop-dead gorgeous was a prerequisite for working at the Colby Agency. Sloan certainly fit the bill.

"I ran his prints, and they were a perfect match for the ones on file with missing persons for Sloan's son," Martinez explained. "It's him. There's no doubt." He gathered the pictures from her and slid them back into the envelope. "If the woman puts up a fuss, they can always do DNA testing. But I'd bet my as—" he cleared his throat "—my next paycheck that the test would confirm my findings."

Rachel frowned, confused. "How did you get the boy's prints?"

Martinez raked his fingers through his jet-black hair. "I salvaged his milk carton."

"You what?" she asked in disbelief.

Aston shook his head, a wry smile on his lips. "You don't want to know."

"I had lunch in the school cafeteria. The female attendant was very friendly," Martinez explained. "It wasn't—"

"That's okay," Rachel cut in. "I'm sure you did what you had to." Mr. Martinez appeared to use those Latin good looks to his advantage when working on a case. Victoria had been right in choosing him.

"Mrs. Colby is anxious to notify Sloan," Mr. Ashton began, "but she asked that we get word to you first. She thought you might want to tell him personally."

Rachel wasn't sure that was a good idea now. She hadn't heard from Sloan since that awful morning... with Angel. Maybe he didn't want to see her again. He'd done what she hired him to do, what else did she expect? He hadn't made any promises. *I won't hold you to any promises you make tonight.* Sloan's words echoed inside her head. They had no future together. She had known that from the beginning.

"Maybe you should tell him," Rachel suggested. "I'm not sure—"

A knock at the door interrupted her. She looked from the door to Martinez, then to Ashton. "Did someone else come with you?"

"No. Just the two of us." Martinez stopped her when she would have reached for the door. "Would you like me to answer it?" he suggested.

She shook her head. "No. I'll get it." She was through being afraid, through hiding. Angel was dead.

Rachel tamped down the foolish hope that it might be Sloan. If he had wanted to see her, he would have come already. Or maybe it would be him. After all, he hadn't collected his fee yet. For that matter, he hadn't even named an amount. Whether he wanted her or not, he would probably want his money.

"Excuse me." Drawing in a deep, steadying breath, Rachel stepped between the two men and pulled the door open. She stared up into Sloan's piercing blue eyes and her heart lurched. Unable to utter a word, she drank in the beauty of him as if it had been a lifetime since she'd seen him instead of only a couple of days.

"I was afraid you'd be gone." His gaze flicked to Martinez and Ashton then back to her. "I had an emergency that couldn't wait." He glanced at the two strangers again. Something changed in his eyes. "Is this a bad time?"

She knew better than to hope that what she saw in that translucent blue gaze was jealousy. "No." Rachel stepped back. "Please come in." She'd been so caught up in staring at him that she hadn't thought to ask him in. "This is Ric Martinez and Zach Ashton from the Colby Agency."

A line of confusion marring his brow, Sloan accepted the hand Martinez offered first, then Ashton's.

"It's an honor to meet you, man," Martinez said eagerly. "You're a legend at the agency."

A ghost of a smile twitched Sloan's lips. "A legend, huh?"

"Absolutely." Martinez was clearly impressed.

"Well after forty-eight hours of surveillance and nonstop travel, I definitely feel old enough to be a legend."

"Sloan, Martinez brought some news," Rachel told him, broaching the subject, but not quite sure how to begin.

Sloan turned back to her, his eyes full of something that looked a lot like hope. She would gladly have traded a year of her life to kiss him right then, but she had to do this first. He'd suffered too long already.

"What news?" He looked from her to Martinez and back.

"I spoke to Tanya after her surgery," Rachel ventured, not sure how you told a man this sort of news. "She confirmed what Angel told you about your son."

Sloan's expression grew wary. "What do you mean?"

"She said your son is alive." Rachel took the envelope containing the pictures from Martinez's hand and opened it. "Angel's sister has been raising him in Detroit." She passed the photographs to Sloan.

Rachel watched, holding her breath, as myriad emotions stole across Sloan's face. He looked at Rachel then, afraid to believe, but desperate for someone to make it all right.

"Martinez—" she stopped to compose herself "—he managed to get the boy's prints. They match your son's." A sob caught the last word.

Sloan turned to Martinez. "How close was the match?"

"As close to perfect as you can get. The kid has to be your son. The woman suddenly shows up in a new town seven years ago with a three-year-old boy. There's no adoption papers, no history of the kid prior to that."

"Take me to him."

The softly uttered command was directed at Martinez.

"We can leave now," Ashton suggested. "We'll discuss the legal ramifications and steps we'll need to take en route."

Sloan nodded. "Good." He turned to Rachel. "I have to go, but I will be back."

Rachel nodded, unable to speak without losing her grip on the tidal wave of emotions looming over her.

Sloan grabbed her and kissed her. The taste of his lips sealed her fate. She would love him for the rest of her life, whether he ever loved her or not.

Late the next afternoon Rachel and Josh left for New Orleans. She couldn't bear to stay in Mexico another day. Sloan hadn't called. She was very happy that he had found his son, but it was clear to her that he wasn't interested in her and Josh. He had said he'd had an emergency and that's why he hadn't been to her hotel before, but he could have called. He could call now. She couldn't do this to herself any longer.

She sighed. He probably had his son back by now. What did he need with her and Josh? He had his own family. Besides, what did they really know about each other? Nothing. Two people with a connected past had reached out to each other during a time of horrendous stress, and now it was over.

Rachel had to get on with her life. It wasn't fair to Josh for her to mope around like this, and it wasn't fair to her. The fall semester would begin in a few days. Josh would be starting preschool, she might as well sign up for a few classes at the university. Her father would have wanted her to finish her education. And she had to find something to do with herself if she couldn't be with Sloan. Her heart ached at the dream that would never come true.

It was time she and Josh started a normal life. With or without Sloan. He had come to her hotel that day. Maybe he planned to tell her how he felt but had gotten derailed with the news about his son, which was entirely understandable. Or maybe he simply wanted his fee.

Enough, Rachel, she chastised. *Time to put the past behind you.* She had Josh to think of.

Early the next morning, Rachel determined to do something about her state of depression. She dressed in the lovely print dress Sloan had bought her the day they'd gone shopping. He might never be a part of her life again, but she would never forget him. He had changed something inside her. Given her back the confidence and trust Angel had taken away. He would always be more than a hero to her.

Determined to take the first step in getting on with the rest of her life, Rachel left Josh with her neighbor, Detective Taylor's wife, and visited the nearby university campus. Though she admired the lovely campus and the offerings were extensive, she couldn't bring herself to actually sign up for anything. She gathered all the necessary forms and a schedule of what classes were offered just in case. She could look everything over tonight. Maybe then she could make a decision about what to do. There was still time.

Halfway across the deserted parking lot, Rachel stopped dead in her tracks. Sloan was leaning against her car, waiting for her. He looked wonderful. From the plain white T-shirt to the faded jeans that gloved his muscular body, he looked like the man she loved. His hair was loose, the way she liked it. He looked amazing, like some Greek god come to rescue her from the humdrum of everyday life.

Ignoring the hope soaring inside her, Rachel covered the distance that separated them with measured steps. She clutched the papers and college catalog to her chest as if she could keep him from seeing what was in her heart. But she knew she couldn't. Her love of him was shining in her eyes, she felt certain.

"Hello, Sloan." She moistened her lips. "What brings you to the Big Easy?"

His gaze lingered on her lips for a very long time

before he spoke. "Unfinished business. We have some settling up to do."

Rachel blinked, taken aback. His fee. "Oh. I'm sorry. I guess you thought I'd run out on you. But you were busy and I couldn't hang around that hotel forever." She shrugged. God, she was rambling. "If you'd like to follow me to my bank I'll have a cashier's check drawn up for you."

"First, I wanted to thank you for helping find my son." He stared at the pavement for a moment. "I really believed he was dead. I wouldn't have asked Tanya." He shook his head. "I couldn't risk that much pain. I would have just spent the rest of my life believing he was gone."

"It was the least I could do." Profound relief washed over her at the confirmation that he did, indeed, have his son back. "No one should be able to take your child and get away with it."

Sloan nodded his agreement. "He's grown so much. It's hard to accept that I've missed all this time with him."

"It'll be fine," she assured him. "What about the woman, is she going to give you any trouble?"

"Actually, she's been very cooperative. She found out a few months ago that she has terminal cancer. She had already written Mark a letter explaining everything. The letter was to be opened upon her death." Sloan blew out a breath. "She's made her peace with God, now she just wants to be sure Mark is going to be okay. Despite how it sounds, I guess

I'm grateful to her for swaying Angel from his original plan."

He fell silent then.

Rachel blinked back the tears threatening to expose her turbulent feelings. "So what happens now?"

"Since she only has a few days to live, I've agreed to let Mark stay with her until the end under my or Martinez's strict supervision. Then I'll bring him home."

"I'm happy for you, Sloan." She shifted the load in her arms. "If you'd like to go to the bank now, we'll settle up."

"Actually, I know a little wedding chapel in Vegas where they do the kind of settling up I had in mind."

Rachel almost dropped her load. He couldn't mean what she thought he meant.

Sloan took the papers from her. "Your keys?" He held out his hand.

Rachel fumbled for the keys in her purse, then passed them to him. He opened her car door and tossed the papers and the catalog onto the passenger seat. He reached for her purse and tossed it inside, as well. Shoving her keys into his pants pocket he turned back to her.

He pulled her close. "I don't know how you did it, but you got under my skin, Rachel Larson." He tucked a tendril of hair behind her ear. "You blew me away. Every time I tried to push it away, the feelings just got stronger. I want to spend the rest of my life with you."

"You're sure about that?"

He tightened his hold on her waist. "Oh, yes. Very sure."

He brushed a tender kiss across her lips.

"What about your fee?" she teased. She fiddled with the collar of his shirt, wishing she could tear it off him right now, right here, and touch that sculpted chest beneath.

"How about you pay me in installments?"

Rachel frowned petulantly. "Installments?"

He kissed that ultrasensitive place next to her ear. "Sounds like a good plan to me. I'll collect every night, maybe even every morning, too."

Rachel shivered as he trailed a path of kisses along the line of her jaw. "When did you plan to start collecting?"

"Right now," he growled against her skin.

She shivered again, then drew back slightly. "What about Josh?" She held her breath. How could he ever accept Josh as his son?

Sloan looked directly into her eyes, his expression suddenly serious. "Josh will be my son, too." He hesitated, then added, "If that's acceptable to you."

Tears welled in her eyes. "That's very acceptable to me." She moistened her lips, tasting the man she loved with all her heart. "I love you, Sloan."

He smiled, a gesture that squeezed her heart. "I have something for you." He fished something from his pocket, then held it between his thumb and fore-finger. "Just a little something to seal the deal."

Rachel stilled, her gaze fixed on the delicate

diamond ring he held so gingerly. "I don't know what to say."

He lifted her left hand and slid the ring onto her finger. "Just say yes."

She frowned, uncertain, her heart pounding so hard she couldn't think. "But I don't have anything to give you."

He pressed his lips to her cheek, then nuzzled her neck. "How about a little girl to go with our boys," he whispered.

Rachel's heart leaped for joy. She slid her arms around his lean waist and squeezed her eyes shut. He loved her. He wanted a family with her…and with Josh. "How about two, to make it an even match," she suggested, then moaned as his tongue laved the pulse point at the base of her throat that pounded out her need for him.

"Is that a yes?" He drew back to look deeply into her eyes, his own glazed with desire.

"That's definitely a yes." She tiptoed and kissed his waiting lips.

He squeezed her buttocks, lifting her against the evidence of his need for her. "I'm a firm believer in consummating all important deals."

"There's a hotel only a couple of blocks from here," she said breathlessly. "We could be there in three minutes."

He ground her hips into his once more. "I was thinking more along the lines of your backseat and *now*."

Rachel surveyed the empty parking lot and reached behind her to open the door. "You are wicked."

He grinned. "Nobody ever accused me of being a saint."

Rachel pulled him down for another kiss. He might not be a saint, but he was her savior. And she loved him all the more for his wicked ways.

* * * * *

THE HARLEQUIN BESTSELLING AUTHOR COLLECTION

CLASSIC ROMANCES IN COLLECTIBLE VOLUMES
FROM OUR BESTSELLING AUTHORS

Available September 2010

SHERRYL WOODS

DREAM MENDER

and

LINDA LAEL MILLER

PART OF THE BARGAIN

Available wherever books are sold.

THE HARLEQUIN BESTSELLING AUTHOR COLLECTION

CLASSIC ROMANCES IN COLLECTIBLE VOLUMES FROM OUR BESTSELLING AUTHORS

On sale
September
2010.

SAVE $1.00

on the purchase of 1 or more books from the HARLEQUIN® BESTSELLING AUTHOR COLLECTION

Coupon expires March 31, 2011.
Redeemable at participating retail outlets. Limit one coupon per customer.
Valid in the U.S.A. and Canada only.

52609204

5 65373 00076 2   (8100)0 11670

BSCCOUP0610

HARLEQUIN® A *Romance* FOR EVERY MOOD™

SUSPENSE & PARANORMAL

Heartstopping stories of intrigue and mystery—
where true love always triumphs.

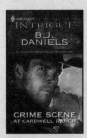

Harlequin Intrigue®
Breathtaking romantic suspense. Crime
stories that will keep you on the edge of
your seat.

Silhouette® Romantic Suspense
Heart-racing sensuality and the promise
of a sweeping romance set against the
backdrop of suspense.

Harlequin® Nocturne™
Dark and sensual paranormal
romance reads that stretch the
boundaries of conflict and desire,
life and death.

Look for these and many other Harlequin and Silhouette
romance books wherever books are sold, including most
bookstores, supermarkets, drugstores and discount stores.

REQUEST YOUR FREE BOOKS!

2 FREE NOVELS
FROM THE SUSPENSE COLLECTION
PLUS 2 FREE GIFTS!

YES! Please send me 2 FREE novels from the Suspense Collection and my 2 FREE gifts (gifts are worth about $10). After receiving them, if I don't wish to receive any more books, I can return the shipping statement marked "cancel." If I don't cancel, I will receive 3 brand-new novels every month and be billed just $5.74 per book in the U.S. or $6.24 per book in Canada. That's a saving of at least 28% off the cover price. It's quite a bargain! Shipping and handling is just 50¢ per book.* I understand that accepting the 2 free books and gifts places me under no obligation to buy anything. I can always return a shipment and cancel at any time. Even if I never buy another book, the two free books and gifts are mine to keep forever.

192/392 MDN E7PD

Name	(PLEASE PRINT)	
Address		Apt. #
City	State/Prov.	Zip/Postal Code

Signature (if under 18, a parent or guardian must sign)

Mail to The Reader Service:
IN U.S.A.: P.O. Box 1867, Buffalo, NY 14240-1867
IN CANADA: P.O. Box 609, Fort Erie, Ontario L2A 5X3

**Not valid for current subscribers to the Suspense Collection
or the Romance/Suspense Collection.**

**Want to try two free books from another line?
Call 1-800-873-8635 or visit www.morefreebooks.com.**

* Terms and prices subject to change without notice. Prices do not include applicable taxes. N.Y. residents add applicable sales tax. Canadian residents will be charged applicable provincial taxes and GST. Offer not valid in Quebec. This offer is limited to one order per household. All orders subject to approval. Credit or debit balances in a customer's account(s) may be offset by any other outstanding balance owed by or to the customer. Please allow 4 to 6 weeks for delivery. Offer available while quantities last.

Your Privacy: Harlequin Books is committed to protecting your privacy. Our Privacy Policy is available online at www.eHarlequin.com or upon request from the Reader Service. From time to time we make our lists of customers available to reputable third parties who may have a product or service of interest to you. If you would prefer we not share your name and address, please check here. ☐

Help us get it right—We strive for accurate, respectful and relevant communications. To clarify or modify your communication preferences, visit us at www.ReaderService.com/consumerschoice.

MSUS10R

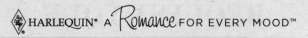